About the aut

Allie Cresswe
and began writing fiction as soon as she could hold a pencil.

She did a BA in English Literature at Birmingham University and an MA at Queen Mary College, London.

She has been a print-buyer, a pub landlady, a book-keeper, run a B & B and a group of boutique holiday cottages. Nowadays Allie writes alongside teaching literature to lifelong learners.

She has two grown-up children and one granddaughter, is married to Tim and lives in Cheshire.

Tiger in a Cage is the fourth of her novels to be published.

You can contact her via her website at www.allie-cresswell.com or find her on Facebook

Also by Allie Cresswell

Relative Strangers

The McKay family gathers for a week-long holiday at a rambling old house to celebrate the fiftieth wedding anniversary of Robert and Mary. In recent years only funerals and sudden, severe illnesses have been able to draw them together and as they gather in the splendid rooms of Hunting Manor, their differences are soon uncomfortably apparent.

For all their history, their traditions, the connective strands of DNA, they are relative strangers.

There are truths unspoken, but the question emerges: how much truth can a family really stand?

The old, the young, the disaffected and the dispossessed, relatives both estranged and deranged struggle to find a hand-hold amongst the branches of the family tree.

What, they ask themselves, does it really *mean* to be 'family'?

Available on Amazon and Smashwords or via the author's website at www.allie-cresswell.com

Readers' Reviews of Relative Strangers

….makes you think, laugh, and cry

Beautifully written and observed.

…a pleasure to read

a very fine observance of character …. as though she is watching developments from a hidden corner

…..keeps you guessing right up until the end.

I was drawn into the family.

….the complex politics, desires and heartache of family relationships are at the heart of this book

a truly compelling read [with] a rich lexicon

Lost Boys

Kenny is AWOL on a protracted binge. Michael is a wanderer on the road to wild and unfrequented places. Teenager Matt is sucked into the murky underworld of a lawless estate. John is a recluse, Skinner is missing, Guy is hiding, Ryan doesn't call.

Then there is little Mikey, swept away by a river in spate.

These are the lost boys and this is their story, told through the lives of the women they leave behind. Mikey's fall into the river sucks them all into the maelstrom of his fate; the waiting women, the boys lost beyond saving and the ones who find their way home.

Lost Boys uses some disturbing, contemporary phenomena; an unprecedented drought, a catastrophic flash-flood, a riot, as well as the much more enduring context of a mother's love for her son, to explore the ripples – and tsunamis – which one person's crisis can send into another's.

Available on Amazon and Smashwords or via the author's website

at allie-cresswell.com

Readers' Reviews of Lost Boys
A clever interweaving of fate and consequences

....draws upon emotional experiences at many different levels

The joy of the novel is to discover how the characters all have overlapping and intertwining stories

I was utterly wrapped up in the story

Allie Cresswell has the ability to flesh-out all her characters into a reality that kept me totally engrossed right to the last page.

...linguistic banquets of colour, texture, and imagery.

Lost Boys is a treasure

Game Show

It is November 1992 and in the suburbs of a Bosnian town a small family cowers in the basement of their shattered home. Over the next 48 hours Gustav, a 10 year old Bosnian Muslim boy, will watch his neighbours herded like animals through the streets, witness a brutal attack on his sister and be caught up in a bloody massacre perpetrated by soldiers who act with absolute impunity; their actions will have no come-back. The only way he can rationalize events is as 'a game without rules. No-one was in control.'

Meanwhile in a nondescript British town preparations are being made for a cutting-edge TV game Show. It promises contestants dangerous excitement and radical self-discovery in a closed environment where action and consequence bear no relation to each other; the game has no rules, no structure and no-one is in control. 'Game Show' explores issues of personal identity, choices and individual accountability against a backdrop of a war that becomes a game and a game that becomes a war.

Available on Amazon and Smashwords or via the author's website

at allie-cresswell.com

Readers' Reviews of Game Show

A powerful, disturbing book.

'... Gripping.' 'Compelling.' 'A real page-turner!'

Love this idea and the way the author handles it.

The tension builds up beautifully

All the strands are pulled tighter and tighter together then tied into a very satisfying knot, complete with bow, at the end.

This book is dedicated

to my Mum

Jean Cresswell

1930 - 2013

Tiger in a Cage

By

Allie Cresswell

Present Day: By Firelight

'Do you think you'll ever marry again?'

The question drops like a nuclear bomb into the unsuspecting peace of the fire-lit library. We are lounging on the saggy sofas, spread-eagled and spent by the rigours of the remote seaside holiday. We have hiked over tufted sand-dunes, and scrabbled along rocks treacherous with slimy seaweed, and shrieked as the tide chased us, and been buffeted all day by late autumn breezes as boisterous as ourselves. And then, arriving back at our temporary home, we have gorged on tea and toast, and now we roast by the roaring sea-logs which burn blue with salt. Someone has closed the curtains, but no-one has bothered to switch on the lamps, and so the library is mercifully gloomy, and in any case the glow of my face can be attributed to my position on the hearthrug beside the fire.

'Oh Lord!' I exclaim, perhaps a little too shrilly, 'I shouldn't think anyone will ever ask me!'

'Why not?'

I can feel the heavy, comfortable exhaustion in the room shift, fractionally. There is a draught of consciousness being drawn back from somnolence. Nobody moves, or, at least, I don't see that they do, but I sense the lifting of an eyebrow, the slight intake of breath which denotes that the interest of the others in the library has been engaged by my daughter's question. Or perhaps they are all asleep, and the draught I feel is only the lifting of my own shroud.

Somewhere in the inner reaches of the rambling, cliff-perched house, others of our party are beginning to emerge pinkly from early baths; the rattle of cutlery drawers denotes that they will begin the preparations for dinner. Presently there will be the plink and fizz of generous gin and tonics.

'Why not?' Lucy asks again.

I sigh, and stroke her hair back from her forehead; she is lying full stretch on the hearth rug and has her head in my lap. In answering her, I lower my voice: the reality is nothing to boast about; it's a hard reality, one I would rather not face, let alone voice, even to myself, much less in this room at this moment with its silently attentive listeners.

'Oh, you know. Once was something of a miracle, really, for someone like me. Who'd be interested in a plain old bird now?

'You're not old,' Lucy says, soothingly.

There is a muffled snort from the person who is lying on the sofa behind me, which could be a snore, but which eerily expresses my own inner indignation that she has chosen the age, and not the plainness, to deny. But in fact there is no point in denying either: I *am* old. At forty nine I am well past any prime I may fleetingly have enjoyed. My back aches and I have a map of thread veins on my inner thighs. My hair is going grey, something I do absolutely nothing to hide although I notice that I am unusual in this amongst women of my age. My figure is losing its delineations. This is something I do attempt to counteract, with a good diet and plenty of exercise, but feel increasingly that I am merely clinging on to the top of a slippery slope. I wake up with creases in my face which do not smooth away with the application of moisturiser, even the expensive ones which promise to restore seamlessness. Sometimes I sit in front of my mirror and with one hand on either side of my face, crease the flesh inwards towards my nose. The result is instant ageing and an appalling likeness to my mother. Oh God! 'This is what you will look like when you are seventy,' I say to myself, sternly. When I let go, the difference seems slight. 'This is what you look like now. Face it; your fantasies are girlish and ridiculous. Wake up, and smell the Steradent.'

'There must be *some* men who don't go for looks,' muses Lucy. It isn't a question, it's a thesis. She is pondering the idea. Oh! The naivety of the young! She is a strikingly beautiful young woman who has always attracted hordes of adoring swains and has already, at only twenty seven, had two quite serious proposals of marriage.

'Not many,' I comment. 'It's all to do with natural selection, you know - survival of the fittest. A man will be keener on procreation if he has a wife he fancies.' I hope, by this deliberately provocative gambit, to open the conversation up to include the others in the room, and to divert the subject of the discussion from my own personal prospects to the dynamics of relationships in general.

I fail. A slight movement of the sofa behind me suggests that its occupant has marginally changed his position; uncrossed his ankles, perhaps, or turned his head on the cushion, but whether that is in order to take more interest in the dialogue or to facilitate sleep I don't know. Julia, on the sofa opposite, has her eyes open and is staring with intensity into the fire. Her husband, Gerald, the fifth and final occupant of the room, fills an armchair next to the low table where our tea cups and crumby toast plates are stacked. He smiles vacantly at me and shifts his unlit pipe from one side of his mouth to the other. No-one speaks, and it occurs to me that my daughter's initial question was one which they had each asked themselves (and probably one another) about me in the past, and now they are simply waiting to have their curiosity satisfied. If that is the case, I wonder why none of them has come out and just asked. We have known each other well for years, thrown together as neighbours when we all moved into Combe Close and even after our enclave broke up, have continued to holiday, like this, on a regular basis. They knew my husband, and witnessed for themselves the less than happy relations which existed between us. Perhaps they are just curious to know whether my failure to make one marriage happy will make me less, or more likely to repeat the experiment. Perhaps this idle curiosity was just what had prompted my daughter's question, out of the blue. Perhaps I have no need to feel threatened. It is possible that I have not been rumbled at all. I am sure, as sure as I can be, that I have never betrayed myself by any conscious word or gesture. My tiger is safely in its cage.

'But just suppose...' Lucy says, sitting up and throwing another log onto the fire, '....just suppose that you did meet a man ....'

'A partially-sighted one, do you mean?' I interject, with an attempt at hilarity.

'If you insist.'

'And single, necessarily,' I add.

'I suppose so.'

'Of my own age?'

'Or older. Slightly older.'

'Well, there you are then,' I conclude, triumphantly. 'How many of those do you meet? You see, darling, the possibility gets more and more remote the more you think about it.'

Lucy gives me one of her looks, and throws herself back down onto the rug. Julia drags her eyes from the mesmerising flames and gives me a baleful smile. She evidently concurs with my conclusion. She heaves herself to her feet and announces her intention to go for a bath. Gerald makes no response and she leaves the room.

It is my belief that I have quashed the topic of conversation for good. It is particularly important to me to do so. To continue it in any kind of earnest might result in my revealing that in spite of the fact that I have no earthly expectation of marrying again I am utterly unable to quell the irrational and pathetically juvenile hope that love might come within my reach. Oh! I don't under-estimate the unfeasibility of it; my age, personal attractions and history of failure are decidedly against its likelihood, not to mention the strict conditions of integrity with which I am constitutionally prone to strangle its first tentative mews of life. Yet, there it is.

I am mistaken in my belief. 'So? Would you?'

'It's *so* unlikely,' I laugh, but there's an edge to my laughter which I recognise instantly as being the precursor to tears. The others recognise it

11

too. Gerald sits up and begins to grope around the floor with his toe, searching for his slippers. Lucy gets up from the floor and takes possession of the vacated sofa. I assume that from my tone she detects that she has almost broken me and will soon have got at the truth, and chooses this elevated position to further pressurise me. I wonder at her cruelty; but then I remember her father. The man behind me makes the smallest noise with his tongue, like a tut, which I interpret, for the time being, as being impatience at my overly emotional response to a perfectly straight forward hypothetical question.

I grasp the nettle. 'Probably not, no.' I say. 'Even in the extremely unlikely event of anyone being prepared to overlook my age and unarguable hideousness, I would probably not marry him.' Marriage, indeed, makes no appearance on my horizon. But love, yes. Closeness, companionship, understanding – oh yes, all of those. I have, in the face of unattainable odds, pinned my hopes upon them, and the vision sustains me. I do not underestimate the impossibility of it, but then what evil spell of ugliness ever kept a prince from his princess? What enchanted forest of thorns ever separated a knight from his damsel? Doesn't love thrive on the impossible? Doesn't hope defy likelihood, and flutter its wings in the face of an onslaught of probability? Certainly mine has; though imprisoned in a tower of silence, it has refused to be reasoned out of existence.

'Humph.' Gerald says, suggesting that I have made a satisfactory answer. He gets up and stretches, then picks up the tray and carries it out. Evidently all my friends have felt it needed confirming that I had no matrimonial aspirations whatsoever. I wonder why this should be. Charitably, I conclude that they all see how much happier I have been since Stan died; it's undeniable, I *have* been happier, in many ways. *They* have caused me happiness, through their friendship, but it is possible that they do not realise how important they are to me and just assume that I am unsuitable for the married state; that I am doomed both to make and to be made unhappy. Maybe they are better realists than I. They do not suspect the absurd aberration which is caged in the fortress of my matronly heart.

From the kitchen, I hear the jolly chatter of friends making dinner. The men joke and lever the tops off bottles of Schweppes, pretending to help with the cooking but getting in the way. The women clatter pans and gently scold the men, while the younger people are sent to set the table. In another room, someone is playing the piano, rather well. The noise from elsewhere seems to have relieved the intensity of the atmosphere in the room. It is as though a scene has ended in a play and we have found ourselves in the wings while the lights blaze on others posturing on the stage. The fire needs more fuel but we don't normally use this room after dinner and so we will allow it to die down. Later, we might play charades, or cards and there will be an elaborate effort made to ensure that I do not feel awkward about having no partner. These are my friends, and I have betrayed them all. My hope is not abstract; my vision no hazy anonymous fantasy. He has a name. He has a face. He is here.

Yes I have betrayed them, I think, but not more than they have betrayed me, with their secrets and private eccentricities that I have struggled, for twenty odd years, to contain. I have been the stopper on the bottle of the evil genie of their wayward impulses. It has cost me, though.

Lucy is lying on her stomach, now, reaching down with a languid arm and playing with the fringe on the bottom of the sofa. I really feel that I might have satisfied her curiosity this time and that she will leave the subject alone, but I am wrong again.

'Why not?'

I heave a testy sigh. 'Why would I not marry him?'

The man behind me is as still and silent as the sofa he is lying on. He must be fast asleep.

'Mmmm.' She doesn't look at me.

I cross the hearth rug and lean against the sofa where she rests her head, and lower my voice to a whisper. 'I wouldn't marry him just because he was available, or just because he asked,' I say, resolutely, 'I'm not *that* desperate. I know where *that* leads you.' I am speaking with a lock-and-key finality but before I can shut the door on it a gleam of light escapes from its prison, 'but if there was a man I loved, and if I was truly convinced that he loved me, and if we were free to be together without any......' shadows, I want to say, but I let the sentence trail away. Indeed I am appalled that I have said so much.

There is a sigh of breath long held but now released, like a dreamer moving from one dream to another. Simultaneously, my daughter says, 'Ahhh. You hope for that too, do you?'

'Of course! But I don't expect it. People my age have so much....baggage. Too many attachments. They're not free to make the choices that younger people can.'

We are silent for a while. Then she says, 'This man, what does he look like?'

Her penetration stupefies me. 'Looks!' I bluster, 'it doesn't matter what he looks like!'

'No, it doesn't matter, but what does he look like?'

I smile, nervously. This is becoming very risky. 'Oh,' I laugh, seeming to dismiss the question, 'he has a quirky smile, and very kind eyes,' I say, as if I am plucking irrelevancies from the air, like motes.

She nods, satisfied at last, and gets up from the sofa. Without a word, she leaves the room.

Slowly, I dare to raise my eyes to the man on the other sofa. He is not asleep. He has not been asleep. His eyes are wide open and they are looking at me, not for the first time, in a way which feeds my poor incarcerated hope.

He will not stay here in this room alone with me. I know he will not stay.

That is one of the things I love about him; his goodness, his self-control; his and mine together form a bulwark which has kept us on the straight and narrow. He gets up from the sofa, but reluctantly. He walks to the door, then turns.

'You are not plain,' he says.

It only lasts a moment, and then the look is gone. Soon I will be left alone in a cold, dark room. But he looks at me before he goes, and smiles.

He has a quirky smile. And very kind eyes.

Combe Close: The Crescent Set

I think I had better begin these reminiscences by telling you about Combe Close. Perhaps you won't recall that in the early Eighties there was a rash of 'executive' building developments catering for the newly affluent Yuppies and Dinkies that Mrs Thatcher's Britain was spawning. You could say that Combe Close was of that ilk. The original plans for it raised a storm of objections from local residents. A developer got hold of a property on a staid and established residential road known simply as 'the Crescent'. *Combe House* had a wide plot with extensive lawns in front and an orchard behind and further gardens to each side. The house itself was every bit as imposing as its neighbours, built at the turn of the last century; solid, red brick, with commodious rooms carefully laid out for gracious living; the gracious living itself augmented by the provision of servants' quarters. Unlike its neighbours, however, it had been subjected, over the years, to no improvements and precious little maintenance. It had been inhabited at last by an elderly lady and her reclusive brother. They had allowed the trees and shrubs in the garden to creep up to the house, casting its interior into perpetual gloom and infesting its brickwork with a greenish damp which penetrated through to the ancient stucco of the elaborate plaster cornices. They had retreated, these two siblings, fusty and shy, lost and confused by the modern world, to two rooms at the back of the house; the chilly, echoing kitchen and the butler's pantry. Meanwhile water pooled in the centre of the ornate drawing room and ivy inveigled its way through a broken upper window to embrace the antique bedroom suites. Swifts nested every year in the heavy walnut tallboy of the master bedroom and above their heads, crows raised clutches of clamouring young in the roof space made accessible by slipped tiles and disintegrated felt. The old lady and her brother shuffled with ever more arthritic difficulty down the scullery passage to the servants' lavatory. Her weekly shopping expeditions, on foot, became too much and in time they were reduced to living on whatever the milkman would deliver. The macadam of the drive broke up and became treacherous with slick moss and un-cleared leaves. Unable to get to the gate they piled their rubbish up outside the back door and it attracted rats, then cats, which all bred and infiltrated the house and its environs.

The Crescent set complained. The place was an eyesore and detracted from their own immaculate properties. It constituted a health hazard; they feared for little Cameron Jnr and darling Chelsea-Marie. Almost as an after-thought they postulated that perhaps the inhabitants were 'at risk', clearly not able to cope, in need of governmental intervention. None of them, for a moment, considered what they might be able to do to ameliorate the sad condition of the old folks at *Combe House*. In the end Social Services removed the old people, blinking and remonstrating feebly, to a municipal nursing home, and put their house on the market. The Crescent set were quietly jubilant, imagining a moneyed family who would replace the roof and install new windows, clear the tangle of shrubs and ivy from the garden, put in en-suite bathrooms and the latest thing in kitchen units, join the golf club. Their horror on learning that the house was to be bulldozed, the site cleared and eight bijoux, 'executive style' homes built on the leafy, well-heeled sweep of the Crescent was beyond articulation. They held a hurried meeting, over sherry, and deputed the barrister from *Hazelwood* and the television presenter from *Hillside* to head up their campaign of opposition, with the car 'phone millionaire from *Westerly Gable* to co-ordinate communications. They attended the Planning Committee *en masse*, choking up the council offices car park with their Range Rovers and high end BMWs and getting the committee secretary's minutes in a muddle with their continual interruptions and apostrophic cries of indignation. The barrister and the television presenter each spoke for three minutes covering their concerns; the over-crowded site, the lack of adequate gardens, the design-scheme which was not 'in keeping' and 'would look too new', access and possible disruption to traffic. Their real objections, of course, remained unvoiced; the development would lower the tone, the people would be the wrong

17

sort, the houses would lack the éclat and the inhabitants the élan of the Crescent and its set.

The developer, a stolid, unflappable entrepreneur, argued cogently in favour of the plans, countering the opposition's points with relentless logic. The plot was quite large enough, he said, for the homes, in the arrangement as suggested; the angles, the sight-lines all calculated as per regulations for privacy. Each garden while, admittedly, being much smaller than the norm for the Crescent, was quite in keeping with the scale which most householders found adequate and manageable 'in these modern days'. The architect had incorporated aspects of design from nearby dwellings into his drawings. He presented photographs which the startled opposition lobby recognised as their own fascias and soffits, gabled windows and pretentious porticoes. The scheme would be artificially 'aged', its newness softened by the use of reclaimed, rather than new brick, hardwood windows rather than uPVC, proper brick chimneys rather than flues. Access posed no difficulty. Traffic, in that sequestered, affluent, residential area, was negligible. Apart from Crescent residents the only significant 'through' traffic were golfers accessing the club at its far end and most of those preferred the more direct route via the Avenue.

The planning committee deliberated, with an eye to their quota for new housing provision, reviewed the plans with minute attention and circulated the architect's schematics. One councillor, a zealous newcomer to the committee, suggested a site visit, but the idea was quashed by longer-standing, more languid colleagues. In the end, by way of compromise, they passed the plans but reduced the number of dwellings from eight to six. The developer allowed himself a grin; it was exactly what he had anticipated. The Crescent set withdrew in disgust.

All this is important because it explains why it was that we in the Close came to rely so quickly and so strongly on each other; we had no choice - we were simply ignored, even ostracised, by the existing residents of the Crescent. We could feel their animosity gusting towards us across the wide swathes of their lawns, resentment as brittle as the glass in their orangery panes. While the builders had been at work so too had the householders immediately adjacent to the site. Alan and Sheila's house, and to a certain extent ours too, was perennially gloomy until midday due to a towering hedge of leylandii now left purposefully unchecked which belonged to *Eventide* on its eastern border. Marcus and Carla moved in to find a twelve foot brushwood fence at the bottom of their garden. Carla, with her usual gay flippancy remarked that it made her feel like something unsightly which had to be shielded from the sensitive public eye - like a municipal dump or sewage works, or even like a wild animal that had to be kept at bay. It was an eyesore until Marcus had the good idea of training espaliered peach and pear trees up its south-facing elevations. (They fruited beautifully after a year or two and Carla and I experimented with poached pears in Amaretto, peach schnapps and various preserves.) Pete and Pam had a running battle with their Crescent neighbours over the children which went on for years. The boys had only to squeak in the garden and the harridan from *Hazelwood* (the barrister's wife) would be round crying 'noise pollution' and threatening the environmental health officer. Pam and Pete had four boys, all told, and they cost her a fortune in footballs which went over into *Hazelwood* and whose reclamation was refused. Pete got his own back, though, when, in the guise of encouraging their musicality, he bought the three oldest electric guitars and the youngest a drum kit.

When we moved in, nobody from the Crescent called in to say hello. We were not invited to join the Neighbourhood Watch scheme. We were pointedly excluded from their round of entertaining at Christmastime and the Round Table Christmas float with Father Christmas aboard did not stop for us. One winter, in a terrible blizzard, we were without power for four days and our cars were useless against the drifts. We ran out of milk and bread while the Crescent set organised jolly emergency shopping expeditions in their 4 x 4s. Randomly thrown together we found ourselves required to rely on each other, almost forced into friendship. We threw ourselves into neighbourliness; *I* did, anyway, rather to Stan's disgust. Combe Close, and the years we spent there, represented to me, at the time, and since, a sort of watershed, an idyll. I entered into that period eagerly, full of expectation which was perhaps naively idealistic. I was determined that, after the unpromising start I had made in life, there, I would make good. I think I did; I certainly have the scars to prove it. And now, even though it is over and we have scattered to other areas, I like to think there is much that remains. It does not remain intact. But it remains.

That's more than the Crescent set can say. Where the car 'phone millionaire is now, or the Pizza Hut impresario, or the television presenter, I do not know but I doubt that they are in touch with each other. One by one they sold up and sold out. Eight out of fifteen houses on the Crescent have now been demolished to make way for two or four or six smaller dwellings, or small blocks of apartments. Extra houses have been squeezed onto spare acres of garden. In fact of all that original Crescent set only the barrister and his sharp-tongued wife remain. She has been incapacitated by a stroke, I believe, and is confined to bed in one of the downstairs rooms of *'Hazelwood'*. He has taken to drink. The house is in a terrible state.

Combe Close: Stan and Molly

Stan and I were the first to move into Combe Close. Really the site was barely ready for occupation but Stan was so keen not to waste another month's money on rent that he harried the builders to complete our house ahead of schedule. They must have been sick of the sight of his car turning up at all hours of the day, his tall, angular figure picking its way over the unmade road and between the pallets of bricks. He had managed to get – goodness knows how – his own set of specifications and he would check them rigorously against the actuality of the emerging house, thinking nothing of hauling the electrician or the plumber from another job to change something he thought wasn't quite 'to spec'. The site manager, whose job that really was, gave up remonstrating with him after a while and even issued Stan with his own hard hat in line with health and safety policy, clearly reasoning that the quicker he completed the build the quicker he'd get Stan off his back.

We moved in before the road was made up even with its initial layer of tarmac. In March, dust eddied round the close in mini tornadoes, all-pervading, coating everything; it gave the site a desiccated, parched, colour-drained appearance and you could feel its grit between your teeth and on your skin if you ventured outside. Not that there was much incentive for going out: noisy delivery trucks came and went all day long with loads of timber and bags of cement and plaster and leering, cat-calling drivers. The garden was like a land-fill, full of bricks and builders' lunch wrappings and those indestructible lengths of plastic strapping and solid clods of clay. It rained solidly throughout April and the road turned to a quagmire, ankle-deep in squelching yellow mud, virtually impassable. Water pooled on our hastily-laid patio and dripped from the incorrectly angled gutters. It was like living on a floating island, then, and I would watch the oil-skinned builders, like battling mariners, toiling across the sucking wastes, and the lorries reversing like liners through the torrential rain, incarcerated in my echoing, uncarpeted, sparsely furnished lounge. It wasn't very auspicious, to tell the truth, at first. Looking out at the wasteland of mud; it was hard to see how I would make it into all I dreamed, and all I needed it, to be.

At weekends it was quiet, and Stan would prowl around the site, into the other houses, pacing out the room sizes to compare with ours, assessing the prospective occupants' choices of bathroom fitting and tile. He filched paving slabs from where they were stacked in the yard beside the site manager's office and laid paths down the sides of our house, saying only, in response to my objection; 'Who's to know *where* they came from? You can get these at any DIY store. And in any case, they *ought* to have done it for us.' One Sunday he laboured from dawn till dusk to reposition by a foot the temporary post-and-rail fencing which divided our plot from next door's, giving us a full extra thirty-odd square foot of rubble-and rubbish-choked garden. I played no part in the escapade. I was five months pregnant with Lucy by then, but in any case I disapproved. No amount of Stan's striding from side to side, counting up the paces, or jabbing his finger at the plans could convince me that he was only correcting an error made when the site was originally laid out. It was stealing, plain and simple, but if I did not abet, I knew better than to thwart him.

What can I tell you about Stan and I? He was tall and skinny, with perennially pale skin, like a plant raised in the dark. He was hairy, too, surprisingly so, all over, with a regular bluish shadow on his cheeks and chin which needed relentless shaving to keep at bay. Once, during a holiday, I persuaded him to try a beard and it grew luxuriantly, but on his spare face and over his fleshless, concave body, and especially in conjunction with his restless, strangely demon-haunted eyes, it made him look like a species of deranged hermit or an old testament prophet, and the experiment was abandoned before we went home.

He worked for the council, or, as he preferred to say, with self-aggrandising pomposity, was a Civil Servant. He was always theatrically vague about his specific role, implying official secrets and corridors of power, but in fact he worked for most of his career in traffic management, devising tortuous one-way systems and scattering mini-roundabouts across the borough, and causing pelican crossings to sprout in places where nobody needed them. It was the perfect job for him. He was part of an inexorable and irresistible machine, imposing edicts, managing changes which, while not necessarily paying much lip-service to what was practical, were unanswerable because they were 'policy'. He liked the power it gave him. At the same time the facelessness of it suited him too. He was sly. But he was also relentlessly dogged, waving away objections to any scheme he had in view, stonily determined, and I used to believe that nothing was impossible for him. As a preternaturally ingrained respecter of authority myself, imbued from the cradle 'not to put myself forward' and to 'know my place' I suppose I was the perfect foil for him, and he for me. At first I saw his determination as manly and admirable but gradually – too late – I recognised it for what it was: insistent self-assertion which brooked no denial. He domineered. He cheated. He bullied.

And me? I had very strict, old-fashioned parents. As well as being old-fashioned they themselves were old, older than the average, anyway. I was their only child, something of a surprise; I think I would even go so far as to say something of an embarrassment – my appearance a patent proof of the nocturnal interaction which must have gone before. They were ultra-conservative, teetotallers, dour and humourless with an in-grained suspicion and a kind of in-built, inherent criticism of everyone and everything else. My mother's lip was almost permanently curled in what I can only describe as a disapproving sneer. They expected – and, to be fair, engaged in – behaviour of the very best, rigidly self-controlled, morally upright kind, inculcating me with the standards of an era which was already long-gone. I was brought up to be 'good', where the watch-words for goodness were 'clean', 'tidy', 'healthy', 'wholesome', 'honest' and 'decent'. Anything which was one – or more – of these things was considered safe, and, as far as it went, I think it was a solid enough foundation. The problem was that it was too narrow and much too rigorously imposed. We rarely laughed at home. Any spare time, and our few holidays, were spent in self-improvement; visiting museums and stately homes, and reading educational books. Although my parents had money there was a perpetual sense of parsimony, a pinched meanness, and any kind of fun was eschewed as being in some way reprehensible, almost sinful, although I do not mean to imply that my parents were church-goers; they preferred to live by their own unyielding, unforgiving standards. There were no treats or surprises, no frills, no softness. As a result things at home were never what you could call *nice*. My childish idea of niceness was bathed in a golden glow of forbidden fripperies, soft-edged, sweet and insubstantial, like candy-floss. As I got older it mellowed; I would have settled for cosy, relaxed, affectionate and happy. No, things are home were not nice, but they were unimpeachably *good* and I was never really able to understand why those two things had to be mutually exclusive.

I mourned niceness, I think, throughout my childhood, and set my sights on achieving for myself a life which would be nice *and* good.

I was one of those mousy and insignificant girls - never top of the class but never at the bottom of it either. Clumsy at games, I was a liability on any team. My parents' strictness, and my own lack of assertiveness, made me afraid to try the kind of uniform adaptation which allowed other girls to look attractive even in grey pleated skirts and blazers. I was not allowed heels higher than an inch. Platform soles, when they were in fashion, were forbidden as likely to inflict permanent malformation of the pelvis although I yearned to own a pair even at the risk of possible disablement. My mother did not believe in diets or in washing the hair more than twice a week and make-up was frowned upon; my cautious efforts with eye shadow and mascara did not impress. 'You can't make a silk purse out of a sow's ear,' she said, and I think she meant it kindly, trimming my expectations to an achievable realism. I liked boys and worshipped a few from afar, but they didn't take any notice of me and in those excruciating sessions of country dancing which took place in the gym on days when it was too wet to play hockey I ended up with the spectacled, the spotty and the stout, boys with perspiring palms and protuberant teeth who were probably as unhappy with their partner as I was. I took A levels – and did quite well, actually – but when I floated the idea of going to University to study English literature it was quashed with 'Well what good will *that* do you?' so I got a job as a telephone banking helpline operator and spent each day sequestered in my cubicle helping irate customers with their PIN numbers and standing orders and trying to fill my quota of additional sales and services. At twenty two I already felt like an old maid, like Charlotte Vane in *Now Voyager*, almost demented by frustration and repression and self-loathing and hopelessness. I was ready to be rescued and it is little wonder that I fell into the arms of the first man to look at me twice.

Combe Close: Gerald and Julia

Ours was the second house on the right, the smallest of the available designs. It stood cheek by jowl with its next neighbour along, the two dwellings quite close but the gardens spanning out behind them into the far corner of the site, what had been the orchard of *Combe House,* and indeed a few of the gnarled old apple trees had been spared the bulldozer. The houses were mirror images in every way from the outside, their opposite drives embracing an expanse of shared lawn at the front – bitter bone of later contention - but whereas we had chosen to leave the lounge and dining room open-plan, the neighbours had opted for two separate rooms. They had picked an old-fashioned design of kitchen unit and utilitarian white for the bathroom, en-suite and downstairs cloakroom. Their utility room had been enlarged by the reduction of their garage – clearly they never anticipated keeping a car in there – and was bare apart from a large, low sink, and that puzzled me, until Julia and Gerald moved in, with their three shaggy, shambolic, bearded collies which they showed and bred. Julia referred to her utility room as 'the whelping room' and three times a year there would be a litter of puppies, a cacophony of yelping and an overpowering aroma of fecund dog.

If memory serves me correctly, they were the next to move in after us and my relief at having a neighbour and my eagerness to bring to life my vision made me oblivious to the obvious disparities between us. After weeks marooned in the house, on doctor's orders signed off work, prevented from taking the bus into town or even the walk down to the local shops, I was desperate for company so I hurried round to say hello before the removal van had got its doors properly open. They were the first to arrive in what I had been constructing in my imagination as my advert-perfect Combe Close world.

They had had their carpets laid already but they were not new ones, garishly patterned ancient Axminster, dark in places where furniture had stood in their previous house, otherwise faded and showing some wear and bringing the scent of dog into the house as much as the three animals corralled in the kitchen, whose claws I could hear clicking and scrabbling on the new floor tiles and already scraping at the thin gloss of the door. Julia was in the lounge surrounded by a number of cardboard boxes she had lifted from the car and holding a table lamp for which there was no suitable surface. She looked dishevelled; her grey hair wild and unkempt and the buttons of her quilted nylon body-warmer done up wrong. At the time I took this to be the understandable distracted disarray of house-moving but now I know that it is her perpetual condition. I never met a woman less bothered about dress or personal appearance. I introduced myself and, spying the kettle peeking from the top of one of the boxes, offered to make tea.

'Oh tea, by all means, m'dear,' she bellowed. 'The universal panacea, what?' I wanted to laugh at what seemed to be the most affected St Trinian's hockey mistress accent I had ever heard. I only just stopped myself from rejoining 'tally-ho' before she marched past me, thrusting the table lamp into my hands, and began to harangue the removal men on the drive with exactly the same marble-choked, home-counties drawl.

She was at least twenty years older than me, rather on the heavy side; stocky would be the polite word for her build, I suppose. Properly attired she could be as stately as a galleon in full sail, with the kind of full figure which Hattie Jacques in her prime or Diana Dors managed to make voluptuous and attractive. But she only ever wore tweed skirts or sometimes thick woollen trousers which she called 'trews', and layers of jumpers and cardigans which she peeled off or pulled on according to the weather, almost invariably topped by her green gilet. Even back at the time I am recalling her face was weathered, mottled by thread veins, its lower delineations obscured by heavy, quivering jowls. She had a largish wart or other kind of fleshy blemish just above her eyebrow but the hairs which sprouted from it melded conveniently into her brow which was black and thick. Her hair was always wild, steel-grey, crammed into a waxed sou'wester if it rained or an ugly knitted bobble hat if it was cold, or a broken old straw hat in summer. Her hands were large and strong, calloused and not always very clean, but very gentle. I have seen her restore fallen featherless chicks, all beak and outsized eyes, into their nests, and ease puppies, blind and slimy, from their mother, and she was always the one we went to when our children had bee stings or splinters or worse. She has a tender competence with all living things. It is a shame she never had any children and I know it is a sorrow to her but one which, even by the time I met her, she had accepted with a sigh.

In the weeks that followed I observed that she did little in the way of housework, as though relying on some invisible functionary to come and tackle it at some stage, but frankly not caring much about it either way. Her garden, though, was immaculate, with its steep slope disguised by terraced beds minutely weeded and broken up by well-behaved plants climbing up trellises, fruiting and flowering under her beetling eye. She was almost always to be found there, when she was not at the local garden centre where she soon got a position working two days a week, happily potting up cuttings and hefting bags of compost. Other than that she walked her dogs twice daily with religious regularity.

The dogs, although exuberant, were obedient to her word, and Stan's fears, (that they would make our lives hell with their infernal barking), turned out to be largely unjustified. Gerald, less exuberant than the dogs, indeed, somewhat ponderous, was also deferential, not with mute submissiveness but with a crusty chivalry which is sadly rare, always ready to hold out a chair or open a door, and although not a big conversationalist could always be relied upon to come in with some affirming comment like 'Splendid!' or 'Quite right too'. In those early days he impressed me as being a deep thinker, staring at a point in the middle distance with his pipe clamped between his teeth, his brow contracted with concentration. You hesitated to distract him with anything as mundane as a 'Good morning' and would content yourself with a waved greeting, which he would soberly return with a Churchillian nod. Like

Julia he was large, more than portly, with a chesty wheeze and a bow-legged gait. He helped make ends meet by teaching people to drive in a tiny hatchback which he levered himself with great difficulty into and out of. I know he was a patient and unflappable tutor because, later, he was to teach me, politely letting me crash and grind at the gears and kangaroo along the Avenue without comment until I finally got it, when he would appear to come out of a reverie to declare 'Jolly good, Molly m'dear! That's the ticket!'

I helped them for the rest of the day – not with the heavy work, of course – but making myself useful in other ways; unpacking boxes of kitchen things and folding up the newspaper they had used to wrap their ornaments and framed photographs – almost all bearded collie related – and making endless pots of tea. They seemed to accept my assistance as a matter of course, and I wondered once or twice if they assumed I was a member of the removals team or even a maid-of-all-work who came with the house. Julia gave me the occasional breezy direction ('That goes with the Crown Derby in the sideboard, left hand side, m'dear.') while she hefted their heavy furniture about and wielded packing cases with the strength of a seasoned caber-tosser. She was everywhere, chivvying the removals men, unpacking boxes, making up the beds (they were to have separate rooms, I remarked, she the larger with the en-suite bathroom, he the second, but the style of the furnishing in each was equally dour, of a style long passed; heavy carved bedsteads made up with sheets and blankets, slippery eiderdowns and candlewick bed-spreads).

Gerald oversaw the unloading and manoeuvring of the furniture in a nominally supervisory role and, when called upon for an opinion removed his pipe from between his teeth and said 'Just the thing!' and 'Quite the best plan!' The dogs, released from the kitchen, spent a mad half hour careering round their garden (and also around mine) before flopping spent on the patio, ready to watch the show. Their mouths gaped in perpetual laughter, their bellies rose and fell in silent guffaws, their tiny, twinkling, mischievous eyes, only just visible behind their fringes, glinted with raffish humour.

There was far more furniture than could be accommodated in the house, and the furniture itself was all too big – huge high bureaux and massive chests of drawers, tall glass-fronted display cabinets, spreading, heavily-upholstered, claw-footed sofas – all clearly antique, probably very valuable and wholly unsuitable for the restricted proportions of a modern house. As it continued to disgorge from the van on the bowed shoulders of the puce, sweating men, it began to create a gaggling queue up the drive, like a Disney furniture parade, while the pieces which had gone before struggled to find their appropriate situation inside. Itinerant bits of it even began to wander onto the newly turfed expanse of shared lawn in front of our two houses, while, within, Julia shifted and lugged and contrived to accommodate it all. It turned into one of those games of logic where you have to move six or seven things which you've already got in the right place out of the way while you negotiate an eighth thing into position. Eventually, as the sun began to set, and the removal men to make frequent, glowering reference to their wrist watches, the surplus had to be carried into the garage as a temporary measure.

For weeks afterwards I would draw my bedroom curtains in the morning to find Julia and Gerald in the process of rearranging their furniture. Odd bits of it would be on the drive – or even, once, poking out of an upper window - while more items were inched into place. Sometimes they would carry a piece of it round to the back door or inveigle it through the French windows, like a guerrilla tactic, in an effort to catch the rest off-guard and surprise it into making room. It was as though they sincerely believed that somehow it could all be accommodated, perfectly tessellated into their inadequate footprint, if only they could get the sequence right. I imagined them pondering the puzzle as they went about their daily tasks, poring, perhaps, over sheets of squared graph paper in the small hours, like a fiendishly difficult jig-saw they just couldn't leave alone, and then, in the morning, starting again with a new strategy. But it was clear to me that unless they were prepared to compromise on the matter of fully opening drawers or easily accessible whatnots, or could live with having to physically scramble over the back of the sofa in order to enter the lounge, all their attempts were doomed.

When Stan got home that evening my cheeks were flushed and I was garrulous with the news of it all, and dinner was late. He sat at the table and scowled while I hastily grilled chops and mashed potato.

'They seem such nice people,' I gushed, 'but so funny, like escapees from a Barbara Pym novel.'

'Did they say anything about the fence?'

'Not that I heard. But they were too busy. They will be for days, I'd think.'

'I don't want you over-doing it.'

'I didn't. I enjoyed it, really.'

'Haven't you enough to do here?'

I looked around the room. Our two-seater settee and single arm chair. Our nest of tables. Our TV on its plastic pedestal. Our little gate-leg dining table and two chairs. Our still uncarpeted floor. Our still naked light bulbs. How much dusting, how much polishing, how much hoovering did he think they needed? How much time could they possibly occupy in my endless, lonely day?

'I just enjoyed the company,' I said. 'And it's nice, anyway, being neighbourly, isn't it?'

'They'll start putting on you, two old people like that.'

'They aren't *that* old!'

'All the same.'

Present Day: Jury Service

It is a strange feeling to come home to an empty house. As I open the door I often have a powerful sense of things whisking away; whisperings, sighings, settlings; the last ripple of a billow.

'It's just the draught as you open the door,' Lucy tells me, practically, when I confide this feeling.

Our holiday is over and she and I have parted company at the station, she to return to her south London flat, her commuter life-style, her days spent at a dizzying height in some city high-rise – it is a mystery to me what she does there – I to this quiet little terrace where nobody bothers me and I can get on with the circadian round of my life.

I miss Combe Close, the comings and goings, the spontaneous social gatherings, the sense I had of being a useful part of something. I try, with all my might, to maintain it, rallying people for dinners, keeping abreast of everyone's news. The holiday we have just enjoyed was arranged at my behest. Friends, I think, are so important, perhaps even more than family; the connections you choose and which choose you.

My bedroom is at the back, over-looking the communal garden in which I envisaged – wrongly – a similar interaction between neighbours, a community activity of mowing and planting and resting on the benches leading to the sharing of a bottle of wine or even the occasional impromptu meal; it was what, in Combe Close, was normal. But instead of being a shared responsibility the garden is collectively neglected. The kids play football on it sometimes but none of the adults take any interest in the shrubs or flowers and it has been felt necessary to impose a rota for mowing or nobody would do it at all. It is loveliest at night, in moonlight, when its raggedness is bathed in pearlescence, and cats and foxes, like silvered spirits, range across the colour-leeched lawn. The people are not friendly. I think that they purposefully avoid eye-contact if they can. I can go days without speaking to anybody.

Amongst my post – a mountain of junk mail and pizza take-away menus and the odd bank statement - there is a letter summonsing me to Jury Service. I am to present myself at the Court toward the end of the month and should make arrangements for at least two weeks leave from my work. That is easily arranged. I work at night, mainly, on-line, tutoring distance-learning students in alien time-zones in English literature.

Before I begin the process of home-coming I send texts: 'Home safely. You? Thanks for a great time. Molly Xxx.' Periodically I check my 'phone for replies. Eventually a 'xxx' drops into the in-box from Pam and a :-) from Anya. Meanwhile I methodically unpack my case, load the washing machine, write a shopping list on the back of an envelope. I am a strict uni-tasker. The days of hurrying through chores, doing several things at once, are gone. I find, now, that if I rush things I run out of jobs before I run out of day. But while I plod through the work, my disappointment at the lack of response from my friends is off-set by the delicious stir of my imaginative juices at the prospect of being a Juror. The case, the pomp and process of the court, my fellow-Jurors. It is an unexpected boon, something to look forward to. So many of my weeks are spent on a dogged trek of days through – not the doldrums, not a slough of despond, nothing as bleak as that – but a landscape which, while benign, tends to be fairly featureless; a savannah, perhaps, or a wide prairie. Internally my topography is enlivened by landmarks of my own devising – a constant supply of good books, my daily swim, calls to or from Lucy, my Friday gin and tonic – which relieve the tedium of poorly phrased essays on Dickens and students' inability to appreciate Henry James; ('What does he mean Molly?' 'It doesn't matter what he means. What matters is what the other person THINKS he means.') Then, in the misty distance, a geographical feature will rear up – an escarpment of excitement – a lunch date with Sheila or Pam, an invitation to dinner with Gary and the twins, or even a weekend away, tickets for the theatre, a prospective party, and I begin to measure the distance to it; it fixes my eye as I trudge the unvarying pathway across the plain. I savour it in anticipation as its outlines become clearer, considering my options of ascent, choosing the places where I might pause and take in the view. I am especially thoughtful about equipment – clothing, of course – and essential accessories so that by the time the day arrives I am ready and in peak condition. Then I begin, not in a rush, but gently, sparingly. I sip and nibble, I sniff and savour, I wring every ounce, every moment of pleasure from the climb and always, at the top, I take time to look back at the endless acres of lowland which brought me to this heady height. It will cheer me, the remembrance of it, as I descend and go on, before the next peak shimmers in the distance.

There is a leaflet with the letter and over the next fortnight I read it several times; the roles and responsibilities of a Juror. Travel into town is an issue: nothing on earth would persuade me to take the car into town. Stan's legacy is too intimidating, designed to ensnare an inexperienced city driver like me. Emails to my Combe Close friends (I still think of them as such, although none of them lives there, now) asking for advice come up empty; only Sheila replies and has no suggestions to make about how I'm going to get myself to court every day. So I print off a train time-table and study the A – Z to plot my course across the city to the Crown Court. I look into, and reject, the alternative of buses. After a while I make an experimental excursion to familiarise myself with the route, and time it, carefully. The building, when I reach it, easily and much sooner than I had anticipated, is suitably imposing, its wide shallow steps thronged with people coming and going, a knot of smokers, the occasional barrister, un-wigged but satisfactorily robed, even some members of the press. Witnesses, victims, the accused and their counsel, Jurors, it is impossible to tell them apart. Although I know that these are real people immersed in personal dramas which are potentially painful they are also, to me, a cast, a troupe with stories to tell and my sense of proper responsibility is more than tinged with a thrill of excitement. I cross the road and mount the steps and loiter, for a while, amongst them, enjoying a foretaste of what is to come.

Back at home I contemplate my wardrobe, selecting clothes which are smart and comfortable. The November weather is truly awful; wet, dark, cold and unrelievedly miserable, and I buy a new Macintosh which is warm and waterproof while also being, I think, rather elegant. I buy, also, a commodious but business-like handbag which holds a notebook and a novel and a bottle of water and some snacks – we have been warned, in the leaflet, to expect periods of inactivity and delay. Then I am ready and, between marking essays and explaining for the two hundredth time the difference between quoting a critic and plagiarising one, I re-read *To Kill a Mockingbird* and *Rumpole of the Bailey*.

The day arrives and I rise early, shower, dress and walk to the station. All my planning pays off and I arrive at the Court in perfect time. Up the steps and through the imposing entrance, I am met by a security guard who searches my bag, ushers me through a body scanner and directs me across the hall towards a corridor with a double door at the end marked 'Jurors Only'.

Then I see him.

In the high, ornately decorated hallway, he is standing at the bottom of a flight of steps, immaculate in a dark suit and stylish tie, holding an important-looking briefcase. I must admit that I do a sort of double take. This sudden and unexpected collision unnerves me; he doesn't belong on this mountain. He, the thought of him, is always in my mind, not at the forefront of it, but residing in a peripheral backwater of consciousness, like a treasure locked away; the knowledge of its possession gives a quiet pleasure which, I have trained myself, must suffice. I never engineer contact – emails or telephone calls. I never put myself in his way. To get the treasure out of its vault, to handle it, to display it, to contemplate it at all is just too dangerous and I have schooled myself to do without either the sensuous indulgence or the terrible potential of it. On the other hand there are occasions – like the holiday we have just enjoyed - when he is presented to me without any proactivity on my part. I am innocent of prompting or manoeuvring in any way, and at those times I confess to indulging in my usual programme of anticipation; he is the most longed-for high point in my landscape and the preparations I make for it are both disciplined and delightful. I wonder, I ponder, but I am stern, so, when the time comes I can bask, with clean, still hands, in the encounter.

So the sudden actuality of him is a shock, unexpected, it throws me. I haven't steeled and neither have I preened myself and my first instinct is to put my head down and hurry by amid the crowd. But my sense of connection with him is already drawing me. For all his outward composure I know him well enough to detect the tension in his jaw and shoulders. He is wrestling with a sodden overcoat and a wet umbrella, indispensible for the deluge outside but now annoying encumbrances. He is anxious, and – I can't help it - I walk up to him and put a hand on his arm.

'Molly!' His face clears as though illuminated by a shaft of sunlight through the high, domed glass of the roof. 'What are you doing here?'

'Jury service,' I say. 'What are you?'

'Bankruptcy case – I'm a creditor,' he frowns. Over my head his eyes fix on something. 'There's my brief,' he says, 'I'll have to go. Have lunch with me?'

My breakfast turns to Bollinger. It fizzes inside me. To quell it I look over at the security guard. 'Are we allowed out?'

He gives me an indulgent smile; timidity is one of my defining characteristics. 'Sure to be. I'll wait outside for you.' He squeezes my arm and is about to go but I take the umbrella from him.

'Let me look after this then,' I smile.

'Oh yes, thank you Molly. Bloody thing...' he hands it over and is gone

Combe Close: Gary and Anya (and Katrina)

I ought, perhaps, at this stage in my recollections, to mention that Stan and I moved to Combe Close from another, very much less salubrious area of the town; it might explain my gushing, over-idealistic expectations for our new situation. There was no doubt that the move took us 'up' in the world, but it was facilitated by Stan's promotion at work and by the sale of my recently deceased mother's house and not by any nefarious circumstances. Nevertheless one of Stan's three-line-whip edicts was that we should keep our provenance to ourselves. I couldn't understand why he wanted to be so cagey about it, but that was Stan for you; he was conspicuously close. It wasn't enough for him to have – or to appear to have – secrets; he wanted people to *know* that he had them. It gave him a smug superiority and he would often be darkly mysterious about matters that were easily discoverable and not even very interesting, like how much he had paid for things from high street shops.

One late May day perhaps three weeks after Julia and Gerald had moved in, I saw a natty black sports car pull up and park on the drive of the house almost opposite to ours. The driver helped his companion from the passenger seat and they hurried up the drive and let themselves in with a key.

'New neighbours!' I cried, and levered myself from the chair in the window.

By then the road had been properly surfaced and the front lawns were all turfed. Although the site office remained, perched on the corner of what would become Pam and Pete's front garden, it was deserted for most of the time. All the actual building work had been done and the pallets of blocks and the mounds of sand had been removed. The Close was beginning to look almost residential, but strangely ghostly, like a deserted film-set and indeed I did think of it more and more in those terms – a stage ready for the play of my life to begin. The air was eerily quiet during the day, without the drone of the cement mixer and the put-put-put of the dumper trucks. I quite missed the cheerful, slack-trousered brickies. The plumbers and decorators and tilers and kitchen-fitters were another breed altogether, much less garrulous and more difficult to encounter. I was more ready than ever for the entrance of the actors, the characters whom I was already predisposed to admire.

I tapped on the front door and it swung open. I could hear the couple upstairs, laughing and in high spirits. The echo of their hurried footsteps on the bare boards rang through the house.

I called out 'Hello!' in a sing-songy voice and stepped into the hall.

Their house had a different lay-out to ours; a nice square hall with four doors and the stairs off it and a galleried landing above. At the back of the long living room they had added a conservatory. I knew (witheringly, from Stan) that their en-suite fittings were all 'Barbie' pink.

The man began to descend the stairs and that's when I recognised him, from my old school across town. Taller, of course, and broader, and without the acne which had plagued his teenage years, but still with the same shock of unruly red hair, rather small but very blue eyes and the distinctive broken tooth – the result, I recalled, of a moped accident - which gave his easy grin an urchin appeal. I gasped and said 'Gary Broadbank!' and then immediately regretted it in the sudden clutch of realising that I had instantly and unthinkingly broken Stan's cover. Gary got to the bottom of the stairs and looked at me a bit awkwardly, his hand half extended to take mine. 'Mr Taylor's maths class? Miss Henshaw's English?' I prompted, but hesitantly. Perhaps he, too, might want his origins to remain obscure. But no.

'Molly Cotton!' he laughed, and took my hand firmly in his.

'Molly Burton now,' I corrected him.

He eyed my distended belly. 'I always was fat,' I laughed. 'But at least I have an excuse now.'

He frowned a little. 'No, you weren't,' he said. He looked a bit lost. 'What brings you here?'

We had moved into their lounge. It was brighter than ours from the light that streamed in through the conservatory. I felt a pang of envy.

I pointed through the front window. 'We live opposite. In that little one, there, on the right. I just came over to say hello.'

'How wonderful,' he said. 'Let me fetch Anya.'

He went back upstairs and there was a whispered conference before they descended and he ushered Anya into the room. She hung back in a shy, almost child-like manner, and Gary put his arm around her shoulders and hugged her into his side.

'This is my wife, Anya,' he said.

I smiled and said 'Hello' but she looked so nervous and shrinking that I didn't dare make any kind of gesture beyond that. She was so perfect as to be almost unreal, with all the things that should be small – waist and nose and feet – very tiny indeed and all the things that should be big – eyes and bosom – just a bit too big to be true. Her eyes were enormous, deep liquid brown, thickly fringed with lashes and over-arched by immaculately even and neat brows. Her hair was as sleek and shiny as black silk, and hung down her back in an almost fluid cascade, like treacle. She had long – impractically long, faultlessly manicured – nails. Her lips were full, slicked with pale lipstick and she had perfectly symmetrical white teeth. Her skin was flawless, without crease or blemish and all of it that I could see was tanned and dark. Her dark colouring gave her an exotic air and her high collared, close-fitting black satin dress was very oriental. She remained silent and it occurred to me that she might be foreign and I speculated fleetingly about remote south-sea islands. As she stood in the light, white room, she looked like nothing so much as a dusky Disney cartoon princess, impossibly beautiful, doe-eyed, coltish and insecure, and as two-dimensional.

'I'm Molly,' I said. 'We're going to be neighbours. When are you moving in?'

Anya looked up at Gary as if unable to answer – or perhaps to understand – my question. 'End of next week, or maybe the week after,' he said. 'The floor people are coming in tomorrow, hopefully. We're having parquet, down here.'

'That's wonderful,' I said, with exaggerated wistfulness. 'We still have bare boards.' I hoped my rueful smile would draw some kind of sympathetic response from Anya – establishing a 'what we women have to put up with' commiseration, but she said nothing and her face was devoid of expression. Only her eyes continued to evince an unfocussed uncertainty.

'I ended up going into estate agency,' Gary laughed. 'Bet you couldn't have seen *that* coming back in the fourth form. How about you?'

'Banking,' I said, vaguely. I put my hand on my stomach. 'Not now, of course.'

A glimmer of light came on in the dark depths of Anya's eyes. I could almost see the penny drop. One hand flew to her mouth and the other pointed across the echoing room towards me. Her expression, when she spoke, was a mixture of awe and awfulness, the equal shock and thrill of a strictly schooled child on hearing a hitherto prohibited word, and her voice, indeed, had the shrill timbre and childish enunciation of a six year old.

'You've got a *baby* in your tummy!' she said.

I started to gush; about their house – how lovely it was; their conservatory – what a useful room. The neighbours – how nice they were all sure to be and what wonderful times we would have, and I started to usher myself out, back into the hall and through the still open door onto the drive.

Gary's car had been joined by another, an identical model except in red.

Another Anya had just got out of it. Another Anya in so far as size and shape and colouring was concerned, but this version had substance. She was loud and confident. Her eyes were full of roguish laughter and her lips were luscious with red lipstick. Her hair, just as dark and thick as Anya's, was a mass of tangled curls and toyed tendrils as though someone had recently run their hands through it, clutched and pulled at it, held her down by it, panted and gasped into it. She exuded sensuality even in the few steps it took her to cross the driveway; sassy, savvy, with swaying hips and an impish light in her eye. She was greeted with pleasure by Gary and Anya and I noticed, with my last glimpse of them, that while Gary took her jacket and hooked it over the newel post, Anya had taken hold of her sister's hand; an oddly confidential, childish gesture.

In the years that were to come I saw the two of them – Anya and Katrina – constantly together and wherever Gary and Anya were invited it went without saying that Katrina would go too. Katrina would always be at the hub of any party, where the laughter was loudest, not far from the drinks and within easy reach of the stereo, the first to dance, moving and talking with a magnetic, flirtatious vivacity. She was torrid with a natural feminine raciness that men – and some women – found irresistible, without ever being coarse or offensive. Anya, meanwhile, would spend the evening perched on a cushion at the end of a sofa solemnly observing proceedings, impeccably dressed but difficult to engage in conversation, hopeless at games like Pictionary or Taboo which were big favourites of ours then. She reminded me at times like that of the Childlike Empress from *The Never Ending Story*; fragile and remote, helpless and in some way I could not fathom, tragically doomed.

Neither of them seemed to work. I was to gather at some later stage that there was money from a trust fund which supplemented their means. They shopped, they watched television, they did each other's hair and nails and make-up. They liked celebrity magazines and spent hours poring over the details of fashion and jewellery and interior design revealed in their pages. I suppose that Katrina took care of things domestically; washing and cooking and so on. I know for a fact that Anya could scarcely boil an egg. She once came to me, in distress, because she wanted to bake her sister a cake as a surprise and she didn't know how. We set to in my kitchen. Lucy was three by then and wanted to help, and it was like supervising two children as we weighed and mixed ingredients and discussed the niceties of decoration and filling.

Theirs was a special twin-hood – I don't know if you have ever come across it - of that uncanny kind in which lives are looped and linked inextricably. They were interdependent but not interchangeable; night and day, dark and light, fire and ice. Some unequal exchange had taken place in the womb whereby Katrina got all of the zest and nous, the sparkle and spontaneity leaving Anya empty; beautiful, but as lifeless as a porcelain figurine, or that kind of ornate doll which is too delicate to play with.

I broke the news to Stan that evening. He was digging over the garden preparatory to having turf laid, accumulating a pile of bricks – the former fabric of *Combe House* - which he intended to use, he said, to construct a barbeque (he never did). For a wirily thin man he was very strong, but the garden was solid clay, impenetrable as concrete after a few weeks of dry weather and steeply sloping towards the back. He liked me to watch him working and every so often would throw a resentful look over in my direction as though the density of the clay and the angle of the slope were my fault and my pregnancy a deliberate ploy to avoid helping him.

I took a deep breath. 'I met the people across the road today,' I said.

'Oh yes?' he flung a brick onto a heap. 'How come?'

'I went across to say hello. I think they'd just collected the keys.'

He frowned, 'People will think you're a real busy-body.'

'Oh, well. It's a good idea to start off on the right foot, I think.'

'I don't see why we should have anything to do with them.'

I let this pass. 'In fact,' I forged on, 'by coincidence, I already knew the chap, from school.'

Stan stood up from his toil and rested on the handle of his fork. 'That's unfortunate,' he said.

'I don't see why,' I muttered.

'They'll all know.'

'Know what?'

'Our business.'

'We don't *have* any 'business'. Anyone would think we were on a witness protection program.'

'When they find out that we moved here from (he named the large and admittedly notorious Council estate where we had previously lived) we'll be outcasts,' he prophesied, gloomily. 'They'll be screwing down their garden furniture and anything else that can be nicked.'

I was standing outside the back door, leaning against the corner of the house. My eyes slid down to the purloined paving slab on which I was standing, and to the re-located fence between our garden and Julia's. 'What will you care *what* they think of us? You don't want to have anything to do with them anyway,' I retorted.

Stan hated it when I used his own logic against him. He had an arsenal of unpleasant consequences he liked to inflict on me and he used one now. 'I've invited my mother over on Sunday,' he said. So I went indoors and didn't tell him anything about the twin sisters or Gary.

Combe Close: Alan and Sheila

Gary and Anya's parquet people took a long time to finish the job, and then there were fitted wardrobes to be installed, upstairs carpets and a complex system of blinds for the conservatory and so in fact Alan and Sheila moved in to Combe Close before they did. The Stillers moved themselves in next door to us, the first house on the right hand side of the Close, a house of a similar lay-out to Gary and Anya's but it would never have the light, spacious feel of theirs; it was already sadly shaded by the towering leylandii between them and *Eventide*.

The contract landscapers had been in the week, planting emaciated saplings and sorry-looking shrubs at strategic points around the site. It would take them a while to establish but in fact, in time, the Close did become a pleasant, verdant enclave. The street furniture had also been established; attractive Edwardian-style iron lamp-posts and a more prosaic municipal street sign supported by two sturdy concrete posts where, in future years, the children used to meet up for the walk to school. It was positioned alongside the border of Sheila and Alan's front lawn and Sheila seemed to consider it in some way under her jurisdiction; she went out and cleaned it, anyway, every month or two.

It was one Saturday afternoon when they arrived, in a self-hire van, and methodically carried their scanty – but perfectly adequate – furniture inside. Because it was Saturday, Stan was home, and so I felt hesitant about popping over to say hello, knowing he would refuse to come with me to make neighbourly overtures. I noticed, however, that much of what they carried into the house seemed to be MFI flat-packs and so I made what I considered to be the inspired suggestion that it would be nice if he went and offered to get busy with a screw-driver.

'You need allen keys for flat-packs,' Stan muttered, pedantically. 'Anyway,' he indicated the lawn, now turfed but rather parched by the recent good weather, 'don't you think I've got enough to do?'

'I could water the lawn,' I offered.

'Don't be ridiculous,' he said.

I waddled slowly inside. Perhaps he was right. I was just over seven months pregnant and the recent heat had completely floored me. My blood pressure was under weekly review and there was something wrong with my urine samples.

'Sit down and put your feet up,' Stan called after me, perhaps realising that his previous comment could be unkindly interpreted. 'Read your book.' I knew what this last suggestion had cost him. He resented my love of books, of fiction, thinking them pointless. He liked DIY manuals and maps, *useful* books, he called them.

I did as I was told and retired to my chair by the lounge window to watch our new neighbours move in. Of all of the ones I had so far encountered Alan and Sheila seemed to be most like Stan and I; not dissimilar in age and similarly circumstanced financially. (We, too, had moved ourselves, a low-budget option.) Like us, the Stillers had no carpets laid and had made (according to Stan) no additions to the standard specification.

Sheila was slim and, from the way she lifted and carried, I surmised she was pretty fit. Later I found out that she was a member of a local harriers club and regularly ran marathons for charity – she was often on the doorstep asking for sponsorship. She had short-cropped mousey hair and wore, from what I could see, no make-up, but her face had a natural radiance and she had a very ready smile which I later came to recognise as somewhat automatic and lacking in warmth. But I will say this for her: Sheila was an assiduous and efficient home-maker, almost obsessive about dusting and polishing and with a creative flair in haberdashery I have never seen matched. Their house was always as immaculate as a magazine feature, with artfully draped throws over the chairs and a plethora of hand-made textile artefacts both decorative and practical in nature. Sheila became locally quite renowned for her skills in soft-furnishing, running up curtains and cushions with apparent ease, and also in decorative floristry, producing, for example, simply stunning dried Christmas arrangements from foliage gathered locally, preserved and sprayed with gold and silver paint. Indeed, their house, at Christmas, was a veritable grotto, stylish and elegant, the equal of any display in Harrods' window, and as artificial.

Alan, her husband, was quite tall, with light, fine sandy hair which flopped over his forehead, and a fair complexion. He wore glasses but they were rimless and so hardly noticeable, especially because his eyes – I later observed – were so very arresting with a kind of sad, penetrating sympathy. He was also athletically built although he never appeared to do anything sporty and certainly did not accompany Sheila to her training nights or running meets. I sometimes wondered quite how comfortably he existed amongst the fabrics and threads, beads, needles and pins which were the trappings of Sheila's industry.

The two girls, with whom they returned later that day after taking the van back, were, then, about six and nine. They were very quiet, nicely behaved but unremarkable little girls. I did not find out for quite a long time that Alan was not their biological father and when I did I was amazed, as no man could have cared more or been more loving than he was towards those children. I watched him, over the years, playing with them, reading to them, helping them with their homework, and, when they became teenagers, turning out in the small hours to collect them from parties and nightclubs.

It used to make me very sad, because Stan never became that kind of father to Lucy. Perhaps it was because she arrived so unexpectedly that he never bonded properly with her. Or perhaps it was because she was not the boy he had hoped for and, as was forcefully impressed on us by the doctors, must remain our only child unless we were prepared to consider adoption. Whatever it was, it was almost as though he considered her to be some kind of rival for my attention. In spite of her early desire to love and please him, he proved himself, again and again, to be awkward and unapproachable. So of course she called for me in the night when she was ill or had nightmares. Why would she not, when all the sympathy she got from him was a brusque command to 'Stop being silly'? Of course it was me she looked for in the audience of school plays and concerts, when it was me and only me who had taken the trouble to help her learn her lines and who had shared all her excitement. Naturally she brought her troubles to me when she knew that, from me, she would get a patient hearing and a genuine attempt to try to understand things from her point of view, as opposed to a half hour lecture from him. He alienated himself from his daughter. At his funeral she did not shed a tear.

Present Day: Lunch

The prospect of my lunch date almost over-shadows the first morning of Jury service. It is a delicious and unexpected boon and I have to really steel myself not to exhibit signs of glee. Not only are they inappropriate, I tell myself firmly, they are unwarranted. It is just lunch, a hasty sandwich, probably. I mustn't let things get out of perspective.

But every so often I reach down and caress the handle of his umbrella.

As luck would have it my name is one of the first to be called out and myself and eleven other assorted good men and true are taken to one of the courtrooms by a robed clerk and installed in the benches. There follows a lengthy time of debate between the defence and prosecution representatives, and a few of us are asked questions about any strong religious biases we might have before we are, one by one, sworn in. It seems ironic that, having denied any particular religious leanings and being offered a secular alternative, we all opt for the bible and the 'so help me God' to make our vows. Then the defendant is brought into the dock, a heavily bearded Asian man with yellow eyeballs threaded with burst capillaries and a huge nose with thick black hair sprouting from each nostril like the tentacles of some deep-sea anemone. The charges are read out; there are several of them but the gist is that he is accused of abusing two girls, the daughters of his wife's sister.

Because of the young ages of the victims they are to give their evidence by video link and the first girl, a petite, glossy-haired little thing of about ten, answers the questions posed to her by a female police constable. We watch on a largish television set wheeled out in front of us. I can understand why it is easier on the victim but for the jury, who see harrowing crime played out every night on their televisions, it is distancing.

It turns out not to matter. In error, the child's evidence has been relayed into the witness waiting area and the second victim has seen it. The defendant's barrister immediately requests a mistrial but the judge decides that the trial will re-start, with a new jury. Frankly I am flabbergasted. How will *that* enable the second child to forget all that the first child has said? Surely (remember, I am fresh from Rumpole's courtroom) the thing to do would be to rule the second girl's evidence as inadmissible? But nobody asks my opinion and we are dismissed, and not only from this trial. To prevent any possibility of us encountering members of the new jury, we are told to report to another courthouse on the other side of town, first thing in the morning. We collect our belongings from the jury room and are ushered from the building.

It is barely eleven thirty and I am in a quandary as to what to do about my lunch date; my lunch *appointment*, I mean. Lunch recess is one till two, I have discovered. An hour and a half is a long time to wait in the rain. Might it not look – a little *desperate?*

But he is already waiting on the steps, in the lee of an imposing statue, the collar of his overcoat turned up against the rain. He doesn't look in the least desperate. He looks.... determined. I wrestle with his umbrella but he takes it off me and slips his hand under my elbow.

'Sack that,' he says, waving down a passing taxi.

'You're out early too,' I say, when we are installed in the car. The air is charged and humid, as though a procession of ghostly passengers have left their soggy auras behind them. The taxi floor is slick with their ectoplasm.

'Bloke didn't show up,' he says. He sighs. 'We had to re-schedule. You?'

'Oh,' I give a little laugh and roll my eyes. 'I don't think I'm allowed to explain. Let's just say a cock-up on the procedural front.'

He leans forward and gives some directions to the driver. The cab is inching through heavy traffic. The road is awash with water, and treacherous with hurrying, umbrella-wielding pedestrians making ill-advised attempts to weave between the crawling vehicles.

'You really didn't have to wait for me,' I say, self-effacing as ever. 'You must want to get back to the office.' I don't, under any circumstances, want him to feel compromised.

He pushes the 'get out of jail free' card I have just offered him away. 'You must be kidding,' he says. 'I'm booked out of there for the whole day. You never know how long these things will take.'

I can't believe the way things have turned out. We're both at liberty for the afternoon. This is getting better and better, I think to myself, even as I am desperately struggling to give him a way out. I am scrupulous, you see; not only will I lift no finger, set nothing in motion, I will, to a point, scupper the few golden chances that fate puts in my way. I plough on relentlessly: 'But, obviously, as it was cancelled...'

He takes my hand and pats it. 'Little Molly,' he says, with an avuncular smile, 'such a conformist. Are you worried I'll get into trouble?'

He takes my silence as confirmation although in fact I am trying to decide if there hadn't been the lightest possible note of scorn in his question. It makes me squirm, that he should have such a view of me; mousy, timid 'little Molly', and that his view should be so apposite. He *sees* me, I realise, with a thrilling, sinking heart.

'I am quite senior, you know,' he says, gently, laying my hand back onto my lap. 'Don't worry. If it makes you feel better I'll send myself a ferociously worded email.'

'Yes,' I laugh, 'I think you should. Condemning in the strongest possible terms.....'

'Shocking dereliction of duty....'

'Appalling example to the junior staff...'

'Yes, yes. All of that.'

I revel in the silliness of it, the banter. It is something I never had with Stan.

The taxi stops outside one of the best hotels in town. The door is opened by a concierge and another one hurries down the steps with an umbrella. In the lobby, a vast acreage of crimson carpet and ornately carved architecture, our coats are taken and we proceed to the cocktail bar. I scramble onto a bar stool and sit blinking around me like some subterranean invertebrate suddenly exposed to the light while he orders drinks. The room is discreetly lit and piano music tinkles in the distance. Our companions at the bar are florid, droop-jowlled businessmen in pin-stripes. The atmosphere is heavy with wealth and cholesterol-rich complacency. They are loud and overly-jocular; one or two of them actually guffaw. But in the peripheries of the room, in the shadowy corners, there are couples 'necking' (this word dredges itself from my sub-conscious and is pronounced in my mother's prim and darkly disapproving voice). I experience a sudden frisson of panic. I am absolutely and sinkingly certain that after their cocktails and Michelin starred lunch there will be abandoned sex in the chambers above our heads. All the women are beautifully groomed, flashing stocking-tops and knowing, seductive smiles. In a clash of fight and flight I have an overpowering desire to visit the cloakroom but whether it is to re-lipstick my seductive smile or to climb out of the window I can't say.

Then I check myself. Whatever the afternoon holds in store for those women, mine will be a civilised and companionable lunch and nothing more. It is ridiculous to imagine, or to fear, anything else. Good grief! I am a grey-haired cellulosic widow! A look across at him reassures me. He is gesturing for menus, exchanging a joke with the bar steward; the only thing on his mind is food. As stupid as I feel perched here on this stool I am glad that he has not led me to one of those shady tables. Here we are decently in full view and our intentions are unassailable.

I think I am glad, anyway.

We are presented with a menu in a heavy leather folder and I stare at it blindly as I wrestle with my conflicting feelings.

'This isn't what you expected,' he says. There is a hint of smugness in his tone, as though he'd wanted to surprise me and knows he's succeeded. But then his demeanour changes. 'Perhaps it isn't what you'd like,' he says, I think, with some suggestion of significance. I am mired in more confusion. What does he mean? The venue? The menu? He compounds my perplexity by adding: 'Would you like to go somewhere else?' My confidence of only a moment ago shrivels. Can he mean, I wonder, straight upstairs? Or just to a location less loaded with sub-text? Is this *my* 'get out of jail free'?

I take a deep breath. 'You must be kidding,' I say, echoing his own words from earlier.

The dining room is reassuringly bright and respectable. We are seated in a window alcove with a view through gauzy curtains of the street below. We order: he, pate and ricotta ravioli; I, goat's cheese and sole. He requests a bottle of wine which turns out to be Chablis – one of my favourites.

The wine, combined with my aperitif, relaxes me as, perhaps, he intended that it should. 'Well,' I say, leaning back and looking around me, 'this isn't what I expected, you were right about that! I thought we'd be going to some greasy spoon or other....'

'I knew as soon as I saw you that I'd bring you here,' he says.

We chat about our shared gastronomic experiences; a succession of Combe Close barbeques; a hilarious but doomed murder mystery dinner party at which the planned bœuf en **Croûte** had had to be substituted at the last minute for Matthews Turkey Roast and at which, to top it all, the hostess had tripped over the corpse and ended up in A & E with four stitches in her forehead; the more recent occasion on one of our holidays at which Julia had almost choked on a fish bone. We laugh about it all – even the fish bone – and move on to recollections of absurd games of sardines and the year we had decided to 'do' Christmas in October complete with tree and secret Santas and Turkey with all the trimmings.

He reminds me of the time I had almost missed the ferry to Mull because of a last minute dash to the book shop, declaring, innocently, to the restive assembled passengers; 'I'm sorry, but I just *had* to have that Trollope.'

'You looked so flushed and tousled,' he says, 'as though you *had* just had a trollop.'

We agree that those holidays are the best. We agree about everything. I can't think of anyone else I have ever been in such accord with. The conversation flows like silk between us, without snag or interruption. I feel that I am wrapped up in it, warm and cool at the same time, carried along in its sinuous, absorbing flow. I am positively wallowing in it and I realise that I am probably a little drunk, and I take a moment while the waiter clears the plates, to take a few deep breaths and sober up.

He seems to sense it. He suddenly becomes serious. 'I was glad,' he says, swirling the last of his wine in his glass, 'about what you said on holiday.'

Of course I know what he means. My man with the quirky smile and the kind eyes. 'Were you?'

'Yes. He sounds a nice chap. You deserve someone nice. I hope you find him.'

I feel, all at once, more than sober. I feel alert and almost super-charged, as though I have blundered through innocuous undergrowth and found myself on a precipice. 'Do you?'

He nods and drains his glass. He looks across the table at me levelly. 'Perhaps you already have?'

I am saved from answering by the arrival of the waiter with the bill. I fumble for my handbag but by the time I have my purse out he has already sent the waiter away with a credit card. 'My treat,' he smiles – that adorable, quirky smile.

'Perhaps,' I say, quietly.

The journey from the restaurant and across the lobby to the cloakroom is fraught; passing the wide, inviting stairs, the eager, accommodating reception clerk. Almost no part of me expects him to make any kind of gesture which would suggest that these avenues are open to us but that treacherous remnant flutters its hapless wings. But we survive, and by the time we get our coats and stand on the hotel steps the rain has stopped and there is even a watery glimmer of washed sun in the west, palely roseate, the shortest day is almost upon us.

I indicate the way to the station. 'It's been so lovely,' I say, inadequately.

'Yes,' he says, 'it has. Thank you.'

'Thank *you*,' I laugh.

We are both hesitant, somehow reluctant to part. There are shops, there are galleries and museums. There are still the bedrooms, clamouring like maniacs incarcerated in a sound-proofed cell. At the thought of them, to silence them, I name, at last, his wife.

'She'll be jealous, when she hears!' I say, too shrilly.

His face immediately darkens. The animation I have seen in it all afternoon just dies away. 'Oh,' he says, 'no. It won't even register.'

'You'll tell her, though?' It seems, suddenly, very important.

He turns to me. 'I don't know,' and then, penetratingly, 'will you?'

I look up at last into his face, into the kindness of his eyes, and see something else, something half hidden or, perhaps, more accurately, half hiding in them. I recognise it immediately because I see it in my own every day in the mirror. It is abject, fathomless loneliness.

He leans towards me and I turn my cheek for his kiss. He makes the slightest possible little sound of impatience, recalibrates his intention and kisses me on the lips. It is swift and chaste.

Then he is gone into the hurrying crowd and I am alone on the hotel steps and the question remains unanswered.

Combe Close: Marcus and Carla

Memory is a little blurred as to whether Gary and Anya or Marcus and Carla moved in to their respective houses next. Pre-eclampsia and an emergency caesarean put me in hospital for ten days towards the end of June. Little Lucy remained in the premature baby unit for a further fortnight and my days were spent by her cot, holding her tiny hand in mine. Combe Close, and the little world I imagined I was building for us there, disappeared entirely off my radar. Stan took me to the hospital every day and went on to the office; he would take leave, he said, when the baby came home.

But when we brought her home he continued to go to work each day, having provided me with an alternative carer, his mother, installed in the spare room for a stay which she clearly expected to be of some duration; she had brought two big suitcases of clothes and her ancient and anti-social cat. She was presented to me as a 'surprise' when I came home from hospital, standing with a more proprietorial air than I liked on our porch as the car pulled into the drive. Freda, like Stan, was dark and hairy, and reminded me of nothing so much as a predatory spider; I could feel the threads of her control in every room. She had been meddling; the crib and changing station I had arranged in the smallest bedroom had been moved around. I could feel her interfering hand in my wardrobe and even in my underwear drawer. The kitchen cupboards were not as I had left them and the stock of food I had laid in had been added to by cheap convenience groceries I would never buy, and cat food. In my absence they had had carpet laid; Stan presented it to me with an artificial 'ta DAH!' as though he had conjured it from a hat. Like Freda, it was not what I would have chosen; dark, old fashioned and eminently *sensible*, and calculated to show off to their best advantage the feltings of white hairs left behind by the irascible moggy. But I didn't complain. What was the point? It was done, and I supposed that any carpet was better than the

55

hard and dusty boards.

For a month or so I just shrank into a little world which contained only Lucy and me. I gave up the house, the catering, the laundry and everything to Freda but I was fiercely possessive of the baby, finding an unexpected strength in myself to do things my own way when it was suggested that I was 'spoiling' her and 'making a rod for my back' because I couldn't leave her to cry and breast-fed her on demand rather than using the ancient bottles Freda had triumphantly unearthed from some fly-spotted box in her musty attic.

Finally Lucy and I were both pronounced fit. My scar had healed and my gynaecological check-up signalled that 'normal relations' could be recommenced. Lucy, though small, was feeding and sleeping well. She had had her first immunisations and survived. She smiled at me when I came into her field of vision. I loved her with a passion so wild it made me want to weep. Her pale, peachy flesh – the smell and taste of it – brought saliva to my mouth. It was the most overwhelming thing I had ever experienced; a maelstrom of primordial instincts and compulsive pheromones and savagely protective impulses. They emboldened me. I felt, for the first time, like a woman rather than a girl.

'I can't tell you what a wonderful help you have been,' I said to Freda over one of her signature dishes – I think it was pilchard casserole; she bought a great amount of tinned fish both for human and feline consumption and I occasionally wondered if she ever got them mixed up – 'but I really can't expect to keep you away from your own home and your friends any longer.' (The idea of Freda having friends was a joke. The closest she came to exchanging pleasantries with her neighbours was throwing them a beetling scowl as she snatched her milk off the step each morning.) She and Stan exchanged a look across the table but nothing was said until we were undressing for bed that night.

'I think it's too soon for Mum to go home,' Stan said, arranging his trousers fussily over a hanger.

'Whatever you think,' I replied, as nonchalantly as I could. 'But, you know, these are only stud walls and it wouldn't be fair for us to really get back to *normal*,' I cast him a significant look, 'while she's still here. Think how embarrassed she'd be.......'

She was gone by the weekend.

It wasn't my idea – I am sure you can guess that – it had been Carla's.

Carla was the only person in Combe Close who came to say hello to me, and I was touched and rather overwhelmed by the gesture. For all the others; Julia and Gerald, Gary and Anya, Sheila and Alan and, eventually for Pam and Pete, I was the one who popped across to say hello. Perhaps you will say that I had hardly given them chance – Stan certainly did – and I suppose in the scheme of things it doesn't really matter who initiated contact; relations were established within our little enclave and that was what was important. But somehow it *did* make a difference to me. To have an overture of friendship reciprocated is one thing but to be the object of an overture is something else especially if you are the kind of person – as I am – who had never experienced what it is to be sought out. And to be sought out by someone like Carla was particularly gratifying.

I think, now, I was sort of mesmerised by her. Stan, I know, thought that I was 'besotted' by her. It's true that particularly at the beginning of those Combe Close years I did hold her up as a kind of model. She swept me up in her gaiety and in some way made me part of it; me, the perennial wall-flower, the shrinking violet. I found her deliciously shocking – she was blunt and frank about things that, in my up-bringing, had been literally unmentionable. She behaved as if I was her equal and I felt elevated by her attitude.

Carla was tall, with that easy, classy elegance that tall women have, and effortlessly slim. Her face was perfectly proportioned with high cheek bones and a finely honed jaw-line and a frank forehead. She had a wide, expressive mouth and green eyes under mischievously mobile brows. Her hair, then, was fashionably big and trendily tousled (this was the eighties, remember), and naturally blonde. She wore flowing skirts and stylish dresses and loose, fine knitwear while the rest of us thought we looked good in nylon shell suits. She had a way of throwing an outfit together and adding seemingly haphazard accessories – a scarf, a chunky necklace, a pair of sunglasses – which resulted in something really stunning. Inevitably men found her attractive but she didn't seem to care anything about them; she was a woman's woman, one of the girls, having a slightly dismissive, eye-rolling, almost patronising attitude towards men. Wherever she was in the Close you could always locate her by her ringing, pealing laugh and I would find myself drawn by an almost irresistible tug of some magical cord into the musical circle she cast around her. She was confident and up-beat, but I am afraid that when trouble came to her, which it did, in time, these positive resources proved to be no match for it. I think I am still in a kind of mourning for the person that she was.

She breezed into my house one afternoon while Freda still held sway, brushing past 'the black widow' (as she immediately, *sotto voce*, labelled her) and bringing with her a gust of summer air and some exotic perfume and a peal of enthusiasm for Lucy who lay peacefully sleeping in her Moses basket.

'Just look at that perfect *angel!*' she cried. Of course nothing could have enamoured me to her more. She gave her own, slightly rounded belly a fond stroke. 'They'll be the best of friends,' she said. She perched familiarly on the arm of my chair and put her arm around my shoulders, 'and so will *we*,' she sighed.

Freda offered to make us tea and shuffled off into the kitchen.

'Oh my *God!*' Carla gave a muted shriek. 'How long have you got to put up with *her?* I swear to God that even on a clear blue day like today there's a big black *cloud* over your house with forks of lightning coming out of it. Is she a witch? Has she put a spell on you?'

'She's my mother in law!' I laughed. 'Stan thinks I need her to help me.'

'Of course he does! What do you expect?' Carla cried. 'We've all been worried to death about you, *incarcerated* in here with *her*. Tell me she doesn't have a spinning wheel!'

'She has a cat.'

'I knew it. I *told* them.'

'Them?'

'The neighbours! I'm their rescue party, sent in to scope out the territory and see if I can't release you from her web.'

It seemed that, while I had been preoccupied with Lucy, social interaction in the Close had moved on. 'I hadn't realised you'd all got so friendly,' I said, perhaps a little sourly, feeling with gloomy certainty that Stan and I would have irrevocably have missed out on the essential foundation-laying of Combe Close friendships.

But Carla put my mind at rest. 'Only because of *you* and this little poppet. We're all *agog* to see her, especially Anya – *she's* such a pet, isn't she? Why don't you come over tomorrow afternoon and I'll get the girls together....'

I cast an uneasy eye in the direction of the kitchen. Carla gave a hoot. 'You *are* allowed out, you know! But,' in a somewhat lowered voice, 'for God's sake, don't bring her (indicating Freda) with you.'

Freda brought tea and settled herself on the sofa opposite to us. She made no contribution to the conversation but her presence quashed the friendly frankness we had been enjoying and Carla moved on to more general topics, chatting breezily about the troubles they'd had with their removals company. Far from being stressful and annoying, she made it all sound like a comedic series of farcical events straight out of that Bernard Cribbins number 'Right said Fred.' She stayed about half an hour and then rose to go. Freda took the tea things back into the kitchen.

'You do *know*, don't you, Molly, that there's one thing that men love more than their mothers....' Carla said to me, waggling her eyebrows significantly. 'Take my word for it: put bedroom activities back on the agenda and he'll have her out of here like a shot.'

And, as I have told you, she was right.

The following afternoon I set out with the newly erected pushchair and walked to Carla's house, followed by a barrage of dire warnings from Freda that I was exposing my baby to a myriad of noxious foreign germs; a joke, considering her crusty ancient cardigans and mangy cat. Being outdoors, for the first time in weeks, made me feel all trembly; it was almost as though the warm tarmac of the pavement quivered beneath my feet. Lucy, too, gazed in wonder at the big wide world which had suddenly opened up to her. Her translucent eyelids and fine, dark eyelashes fluttered against the balmy breeze while her little toes arched and curled in a kind of ecstasy.

The Close was transformed; the lawns trim and tended, the houses looking for the first time in some way alive, their window-eyes sentient; small personal touches – a window box, a bird table, a doormat declaring 'welcome' – had turned them from houses into homes. Even at Pam and Pete's – so far unoccupied – the foreman's cabin had been removed from the front lawn and a landscape gardener was busy turning the bald patch where it had stood into a rockery. On the drive, a carpet-fitter's van declared the owners' imminent arrival. I walked slowly around the circuit of the Close, and took it all in, the almost-completion of this little commune that I had such high hopes for; these safe, happy houses and their genial occupants – the people who would be my neighbours, the people I so hoped would become my friends.

Along with the house on the corner which was to become Pam and Pete's, Carla's was the biggest on the site, with a large, open-plan kitchen and breakfast area with patio doors, and a family room as well as a lounge and dining room. I already knew that they had had numerous 'optional extras' like granite worktops, a whirlpool bath and an inglenook fireplace.

Because of Stan I even knew what they had paid for these things – the design specifications and price list had a permanent place on his bedside table. It was a house designed for entertaining, with a range cooker and an American style fridge, and lots of comfortable sofas arranged to facilitate large groups in amiable conversation. They'd had a sort of canopy attached to the back of the house which stretched over the patio so that even on wet evenings they could open the French windows and use the terrace as part of the space. But it wasn't the house so much as Marcus and Carla's free, hospitable style which resulted in our Combe Close parties being held, more often than not, at their house. You just felt instantly welcome and at home there; they were always pleased to see you no matter what time of the day or night you turned up. Anything they had they were pleased to lend or to give; it was perpetually 'open-house'. You could stroll in and put the kettle on, run in to borrow a cooking ingredient you had suddenly found you were short of, and they would take it absolutely in their stride. I truly believe you could have walked in and run yourself a bath and they wouldn't have turned a hair. Carla was somebody who just thrived on company; more than that, she *thirsted* for it, opening up like a spectacular flower when she was amongst people. And Marcus, as I was to find out, and to his cost, loved to give his wife exactly what she wanted.

I didn't meet Marcus until later. Against Carla's flamboyance he seemed quiet, perhaps even a little dull. Whatever authority and drive he used at work to build up his company it got left behind when he came home. He would change out of his suit and then submit himself to whatever agenda Carla dictated; running Sophie to Brownies, putting away the shopping she had bought during the day and left abandoned on the worktop, cooking dinner, or, if nothing seemed required of him he would potter in the garden or dabble with DIY. He was very handy in that way; throwing up shelving with ease – nothing like the full scale production Stan made of such tasks, the DIY books notwithstanding – tiling, installing a sound system. *They* had a block-paved patio and barbeque in no time, also a pergola with a trained vine and, as I have mentioned, espaliered fruit trees. I must admit to times when I compared Marcus' easy-going nature and effortless ability with things to Stan's awkward, ham-fisted efforts and sighed inwardly, identifying a spark of envy; why couldn't Stan be more like Marcus?

Marcus and Julia got on like a house on fire, often swapping cuttings over their shared fence, but while hers was a species of market garden, productive, with terraced vegetable beds, phalanxes of tomato plants and runner beans, relentless raspberry canes and even a bee hive, his was an oasis of flowering shrubs and perennials, with shady arbours, tinkling water features and considerately placed seats, and a shed, what Carla called his 'man-cave', where he kept his tools and could often be found tinkering with a bit of carpentry at times when Carla had no use for him in the house or running errands. He got on with Gerald too; the two of them quietly contemplative, facilitating with rock-like dependability the wiles and enthusiasms of their respective wives. He was, then, a large, solidly-built man, not especially handsome, with a round, sympathetic face and thick wavy hair. In company with Carla he was always somewhat in the shadows, but from them he implemented his generous, open-handed nature, dispensing largesse with the quiet, hugged-in pleasure of an anonymous benefactor; poised to supply drinks, meals, a shawl around shoulders that he has spied in the act of a discreet shiver. He is such a kind man; one of the kindest men I know.

Combe Close: Pam and Pete

I have often, in the intervening years, wondered if Pam felt cheated about being the last to move in. There's a moment, isn't there, in any social setting, when things sort of coalesce, a tone is struck which endures from then on. Did she feel that she had missed that essential instant of synthesis? It is true that, by the time she had arrived and got herself unpacked and into what passed, in that tumultuous household, for order, the rest of us had already embarked on what was to become a mesh of intense, interconnected relationships. Sheila had latched on to Carla – as I did, and indeed, who could resist her? We were in frequent contact, popping across for coffee or out shopping, or giggling over glasses of wine like new undergraduates at Freshers' week. My preoccupation with my new-found friends infuriated Stan but I was too caught up in it to care. The twins had each other of course but Julia took an especial shine to Anya, gathering her under her matronly wing as though she was an orphan refugee or a stray kitten. It seemed that Anya hated being on her own, and at times when Katrina was off somewhere and Gary late home from work, or having to work over a weekend, Anya could invariably be found in Julia's house, or, more often, her garden, wandering between the nascent cabbage plants or in the orchard while Julia turned the compost heap or double-dug the potato plot. Julia included me in her flock, too, buzzing in with pies and bags of home grown produce and stroking Lucy's cheek with an affectionate, calloused finger, and Lucy soon got used to the booming cadences of Julia's endearments.

We included Pam as soon as she arrived. Carla and I went over together and introduced ourselves and I wondered if, possibly because of that – our going together – or perhaps because we had chosen a bad time (her washing machine was leaking), or just because she was preoccupied with two boys and another on the way, she seemed to hold herself at a distance. She invited us in and made us tea but it was with a slightly wary, withheld, almost suspicious air.

Pam is small and tubby. She was as pregnant as Carla at that time but looked to be much further on. I concluded, sympathetically, that she had not lost the baby-weight from the second child before conceiving the third. (I was all too aware of a slackness about my own body which had not been there before Lucy.) But in fact when she stopped either being pregnant or breast-feeding (one or the other being her constant state for about six years) she did not perceptibly lose any weight. I am afraid she is just one of those women genetically prone to fatness, with vast hips atop thick, inelegant legs. She is a slow mover, seeming somehow out of her natural element; as lethargic as moon-walker or a beached walrus. And yet she is in perpetual motion – slow motion – cleaning, ironing, tidying, fetching and carrying, from dawn till dusk, a constant diurnal round of repetitive household tasks. She has very dark hair, somewhat thin and lustreless, a fleshy nose and smallish eyes under heavy brows. She is not an attractive woman, there's no getting away from that, but once I broke through her suspicion and reserve I found her to possess a kind and caring heart and an innate desire to nurture and protect, and in this she did find a kind of soul-mate in Julia, although the older woman's incisive intelligence and brisk, authoritative manner leaves Pam blinking and bewildered. Pam is not a deep thinker and neither is she much of a talker; she is a doer – practical, home-loving. Her boys – and her husband - are her life and she accepts their rumbustious temperaments with a kind of quiet, poignant acquiescence. She accepts everything that life throws at her, almost, with the same stoical strength. Pam is a whizz in the kitchen, able to turn out vats of wholesome, delicious food. Food is the physical manifestation of her caring, giving nature. When Stan died there was a constant stream of it from her house to mine, a river of casserole, lakes of soup, endless spigots of tea. Mass catering seems to be second nature to her, which is a good job given the voracious appetites of her boys and Pete, and it is true to say that while the majority of our parties were held at Carla's house, Pam provided most of the food.

Pete is as loud and brash as Pam is self-effacing. He is enormous, easily twenty stone, testament to Pam's great love for him. His shirts strain over his belly, his thick neck spills over their eighteen inch collars. He has a huge head and thinning hair, as though one is consequent on the other, the hair inadequately stretched across his bulging scalp. He has dark seductive eyes and a full, sensitive mouth. Pete is large – larger than life – with an enormous appetite for everything life has to offer. And he is a potent catalyst; once he has entered a room nothing remains the same. He comes in with a gust of laughter and sends out eddies which energise everything, like a vast cruise-liner entering a harbour, the lesser fishing vessels and tugs begin to bounce and strain at their moorings. At the time I understood – vaguely – that he was something in sales – what else, with that irresistible laugh of his, his beaming, friendly smile, his persuasive line of chat? – and personal finance. His sons adored him, throwing themselves into his arms and scrambling onto his shoulders the moment they saw him. Men are drawn to him – even Stan was lost in a reluctant admiration for his sheer machismo, dazed by the compelling charisma of that enormous, ebullient character. Women too.

*

And so, with the arrival of Pam and Pete to Combe Close, the scene was set, the troupe assembled, the die, I almost want to say, cast, for that glorious, golden era which fused and at the same time, in spite of my best efforts, warped us. At the beginning of it I didn't see the outcome. I ask myself; who could have done? But I think now that I didn't *want* to see it. I so wanted it all to be perfect – I wanted *them* all to be perfect. I had pre-imbued them with noble qualities and I was determined that they would not let me down. In the same way that I had with Stan, when fissures and flaws began to appear, I skimmed over them. With dogged resolve, a bigger than average dose of immature optimism and a deeply ingrained conditioning I simply refused to see anything unpleasant. Everything, to borrow from *Candide*, was to be for the best in the best of all possible worlds. But we did not live in a vacuum and so things from outside the circumference of our lives did invade and impinge. And none of us was perfect; we arrived contaminated by prejudices and predispositions and those deeply seated personal flaws; our weaknesses and insecurities and hungering desires.

They are like tigers, those little peccadilloes, starting off cute and harmless enough; we think we can keep them in tight restraint. Innocuous, we tell ourselves, and completely under control. But exciting, none the less; warm to the touch and so pleasurable to stroke and cosset. But then they grow, and fret at the cages of discipline we have built. They raven to be let loose until their roaring importunity is too much to bear. We let them out and they wreak havoc, if not absolutely tearing us apart, scarring our souls.

Combe Close: Putting down roots

That first summer – how long ago it seems, now - was a time of settling, establishing ourselves in our new environment; like new plants we sent out tentative roots and assimilated the soil. For those who had moved from other towns, there was all the bother of orientation; finding the best supermarkets and DIY stores and a decent hairdresser and learning not to get lost in Stan's interminable one way system. It was all about making ourselves at home. In the same way we took possession of our houses, not just in the sense of unpacking boxes and putting up pictures, but more in the way that you wear in a new pair of shoes – we shaped them to fit, we moulded them to ourselves. We tested them – and each other – for comfort and style and practicality.

Julia and Gerald's efforts with their recalcitrant furniture continued but with less fervour; perhaps they had grown tired of it or had discovered that they just didn't need it all. They occasionally finagled a few more pictures and the odd rug through the lounge window and came up with the inspired idea that by putting a sign reading 'front door not in use, please go round the back' they could block off the hallway altogether and use it for a large and astonishingly ugly hall stand.

They were, as I have described them to you, an unprepossessing enough pair, wholly unconcerned with the outward appearances of things; Julia's hair always awry, Gerald's shirts less than pristinely laundered and both of them indelibly permeated with a pungent whiff of dog which they carried with them wherever they went. But the life they lived was anomalous to their humdrum surroundings, imbued with a certain old-fashioned pomp and ceremony. They ate a proper cooked breakfast every morning at the dining table – kedgeree or mounds of scrambled eggs with bacon, washed down with tea as they read The Times and The Telegraph from cover to cover with every appearance of leisured refinement. When at home they had a cold 'luncheon' of sliced meats and salad. Afternoon tea was more informal; scones or toasted tea cakes in the lounge (they called it the drawing room), but their evening meal, which they referred to as 'supper' – a meal I associate with ill-advised cheese and biscuits eaten at bedtime – was very grand; preceded by sherry or gin, accompanied by wine, and concluded always with proper pudding with custard. Julia prepared their meal in her disorganised and doggy kitchen, served it and then sat down to it as regally as though some lowly menial had done all the work. It was behaviour which scarcely belonged in a modern house or the 1980s but then in some strange way Julia and Gerald didn't quite belong there either. When I had placed them in a Barbara Pym novel I had been something wide of the mark: Evelyn Waugh would have been more apposite. I admit that I thought them eccentric, rather absurd and perhaps just a little ostentatious with their pretentions of grandeur.

They spent a good many days that summer visiting various horticultural and Country shows, arriving home late at night with a car rammed to the gunnels with limp, travel-shocked florae and hot, salivating Collies. On one occasion, Gerald being unwell with a chest complaint – a malady which was to plague him, on and off, throughout our acquaintance - I was invited to go along in his stead.

'Shame to waste the ticket, m'dear, don't you think?' said Julia as she stood on my doorstep in the gloaming on her way back from taking the dogs for their evening constitutional around the golf course. 'Bring the baby, of course. Plenty of room, and all that.'

We set off early the following day and arrived at the show-ground mid-morning. Julia drove slowly, heedless of the fulminating gesticulations of drivers trapped behind her on the A roads and those who roared past her on the motorway. She maintained a dignified, formally erect posture in the driver's seat as though in some way *on show,* a participant in a solemn procession or a funeral cortege. As she drove she told me something of her girlhood as a farmer's daughter - or, I might say, more specifically, a *gentleman* farmer's daughter – she had been brought up to the hunt and weekend house-parties at a time (just after the 2nd war) when such things were already relicts of the past. She told me she had liked nothing better than to be riding across the acres with her father, inspecting fences and helping out with the lambing.

'Which was as well, in the circumstances,' she admitted, sadly, 'labour was in such short supply and both my older brothers had been lost in the war.'

Her story explained to me the oddly bygone air about Julia and Gerald. The family home and estate were gone, sold to pay death duties, but they continued in their happy, shabby gentility to all intents and purposes as though nothing had changed. Their little house on the Close was their castle, the dogs their stock, the garden their grounds.

I fed Lucy in the car before we set off across the rutted parking field. Julia showed what turned out to be VIP passes at the gate and we plunged into the melee of farmers, farriers, horse-enthusiasts and horticulturalists. Several large marquees had been erected at one end of the main arena for the specialist exhibitors while ranks of stalls radiated outwards across the field selling every conceivable – and some inconceivable - countryside appurtenance. To my surprise Julia was greeted by stewards, exhibitors and officials alike with demonstrations of great warmth and also enormous deference – clearly, she was something of a celebrity in this milieu. Everyone she met remarked on the absence of Bearded Collies – left behind with Gerald – and cooed over Lucy, whose buggy Julia had eagerly appropriated. It turned out that Julia was to judge one of the canine categories and she went straight to work in one of the marquees, running her hands over the flanks of three dozen panting, pent-up pooches and observing their gait from beneath her beetling brow before giving their ears an affectionate fondle and rummaging a treat for them from the pocket of her gilet.

At lunchtime we were escorted to a private hospitality area where we ate poached salmon and salad and drank white wine and when Lucy grew querulous she was taken imperiously off by an elegantly dressed lady in pearls and sensible lace-up brogues who turned out to be an Honourable Lady Something-or-Other while I listened to Julia make enquiries about mutual acquaintances of a tweedy, craggy-faced gentleman who she called Arnold but who somebody else addressed as 'm'lord'. All at once Julia, amongst these well-to-do, perfectly agreeable but distinctly superior county types, was looking less like an aberrant throw-back from the thirties and more like an indigenous constituent. She was at home.

Later, in the botanicals marquee, she was absorbed into a circle of fervent horticulturalists and even as Lucy and I wandered amongst the stalls I could hear her strident, plummy boom extolling the virtues of this or that specimen as though still the possessor of a stately home with extensive formal gardens: 'One has to ensure that these are moved into the hot-house at the first sign of frost, doesn't one?'; 'Soft foliage always shows off the statuary so charmingly, don't you think?' But now, rather than finding her quasi-grandeur affected, I thought it poignant. The disposal of her inheritance might have left her and Gerald impoverished but they struggled on with dignity and without rancour.

As we made our stately way home through the cooling evening air it occurred to me that Julia's story was Cinderella in reverse and afterwards I never thought her eccentric or silly but only noble and rather brave.

What with these outings, and their jobs, Julia and Gerald were out a good deal and when they were home the garden occupied all their hours so that when I made social calls on them, although always graciously received, I couldn't help but see that the removal of outdoor shoes and the washing of hands and the arrangement of cakes on a doily was a nuisance and a distraction.

Carla, on the other hand, was always delighted to see me, usually to be found at home unless visiting her aged parents and one way or another I saw her almost every day. Indeed I would say she acted like a sort of magnet to me, with a silvery, mercurial appeal I found it impossible to resist – not that I tried to, anyway. Even while I was doing my housework or playing with Lucy I would find myself wondering what *she* was doing; if she was out, or in, or busy, or bored. I kept an eye open for movement in her driveway or even through her windows which would denote an excuse to see her. Once or twice I even stood in the Close and waved my arms about to attract her attention, and when she beckoned me over by making a T sign with her hands, I'd grab Lucy and hurry across.

She was such fun to be with, even if she was just spending the day at home. I might find her rummaging through a pile of old singles and slapping them onto the record deck, reliving school discos, dancing barefoot across her lounge regaling me with her memories, ('Michael Foster and I danced to this at the fifth year Christmas party. Oh! How I loved him! I let him put his hand down my dress in the gym...'). Or she would be busy cooking up some exotic dish, the kitchen strewn with bizarre ingredients, the radio blaring. 'Stir this,' she'd cry, or 'Grate that, will you? How does it taste? Awful? Put more wine in. You can never have too much wine!' Or she would pull me up to her room and drag clothes from the wardrobe for us to try for fun – her wedding dress, a wet-suit, Marcus' dinner suit ('to see how it feels being a man'). And then in the middle of it all she would suddenly look at me and announce 'You *must* have your eyebrows waxed, Molly,' and off we'd go, right there and then, leaving the mess as it lay, bundling Lucy into her car seat, to have our eyebrows waxed or our nails done just to tour the shops. As her pregnancy advanced she became less active, less able to amuse herself, less inclined to go out and so all the more available to me. I went across sometimes more than once a day until she began to go to bed for a nap in the afternoons, and then I patrolled the Close to intercept any delivery man or Jehovah's witness who might ring her bell and disturb her rest.

Occasionally I would walk across to Pam's house to pay a visit but she, like Julia, rarely had time for leisure, slavishly washing and ironing, cooking and trying – in vain, mostly – to keep things in order. Everything inside their house was over-sized, to accommodate its larger-than-life owners; huge squashy sofas and wide reclining armchairs, all slightly the worse for wear. They had what was – in those days – a gargantuan TV set. What with the out-sized furnishings and the tide of toys which perpetually washed out of the family room, and Pam herself – bulky and clumsy and likely to knock into things – her house was a picture of disorganisation which had none of the fun and frivolity of Carla's sudden eccentric enthusiasms but which made me feel tired and harassed just looking at it. Even the garden had become cluttered, with an enormous climbing frame (it had a slide and a selection of swing accessories and a sort of tent incorporated into it), soon joined by goal posts, a basket-ball hoop and, in time an aluminium-framed, vinyl-lined pool. A long washing line looped from one side of the garden to the other and I think it was strung with clothes every single day that the weather allowed as a result of Pam's steadfast industry. While the rest of us – even Stan and me – attempted to put our own decorative stamp on our houses, Pam and Pete never got around to it but in no time the standard magnolia decor of their interior walls were covered by the boys' abundant artistic efforts.

I found Pam's conversation somewhat hard-going at times, doggedly hum-drum and plebeian.

'Stuart woke at one and was awake for twenty minutes, and then again at three,' she would intone. Or 'I could only get three spoonfuls of Weetabix down Colin, this morning. I expect he's going down with something.'

Her speech – like her person – was slow and ponderous, with a tone of hopeless, helpless gloom which reminded me of Eyore and the effort of looking on the bright side was sometimes more than I could take. But I persevered with it for the unity of the Combe Close coterie and I'm glad I did because underneath her stodgy, prosaic exterior Pam is really a good-hearted, genuinely nice woman.

In contrast, next door, Anya and Katrina provided lots of high-spirited if intellectually unchallenging chatter and they adored Lucy and so taking her round there provided something of a break for me. Anya even kept a little collection of toys in a basket in the conservatory for Lucy to play with. On the odd occasion when I caught Gary at home I enjoyed hearing about our old class-mates with whom Gary had kept up contact. He always had been one of the popular boys, I remembered.

Gary and Anya decorated lavishly – or, I should say, Katrina and Gary did, Anya mainly watched – with intricate stencils and various other cutting-edge paint techniques. Gary wired up a music system so that it could be heard in every room (even the bedroom, I discovered, deliciously aghast). The girls made dream-catchers and wind chimes for the conservatory. Everything was white; the leather suite, a large, deep-pile rug, and the fancy linen covers on the dining chairs which, I don't believe, they ever used day-to-day. They didn't do much with the garden except to erect a high panelled fence all around it, rendering it entirely private. It was south-facing and it did occur to me to wonder whether the girls used it for sunbathing. I know that Katrina had an all-over tan because I saw her naked, a couple of years later, at the impromptu pool party we had at Pete and Pam's. That was the night that she told us she was pregnant and another layer of the veil of innocence was ripped from my eyes.

But it was Sheila who put us all to shame in the matter of home-improvement that first summer. As well as working three days a week as a dental receptionist, and two evenings at a wine bar, from the moment they moved in she was relentlessly at work on and in the house, on a programme of decoration and ornamentation. She was never still, always busy at her sewing machine or with her art materials. At first I considered her to be simply very house-proud and extraordinarily creative. As well as making all her own curtains – opulent swagged ones with fringed tie-backs – and a range of co-ordinating cushions variously embroidered and appliquéd, she worked needlepoint pictures and framed them and hung them on her walls, together with collages of pressed flowers and cleverly arranged seashells. She crocheted intricate doilies and antimacassars. The children's bedrooms had hand-painted murals and there were hand-stitched quilts on all the beds. The house was always immaculately – dare

73

I say even uncomfortably - clean and tidy, even the impractically pale carpet they had laid soon after moving in. Sheila thought nothing of re-glossing all the doors and skirtings every couple of months or appending a decorative border or other embellishment to the rooms. The girls' beds were always neatly made and fussily covered with soft toys in endearing poses, scatter cushions and artfully draped throws. I never saw a crumb on Sheila's work-top or so much as a smear on her gleaming draining board. But I found the house impersonal, staged and artificial, and it was the one I found I was least likely to spend time in, if I could help it.

Sheila herself, her creativity notwithstanding, was a hard-nosed realist, tackling life's obstacles as I assume she tackled the Harriers' events: with steely determination. She was what would today, perhaps, be described as 'results-driven'; she positively wrestled with the nuts and bolts of life, or, perhaps it would be more accurate to say, its pounds and pence. She knew where the bargains were, travelling far and wide to obscure mills or doubtful-looking trading estates to buy things at discount prices, enjoying each successful foray as a kind of triumph against an invisible foe who would out-do her if he could.

But Sheila, once she had things to her liking, became very sociable, with a targeted, determined affability. She began to throw those parties where you know you are expected to buy a piece of Tupperware or a book or a kitchen utensil or some cosmetics – perhaps you remember the kind of thing I mean? Party-plan was very prevalent back then. I think that she managed to take almost all of us in before we caught on that the Tupperware was not the only thing she was trying to sell. You had only to admire a cushion or a prettily painted piece of china before she would offer to make one for you, and, only when it was too late, did you realise that she did not intend it as a gift. Her house was, quite literally, a show-house, and I know that over the years she got commissions decorating children's bedrooms and making soft furnishings and even 'dressing' homes for sale from women unsuspectingly lured into her house on the promise of a cup of coffee and a glance through the Avon catalogue.

Those parties – and I went to almost all of them because I was too cowardly to refuse and too ingenuous to think of a ready excuse - were for women only and Alan was never to be seen. I used to wonder, as I perched on her cushion-strewn sofa and sipped from a hand-painted wine glass, if Sheila had hung him tidily in a closet or folded him into a drawer for the occasion. I imagined that, on the evenings she went out running or was working, he would take pleasure in slouching with his feet on the sofa and the cushions scattered all awry, drinking from a can of beer placed defiantly *not* on the nearby hand-enamelled coaster. Perhaps that is why he made no move to arrest Sheila's unremitting acquisitiveness; although it reflected negatively on his ability to provide for them all – which, as an associate in some highly specialised accounting firm, he was surely able to do, as Stan once bitterly pointed out – at least it afforded him these opportunities to relax.

Present Day: Shopping

I wait two days in the soulless waiting room of the other Court in town. This one is in a modern, astonishingly ugly building where everything is square and practical and lacks any sense of romance or drama and correspondingly seems to deal with the mundane, slightly shabby and lacklustre cases. When I am eventually put on a case it is something and nothing, and quickly dealt with. The manageress of a suburban convenience store accuses two local women of barricading her behind the counter and beating the living daylights out of her after she caught the son of one of them (allegedly) shoplifting. The two women in the dock, sisters, are coarse types; hook-nosed and heavy-browed, and I can easily imagine them being extremely free with their fists first and asking questions later. The Manageress minces and winces her way through her testimony, as innocuous as skimmed milk, so that when it is the sisters' turn to accuse her of having locked the child in the stockroom and terrified him into handing over a bottle of pop and a chocolate bar he had legitimately bought in another shop, it hardly seems credible. The sisters admit to having visited the shop to 'remonstrate' (their barrister's word, not theirs, I doubt it is in their vocabulary) with the Manageress and yes, they admit, unfortunately, during that encounter, the Manageress did accidentally trip over something and fall. But they deny the vicious kicking and punching, the head-slapping and hair-pulling, the black-eyes, the broken nights, the emotional distress and the post traumatic shock syndrome which the Manageress asserts were the results of their actions. In the jury room the twelve of us discuss the case at length and in the end I have to bring them back to the medical report which describes nothing like the level of injuries which would have ensued from the kind of attack the Manageress has described.

'I can quite believe those women beat her up,' I say, 'they look the types. But the judge made it clear that we can only decide based on the evidence. Our knowledge of human nature doesn't count. The only evidence for this attack is a few grazes and bruises which could easily have been caused by a nasty fall. I don't think we can find them guilty.'

We deliver our verdict and I make my way home. The journey is far more tortuous and difficult than from the other court, involving quite a walk and then a sinuous tram ride before I get to the station. The weather remains appalling and I sit in the steamy tram and on the draughty platform and then in the airless train in a soaking coat with wet feet and hands like ice. By the time I get home I am feeling distinctly unwell. I struggle in to town on the following day, Friday, and huddle in the corner of the waiting room by a radiator giving out meagre heat, shivering and nursing my pounding head. As I drag myself home at the end of the day I am assaulted by the dramatic contrast between the beginning of the week and the end. The promise of the elevated plateau in the plain of my days, further heightened as it had been by my chance encounter, has turned into an undignified plummet from a treacherous cliff.

I don't remember anything about the weekend and not much about the following week, although I do recall 'phoning the court on Monday and giving them to understand, through a throat lined with razor blades, that I was too ill to attend.

One of the saddest things about living alone is being without succour during times of illness. Although Stan eschewed the sick room at least he was *there* on the rare occasions during our married life when I had to take to my bed. He would bring tea in the morning and provide some kind of sustenance in the evening and once even changed the sweat-soaked sheets, although I suspect this was more for his own comfort than for mine. The only part of nursing he really took to was doling out the medication, something he did with a finicky perusal of all the small print and meticulous time-keeping. As far as a cool hand on a fevered brow, the comforting drowse of a voice quietly reading, the little attempts to pique an appetite dulled by malady are concerned – forget it. But now, for the little comfort he was, he is gone, metamorphosed into a piece of vegetation in the garden of remembrance – probably the most vicious thorn on a blighted rose.

Lucy was more of a help, understanding the relief of a damp flannel on the head, iced juice to the flayed throat, but she too is beyond my call, converted into a scythingly efficient something-or-other in a blooming big-city business, and I crawl into bed with two paracetamols and alternately shiver and sweat, shiver and sweat, losing track of the days, confusing dawn with dusk, beset by hallucinations and raging thirsts and the feeling that every bone in my body is broken. I cough and dribble and snivel, my lungs and sinuses a spigot of evil, blood-streaked phlegm. In the darkest hour I quite expect to die, drowned in my own sputum. Of course the neighbours do not take any notice of the fact that my curtains remain closed. The telephone does not ring and for a brief, feverish period I nurse a bitter resentment against my so-called friends until I recall that I have told them all that I'll be busy with Jury service for two weeks. I cannot face the prospect of sitting in my freezing office long enough for the computer to boot up to see if there are any emails. My twisted, malodorous sheets become a nest I burrow into and feel sorry for myself.

The next time I lift my head my room is flooded by a strange, unearthly bluish-white light which pours in through the half-open curtains and paints the dusty, heavy-aired room with pearlescent glaze. My head is clear. I swallow gingerly and the blades have gone. I am weak and desiccated and sort of furred with dead skin and old crusted sweat, but I know at last that I am well. As I step out of bed my legs feel boneless as I wobble over to the window and look out. The communal garden is shrouded in a thick layer of new snow. A full moon pours light like milky gauze from a silver-grey sky. In the downstairs windows of the houses opposite coloured lights twinkle and flicker and I realise with a sinking heart that it is December, and almost Christmas.

Lucy and I gave up on traditional Christmas after a couple of years. Decorating the house, amassing piles of parcels, producing the usual festive food all seemed so pointless for just the two of us. We have no other relatives in the world but each other and we were never invited to join any of the Combe Close set. We spent a few enjoyable Christmases ski-ing in Austria. One year we went to stay with the family of Lucy's then boyfriend but the relationship broke down on Boxing Day and we beat a hasty retreat. For the past few years we have booked ourselves into a country hotel with a spa where we treat each other to facials and massages and other forms of flagrantly decadent pampering. I know, of course, that even these events are numbered. Sooner or later she will marry and have a family, and it won't always be possible to include me in her plans. I don't expect it. I don't even want it. Having to entertain Freda, as I did, for year after year, means that I know what a drag a superfluous mother-in-law can be. When the time comes I will wave away Lucy's guilt and insist that I will be perfectly fine, and promise to join a literary singles' tour of Venice, before incarcerating myself by the fire with a bottle of gin and a two pound box of chocolates and a stock of weepy films.

But that prospect is not with me yet and so I spend the next week or two regaining my strength, getting the house back to rights, easing myself gently back into my swimming regime, writing Christmas cards and setting my students' holiday assignments. Cards arrive on my doorstep and I prop them on my bookshelves, my only concession to Christmas decorations. I can identify the senders of the Combe Close cards without even reading them: Marcus and Carla's is bespoke, heavy cream card, a sketch of their country cottage with an impersonal, printed greeting; Alan and Sheila's is hand-made, of course, and on the back is a small sticker advertising 'Sheila Stiller, Home Crafts, Interior Design, Unique Home Furnishings'; Anya and Gary's is a cute cartoon of a chubby Santa and assorted adorable forest animals; Pam and Pete's is flimsy, supporting some charity. Julia and Gerald's is a photograph of their latest prize-winning dog wearing a Santa hat and encloses an invitation. They are having a party in the New Year to celebrate their Golden wedding anniversary. The prospect of it rises, a towering peak, beyond the cairn of my Christmas.

In preparing my Christmas wardrobe I discover, rather to my delight, that I have lost almost a stone in weight. This necessitates some clothes shopping. At one time I would have called Carla and submitted myself with joy to her ineluctable taste and flair for perfect accessorising. But that Carla is lost to me and so I call Sheila instead, who has a good eye for colour and a hound-like nose for a bargain even if she can be a little brusque and overly business-like. These days she's incredibly busy but she agrees to 'squeeze me in' and so we do a brisk tour of the shops while she assimilates the kinds of things I am looking for and I spend half an hour in the changing room while she whisks in and out with a selection of clothes in alternative styles until I have a collection of outfits suitable for a Country House hotel. Thinking of Julia's party – a black tie event - I take a shine to a beautiful but extravagant evening dress, very elegant, in sheer, pearl-grey silk. It is sleeveless, which can be a no-no for a woman near fifty, although, because of the swimming, my arms are pretty good. It comes, anyway, with a sweet little bolero jacket.

Sheila frowns as I stand before the mirror. 'The colour does suit you,' she admits, reluctantly, 'but isn't it a bit much?'

'Money, do you mean?' I see what's coming.

'Well, yes, for what it is, it's hugely over-priced. I could run you one up in an evening for half what they're asking.'

'No, you're right,' I say. 'Anyway, it isn't suitable for the hotel.'

I take it off and pay for my things and we go for lunch in the department store restaurant. It goes without saying that I will pay for Sheila. Our business concluded we natter about our daughters. Sheila's are both married now. One of them lives in Canada, the other, nearer at hand, has a new baby. Sheila has some pictures to show me.

'Alan must be thrilled,' I say, remembering how fond he was of the two girls.

'Oh,' she shrugs, 'he's so busy these days. I hardly see him. Work, work, work. He hasn't got time for *us.*'

I think to myself that Sheila is getting a taste of her own medicine. When they moved from Combe Close it was to another new-build house, on a much larger estate, where Sheila's industry in the matter of party-plan and personal promotion has had so much more scope that she left the dental practice to work on it full time. The wine bar she had given up on years before, to concentrate on the other extracurricular activities which threatened to tear our Combe Close society apart.

'It's a good job you keep yourself so busy,' I say, thinking that probably, four evenings out of five, Sheila is out when Alan gets back from the office, and feeling, if anything, sorrier for him that I do for her.

'Yes' she says, and checks her watch. 'My lounge is full of curtain material at the moment. I ought to get back to it before too long.' Then she flashes me that bright, brittle smile. 'You do know, don't you Molly, that if you wanted anything like that doing....'

'Of course,' I say, 'I'd only have to ask.'

Our lunch arrives and we begin to eat. Sheila has chosen a substantial meal and I guess that she won't be cooking this evening. Poor Alan will get catch-as-catch-can from the fridge. She prods at the food suspiciously for a moment, lifting the pastry lid of her pie to check that she has not been cheated of her proper quota of filling before asking: 'Have you seen anyone since the holiday?'

'No.' I explain, briefly, about the jury service and the 'flu. 'Have you?'

'I called in on Carla,' she says, adding, bitterly, 'it breaks my heart,' but her strange note of indictment is directed resolutely at her plate.

'Mine too,' I nod, wondering why, in spite of her down-cast gaze, I suddenly feel so defensive. 'How was she?'

81

Sheila shakes her head. 'Droopy. Uncommunicative.' She puts her fork down and leans across the table and now there is more than a hint of blame in her tone. 'Do you know how all this is going to pan out? *Do* you?'

I shake my head. 'No. No, I don't.'

'I do. I've looked into it. Let's just say – not indefinitely.'

I don't know what she expects me to say; that I am sorry? Of course I am sorry, sorry in the way that people are for things that aren't their fault, with an entirely useless, ineffectual sorrow. I press my napkin to my eyes so that I don't have to meet her accusative eye.

'Terrible isn't it?' She actually leans back in her seat to observe the results of her cruelty. She waits until I have blown my nose before delivering her next coup. If anything it appals me still more. 'And yet,' she says, resuming her lunch, 'there comes a point, don't you think?'

She is so hard, I think. Does it not occur to her at all that I, too, have been a victim in all of this? 'A point?' I stammer.

'Yes. Well. What would you want, in her shoes, given the prognosis?'

'Oh Sheila!' I cry, 'That's a terribly defeatist attitude. They're coming up with new treatments all the time.....' Sheila shakes her head, but I plough on, 'and in the meantime we must give them all the support we can, *both* of them. I think the holiday did Marcus good. At least we could share the load. Perhaps we could do it more often – book in a few weekend breaks......'

'About the holiday,' Sheila begins, wiping her mouth with her napkin.

'Yes,' I say, pushing away my sandwich, ready to make a plan. 'I'll have to get on to it in the New Year. What do you think? Shall we try Scotland again? Or somewhere a bit nearer?' It always falls to me to organise our Combe Close holidays. It is no mean feat; we're a numerous party and there aren't many houses that will accommodate us, plus, in recent years, people have had so many other commitments that finding a week which is convenient for everyone has been a nightmare.

'I don't know,' Sheila pulls her dessert towards her. 'I'm not sure we'll be going next year.'

I am dumbstruck. 'Not going?' After what I thought we had just agreed, her statement seems incomprehensible.

'Didn't you..... don't you think.....' She makes a number of attempts to start her next sentence before blurting out, 'Oh Molly, it's just so difficult with Pam.'

'Pam?' I repeat, bewildered. I thought this was all about Carla. Of all of us, Pam is the *least* difficult; if anything, the most Saint-like. But then, there is awkward history between Sheila and Pam. I thought it had been settled years ago, I worked harder than anyone to make sure that it would be. It puts a stone in my chest to think that I have failed.

'Yes,' she says, 'so parochial in the kitchen, all that unnecessary baking and those rich desserts. Don't you come away feeling sickened? I do.'

'You know what Pam's like,' I say. 'Food is love.'

'Food is calories,' Sheila says, spooning trifle. 'Some of us have training schedules.' Then she adds, with more honesty, 'She makes me feel uncomfortable.'

I stir my tea, fighting panic. My Combe Close world is threatening to disintegrate, further, that is, than it has already done, and if that is the case, what has been the use of my own small sacrifice? 'If *she* can get past it, surely *you* can,' I suggest, hearing the note of desperation in my own voice. 'It's all in the past.'

She looks at me then across our untidy little table. Her lips remain tightly closed and I notice, for the first time, that she is developing those vertical stitches around them. I get the sudden impression that her mouth is sewn shut, lest secrets spill out. For all she has just eaten a hearty lunch she is thin, almost hollow, and I realise that her athletic trimness has become drawn; there is a meanness about her I haven't noticed before. Her hair, dyed now, has an unnatural brassiness about it which is unbecoming and harsh, like rust. Her flinty grey eyes flash me a bladelike look before she begins to babble about how difficult it is to pin Alan down to holidays.

'Oh God,' I think to myself. 'It isn't over.'

When I have waved her off from the car park I retrace my steps and buy the pearl-grey dress, because I want to look my best for Julia's party and just now I don't care if I have to pay twice as much as I should. He will be there, of course, and in some convoluted way the possible prospect that lunch with Sheila has just opened up to me has renewed my sense of what might, conceivably occur. It nestles, embryonic and unrealised, as I have always kept it, slumbering within the protective encasements of my friends' enduring marriages and our collective reliances. But if the breakdown of its carapace is inevitable, who is to say what might, from within, emerge?

Combe Close: Invitation

I recall that Stan and I did gradually improve on the somewhat Spartan interior of our house, more as a result of my wistful and repeated observations of the neighbours' activities than due to any real enthusiasm for it on Stan's part. We did, eventually, have light fittings and I chose ready-made curtains (much to Sheila's disgust, I suppose) and we relieved the blank canvas of our walls with practical anaglypta and some prints we both liked, and a couple of wedding photographs. Our garden remained a utilitarian area of steeply sloping lawn (why on earth, I wondered, had Stan wanted to make it bigger?) and because it faced roughly north it got little sun, so when my birthday came round in mid August I asked for a wooden bench for the front garden, which was south-facing and gave me the pretty view of our neighbours' trellises and hanging baskets and the old trees of the Crescent gardens beyond. It was lovely to sit there in the sun while Lucy had her nap, with a book or a cup of tea, and it was the perfect space from which to beckon over one of the neighbours, so quite often I would find myself joined by one of my friends for a little natter in the lulls between their daily tasks.

It was on this bench that I established the common desire to socialise. 'Would you like to?' I asked them. 'Don't you think it would be great?' 'Why don't we have a get together – like a joint house-warming?' It was already clear that we could expect no overtures of friendship from our Crescent neighbours and now that we were settled, now that Lucy had arrived and I had recovered from her arrival, I was keen to make a start on this convivial, neighbourly intercourse I had so anticipated would be an intrinsic factor in Combe Close life. 'Oh yes!' they all said, in full but non-specific accord and I wondered what on earth they were waiting for.

'I don't understand it,' I said to Stan one evening. 'Everyone wants to have some kind of social event but no-one seems to be doing anything about it.'

'For God's sake, Molly! They probably feel you're nagging them into it,' Stan snapped.

'I don't think so,' I rejoined, a little hurt. 'They said they wanted to.'

'When?' Stan asked me. The lawn-mower was in pieces on the drive and he was up to the elbows in oil.

'When I asked them! Every one of them said they thought it was a great idea.'

Stan sighed and threw me one of his withering looks. 'And now you're waiting for an invitation?' He passed me a handful of tiny metal bits and pieces, 'Hold these, can you?'

'Alright.' I held out my hand and took them from him.

'You dunce,' he said, under his breath, selecting a spanner from his toolbox.

'What?'

'They're expecting *you* to issue an invitation!'

I thought about it. 'Do you think so?'

'Of course I do. What would you expect if someone asked you if you thought a party was a good idea? It's like issuing a theoretical invitation. Now they're just waiting for you to name the day.' He was half laughing at me, with a dry, humourless exasperation, but half angry as well. I could feel a 'I told you it would come to this' moment coming on.

'I don't suppose you want us to throw a party, do you?' I asked, in a small voice.

'You suppose right. What do we know about parties?'

He was right. We were woefully under-socialised. I waited while he tinkered with the mechanics of the mower. 'I just want to have friends, Stan,' I burst out at last. 'I want us all to get along.' I swept my arm in a semi circle to encapsulate the Close. 'It's what people do in our situation.

They have dinner occasionally, the chaps go to the pub, the women look after one another's children from time to time, and share the school run and all that. I'm not asking for anything that isn't *normal.*' Even as I described it I felt I was betraying my vision, which was so much more than the practical, emotionally-dry picture I had just painted.

'Give me those screws,' he snapped. I dropped them into his hand and waited for him to unleash a salvo of scorn, and I am sure that he was preparing to deliver one but just at that moment Gary's front door opened and Anya and Katrina stepped out. Anya wore jeans and a pink t shirt with a glittery ballerina on the front, but Katrina wore the shortest shorts I have ever seen and the skimpiest of tops which only just kept her bosom in check. She was bronzed from head to foot, her hair in a carelessly erotic top-knot, her feet thrust into high-heeled sandals. She chasséd across the Close, dark eyes alight, red mouth in a wide smile. Anya walked a step or two behind, smiling also, but more diffident.

'Well Molly,' Katrina said in her ripe, husky voice. 'Is this your husband?' There was a note of, not quite salacious enquiry, but something close, in her voice. Stan leapt from the ground scattering miniscule nuts and bolts all over the drive. She was quite an eyeful and I noticed that he took full advantage.

'Yes,' I said. 'This is Stan.'

Katrina regarded him roguishly, 'She's been keeping *you* hidden away,' she grinned.

Stan blushed and half held out a greasy hand and then withdrew it again sharply.

'Stan, this is Katrina and Anya. Anya and Gary live across the road.'

'I live there too, most of the time, don't I Anya?' Katrina laughed. She surveyed the dismembered lawn mower. 'This looks interesting,' she said, 'what are you doing?' She leaned over the machine and I thought that her breasts were going to topple out of her top. Stan thought so too. Ever the gent, he readied himself to catch them. She began to point out different parts of the workings and ask what they did. Anya slid on to the bench beside me.

'Gary says we'll have the party,' she gushed in the dry, breathy counterpart to her sister's throaty voice. 'Isn't that exciting?'

'Oh Anya it is!' I exclaimed. 'Stan and I were just talking about it.'

'Only it can't be for a couple of weeks because he has to go away on a course, and Katrina will be on holiday, but after that,' she actually clapped her hands together, 'we can have a lovely party and everyone's invited.'

So the date was set and my excited anticipation was almost boundless except that Stan managed to sour it for me, driving the first wedge into the scarcely-set surface of our Combe Close community.

He didn't manage to fix the lawn mower that evening and it had to go off to a repair shop. Our front lawn, as I think I have mentioned, was a piece of shared turf which stretched across the front of our house and also Julia and Gerald's. The landscaping team had dug in flower beds at the outer corners and planted a variety of flowering shrubs in them. They had also put a larger specimen within the lawn itself, more or less in the middle. It was a spindly sapling as yet, but would one day be substantial. Our mower being out of action and in spite of the weather which continued warm, the grass on our side got rather long, and one day Gerald mowed it for us when he was doing his own patch. It was very kind of him, I thought. Just the neighbourly sort of gesture I had depended on. But Stan took it dreadfully amiss and flew into one of his most irascible tirades. I was flabbergasted, frankly, and rather appalled by the ungraciousness of his attitude.

'Who does he think he is?' he railed at me. 'Walking onto our property without a by-your-leave. I know his game. I always did think the idea of open-plan gardens was a law-suit waiting to happen.' He was on his way upstairs to get the house plans and plot specifications from his bedside drawer.

'Stan! Stan'! I cried, helplessly from the foot of the stairs, holding Lucy on my hip.

'Don't you know,' he yelled at me as he came back down, 'that if someone maintains a piece of land for a certain amount of time they can claim it? He's after it. I know it. If not all of it, then at least the lion's share.' Stan started to spread the plans out on the dining room table.

'For God's sake, Stan,' I gasped. 'He did it as a favour.'

'We don't need his favours,' he snarled. 'This tree,' he stabbed at plan, 'it isn't in the middle, you know, it's ours. I bet he thinks it marks the boundary but look - *look!* – it's clearly on our half.'

He was being ridiculous of course, and I think he knew it, and, perhaps because he knew he was completely over-reacting, there was no arguing with him. He was utterly, wilfully entrenched in his untenable position and simply set his face to endure it to the last stubborn ounce of his determination.

There were only a couple of days to go before the party and Stan entered one of his dark, brooding moods which, I felt sure, would result in us not attending. He hardly spoke to me even after I realised the pointlessness of trying to reason with him and the futility of trying to defend Gerald. He went off to work early and came back late, and took to sauntering with an ominously proprietorial, perhaps even defiant air, up and down the front lawn between the houses and the pavement along the line of what I knew he believed to be the border as though he could tread in some indelible margin, like a predatory animal marking off his territory. I walked on eggshells for those two days, and avoided the bench on the front lawn, half as a fretful kind of stratagem – discretion being the better part of valour - half resentfully. I cooked Stan's favourite meals and tried to make sure that I gave no cause for further annoyance by being particularly diligent about the things that Stan was especially pernickety about.

As the hour approached, and with it Freda, hot-foot from the bus stop, to babysit, I made simple preparations for myself and laid out a clean shirt and some light, casual trousers for Stan while he continued to toil, up to the last possible minute, on some project in the garage. As I put Lucy down in her cot I heard the first distant strains of music from across the Close, and peeped through her curtains to see Gary and Anya's lounge windows thrown open, the twinkle of fairy-lights and candles from within, the gay bounce of an endearing but at the same time rather pathetic balloon tied to their door knocker – Anya's doing, I was sure. When I was certain Lucy had settled I stepped into the garage on some pretext, just so that Stan could see that I was dressed and ready, then withdrew without saying a word to wait patiently in the lounge. I was almost breathless with anxiety but at last heard him come in, his heavy tread on the stairs, the rush of water in the shower.

We finally stepped out of the house only about half an hour after the appointed time. The heat of the day had waxed leaving a pleasantly warm evening. The sun had already sunk below the line of trees on the other side of The Crescent. I slipped my arm through Stan's but he said nothing as we crossed the Close and walked up Gary and Anya's drive until we were on the step and ringing the bell, when he gave a sudden heavy sigh and muttered, 'What are these people called again?' I told him and then Anya opened the door.

Combe Close: The First Party

I sensed as soon as I stepped into Gary and Anya's hall that I was not the only person experiencing a frisson of excitement at more than the ordinary level for a simple neighbourhood get-together. There was an air – an almost audible high note – of pent up expectancy in the house and surrounding the guests. It released itself a little as we entered – we were the last, of course – as though perhaps there had been a feeling that things could not really begin until we arrived; as if we were, together, a recipe which depended on every constituent ingredient being properly present to come out right.

From what I could see as I stood on the threshold people had remained more or less in their couples: I could see Marcus and Carla in the conservatory; Julia and Gerald were beached on the low, slippery white leather sofa in the lounge, like basking seals incongruously sipping G & T's from heavy cut-glass tumblers; Sheila and Alan had taken up a position on the hearth rug opposite to them. As I entered they were both drinking from tall glasses of what turned out to be vodka and orange and because they were slim and elegant and because of my initial impression of Julia and Gerald, they looked fleetingly like yellow-beaked, eager sea-birds stranded on a white sandbank. Pam and Pete occupied the area by the window. Pam was looking round anxiously at the small bowls of nuts and crisps which appeared to be the only food on offer. Pete was already dripping sweat and fighting with his tie – none of the other men were wearing them – and he was the one to shout as we entered: 'Here they are, *here* they are at last. *Now* we can get this party started!' and it was this comment which gave me, most of all, a sense of shared expectation that things were going to, in some way, take off; of something momentous and inaugural. I couldn't say what, exactly, but *something*: the pop of champagne corks, a round of applause, even the sudden fizz and crackle of fireworks above our heads, would have seemed appropriate. That there needed to be a launch of some kind Gary must have felt as well, for he suddenly strode over to the space-age stereo and jabbed at the controls, replacing the lull of Spanish guitar music with something much more up-beat, and adjusting the volume upwards too, before seizing bottles with a flourish and topping up people's drinks.

I saw Stan shrink slightly, whether from the sudden jarring jazz cacophony or from the crowd of strange faces in the room I couldn't tell – both, I thought, were likely to unsettle him - and told myself that I would have to watch him like a hawk and be ready to intervene if he looked like saying something sharp or ungracious. But Pete - big, booming, irrepressible man that he is, as different to Stan as it is possible to imagine – immediately stepped forward, clapped him on the shoulder and held out a meaty hand to introduce himself, and at the same time Katrina swooped to his side with a look on her face which suggested that, in her opinion, Stan was the most exciting man in the room and the one whose arrival she had most eagerly awaited.

'Pleased to meet you!' Pete cried, pumping at Stan's arm. 'Know the wife, do you?' he indicated Pam with a jerk of his chin, 'Beautiful woman in blue there. All mine, bought and paid for!' Pam gave an awkward nod of greeting.

'So glad you could come,' Katrina breathed, slipping her arm around Stan's waist, 'let's get you a drink, shall we?'

'Yes, come on! You're two behind the rest of us, at least!' Pete boomed, and they carried Stan off towards the conservatory between them as though he was a prize celebrity. I was waylaid in my pursuit by Pam who wanted to tell me about a cough or sniffle one of the boys had developed but I managed to cut her short and arrived in the conservatory in time to hear Pete introducing Marcus and to catch Stan's studiedly mysterious 'I'm with the Civil Service' line as he shook hands. Later, it was to strike me as odd and a little unsatisfactory that he chose this and not 'I'm Molly's husband' as his main identifier.

I had hardly had a drink pressed into my hand before Carla took my arm and led me out onto the patio with Anya.

'Let's leave them to it,' she said, aside, as we moved towards a pretty wrought iron patio set.

'I mustn't leave Stan by himself for too long,' I replied as the three of us took seats.

'Stan will have to stand up for himself!' Carla laughed archly, throwing out a dismissive arm. 'We have to expect a certain amount of sparring and posturing at first, from the men. It'll take them all night just to establish who does what and who earns what and to rough out some sort of pecking order and then they can get onto football and cars and that's about as deep as they'll go. You know what they're like!' Anya and I exchanged a look. Her face was as blank as mine, which made Carla laugh even more. 'Well they're not like *us* are they? They don't talk about the things that really matter.' She took a sip of her drink – non-alcoholic of course, because of the baby – and placed her glass on the table.

I wondered what Stan would think of this proposal: that his job and salary didn't matter, and decided that it would be poorly received, but then I had to admit that I had rarely seen Stan in company before and particularly not in company with his peers. This view of him was entirely new to me. Suddenly I saw it exactly as Carla had described it; the first skirmish, as it were, the first joining of battle between the men. And with that realisation came a swift dawning of understanding of his ridiculous reaction to the front lawn situation. With the battlefield in view, he'd been compromised before the first shot was fired by the fact that he'd had to make do with an old, second hand mower which, to add insult to injury, he'd proved unequal to fixing. No wonder he'd shown so little enthusiasm for the party!

'Men talk about sport and tools and the news and cars,' Anya offered, as though reciting from memory.

'Well there you are then, darling,' Carla said, implying that Anya had made a new and incisive contribution to the discussion.

'Women talk about clothes and make-up and the television,' Anya went on.

'And men,' I said.

'Oh and a lot more besides,' Carla added, 'with their friends. But it doesn't do to leave the men behind. It's a matter of making sure that they keep up with us.'

I realised how right she was and marvelled a little at the acuteness of her penetration. By the time of the party the women of the Close had progressed several stages along the path to friendship, the route lubricated by numerous cups of tea and coffee and even the occasional glass of wine. We had, in the way that women do, established common ground – predominantly the tardiness of the builder's snag-fixing programme (poor Pam's washing machine was *still* leaking) - and the unvoiced but tacitly understood uselessness of men which unites women the world over when in all-female company. We had swiftly covered those important bases; whether we favoured Tesco or Sainsbury's, how we took our tea, preparatory to getting down to the important stuff, the things which, as Carla said, really mattered: what we felt, what we thought, what we hoped and feared, the kinds of things men rarely – if ever – discuss. We had established above all our openness, our availability for friendship. In all this we were far ahead of the men, and as Carla helped me realise, it was for the men, really, that this party was such a good thing. We needed them to catch up with us and, being men, they could not by any means have been left to make a start on their own. Now, having corralled them in one place and supplied them with alcohol and Katrina, around whom they all gravitated like bees round a honey pot, we could do no better than to leave them to it.

From where I was sitting I could see Stan standing with the other men in a semi-circle around the makeshift bar and Katrina, who laughed and twinkled and flashed her eyes as she poured drinks. She had a way, as the men talked, of reaching with her hand into the depths of her artfully tousled hair to absently tease and tug at its tresses, all the while regarding them with her huge, dark eyes, and then, when they looked at her, of sliding her gaze away, as though to hide thoughts she did not want them to see. All the men, by now, had graduated towards her. Pete's was the voice I could hear most clearly and loudly, even above the music, he called her 'my beauty' and 'my lovely' as he helped her pass round the glasses and handed her ice and slices of lemon, and at the same time incited the men to drink, managing to quaff, himself, glass after glass of beer as though each was only the smallest swallow.

'Get your laughing-gear round this,' he roared at them, pressing glasses and bottles and cans, 'we need to keep this beauty busy or we'll lose her for sure. We mustn't let her escape! Marcus, you cover the French windows there, Gerald, you man the other exit! Now we've got her! Now we've got her lads!' He was working hard at setting the keynote and it was taking its toll on him; his round face was quite florid and beaded with moisture, his shirt stuck to his back. His line was not at all what Carla had suggested – he sounded not the slightest note of brinksmanship – but established himself as leader of the pack just by implying that they were a pack – those six men – for whom the good of one was the good of all. He was relentlessly inclusive, imbuing them all with his hearty appetite and mischievous sense of humour, an attractively encompassing campaign of irresistible 'all lads together.'

Marcus allowed himself to be bowled over by the sheer affability of the man and to be led, by him, into exchanges of banter which soon had everyone in stitches. He must have recognised in Pete an echo of his own nature. I do not mean the animal appetite, but certainly the largeness, the generosity, of soul. They made quite a double act, the two of them, and while Marcus' sense of humour was not at all of Pete's suggestive ilk, they did find common ground in various comedy sketches they both liked and knew by heart and a general boyish, boisterous jocularity.

Gerald, egged them on with cries of 'Capital! Capital!' wheezing and slapping his thigh and getting redder and redder in the face until I thought he was going to have an apoplexy. Alan laughed and drank along with the rest but said little, maintaining more of a watchful stance. I noticed a tick he had, of removing his spectacles and polishing them with his handkerchief, and it seemed to me that he played out this little ritual to conceal some expression he did not want people to read. He was the first to break away from the cluster to seek more personal conversation, though; more at home in a couple than a crowd. Gary, to whom, it turned out, Pete was not a new acquaintance but an existing friend and business contact, just basked in his neighbour's charisma, smiling indulgently from time to time while his bar was systematically plundered. Even as host, with all the responsibilities that entailed, he was relaxed and confident, eagerly demonstrating the electronic wizardry he had incorporated into his home, boyishly enthusiastic about showing us over his house. I must admit to being rather impressed, and in a strange way proud, of the suave, velvety assurance he exuded; not bad, I thought, for a boy from my side of town.

Of them all, Stan, whom I had thought so assured and who, I now realised, had come to the party both girded and ham-strung for battle, looked the least comfortable, the most like a rabbit caught in the headlights of Pete's effusion and Katrina's womanly light. Alternately flattered and bewildered, he looked from one to the other and drank the beers which were handed to him, and forgot (for the time being, anyway) all about the boundary between our house and Gerald's and the question of who owned that wretched tree. I think I saw him, then, for the first time, as he really was. Side by side with those other men it was all too clear to me that beneath the bluster and growl, beyond the finicky fuss-making and the irate tirades Stan was an insecure little man, out of his depths in any but the most restricted sphere (like his small department at work) or the illusory orbit of his own making, which he wove with his silly secrets and self-made mysteries and vague allusions to things which must remain veiled. I felt a pang of guilt: I had brought him like a lamb to the slaughter here to this company of wiser, more experienced, more successful, more confident, more brilliant men. I felt sorry for him.

And then, swiftly, unexpectedly, I felt sorry for myself.

As the night drew in it turned cool and we closed the French windows and gathered indoors. The candles warmed us with a glow that seemed to come from some inner region of golden well-being, and cast a dancing, insubstantial, sinuous light over everything. Gary had changed the music again to something soulful. There was food (to Pam's relief) and its consumption, combined with the narcotic effect of the candlelight and the music turned us languorous, like sea-bathers who have overcome the initial thrill and yelp of the cold water to be able to bask and luxuriate in its cool caress. We all had shared that first anticipated plunge into our new relation and now we took possession of it. Like a married couple after the ceremony; the deed was done and it could begin.

Anya showed Sheila and I around the upstairs rooms of the house. Everything was terribly stylish, but on a distinctly un-cluttered, what, today, would be called 'minimalist' scale, an anathema to Sheila's florid, ruched, embroidered and multi-tasselled taste in home décor. Her continual enquires as to the provenance and cost of things were frustrated by Anya's repeated 'I don't know, Katrina brought it here one day,' and 'you'll have to ask Gary,' as were her numerous offers to supply soft furnishings.

'This would be just the spot for a wall-hanging, don't you think?' Sheila suggested, indicating an expanse of empty wall on the landing. 'Say four foot square – or larger - appliqué, perhaps, lots of colour. I have a design in mind. I'll sketch it out and bring it over tomorrow, shall I?'

'I don't know. You'll have to ask Gary,' Anya said again.

Downstairs Pam had nobbled Julia and was enumerating the symptoms of the child's incipient illness. 'Up all night coughing,' she was saying.

'Oh!' Julia ejaculated, 'Gerald's just the same. I give *him* hot brandy...'

Except for Carla and Pam we had all been drinking; for myself I had drunk a good deal more than I was used to but not so much that I felt inebriated; rather, I felt in some way raised, as though I had become a better version of myself, elevated out of the mundane and plain person I habitually thought myself to be, lifted, certainly, out of the moroseness I had felt an hour before. It was always to have this effect on me – the Combe Close chemistry – a glorious sense of well-being and belonging, comfort and security, and a better, brighter idea of myself, all strung together like pearls on a thread which seemed to carry with it a thrilling, enlivening current.

As people wandered now between the buffet and various seats, the bar, the cloakroom, I revelled in the opportunity for avid, interesting communication, realising all at once how much of my life was spent in solitary silence; at home alone during the day, even with Stan, in the evenings, and before that, at home with my parents, our talk was only functional; what we would eat, what we would watch on television.

I listened to Julia and Marcus discuss plants and their propagation, to Alan and Gary as they rifled the shelves of CDs and established a common passion for Jazz, to Pete and Sheila as they relived a pop festival it turned out they had both attended as teenagers, and I watched them all – their bright eyes, eager gestures, the almost palpable flow of connectivity. Then I was not outside it, not observing, I was in it, carried along by its irresistible tide, and Gary and I were describing to Alan our shared nightmare of country dancing classes at school.

'I always ended up with either Gareth Gubbins or Steven Sligh,' I laughed, amazed how, in retrospect, and from this new perspective, the ignominy of it could be so innocuous.

'You didn't have the worst of it,' Gary said, with theatrical gloom. 'If there were no girls left you had to dance with Miss Higginbottom.'

'Ah yes,' I agreed, 'a very capaciously bosomed lady.'

'Nearly suffocated a little tyke like me,' Gary cried, as though defending himself against a charge I had not made.

'Poor woman,' I said, dryly, 'you had to feel sorry for her. That moustache...'

Alan laughed aloud at the picture we created. 'Sounds like something out of Dickens,' he said.

'You'd have to ask Molly,' Gary demurred. 'She was always top in English.' He gave me a straight, knowing look, in some strange way collusive; in this room of strangers, it said, we are not.

'Were you?' The fact seemed to ignite something in Alan. He opened his eyes more widely, behind their rimless spectacles, and dipped his chin more closely to the stem of his neck, as though taking a mental step backwards in order to be able to appreciate this revelation more fully. I basked in the glow of it, of all of it, like bathing in honey.

Later, Marcus took me to one side. 'I hope I can rely on you,' he said, 'when our baby comes.'

'Of course,' I cried, 'I'll do all I can.'

'Carla's such a maverick,' he smiled, indulgently, watching her across the room as she taught Anya a line-dancing routine. 'She's quite likely to forget all about the baby and go out on some whim....'

'She won't do that,' I said, glancing through the lounge window across the Close to our house where, I noted with relief, Lucy's bedroom light remained off, 'it would be like forgetting herself.'

'No, but really Molly,' Marcus put his hand on my arm, 'she needs a steady friend like you.'

Thus the evening stretched out as we mingled and melded from one grouping to another and I felt deeply happy. From a vantage point on

Gary and Anya's galleried landing I took a moment to take stock of it as snatches of conversation, the music, the occasional shout of laughter permeated up through the building. My vision was being realised before my eyes; these lovely people were my friends and neighbours and Lucy would grow up amongst them. I had stepped from the shadows of drab and vacuous isolation on a soulless estate, and before that the anonymity of my bank cubicle, and before that the grinding emotional famine of school and home, to this perfect community of genial interaction where I would take my long-awaited place.

I found Stan in the dining room with Julia and Gerald. Our neighbours were eating from plates heaped with food. Stan held a plate also, it had hardly anything on it, but in any case he could not have eaten anything because his other hand clasped a tumbler of some amber coloured drink; whiskey perhaps, I speculated. While Julia and Gerald talked, she in that booming, declamatory way that she has, he with his habitual apostrophic interjections, Stan said nothing. He engaged with them, as far as it went, with head movements, nodding and shaking as appropriate, and sometimes when not. His features were screwed into a frown, his eyes narrowed and calculating. As a result the most powerful impression I got of him was of someone massively preoccupied with a knotty arithmetical conundrum from which our neighbours were trying, but failing – just – to distract him. When I stepped up to him and spoke to him he turned almost in slow motion, and I realised that he was drunk, and investing every atom of concentration into appearing to be sober.

I gently disengaged the glass from his hand. 'Eat something,' I urged, brightly, 'these sandwiches look delicious.'

'We were just saying,' Julia exclaimed, in as close to a whisper as she could manage, 'all bought in from the delicatessen in town. Exquisite! But jolly pricey, wouldn't you say?'

'I'd say so,' Gerald put in. He opened his mouth and posted a *vol-au-vent* into it. 'Oh yes,' he repeated, through pastry and creamed mushrooms, 'I'd say so.'

'You mowed our lawn,' Stan said, suddenly, irrelevantly, and rather indistinctly. His voice, hardly recognisable to me, emerged curiously independent of his tongue and lips.

'Yes Stan, it was Gerald who mowed the lawn for us,' I reiterated, by way of translation.

'Good of you,' Stan said, more clearly, 'very good of you indeed.'

Gerald cleared his throat a few times and waved a miniature pork pie dismissively, indicating that it was not worth mentioning. Stan, finding his hand disengaged, took a bite of the ham sandwich I had proffered to him and at the same time raised his index finger to suggest that the topic could not be so easily dismissed and must, indeed, be elaborated on. We waited obediently while he chewed his sandwich, chewed it very slowly, thoughtfully and deliberately, as though he had never eaten such a thing before and must make a minute assessment of its finer gastronomic qualities. At last he swallowed.

'That tree,' he said, slowly. 'The central one,' he cast me a bleary look of triumph at his clever avoidance of the word 'middle', 'what kind is it, do you think?'

'Philadelphus Belle Etoile,' Julia said, promptly, 'more of a shrub, really, although it can grow as high as six or seven feet. Mock orange is its common name of course.'

'Need much looking after, does it?' Stan enunciated carefully.

Julia shrugged. 'Just a good prune once a year. Pretty low maintenance, I'd say.'

'Just the ticket,' Gerald nodded. 'Low maintenance, that's what we like.'

Stan narrowed his eyes and I detected, within their glazed sheen, a glimmer, just a glint of sentient light. 'And *where*...' he placed the question heavily, giving it the significance of an unexploded bomb amongst us, 'just exactly on *whose plot*...' he squeezed the nub of the matter out from

101

between his flaccid, uncooperative lips, 'would you say that *shrub* is situated?' he looked from one to the other of us.

'Oh! If you're concerned about the pruning,' Julia ejaculated, getting the wrong end of the stick, 'it's the easiest thing! Isn't it Gerald?'

'Nothing simpler,' Gerald concurred.

'No, no...' Stan held up that admonitory finger again. I tried to distract him with another sandwich, I knew what was coming. He turned to me, 'No Molly!' he shouted, making us all jump, and giving me a speaking glare before turning back to Julia and Gerald. 'No. What I want to know is;' speaking with infinite, almost comic sluggishness, 'who do you think it belongs to?'

Julia and Gerald looked at each other in bewilderment as if the question was so easy they couldn't believe it had even been asked.

'Oh Stan!' I hissed, under my breath, feeling, all at once, deflated and broken; Cinderella after the midnight chime.

'To us, of course!' Julia hooted, and I saw her lift her arms to embrace Gerald on her one side and Stan on the other, indicating our collective ownership of the disputed shrub, and I saw it, even more, from her gesture, as a symbol of the commonality of Combe Close I so desired. But Stan, his peripheral vision mazed by the unaccustomed beer and whiskey, heard only her words. He put his plate down on the table but misjudged it and it fell onto the parquet with a sickening smash.

'Oh Stan!' I began, but his voice drowned out mine. He had turned very white and I thought he was going to throw up but he leaned across the space between himself and Julia and roared into her face 'I don't *think* so.' She took a step backwards and Gerald, at her side, took a corresponding step forwards but at that moment I heard Marcus' voice, abrupt and surprisingly authoritative, although genial enough in tone, from the dining room door.

'Stan! I think Molly wants to go home. Don't you, Molly?'

'Yes,' I said, quickly, and my own lips were uncooperative now; stiff with shame and shock. 'I need to feed Lucy.'

The colour rushed back into Stan's face and he recovered himself enough to give a lopsided smile. 'Let her go then,' he slurred, reaching for the whiskey glass I had taken from him, 'it isn't far.'

Marcus had been joined by Alan in the dining room doorway. I wondered how much of the exchange they had heard. Whether all of it, or none, I couldn't tell, but they took in the situation at a glance.

'We're all making a move now,' Alan said, quietly persuasive. 'The girls are all tired.'

'Let all the girls go home then,' Stan said, belligerently, 'we chaps can stay, can't we?'

'We could, but it wouldn't be good form,' Marcus said, smoothly. He was in the room with us now, at our side of the table, and, without touching him, began to edge and usher Stan towards the door.

'Not good form,' Gerald agreed, 'oh no, not at all.' I threw him what I hoped he would understand as a grateful glance. He could so easily have insisted that the matter should not be dropped. At his side, Julia was rummaging a handkerchief from her handbag. I gave her a baleful look; we were both close to tears.

When we got into the hallway I cast a woebegone eye across the scene, forcing myself, but hardly daring, to meet anyone's eye. I glimpsed Pam, in the kitchen of course, her arms elbow-deep in sudsy water, with Anya at her side looking pale and tired, poor thing, it was way past her bedtime. But then I picked myself up on the thought; how patronising of me, I thought. Anya was not a child.

Through the lounge door I could see the heads of Pete and Sheila on the sofa, still in animated recollection of their pop festival, I supposed, and seemingly unaware of the scene which had just played itself out in the dining room. Pete had his arm draped across the back of the settee. In the doorway stood my friend Carla. Her face spoke volumes of sympathy and sadness for me; *she*, clearly, was not unaware. She came and kissed me and gave me a hard hug. It was the first physical demonstration of our budding friendship.

Alan had the front door open and Stan and I were shepherded, with great finesse, onto the front step. I turned to thank my hosts. Gary and Katrina were in the conservatory, where the candles had been extinguished and only a string of fairy lights looped amongst the supports of the roof gave a dim, pixie-grotto glow. I could barely see them because my eyes, now, were awash with unfallen tears.

'Do thank Gary and Anya for me,' I muttered.

'Of course I will,' said Alan, taking my arm and stepping with me into the black, moonless night. Ahead of us Marcus had already got Stan halfway home. I could hear Marcus talking discursively about something and nothing. He gestured occasionally and used phrases like 'Of course you're aware,' and 'You don't need me to tell you,' which gave Stan the dignity of complicity in the discussion without requiring him to say anything. He was incapable of saying anything, anyway. The fresh air had extinguished what little flame of acumen he retained. The two of them arrived at our porch and Stan made an elaborate search of his trouser pockets for our door key, which I had in my handbag. I handed it to Marcus who opened the door for us. As he released my arm Alan murmured, in a voice so low I could hardly catch what he said, 'You'll be alright?' and I nodded dumbly and followed Stan across our threshold.

'Goodnight Molly,' Marcus said. 'See you tomorrow.' He and Alan, my knights, remained until the door was shut and fastened behind us.

'I need to feed Lucy,' I said. In fact my breasts were swollen with milk and at the thought of her I could feel the let-down reflex kick into action. I pushed past Stan and ran up the stairs, leaving him to follow as best as he could.

Present Day: Christmas

Lucy and I enjoy our Christmas at a Country House Hotel situated about half way between our two homes. The weather is nondescript outside but we scarcely notice it from our horizontal perspectives in the gloom of the treatment rooms or in the artificial south-sea isle of the spa, where we wallow in the Jacuzzi until our finger-ends are shrivelled, flesh-coloured raisins. I have a series of anti-ageing treatments which address my crow's feet and laughter-lines and she sweats and frets inside layers of seaweed and generous lardings of cellulite-reducing mineral mud.

Although there is a tree and the traditional festive lunch is served on Christmas day there is a distinct – and agreeable – lack of Christmas hype about the hotel. The management have cottoned on to the fact that the season is not necessarily a source of unalloyed joy and excitement. Most of the guests, like Lucy and I, just want a quiet break. There are a number of withered female parties; a set of spinster-sisters who knit and read murder mysteries and drink sweet sherry, and a widowed bridge-four which spends every afternoon at a reserved table in the lounge frowning over their hands of cards and occasionally barking things like: 'Oh Muriel! We are in three *spades* you know!' They break at five for large gin and tonics all round, are the first into the dining room and the first out again, back at their three no-trumps by half past seven and in bed by ten. A pair of hirsute, sensibly-shoed women go out walking every day, apparently exploring grave yards and doing brass rubbings in sequestered country churches. They occupy opposite corners of the sofa by the log fire after dinner, engrossed in Sudoku and cryptic crosswords. The more moustachioed of the two presents the other with a box of liqueur chocolates on Christmas Eve and proceeds to eat them all before the nine lessons and carols are done. There are a few married couples who eat breakfast in silence and then disappear for the day, returning for a dinner consumed entirely without the inconvenience of conversation. There is a family, experimenting with a Christmas away from home, they tell everyone, but seeming to want to insist on having everything exactly as it would have been if they had stayed there, including placing their presents under the tree in the hotel lobby and watching *White Christmas* on the television. They are the only people who make anything of it other than the restrained exchange of 'Happy Christmas' which percolates, along with the coffee, amongst the breakfast tables on Christmas morning.

There is a father and son combo, the mirror image of Lucy and I. Freddie, the son, makes an immediate bee-line for Lucy and his father, who introduces himself as Mac, a well preserved, indeed rather handsome man perhaps five years older than me, is scarcely less eager to form our acquaintance. I had already spotted him, in fact, in the gym and the pool. They invite us, twice, to share their table in the dining room but we decline. We do, however, join them for Scrabble one afternoon and another evening we sit at the bar with them and have drinks. I discover that Mac is recently divorced, an amicable arrangement, he tells me, although a sad decision to have to come to, after twenty five years. He and Freddie's mother are still good friends but she has already taken up with somebody new, an old University friend she had rediscovered on Friends Reunited. Freddie, apparently, their only child, has been marvellous about the whole thing, very supportive to both parties.

'He's keen for me to move on,' Mac says, with a brave smile, 'and I think he's right. I'm ready to think about meeting somebody new.'

'There are plenty of women to choose from here,' I smile, indicating the bridge-widows and spinster-sisters.

'Good lord,' he murmurs, 'I'm not interested in *them*.'

Later, in our room, Lucy is ridiculous about what she describes as my 'conquest.' 'Mac's *rich*,' she gushes. 'Freddie says he's an MD.'

'A medical doctor?'

'A managing director. Of his own company - sounds as though it's a biggish concern. Freddie works for him. He's handsome. Don't you think so, Mum?'

'Who? Freddie?' I say, deliberately obtuse.

'No!' Lucy has undressed and left her clothes strewn everywhere. I make myself busy by picking them up and putting them on hangers. She sits in bed and hugs her knees, flushed with glee and Glayva. 'Don't you think it's amazing, though, when you think of it? That we should have picked this hotel, and that they should? Out of all the ones there are....'

'Just coincidence,' I shrug.

'Oh Mum!' she wails, 'what's the matter with you? It's just perfect. It's fate. I mean,' she counts off on her fingers, 'he's *interesting*, he's *good looking*, he's *wealthy*...'

'He's available...' I say, with more sarcasm than I intend, but, in her enthusiasm, it sails past her.

'Yes, and so are *you*....'

'I'm not,' I snap. It's a mistake and I could bite my tongue out.

She gives me a look which has shock and hurt melded together in it. 'Not available? Do you mean....'

In my heart, of course, I am spoken for, but this is not something I can explain to Lucy. I claw, with rising panic, onto the last conversation we had on this topic. 'I told you in October,' I stammer. 'I'm not interested in any man just because he shows an interest. I want.... connection... something,' I cast around the room with my eyes, as though the word I am looking for might be perched on the pelmet or lost amongst the litter of Lucy's make up bag on the dressing table, 'deeper,' I conclude, lamely.

'Oh.' Lucy just looks at me, 'I see. And you don't....with Mac.... you don't feel it?'

'No.'

107

'Oh,' Lucy says again, and slides down into the bed. 'Well, that's a shame.' She turns over towards the far wall. 'Although I must say,' she adds quietly, into her pillow, 'you haven't given him much of a chance.'

We don't discuss it again, and although we exchange smiles and waves across the dining room with Freddie and Mac, we don't join forces again. I suspect, however, that Freddie has Lucy's number and email address and because I know my daughter's tenacity, feel sure that I haven't heard the last of Mac. I feel bad because I know Lucy only wants me to be happy, but what can I do? There's only one man I'm interested in. He has burrowed his way into my heart over twenty odd years and I am as emotionally entwined with him as ivy on a tree. It's quite hopeless but as long as my feelings are kept strictly under control they hurt nobody but me.

Lucy and I address ourselves with renewed vigour to the strokings and smoothings, the plumpings and pummellings of the treatment room and at the end of four days, despite lavish dinners and unstinting recourse to the house Shiraz, we both look amazing. We go our separate ways the day after Boxing Day. Our relationship is intact and we feel girded for the ordeal ahead.

New Year's Eve, of course, is not an occasion for single people. The moment after Big Ben's first chime is the loneliest in the world for those without a partner to kiss and hug; your arms never feel so empty as they do just at that moment, when everyone else's are full of their special somebody. Your eyes, with no reciprocating gaze, can only see that you are standing alone and spare in a room full of human Pelmanism, and no matter how they might turn to you and enfold you as the second and third chimes fall, or how genuine their wishes for 'a Happy New Year', you are indelibly impressed with your hollow, howling singleness.

So I have no plans for New Year's Eve and as I get back home and let myself into the house, (experiencing, again, that eerie certainty that in the split second before I turn my key and push open the front door, some ghostly squatter has scurried into the shadows), I put a mental full-stop to

Christmas. The few cards which have arrived late I do not even put on display but consign instead to the paper recycling bin along with the others. I restock my fridge and cupboards, buying nothing which has any festive connotations, eschewing the reduced price turkeys and Christmas puddings and even things which have holly or Santa on the packaging. I work, reviewing my students' files and planning their schemes of work for the coming term, emailing them their reading lists and first assignments. I clean the house from top to bottom and I swim every day. I read and I avoid television. In this way New Year arrives without a passing nod from me and I remain immune from its cruelty.

Present Day: The Last Party

Julia and Gerald's anniversary celebration is to be held in a Masonic hall of a small town about ten miles from Julia and Gerald's new place and about an hour's drive from mine. I'm the furthest away so nobody has offered to pick me up and I have decided that it isn't really far enough away to justify a hotel room. It had occurred to me that somebody might invite me to stay the night and I did send a few exploratory emails enquiring about people's arrangements but the days have passed and I haven't received a response. It saddens me beyond words that our friendship has stretched so thin. I had so hoped the frequent poppings-in and –out, and in between the poppings the numerous telephone calls, would go on in spite of our leaving Combe Close; our connection, I had thought, was stronger than mere geography. But I am finding, more and more, that it is something that I have to keep on a one-woman life-support machine; it is always me that picks up the 'phone, me that suggests lunch or the theatre, me that calls in 'on the off-chance' for a spontaneous cup of tea. And increasingly they are out, or busy, their calendars filled up with new friends who are strangers to me, and my invitation has to be juggled with other commitments, compromised and curtailed to fit. Only I have been faithful, I think to myself, bitterly, on the afternoon of the party, over a solitary mug of tea and a Marie biscuit. But I rebuke myself at the thought. Deep in its vault my secret longing is more traitorous than any neglect of theirs. They have just 'moved on' while I have remained stuck, impaled on a hook of useless pining, a relic of a time which is past.

Although all my careful preparations for the party are complete and I ought to be enjoying an anticipatory savouring of the delights to come, I find myself curiously dissatisfied. I am suddenly filled with the need to demonstrate some kind of 'moving on', and as a gesture towards change I go out in search of a hairdresser. It is ridiculously late in the afternoon and I am lucky to find a salon which can accommodate me. It is dark when I come out and the high street looks desolate; the decorations strung overhead, unlit now that twelfth night is past, are tatty and wind-blown. But back at home I shower and put on my face and my new dress and when I survey the result in the mirror the nagging dissatisfaction of earlier is assuaged. My new style is short and layered and in spite of the grey I look younger, I think. Together with my rejuvenated skin and my slimmer figure, even in my own eyes, I look better than I have in years. The woman reflected back at me in my full-length mirror is smiling.

The Masonic Hall is located down a narrow side street and I have to park some distance away. Pushing open the doors there is a gust of humid, beery air and a wall of noise from the assembled guests. The room I can see from beyond the entrance vestibule is packed; I had not thought that Julia and Gerald had so many friends but then, I recall, since moving, they have thrown themselves into various social, cultural and voluntary groups in the upland market town. After hanging my coat in the cloakroom and checking my lipstick in the mottled square of mirror, I make my way towards my host and hostess, who have positioned themselves next to a tray of complimentary drinks. Julia is resplendent in a voluminous gown of emerald green velvet. She, too, has had her hair done; its wiriness welded into iron-grey whorls and steely curls, but the wobbly jowls and beetling brows are the Julia I know and love and she greets me with a fierce hug. Next to her, Gerald is puce and glistening in the heat, his dinner suit straining at its seams. As I hug him I can feel the fat of his back and shoulders like dense pillows packed into the material.

He wheezes 'Splendid! Splendid' and she hoots 'Molly, m'dear, we must talk later. Something of a favour to ask of you,' and the two exchange a conspiratorial glance. Then it is time for me to move on. It doesn't do to hog your hosts even when you're alone in a room of strangers. I take a glass from the tray and edge into the crowd with what I hope is a bright smile of happy expectancy plastered across my face to mask the sudden grip of panic in my heart.

I am oddly in tune with the general tone. The atmosphere is self-consciously jocular with a sense of people determined, against their better instincts, to have a good time. They stand in groups clutching glasses – empty, many of them, perhaps they are holding out for free top-ups although across the room I can see a bar lit up and ready for business - their voices raised to be heard over the din. The noise of conversation is like the roar of the sea in competition with the rush of the wind. No one is really listening to anyone else. Everyone is well turned out; dressed up, made up, buoyed up; their collective inflation makes it impossible for me to see round or over them. I search in vain for a familiar face. Eventually I find myself pushed against a panelled wall which is draughty and dusty and riddled with cobwebs.

It is an L shaped room with the bar and all the people pressed into the shorter wing. In the longer wing they are laying out a hot buffet on trestles against a far wall and in the centre round tables seating eight are gorgeously laid with cream linen and decorated with balloons. I am sorry to see that there is no seating plan, which is always an awkward situation for singles, who must impose themselves onto a group, making the numbers odd, or relegate themselves onto a table with the other miss-fits, and it is hard to say which is the more depressing prospect of the two.

There is a sudden surge towards the bar and all at once the bar steward is overwhelmed by men waving ten pound notes, but the shift means that now I can see more clearly across the room and simultaneously I spy the red hair of Gary and hear the tinkle of Carla's laughter. In essence it is the same trill I know so well but there is something slightly hectic, perhaps even a little hysterical about it, now. In another seismic shift I can see them all. The twins are identically dressed in sheer black silk, their hair artistically piled onto their heads. Carla is wearing a becoming green chiffon top over elegant evening trousers. Her hair, white-blond since the accident, is loose and cut into a fringe to hide the scar. To the casual observer there is no sign that she is anything other than entirely normal, but, even from this distance across the room, I can see the light of bewilderment in her eye and the way her hand rests, for reassurance, on Marcus' arm. His expression of attentive concern is more marked than usual as he stands, rock-like, at her side. Sheila, I am both amused and piqued to see, is wearing a dress identical in style to mine, even down to the little bolero jacket, and I wonder if she dissuaded me from buying mine with the fixed intention of making one for herself. I slip my bolero from my shoulders and drape it over my handbag in an effort to differentiate our outfits. Thankfully the material she has used has none of the pearly lustre of mine and is in a shade of burnt umber which does nothing for her skin tone or hair. I can hardly see Pam; she is obscured by Pete's bulk, as always. He is central to the group, holding forth, making them roar with laughter. I cannot see Alan at all for a moment until my eyes find him in the crush by the bar, assembling drinks with difficulty onto a tray which is too small to accommodate them all.

I stand still, against the cold wall, looking at them with an odd sense of detachment, as though they are strangers, and I am gripped by the idea that I should slip away, discreetly. Nobody will miss me. Julia and Gerald have been absorbed into an influx of late-arrivals, landing en-masse; weathered women in ghastly ruched frocks and ineptly rouged faces and their grizzle-bearded, rugged husbands.

But I cannot deny myself the opportunity of being near him. He is very handsome in his dress suit. He, too, has had his hair cut and a close shave. His jaw is smooth. I know he will smell delicious, of a particular brand – I can even name it - of soap.

At last the flurry of arrivals is over and the buffet is announced. There is a movement towards tables, a yoo-hooing and clannish beckoning of friends and relations. Chairs and heads are counted, people hover, jackets and handbags are placed proprietarily. The Combe Close set filch a spare chair and place setting from another table and squash nine around their table for eight. Alan brings the drinks and distributes them to cheers of approval from Pete. Marcus settles Carla before taking the seat to her

113

right. Sheila has taken a seat between Pete and Pam, leaving Alan to squeeze in between the twins at the place which doesn't really fit. I wait, hoping that one of them will scan the room for me, or even, somehow, make another place and ear-mark it as mine. But no.

At last, people are seated. I slip into a chair on a half empty table in a shadowy corner of the room, next to an elderly lady with two sticks who turns out to be Gerald's distant cousin, and opposite a spectacled man who introduces himself as the driver of the coach which has ferried a cohort of hill-farmers into town, Julia and Gerald's new neighbours — the ruched and rugged contingent. The other two occupants of the table are a husband and wife who have clearly had a row. No sooner are people settled than tables are called to the buffet. I offer to collect food for the elderly cousin. She gives me a long list of foods which do not agree with her.

I cannot help but pass their table on my way to the buffet. I greet them and press their cheeks against mine and wave away their concern that I am sitting on my own by explaining that I am looking after Gerald's cousin.

The other tables are hilarious with good humour, especially the hill-billy table, whose occupants clearly don't get out, much. They have a vast array of drinks and several wine bottles on their table. The man who has argued with his wife kindly offers to buy me a drink. I decline. His wife throws me a positively hostile look and when he returns to the table from the bar the atmosphere between them, already chill, notches down a degree or two. The cousin and I labour on with our conversation. The coach driver eats mechanically and says nothing at all.

There are speeches, and gifts are opened. Then, mercifully, the tables are cleared, lights are dimmed and the DJ begins to play the anniversary waltz. Julia and Gerald sail around the tiny dance floor with surprising grace. Half way through they are joined by a few other couples. I fear that we are in for an evening of foxtrots and quick-steps, but, his duty done, the DJ moves on to disco. There is a surge toward the dance floor. The coach driver goes outside for a smoke. The cousin shuffles painfully away to the toilet. The couple who have rowed leave and I am left entirely alone while everyone else gyrates to the music. I fix an expression onto my face which is meant to denote that I am thoroughly enjoying, vicariously, the dancing, the music and the genial atmosphere, and have every confidence of being joined soon by someone who has just slipped to the toilet or is in the queue for drinks.

Presently my end of the room is crowded again. There is jostling for the bar and a steady stream of people in and out of the toilets. My expression has become a rictus and I can't bear to remain any longer at the table by myself but something stops me from going across to join my friends even though there is room, now. Sheila, Anya and Katrina are dancing. Pete is at the bar. Pam and Carla have passed me on their way to the toilets. Gary, Marcus and Alan remain at the table in huddled conversation. I get up from the table thinking that one of them might catch sight of me, remember me, call me over, but they are all absorbed and I go back to my position by the wall, and feel as though I am invisible. What stops me from just going over? Is it stupid pride? I don't know, but the longer I leave it, the more difficult it becomes.

The rustics are being rowdy by the bar, downing pints as fast as the steward can pour them. Their wives are positively raucous, shrieking and braying at one another as though on opposite sides of a wide valley rather than in the same room. Pete has been sucked into their company; he slaps a wiry, gnarl-faced chap on the back and everyone bellows with laughter as the man chokes and splutters on his drink.

The girls are still dancing round their handbags. Sheila is looking a bit unsteady. Pam and Carla return from the toilets and stop off to speak to Julia and Gerald who are holding a sort of court from a small table in front of a massive fireplace. I am just about to go and join them – Julia *had* said, after all, that she wanted a word about something – when suddenly, there he is in front of me.

115

'What on earth are you doing over here all by yourself?' He is reproachful, and takes my hand to lead me across the room. I want to make some cutting rejoinder ('I've been asking myself what I'm doing here *at all.*') but I know it would be grossly unfair; I only have myself and some stupid notion of martyrdom to blame. Instead I mumble something about waiting for the elderly cousin. I pretend to scan the room, looking for her, and he must see the tears shining in my eyes.

'Oh Molly,' he says, stepping closer to me. His mouth is next to my ear. I can feel his breath lifting the feathery layers of my hair. 'Don't cry. You look so *lovely….*'

At that moment the DJ ups the tempo of the music, the coloured lights are all extinguished and a single strobe flickers across the dancers. They become fantastical, jerking, monochrome marionettes; mechanical and unreal. The whole room is bathed in the black and white of dreams, the people at the bar are in a silent movie, stiffly gesturing, the other guests are automated and oblivious. We stand, he and I, in some oddly separate state. I dare to turn and look up into his face. It is so close to mine that the slightest upwards tilt of my chin would invite a kiss. I was right, he does smell deliciously soapy. I open my lips just a fraction. I don't know if it is preparatory to speech, or to the kiss I feel so sure is coming. I don't know anything; I am completely lost. His brow contracts slightly and later on I will struggle to interpret the expression - a stern summoning of resistance, or a frown of disapproval - but just at that moment I can only register with a vague surprise that there is a little line there, between his brows, which I have not noticed before.

Then it is over. The strobe ceases and the disco lights resume. The manic beat of the music subsides. Everything is back to normal. He drops my hand, which he has continued to hold, and takes a step backwards. 'Come along,' he says.

When we get back to the table the girls are back from the dance floor. They are all breathless and hot.

'Lovely dress, Molly,' Anya says, reaching out to stroke the material, 'such a beautiful colour.' I wonder if she will be able to see that, beneath its pearly membrane, I am shaking.

Sheila gives me an ironic lift of her eyebrows, finishes her glass of wine and holds out her glass to Alan.

'Pete's getting them in,' he says, cocking his head towards the bar.

'He's taking too long,' Sheila snaps. She takes her empty glass and walks across to Pete, who puts his arm around her and pulls her into the jocular circle of agrarians.

'You haven't got a drink, Molly,' Marcus says, 'can I get you one?'

'Not unless there's any coffee,' I say. 'I'm driving, of course, and you know there's only so much orange juice a girl can take.'

It isn't really a serious suggestion but Marcus goes off purposefully towards the kitchen where the caterers are clearing up.

Gary takes Katrina back to the dance floor; she is quite inexhaustible when it comes to dancing. Carla and Pam join us and Carla greets me and kisses me as though she hasn't already seen me.

'How is Sophie?' I ask, choosing some safe ground. 'Did she manage to spend long with you at Christmas?'

'She *did* come,' Carla says, 'but she's gone now.'

'I think she stayed a few days, didn't she, Carla?' Pam puts in, helpfully.

'Oh yes, quite a few days, I think, but not..... not...'

'Not the whole week?' I suggest. 'Lucy and I only had four or five days. They're so busy, nowadays, aren't they, our girls?'

'How is Lucy?' Carla picks up the clue I have dropped for her, and nods and smiles while I witter for a while about Lucy's news, and manages to keep it up while I tell her about the Jury service and the flu. I am in the middle of my story when Carla says, 'I think I'd like to go home now.' Her hands have been toying restlessly with her bracelet. I put my hands over hers and still them gently. 'Marcus will be back in a minute. He went to get me some coffee.'

She brightens immediately. '*I'd* like some coffee,' she says, with animation. 'In fact I've been dying for a cup all evening. It's so cold in here, isn't it?'

I agree, although in fact the room is warm, now, from the lights and the bodily exertions.

Anya says, 'Here he comes now,' and we look across to where Marcus is negotiating the dancers with a tray of coffee cups.

'You star!' I gush, helping him unload the tray.

Presently I turn to Pam and ask her what she thought about the buffet we have just eaten and she begins an item-by item critique (clearly, she sampled all the dishes) but her attention is distracted by Pete and Sheila and the country crowd at the bar. Alan also seems to think that Pete and Sheila have been too long absent from the table, but instead of going over to remind them about the drinks, he asks Pam if she would like to dance. She is so surprised that she agrees and the two of them, an ill-matched couple if ever there was one, stand opposite to one another and jiggle self-consciously, and do not exchange a word.

The evening wears on. People come and go; to the bar, to the dance floor, to the toilet. Our table is an ever-shifting motley and I am forcefully impressed that the cohesion, the link, has simply disappeared. We are no more connected now than the chairs are to the table or the table to the floor. Even my own conversational gambits are no more than an attempt to fill up the empty space. We exchange small talk, and dance, and raise our glasses to our lips, and occasionally one of us will begin to explain something about our new lives and we might as well be speaking in a foreign language; it means nothing, nothing at all, because it is nothing to do with the rest of us anymore.

Periodically I dance; with the twins, with Gary, and just briefly with Carla. I hold her hands in mine and make exaggeratedly cheerful and reassuring motions as though dancing with a shy toddler, communicating a forceful sense of *fun*, but she is stiff and uncertain and we soon retreat. When we return to the table Marcus stands and holds out Carla's wrap. The gesture, considerate though it is, seems, unaccountably, to rile Carla. She snatches it off him and throws it onto the floor. 'I don't want *that,*' she snaps. 'I want a drink! I'm parched!'

Marcus reaches for her wine glass but that, too, turns out to be wrong. 'Not wine! Water! Why can't you get me some water?'

'Of course darling,' he says with a smile which does not reach his eyes. When he returns with it I notice that his hand is trembling. She takes only the slightest sip before pushing it away. 'I need the toilet now,' she says, nastily, as though it is his fault.

'So do I,' says Anya, before I can speak. 'Let's go together.'

When they are gone I throw Marcus a questioning look. 'This is new,' I say. 'There was nothing like this on holiday.'

He shrugs. 'It's happening more and more frequently,' he says, with a bravery which has broken edges, 'what the doctor calls 'volatile moods'.'

'I can't even...' I begin.

'No,' he cuts me off. 'Best not to.'

The DJ switches to one of those dreadful party numbers with ridiculous, set dance moves. Many people beat a hasty retreat from the floor but there is a simultaneous rush of people from the agricultural faction to join in. Corpulent country women drag their hoary men-folk onto the dance floor and amongst them Pete and Sheila, for some time firmly ensconced into their company, throw themselves into the prescribed actions of the song. It is quite clear that Sheila is tipsy; more than once she stumbles and Pete has to shoot out a supportive arm to stop her from colliding with other revellers. We all sit and grimace at their antics but poor Pam looks close to tears and Alan is busy polishing his glasses and so manages to see nothing of it. I throw Pam a sympathetic look.

'They're in another play together, did you know?' she mouths, miserably.

'No,' I shake my head and frown my disapproval, hypocrite that I am. 'I thought they'd given all that up.'

'Porgy and Bess,' she says.

'Good God,' I exclaim, 'at *their* age? I didn't know Sheila could even sing!'

Pam shakes her head. 'She isn't *in* it, in that way. She's dialogue coach, or something, I don't know,' she trails off. 'Has to attend all the rehearsals, I know that much,' she sniffs. It is the only conversation I have had so far which means anything, which has any underlying strata of understanding at all.

Julia and Gerald have been persuaded – I might even say coerced – onto the dance floor, and they put themselves through the unseemly motions of the dance routine to the clapping encouragement of their new friends. There is something quite grotesque about it and I can tell from the looks of mute haplessness that they occasionally throw to one another that Julia and Gerald feel exposed and ridiculed. The spectacle is so contrary to the quiet inner nobility of these two lovely people that I cannot continue to watch and hurry to the ladies.

Perhaps the DJ feels the same. When I get back the tempo has changed and people are slow-dancing in the gloom. I arrive in the middle of an altercation. Sheila, clearly, wants more wine. Alan has demurred. 'It's getting late,' he says, consulting his watch, 'we'll be leaving soon.'

'I'll be ill if I have any more,' Katrina observes, judiciously. 'I just hate hang-overs.'

'Alan!' Sheila barks, holding out her glass, 'if you *don't* mind.'

'Get the girl a drink,' Pete says, equably, leaning back in his chair. His tie has disappeared and the top few buttons of his dress shirt are undone. There are damp circles under his arms but his powerful geniality is irresistible. He winks and adds: 'Get me one, while you're at it.'

'Oh *Pete*,' Pam murmurs.

Gary says 'My round, I think,' and goes off to the bar. It is kind of him, I think, to bail Alan out like that.

'Want to dance, flower?' Pete holds out his hand to Pam but she shakes her head.

'I will,' Sheila is on her feet in a moment, and the two of them disappear amongst the couples. I am stupefied by their barefacedness. Marcus sits down next to Pam and begins to ask her about the boys. I notice that he positions his body so as to block her view of the dance floor. Katrina removes her shoes and rubs the balls of her feet but when Alan asks her if she is tired of dancing, she denies it and lets him lead her onto the floor.

Carla turns to me. 'How's.... erm..... how's...'

'Lucy?' I provide, and embark on a reprise of my Christmas. Carla interrupts me again but this time to ask, in a confidential tone; 'Do you mind just telling me: *whose* party is this?'

'Julia and Gerald,' I point them out, across the room, recovered from their ordeal and sipping from large brandy balloons. 'You remember? Our neighbours in Combe Close.' Poor thing, I think to myself, she has no idea who anybody is.

She nods slowly. 'That all seems a long time ago, doesn't it?'

'Sometimes,' I agree, 'but then sometimes, it seems like just yesterday.'

'But it isn't,' Carla is suddenly emphatic. She returns my earlier gesture, taking my hand and pressing it. 'It's a long time ago and we're all very different, now.' It sounds like something she has learned to repeat, parrot-fashion.

'Some of us are,' I say, sadly. Sitting so close to her, I cannot ignore that Carla is changed in both dramatic and in subtle ways. She has pushed her fringe back from her face and the scar is quite visible on her forehead. Her eyes, always so full of mischief and laughter, have an eerie vacancy, like the dusty windows of an abandoned house. Her dress, her gestures, and her voice are all the same, though, cruel reminders of the past, like empty exhibits in a museum.

Over by the bar there is jostling and angry words are exchanged. Soon two men are fighting, with big, blunt-knuckled hands, a shocking contrast to the lugubriously sentimental slow-number playing for the dancers. Chairs are pushed back and a woman becomes hysterical. The music stops abruptly and someone hurries to the back of the room to switch the lights up. In the sudden glare, Pete and Sheila leap apart. I think – I hope - that I am the only one to see their guilty, startled faces. Marcus has helped Pam to her feet and, taking Carla with his other arm, is guiding them away from the hubbub.

Anya grabs my hand and looks at me for reassurance. 'Where's Gary?' she whispers. Then we see him; he is soaked by the drinks which have been knocked from his hands, but unhurt. The twins both rush into his arms. 'I'm quite alright,' he says, but he looks distinctly wobbly.

The room is in chaos, tables awash with spilled wine. Chairs lie on their sides. The crofters – at the centre of the furore - are dishevelled and unsteady. One man is bleeding and belligerent, and another limping. Their women-folk are a mess, hair awry, make up smudged, shouting incoherently at one another, at their husbands, at no one at all. The coach driver marshals them from the room with surprising authority. Pam drags Pete towards the cloakroom. Alan already has Sheila's coat and is helping her into it. Marcus has Carla firmly under his wing as he guides her past the up-ended furniture; the sound of approaching sirens has uncorked a subliminal geyser and she is crying uncontrollably. Gary is perched on a chair with a twin on each knee as they dab ineffectually at his wine-stained shirt with their tiny handkerchiefs.

Clearly, the party is over.

I head for the cloakroom to collect my coat. Julia is pale with tiredness and shock as she says goodbye. Gerald's eyes are bloodshot and when he hugs me his melancholy 'There now, Molly, there now,' expresses all the regret and finality which weighs my own heart.

When I get home the small-hours shadows scuttle behind the curtains; not even they will stay to relieve my loneliness. I make tea and cry into it with a despair which seems fathomless. It isn't fair, it isn't fair. Not for him; condemned by loyalty to tolerate her perversity; not for me, consigned to this empty house, empty arms, an empty bed.

Combe Close: Apologies are in Order

I remember that Stan was 'poorly' for two days after Gary and Anya's party. I took care of him with a detached, brisk sympathy, but didn't challenge his claim that he had eaten something that didn't agree with him. I felt thoroughly ashamed of him and wrestled with the bleak reality that Stan had been right all along; we would never fit in to Combe Close and I had been a fool to think we could interact on an equal footing with the other residents. They were of altogether a different breed from us; habitual party-goers and hardened drinkers, socially competent, while we were gauche and green; unadapted for their proficient, easy revelry.

I went round to Julia and Gerald's house the morning that Stan went back to work, and apologised.

'My dear, my dear,' Julia said, after I had given her my little speech, laying her trowel down and shaking her head until her jowls quivered. But there was nothing she could in all honesty say to reassure me. Stan's behaviour had been outrageously rude. The issue of the shrub we left, for the time being, in abeyance although with hindsight it was a nettle we should have grasped there and then.

'He isn't used to drink,' I said. 'Not that that's any excuse at all.'

'I'm a tough old bird,' Julia said, reaching out to caress the ear of the nearest collie. 'I think Gerald was more upset than I was.'

'Poor Gerald. Stan put him in an impossible situation,' I lamented.

'Stan's put *you* in a worse one, if you don't mind my saying. Sending you round like this.'

I shook my head miserably. 'Stan doesn't know I'm here. I'm not sure how much he remembers of what happened. Even if he did...' I trailed off.

'I understand,' Julia said, stiffly. 'He's one of those men who won't admit when he's wrong.' She picked up her trowel and continued with what she had been doing. 'Insufferable!' I heard her growl, under her breath.

I turned to leave. 'I just wanted you to know,' I said, desolately, 'that *I* don't..... that *I'm* not...' What I wanted to say was that I dissociated myself utterly from Stan's behaviour and even from Stan himself. But I ask you: how can a woman say that about her husband without undermining, with fatal consequences, the bedrock of her marriage?

'Of course m'dear,' she said, but without turning round. 'That goes without saying.'

'We'll be social pariahs now,' I wanted to wail. 'You'll all have your parties without us from now on.' But I knew it would be wallowing in self-pity to indulge in this line. She, after all, was the victim here, not me.

Even so, I knew it to be true, and had to resist my instinct to crawl back home as under a stone in order to call on Anya and repeat my apology. Anya opened the door and invited me in with a smile much warmer and brighter than I had any right to expect. She led me into the conservatory where she and Katrina were leafing through magazines. I never saw either of them do any housework yet the house was always immaculate, without a speck of dust. It was also, perhaps more disconcertingly, empty of the kinds of personal knickknacks which transform a house into a home. There were no photographs, no ornaments which looked like the kind of heirloom which progresses down a family tree looking more and more incongruous with each generation. There were no clothes – shoes kicked off, cardigans laid aside; the stairs were free of that mounting parade of disparate things waiting to be taken up. Everything in the house had an artificial, what would later come to be called a 'designer' feel, coldly chosen with a scientific eye to colour and effect and an almost formulaic flair. There was elegance and art and form but there was no whimsy. And Anya and Katrina, perfectly groomed, glossy-haired, faultlessly manicured, looked like models picked, along with the marble fire surround and the deep-pile rug, to set off the parquet and posed, like the tentacle-like arms of the modern candelabra above our heads, to illuminate.

All traces of the party had gone. The makeshift bar, the fairy lights, the bought-in buffet. How I wished that our disgrace could as easily be cleared from view.

Anya took Lucy from my arms and invited me to sit down. I perched on the edge of one of the chairs while she rocked and swayed the baby around the room. It was hard to address myself to her because she was moving around and more interested in Lucy than she was in me, and while in many ways it was easy to think of Katrina as equally or perhaps even as more obviously the 'lady of the house' I reminded myself that this wasn't the case and that an apology to Katrina simply wouldn't do.

'Anya,' I said, getting up from my seat and going to stand next to her at the window, 'I wanted to say how sorry I was about Saturday evening. Your lovely party..... can you ever forgive me?'

Anya turned her chocolate-brown eyes towards me. I could see immediately that she had no idea what I meant. She looked from me to Katrina. Katrina's expression was equally empty of comprehension and yet I thought I detected, from the slightest twitch of one dimpled cheek, that she knew something; more, anyway, than Anya. But neither of them said anything. They continued to fix me with their incredulous gaze.

'There was.... a bit of a scene in the dining room,' I stammered. 'That's why we left without saying goodbye properly, or thank you. Stan...... broke a plate,' I finished, lamely.

Understanding dawned. My eyes had filled with tears again. Anya's did too, in sympathy. 'Oh Molly,' she gushed, slipping her arm around my waist and laying her head on my chest, 'it was only an accident. You silly billy. Poor Stan. Don't be cross with him.'

'*Are* you cross with him?' Katrina asked. There it was again, that tell-tale quiver in her cheek. It occurred to me, then, that she had been playing him, on Saturday, like a cat with a mouse. I saw her again, in my mind's eye, making a bee-line for Stan, pressing her voluptuousness against his bony, frigid frame, plying him with alcohol. She, after all, had been dispensing the drinks. Perhaps she had even been spiking Stan's. He had been sicker than a few beers and a large whiskey would suggest.... But then again, there might have been more that I didn't know about. In the excitement and interest of the talk I had lost sight of him for quite a long spell. And in any case, looking, now, as I was doing, at sweet Anya and her ever-supportive, ever-patient sister, I couldn't believe it.

'Not cross,' I said, a little untruthfully, 'but we behaved badly and I felt I wanted to apologise. It was,' I finished, '*such* a lovely party.'

I wanted to ask how it had ended and when. Had the others stayed much later? What, I wanted to know, had everyone talked about? I felt cheated of the portion of enjoyment I had lost through Stan's belligerence, and strangely jealous of the bonds which might have been forged without me. But I had lost Anya's attention. She was crooning a song to Lucy; the party and even my apology forgotten, an unreal shadow compared to the vivid vitality of 'little Bo Peep.'

'Will you have a cup of tea?' Katrina asked, unfolding her long legs from underneath her and getting up.

'Thank you,' I nodded, and cast about for some topic of conversation which would leave the party and our ignominious departure from it behind. 'I'd love to see your holiday photographs, if you have them here. I haven't even had chance to ask you if you had a good time.'

'Holiday?' Katrina frowned, caught oddly off-guard.

'Yes,' I laughed. 'You can't have forgotten it already! You had a week – well, I'm not sure where you went – a couple of weeks ago. It coincided with Gary's course. Poor Anya did miss you.'

'Ah!' Katrina nodded, suddenly. 'Oh yes. It does seem such a long time ago. I really must get those photographs developed some time.'

127

It had been during that week that Anya had first started to spend time with Julia and, to a lesser extent, with me. It wasn't just that Anya didn't seem to enjoy her own company or needed to have things to fill her time, it was more an air she exuded of curious incapacity. Whether this stemmed from the fact that Katrina or Gary always did everything for her I didn't know; it was one of those chicken-and-egg conundrums: did they act for her because she could not, or could she not act because they did it for her? But at the heart of it was a sense you instinctively got with Anya that she was in some delicate way unable. She subsisted, while they were absent, on a diet of daytime television and Weetabix, beginning a plethora of little tasks but losing heart before any of them were completed, and wandering over to us with a bewildered, hopeful air like a cat who has been shut out. She would set off, willingly enough, on any task you might give her, but you would always find her a few minutes later perplexed by a basket of laundry you had asked her to fold, or staring dreamily into the half distance with a watering can poised over a plant. That she was dependent on Gary and Katrina emotionally was obvious; the three of them had a bond which was quite uncanny and surprisingly, three never seemed a crowd with them. I thought Gary must be an exceptionally understanding and long-tempered man to accept Katrina so unquestioningly at the core of his marriage. But he must have gone into it with his eyes open. No one who ever saw Anya and Katrina together could ever have imagined that you could have one without the other.

There *were* more parties, of course, after that inaugural one at Gary and Anya's house, lots of them, and of course Stan and I were invited to them. Stan's fall was never discussed, at least not in my presence, but it had been noted, and in some barely perceptible but gentle way at those subsequent shindigs Stan was – how can I put it? – *managed*. I don't just mean that his alcohol consumption was managed (although it was) but that the neighbours cottoned on to the potential in Stan for awkwardness. He was not a social animal. He had no capacity for small-talk.

As I got to know Carla better I confided in her; you know how it is.

Sometimes you just have to tell somebody or you'll explode.

'You must let him find his own level,' she advised, pragmatically. 'He'll find *some* point of connection with *somebody*.'

'I wonder,' I lamented. 'I'll be amazed if anyone can be bothered to put in the work, when there are people who are so much easier to get along with.' I was thinking, of course, of loud, charismatic Pete, of sassy, sociable Katrina, of Carla herself.

'Some people like a challenge,' she chimed, 'I do myself. We had a Korean girl come to our school – her English wasn't good and the rest of the girls gave up on her. I didn't. She turned out to be lovely. We're still friends, as a matter of fact.'

'Stan makes things such hard work. I'm worried people will stop inviting us.'

'Don't be ridiculous. There wouldn't be anything to invite anyone to if it wasn't for you!'

I was marginally reassured by Carla's sanguine attitude. It's possible that she discreetly passed nuggets of information on to the others. I don't know: perhaps the entire Close had a clandestine meeting and mapped out a collective strategy for coping with my irascible and socially inept husband. However it came about, I noticed that Stan was always made much of at first and then asked, as a special favour, if he would *do* something which would give him a purpose in proceedings. Would he help with the barbeque, the film projector, the children's bouncy castle? Sometimes there would be some technical problem in the garage or workshop insoluble without Stan's assistance; would he mind taking a quick look? Having scuppered his own canoe in terms of discussing his work – those dark, inviolable secrets of the traffic management department – he had nothing to contribute while Pete and Alan discussed the niceties of financial management or when Marcus tried to explain the – admittedly very obscure – purpose of the engineering widget he

129

manufactured. But it didn't matter if Stan had something to *do*; *that* gave him the crutch he needed to support his ego if it started to flag. At the very least, I noticed that Stan was, in the nicest possible way, *passed around*. The women did it mainly although their husbands were complicit also and I was unspeakably grateful to all of them, my friends, who saw my need and shored me up. It was humbling and up-lifting, to be the beneficiary of such kindness.

There was another way, also, that the Close managed Stan without compromising its social intercourse. In between the big get-togethers there were smaller ones – dinner parties, outings to the theatre – and no-one took the least offense if they discovered that two couples had been out without the rest, in fact, often, we were called upon to baby-sit for one another. As we got to know one another better we discovered shared interests which we then developed. Julia and Gerald often visited the gardens of stately homes and Marcus and Carla started going with them. Julia began to take Anya with her to dog shows on weekends when Gary had to work and Katrina was busy. Sheila introduced Anya and Katrina to her gym. Alan and I began a programme of book swapping (very much in one direction at first, I am afraid). Gary and Pete were religious supporters of the local football team. Pam, Carla and I began a mid-week mother-and-baby lunch club.

In all these satellites of social interaction, Stan played no role whatsoever. But, him aside, what a busy, bustling group we became, constantly coming and going between each other's houses and in and out of one another's cars, off shopping or to the gym or to watch the football. And there was I at the centre of it, perched on my bench if the weather was fine and my housework done, happily running across to one house or another to help unload a car or to hand over a parcel I might have taken in for one of them. Even as winter came on I would be on the alert for their comings and goings, getting, in an oddly subliminal way, to know their routines so that I would invariably be at the window when one came home or another set out. Hardly a day went by without my exchanging at least a wave but often more with them all, and it made me feel wonderfully pivotal, a little hub of the Combe Close wheel, connected to them all by the radiating spokes of my care and concern. Stan called me an incurable busy-body. The neighbours began to refer to me, affectionately, as their social secretary, or, sometimes, their mother-hen. 'What would we do without you, Molly?' they would agree, when, towards the end of any gathering, I would whip out my diary and cry; 'now, everyone, bonfire night will be upon us before we know it – what about some fireworks for the children?' or 'it'll be Anya's birthday in a fortnight – we can't let *that* go by without celebration, can we?' or in some other way put in motion the wheels which would make inevitable our next get-together.

I was the first on the scene when Carla went into labour, taken across to her house by some deep, instinctive sense that all was not well, and finding her in the bathroom, doubled over by a contraction, her lower garments dampened by broken waters. Similarly, it was me that Pete called on a month later when Pam's planned home birth went wrong and she had to go to hospital. Of course I rushed over and took charge of the two boys, and I changed the sheets on their bed and gave the house a thorough going over as well before Pete's Mum and Dad arrived to take over. I liked it, being the person that they called on in a crisis. It gave me a sense that, out in the Close, I was somebody important, someone who could be relied upon, a stark contrast to the person I was behind the closed door of our house, where I felt, increasingly, that I was merely a functionary; nobody and nothing.

Combe Close: The By-pass

As far as I can recall we had lived in Combe Close almost two years when Stan came home one afternoon with news. It was 'strictly confidential' he said, placing his briefcase, as always, in the cubby hole under the stairs and disappearing into the cloakroom to wash his hands. I had news too. Lucy, that very day, had taken her first steps, pursuing a drunken diagonal across Anya's parquet. She was a late walker – and also a late talker, but you will not be surprised to hear that she made up for that in time! – and I had been getting anxious about her reluctance to take to her feet, but I knew better than to tell Stan; it was the kind of thing it was better for him to see, for him to discover, for himself. He must be allowed to be first. So I threw Lucy a look which I hoped would convey my excitement in our shared conspiracy as she waited in her play-pen for Daddy to notice her.

'Oh yes?' I said, neutrally, folding washing.

'I really oughtn't to tell you,' Stan said, as though I had begged him to. 'It's sensitive, politically.'

'I thought you civil servants were supposed to be above politics,' I observed.

'Oh well if you're not *interested*...'

Lucy, standing in her pen, her legs bowed like rubbery parentheses, jiggled its bars so that the abacus rattled, trying to get Stan's attention.

'I didn't say that. Of course I'm interested. On the other hand, I entirely respect your position. I'm sure you'll tell me when you can. I think Lucy would like you to lift her up, wouldn't you, darling?'

'Yes, alright, in a minute.' He was fetching his briefcase. 'It's a by-pass,' he burst out. 'And it's to be my project. Mine, Molly! What a coup! Bernard's livid, as you can imagine.' Bernard was Stan's senior in the department.

'Of course he is. But a project of this magnitude – he'll be retired, surely, before it's completed.' My attempt at ego-massage was off target, however.

'It isn't a question of *that*,' Stan spat out, 'he isn't up to it, that's the truth of it.'

'Is that what Mr Abel said?' Mr Abel was Stan's departmental head.

'As good as. Would you like to see the plans?' He was lifting them, anyway, from his case, and spreading them across the table. Lucy dropped onto her bottom with a sigh and picked up a toy.

The by-pass was to have far-reaching consequences for our little family. It meant more money, for a start, as Stan at that time wasn't sufficiently elevated on the traffic management ladder to be given such a large-scale project. 'It stands to reason,' he told me, 'when you think of the people I'll be dealing with; Civil Engineers, major contractors, not to mention Governmental deputations. I can't hand people like that a business card that says 'assistant' can I? They've got to promote me at least two pay-scales to Manager.'

'At least,' I said.

It would also mean, he told me, sombrely, especially at first, some considerable time away from home; perhaps even some foreign travel. 'There will be case studies to do, you see. I'll need to see some European equivalents. You can't just slap a new road down, you know. It has to be connected up arterially; that's really where my main involvement will be. I'll have to decide just which is the best way to do it.'

'Gosh yes,' I said, with what I hoped would be sufficient awe. 'It's like a triple heart by-pass, really, when you think of it.'

'That's right,' Stan nodded, pleased with my analogy. 'And before we even break the ground there'll be meetings I need to attend, and planning committees. Are you sure you're going to cope?'

'Cope?' I squeaked, turning exuberant somersaults inside, 'Well, I expect so.'

'You could always ask Mum....'

'I have the neighbours,' I said, very firmly. 'They won't watch me struggle.'

The prospect of being without Stan for extended periods filled me with a sense of what I can only describe as euphoria. It bubbled up quite unbidden from the bottom of my stomach and made me feel at the same time heady with excitement and sick with guilt; I looked forward to it and yet despaired with a bleak blast of cold and shocking realisation that I did so. When Stan was away, my sense of luxuriating in his absence was significantly tempered by the awareness that *this*, and not loneliness, not sadness, not even a brave resignation, was my predominant experience.

'You'll have to learn to drive,' Stan pronounced, as though imposing a sentence on me. It was something he had resisted for quite a while, deaf to my importuning. I don't know how I suppressed a whoop of pleasure.

'If you think so?' I croaked. 'I expect Gerald will take me on.'

Stan frowned. '*I'll* teach you, Molly.'

'Oh of course. But Gerald will know the test-routes and what the examiners are looking for. Besides, how much time will you have? You could ask him at any rate. He might not even have any vacancies.'

Stan frowned again, his eye drawn to the moot shrub on the front lawn. '*You* can ask him,' he said, darkly, 'one or two lessons might be useful when we get close to your test.'

So Stan got a promotion and a rise, and I learnt to drive, so that when he began to be away on what he delighted in describing with his usual pomposity as 'project meetings', he left me to periods of autonomy I had never in my life experienced before. Some of my new freedoms I entered into with mad and almost reckless abandon, setting off on adventures in my little second hand car; to the shops, the zoo, the seaside. I often got lost and once ran out of petrol, getting home after dark thrilled with the independence of knowing I would not have to account for myself to him, or to anyone. Others I enjoyed domestically; trying exotic foods in new recipes which Stan would never had tolerated, watching things on television he couldn't abide. One week I turned the lounge into an approximation of a Bedouin tent where Lucy and I played and picnicked and even slept for three whole days while it poured with rain and the car was at the garage having a gash repaired (which I never told Stan about). I experimented privately, at night (I hope you will not be too shocked to hear), gloriously alone across the whole width of the bed. With the sheets pushed back I experienced my first orgasm and cried out with genuine surprise at the inexpressible sweetness of it as I did so, and the next day I ached with the heavy aftermath of pleasure and smiled with the memory of its glory.

Another benefit of the by-pass was the freedom it gave me to spend time with Carla. We were firm friends by then although she had lost none of that glamour and allure for me that she had had since the beginning. I looked forward to being with her with an almost breathless excitement; you could never tell what might happen or where we might end up and she managed to transform even everyday activities into wondrous adventures. Shopping, for instance, was a white-knuckle roller-coaster. She would snatch garments off the rails and hustle me into the changing room, peeling my clothes off me with deft, business-like hands, oblivious to my shy remonstrations. I tended, in those days, to wear baggy things that were at least a size too big – I was hiding, I suppose – but there was no foxing Carla. 'You've got a *figure* under there!' she'd exclaim, eyeing my curves, then off she'd flounce, leaving me shivering and gasping in my bra and pants while she flicked through the rails for the best cut of trousers for my body-shape or the right coloured top for my complexion, and I would emerge, blinking, an hour later, with a bag full of clothes I hadn't known I needed.

135

It was on one of these impromptu outings that we went to visit a medium Carla had heard about, removing our wedding rings before we went in. I was told to expect several children – something I knew would not occur – and a new career path in later life, which did, in fact, as you know, come to pass. Carla's reading was less specific and in fact the medium seemed to feel so uncomfortable doing it that in the end she returned Carla's fee and explained that some auras were just too obscure.

We howled with laughter about it all, afterwards. If only we had known.

Yes. Being with Carla was like riding a magic merry-go-round; dizzying and disorienting and wonderful. What did I care if the beds weren't made or the ironing wasn't done, with no Stan to come home and complain about it? Carla didn't, and Marcus made no protest. He would just roll up his sleeves and tidy up, throw away the half-prepared food and cook something sensible, hang up the discarded clothes, put the records neatly away in their box. He loved her waywardness with an indulgent, patient devotion I found foreign and rather enviable but which, at the same time, made me feel a bit guilty. Hadn't I promised to be the 'steady friend' which Carla needed?

One evening she came round and we both got so gloriously drunk that I confided in her about my solitary bedroom frolicking and she told me that she and Marcus had a drawer full of what she described as 'toys' to keep things fresh in the bedroom.

'He's ever so keen on my having a good time,' she slurred, 'I must say that for him.'

'Lucky cow,' I replied, 'I don't think Stan knows how.'

'Show him!' she cried. 'For God's sake, draw a map if you must. *I* would. He'll like it, I promise you. Men do, you know.'

'Oh! I *couldn't*,' I said, shocked at the thought.

'*Tell* him then. Whisper to him, 'touch me here, darling.''

'No!' I cringed, 'we don't *talk*...'

'What?!' she squeaked, 'good God, that man needs taking in hand.'

'Oh, he likes *that.*'

I thought we would laugh so much we might make ourselves sick.

Later that same night, when inebriated hilarity had mellowed to uncorked truthfulness, she told me that she'd had a brief affair with Marcus' older brother. 'We needed him to invest in the company,' she said, 'he'd always liked me and it seemed like a small price to pay.'

I stared, aghast. Surely, through the fug of alcohol, I'd misheard?

'Marcus didn't....?'

'Oh God no. He hasn't a clue.'

I must have made some face; utter amazement, shrinking disgust.

'Don't look at me like that, Molly.' She frowned. 'What did it matter? I did it for Marcus. You do anything, don't you, for the people you love?'

'But how..... I mean, how could you bear it?'

She shrugged. 'It's like when you have to have an internal at the doctors – you sort of dissociate yourself. I didn't feel it was anything to do with me, really.'

'But what about afterwards? At family parties and so on? Didn't it feel dreadful?'

'Oh. We don't see them, now. It's a shame; we all got on so well. I really liked his wife. But I don't think he can live with it, so in the end, I suppose you're right, it ruined everything. But it *needn't* have. I'd do it again, if I had to.'

As she was leaving Carla wrapped her arms around me and held me close. 'I love you, Molly Burton,' she said incoherently.

'I love you too,' I replied, 'you're the best friend I've ever had.'

That's the exchange that stayed with me most prominently the next, hung-over day, and underneath it, a disquieting current; Carla's shockingly pragmatic, dismissive attitude to sex.

Those Stan-less periods were calm and golden, and were made even better when I could share them with Carla. But even if she was unavailable – which she sometimes was, caught up with caring for her parents or the bookwork for Marcus' company – one of the other neighbours was usually around. I would go off with Pam to the cash and carry to help her manhandle catering-size boxes of cereal and industrial quantities of laundry powder into the back of her estate car, or accompany Sheila to a discount fabric wholesaler in some seedy backstreet of a nearby mill town. I needed the respite. When Stan was at home he was more difficult than ever, intensely agitated by the by-pass scheme, puffed up both with the status and the stresses it entailed. He would pace around the lounge haranguing me about the 'idiotic bumblings' of one person and the 'lunatic incompetency' of another, or have me make notes for meetings he was due to attend. I was never sure if this was to impress me or himself with a suitable concept of his importance.

The battle over the disputed strip of front lawn was on-going but never directly addressed. Both Stan and Gerald mowed it assiduously, with the result, infuriating to both parties, that the grass there grew greener, taunting them both.

But of all the ramifications of that by-pass, there was one which turned out to be nothing short of momentous. It was during that period of the eighties when everyone was making money hand over fist; making money out of money – it seemed to self-replicate like cells in a petri-dish. If you had money you only had to turn your back on it for a day or so and it would have multiplied into more. House prices were escalating and although interest rates were high for mortgages they were correspondingly good for savings too. People were leaping up the property ladder making thousands as they went, and earning more as salaries boomed, and splurging money like water on foreign holidays and cars and meals out and mobile 'phones and computers so that it flowed out into shops and businesses and service industries, benefitting everyone. Of all sectors, the financial sector seemed to be doing best of all, and Pete found himself inundated with requests for advice on pensions and investments and stock brokering and tax efficiency everywhere he went. Seeing an opening he left the company he worked for, took a course which qualified him as an independent financial adviser and started his own business.

'I am a bit worried about it,' Pam told me, gloomily, one afternoon as she raked stickle bricks and Lego into a heap in one corner. We had Sophie with us that afternoon, while Carla took her Mum for a hospital appointment. She and Lucy were playing happily in the family room. I was doing Pam's ironing for her, keeping my eye on them through the doorway. 'It's such a big step and we'll lose the security of a regular salary.'

'That would worry me, too,' I sympathised, 'but surely Pete's such a good salesman, and he knows his stuff...'

'Yeeesssss but......' Pam was so prone to see the negative side of things.

'And he knows so many people – I mean, it's all about contacts, isn't it?' I hung one of Pete's voluminous shirts on a hanger and turned to a pile of boys' tracksuits.

'That's what worrying me,' Pam said, throwing a subconscious look across the Close to Sheila's house. 'I don't want him to become like.... like one of those people who prey on their friends for business.'

'I'm sure he wouldn't *prey* on them. But if people *ask* for his advice and want to support him...'

'But what if they do and then things go wrong? I mean, the way things are now, it can't go on forever, can it?'

'I'm sure that's a risk people will understand has nothing to do with Pete. *He* can't dictate the markets, can he?'

'Let's hope they remember that when their pensions aren't what they'd hoped,' Pam said, glumly, falling into a chair.

'I'll make you a cuppa,' I said, putting the last garment onto the board.

Pam's fears were realised in so far as almost everyone in the Close chose to ask Pete's help with their finances, but, so far as I know, no-one was the loser by it. He spent hours with Gerald and Julia, delving way back into their tax affairs and discovering a large tax rebate they had never claimed. He re-organised their pensions and Gerald's business accounts so that their straitened circumstances were substantially relieved and they were enabled, in time, to buy the country small-holding they had always dreamed of. With Pete's assistance Gary began a property development business alongside his estate agency work. It was fronted by Katrina for tax purposes and the two of them were soon travelling far and wide to view likely prospects. Anya rarely went with them. 'The houses are dirty,' she said, 'and cold and damp. I don't like being in them.' I am not sure exactly how Pete helped Marcus and Carla, but when Carla's parents died, which they did, conveniently, within six months of one another, I heard them discussing probate and inheritance tax. And us? Well as you can imagine Stan was intensely resistant to telling anyone anything about our personal finances, but he did take out some life insurance when I impressed upon him my perception of how *dangerous* his new role was, implying that he dangled from cranes and frequented deep and perilous excavations on a daily basis.

The only people in Combe Close who I know Pete did not advise were Sheila and Alan. It was unnecessary, for a start; Alan was in a similar line and didn't need any additional in-put. And, as things turned out, it would have compounded what was already a terrible trespass.

But when it came to it, nobody had a word to say against Pete. He was, by then, so deeply in their confidence and they had come to rely so heavily upon his sound advice and that air of confident, solid reliability which he exuded. And then, knowing him as they did, it seemed almost natural, almost to be expected, that a man of such large appetite, with such an epicurean zest, would taste and take and enjoy any tit-bit that fell within his grasp. I don't need to tell you that *I* wasn't of that persuasion. I was shocked and disappointed with a prim abhorrence which I did not like but could not rid myself of. I thought of it as a sordid, hole-in-corner affair, sneaking and dishonest. I saw Pam's world threaten to disintegrate before her very eyes. I saw the hurt in Alan's face, the way a muscle in his jaw went into spasm in an effort to keep himself in check. And selfishly I saw the lapse as a fissure which lurked under the surface of my own comfortable and cosy world. *This* sort of carry-on had played no part in the story-book world I had imagined for myself. For my own sake I shored it up, I put it all back together in a way that was convenient to me. I took the moral high ground then, so that now I am marooned upon it with no way down.

Present Day: Cake and Salad

Seeing everyone at Julia and Gerald's party, and especially seeing how disconnected we have all become, makes me renew my determination to try and re-forge our associations; this, ostensibly is my motivation. Privately it is for Pam's sake, and for Alan's, and perhaps also partly for my own, that I resolve to get to the bottom of whatever is happening between Sheila and Pete; it is an unpleasant task and one I would rather not face but if I don't, I reason to myself, nobody else will. And I have to know. I just have to *know*. What, and why, I dare not articulate. So, although my teaching term is now back in full swing and I am spending three nights a week tutoring into the small hours I make it my mission to set forth to visit my old friends.

My assignment takes me far and wide and I am dismally impressed again at the disparate directions the others have taken from our peaceful commune. Marcus and Carla's new house is in fact an old house, the former rectory, at the centre of a sought-after village south and east of the town. It is very pretty, crawling with Virginia creeper, accessed via a tiny gate and through a garden riotous with cottage-garden favourites. Everyone in the village is madly rural at weekends – wearing Barbour jackets and Hunter wellingtons, digging their veg patches and mucking out their hens – and during the week they cruise off in their exquisitely engineered motorcars to sit on leather chairs behind mahogany desks in high-rise city office complexes. Carla and Marcus have become deeply enmeshed in village life; Marcus sits on a number of committees and spear-heads their entry to the annual 'Village in Bloom' competition. Carla does stints as a volunteer in the community shop but she is never unsupervised and has no clue that it is part of her therapy as opposed to a genuinely useful contribution. Marcus works from home as often as possible, and at other times women from the village 'pop in' during the day, apparently to leave a recipe or a basket of home-grown goodies, to remind her about the Reading Group or to discuss a stall at the upcoming fete, but really to check that she is OK. Between these visits she seems to spend her days on the sofa, in a sort of limbo, waiting for the 'cooee' at the back door which will herald her latest caller.

That's how I find her, sitting in semi-gloom (it is a dismal day) and complete silence. Her hands are neatly folded in her lap, neither book nor sewing are near, the radio, the television, the stereo are all mute. She is not asleep; her eyes are open, patient, calm, neither expectant nor despondent, their expression not blank exactly but just neutral. She looks to me like a princess under a spell; all her natural verve and animation, the gusto and flamboyance I used to love so much, the chaos as she whirled like a dervish from one thing to another, simply suspended.

I break the spell, announcing my presence by a firm close of the door and a semi-rhetorical exclamation about the weather, and she blooms back into a semblance of the life she used to have; rising, turning, a smile already formed.

'It's Molly,' I sing out, through the gloom, to help her.

'Of course. Molly,' she says. But in her voice I hear no glimmer of recognition at all. 'Will you have tea?' she asks, and I know that her offer is simply a mechanical response.

'Let me make it,' I say. 'You know how I love to play with your Aga.'

'Do you? Go on then, if you like. Somebody brought cake. They're always bringing cake!' she laughs, but stands, in the centre of her vast farmhouse-style kitchen, eyeing the hand-made oak cupboards, and I know she has no idea where the cake might be.

'I think the clue might be on the tin,' I laugh, indicating a large blue enamel one emblazoned with the word 'cake'.

'Well, what do you know?' She looks as though she has never seen it before. 'I wonder what type it will be?'

She busies herself with serving the cake, using the knife, the plates, the napkins which I put nearby as prompts for the appropriate process, and as she does so she talks about some impending village event, mentioning people I don't know, the arrangements for the hall, somebody's ideas for races.

'And of course there'll be mounds and mounds of.... of erm......' she stalls in her diatribe, lost for the word, and it is only the slightest motion of her right wrist, turned up, clenched as though holding something, giving it a series of flicks, that helps me to cotton on.

'Pancakes?'

'Yes!' she laughs. 'Are *you* going to be making those?'

'I don't think so,' I demur, moving the kettle off the Aga plate.

'Oh.' She is nonplussed. 'Don't you though, usually?'

'I did once,' I agree, thinking years back.

'I thought so,' she says, but hesitantly, sensing but unable to put her finger on the missed connection she has made, somewhere.

'It all sounds lovely,' I say, 'but we don't need to worry about it now. It's a few weeks until Shrove Tuesday. Shall we take our tea through to the sitting room?'

But once we are settled on the squashy sofas – not the ones they had at Combe Close, but animals of a similar ilk – and sipping our tea, I have no idea how to broach the subject at hand. If she doesn't know me, if I am only as delible as words written on the sand and as easily eradicated, how can I expect her to recall the party and what happened there? Less than a week ago, and yet probably consigned to some closet of dreams. And recalling her distress as she left, I am anxious not to rake up unpleasantness. While I consider all this she sits opposite to me, as lovely as ever, beautifully dressed and as perfectly accessorised as she always was – I wonder if Marcus does it, every morning – with a half-smile of polite attention playing around her lips, waiting for me to – engage, I realise, is the term. That is her life: strangers, infinitely kind, visit to bring the kinds of gifts suited to the invalid and to engage her for half an hour with topics calculated not to disturb.

Suddenly her passivity makes me angry. She was always the leader, always the catalyst in our relationship – in all her relationships, I think, a little bitterly, and if she has lost something, well, haven't I lost more? And yet Carla is the focus of all our care, Carla is the one we all feel sorry for.

'Don't you remember me at all?' I blurt out. 'Don't you remember anything about us, about Combe Close? There's so much I want to talk to you about, Carla, things that I need to tell you, to ask you, about Sheila and Pete...' I trail off, hearing a mosquito note of self-pity in my voice.

Carla frowns slightly and puts her tea cup down on the table. 'That was a long time ago,' she says, mechanically, 'and we're all very different now.'

Later, Marcus arrives, coming in through the back door with an air of being girded to deal with whatever situation he will discover. I can only imagine the kinds of things he has had to cope with; charred baking, a tap left running, Carla locked in the bathroom or in the throes of one of the vindictive moods I now know assail her from time to time. He gives a smile of relief when he sees me but still approaches Carla with a kind of wariness.

'Hello darling,' he says, taking her hand and then, when this provokes no adverse reaction, kissing her gingerly on the cheek. 'How has your afternoon been? How lovely of Molly to call.'

'Did she? I didn't know. This lady has come about the thing at the hall,' Carla says. 'She doesn't want to make the pancakes this year. What will we do?'

Marcus takes it all in his stride, which is convenient since I am completely wrong-footed. 'We won't worry about it, sweetheart. Now then, Molly, you'll stay for supper?'

I decline, pleading another – entirely spurious – engagement, and fetch my coat. As I leave the lounge Carla relapses into that torpid, disengaged mode I had found her in. She will remember nothing of my visit.

Marcus walks me to my car and his jolly, confident demeanour evaporates as soon as we are out of the house. His shoulders droop and his eye turns dull and weary. Filled with compassion I take his arm and when he turns on me the kind of look a drowning man might give the rescuer whose rope is out of reach I slip the other arm round his neck to perpetrate the illusion that I can save him.

Briefly, he allows his head to rest on my shoulder. 'Molly, Molly,' he says, brokenly.

'Shhhhh,' I reply, and stroke the hair on the back of his head. There are no words I can say to him, recalling what Sheila has told me about Carla's prognosis. The damage to the brain sustained from the accident can only mean a gradual but inevitable decline in her mental function. The dementia, already quite pronounced although mercifully at present also quite benign in its passive, harmless manifestation, will metamorphose into more aggressive or at least more unruly expression. Day by day, a little less of her will remain until she will be, at worst an unmanageable harridan, at best, an empty casing. It will spread and affect bodily function also. She will atrophy, insidiously, the brain failing to send the right messages to the organs, until the casing itself with fail, piece by heart-breaking piece. The lingering inevitability of it is unspeakably cruel and my heart goes out to Marcus, who will end up with – perhaps already has - a wife who bears no resemblance to the woman he loved, a burden of duty, a tragic tie, the weight of whose care and loss will cripple him, probably, for the rest of his life, unless (and this is the only hawser of hope I can throw) he can come to think of himself as in some way exonerated from it.

He is like poor Rochester, I think, as I drive away, leaving him to stand alone on the driveway, but much kinder and morally averse to allowing himself an alternative outlet. I think of his careful hands washing and dressing Carla's unresisting body each morning, the meticulous selection of the right coloured earrings to go with the scarf. I see him, in my mind's eye, brushing her hair so that the puckered line of scar is hidden beneath its flax. The wasted tenderness of it makes me want to weep.

I hardly get any more satisfactory response at Anya and Gary's house the following day. It is positively palatial, in a gated community on the edge of a championship golf course well west of the town, but in a style I rather witheringly describe to myself as 'McMansion'. I get an impression of enormous echoing rooms sumptuously furnished with granite, marble, ebony, leather, silk, as Anya leads me to a smaller, much more comfortable space beyond the kitchen where she clearly spends most of her time. Katrina is rarely around during the day, off supervising the property empire that she and Gary run between them. She has her own apartments somewhere within the house which makes their joint venture easier to manage.

Now that Austin – Katrina's boy – is away at University, poor Anya – to whom the lion's share of his care and upbringing somehow fell - is left very much to her own devices. She is *very* pleased to see me and offers me lunch, which she decants from cellophane-sealed Waitrose containers. She has hardly aged at all, I think, watching her arrange vari-coloured lettuce leaves around the plate. A very few silver strands in her hair, the slightest possible lacework of lines around her eyes. Essentially she is still the child-like princess I always thought her, empty of passion and untouched by regret, just resolutely good and hopeful and sweet. And while some might find her unwavering naivety sickly and incredible, I am touched by it and hesitate to sully it by introducing the topic which has brought me here.

But I do bring it up, as we nurse our coffee and curl companionably on the sofa. 'And so,' I say, with a look which I hope will encourage a tone of eager but harmless gossip, 'what did you think of the party?'

'I thought *you* looked lovely,' she says, reaching out to stroke my newly cropped hair. Trust her, I thought, to light on something positive, 'and we

147

all had a lovely time.'

'Except at the end,' I demurred. 'Poor Gary got soaked and Carla was upset.'

'Oh yes,' Anya nodded, looking away; her eyes, her mind, sliding away from the unpleasantness.

'And I think,' I forge on, 'that perhaps Pam was a little bit upset too....'

'Oh? Poor Pam, I didn't know.' It speaks volumes for Anya's instinctive and enveloping empathy that her eyes fill with tears at the thought.

'Mmmm,' I persist. 'Perhaps Pete did spend a little too much time with Sheila.'

'But that's the way they *are*,' Anya says, as though referring to two adorable but wayward children, 'those two. They just love having fun!'

'But you don't think, I mean, you don't suspect...' I let the word hang in the air. Anya just looks at me with her doe eyes wide and empty of all, empty even of the possibility of, suspicion. It is a look I have seen before.

Combe Close: The Pool Party

During all those Combe Close years I never did know – I still do not – just how much of their unconventional arrangement Anya understood. I was entirely innocent about it for at least three years. As far as I knew Katrina was just an incredibly supportive and attentive sister to Anya, whose unworldliness and special vacuity meant that she needed delicate and loving supervision. We in the Close, without ever discussing it, fell into the role whenever Katrina or Gary weren't around, instinctively understanding that although a fully grown woman in every physical sense, Anya retained a certain ingenuous vulnerability. Nowadays I suppose we would be encouraged to pin labels on Anya; perhaps she is mildly autistic or has what are called 'special educational needs' or 'learning difficulties.' I hate those terms, don't you? The supposedly deficient qualities about Anya which would tend towards such crass categorisation are precisely the things about her which I find the most endearing; her profound, unquestioning trustfulness, her ability to see and presume upon people's goodness, her calm, patient acceptance of whatever befalls.

It was summertime. Lucy had just turned three. Stan was in the throes of the public consultation which became necessary for the by-pass and was often away or working very late. He was working late, I think, on this occasion; anyway, he didn't join us until much later - I don't recall exactly why but that, I am afraid to say, only illustrates my focus then. After Lucy it was my friends and neighbours who formed my world. My gaze was fixed firmly outward, into the Close, watching over their comings and goings with an eagle eye.

It had been a wonderful, warm summer day, the kind we so rarely get, and we had all gravitated to Pete and Pam's garden where their new aluminium-framed pool was proving an irresistible draw to the children. Pam was pregnant with what turned out to be Quentin, their fourth and final child. Lucy was wearing an adorable pink bathing costume with a

149

sparkly fish on the front. Sophie and Andrew (Pam's third) were naked. I didn't quite approve of that, I remember. But they all had a riotous time, in and out of the water, the sandpit, up and down the slide, while we reclined on loungers and got up only periodically to administer sun cream or cool drinks or to replace discarded sunhats. After a while Sheila and Pam went off to get their older children from school leaving Carla and Anya and Katrina and I in charge. Then Sophie got a thorn in her foot and Carla had to carry her, howling, across the road to Julia.

Katrina stretched on her lounger. 'Later on,' she said, 'when the children are in bed, I'm going to get into that pool.'

'You can get into it now!' I laughed

'I don't think I'd better – you see, I'm going to do it with no clothes on.'

'Andrew has no clothes on,' Anya commented, mildly.

'That's true. But I'm waiting until there's a more appreciative audience.'

To say that I was shocked is an understatement. I was dressed in a skirt and top even though the temperature must have been in the eighties. I'd have needed some persuasion to wear my bathing suit in front of the women and nothing on earth would have convinced me to do it when the men were around. But then again, I thought, eyeing Katrina's svelte, tanned body, I didn't have what she had to show off. But the suggestion placed a gnawing sense of anxiety in the pit of my stomach, testament to my inherited prudery about what was appropriate. It threatened to sour what promised to be a really lovely evening.

We had, that evening, once the men were home, one of those impromptu get-togethers which coalesced from the merest observation that it was a shame to break things up for supper. Pete fired up his barbeque and we all scurried home to bring things from our fridges for him to cook. Julia arrived with an enormous bowl of home-grown salad. Pam produced bread rolls. Carla sent Marcus out to get ice cream. Katrina disappeared next door for a while and came back with tall, tinkling glasses of Pimms and Alan brought a few bottles of his infamous home-brew.

By half past seven all the children were fast asleep. Lucy and Sophie were on Pam's bed, but Sheila had taken her girls home. Julia and Gerald left too; one of their dogs was due to whelp. An hour later, the dishes cleared and the toys tidied away, those of us who remained were languidly relaxing on the patio in the plethora of disreputable deck-chairs which Pete had brought out of the garage. Gary was teaching himself to play the guitar and strummed inconsequential chords. The click of Pam's knitting needles was like crickets in the grass. Somewhere along The Crescent someone was mowing their lawn. The heat of the day had relaxed its grip and the sun, sinking at last behind the trees of The Crescent, cast golden, shimmering rays over everything, over all of us, in our contented, companionable circle. I felt drowsed and torpid; the Pimms and the homebrew had dispersed my disquiet of earlier on. With Lucy safely asleep and no Stan to worry about I was conscious of a sense of enormous blessing, as I looked around me with sunset-dazzled eyes. I was as close to the apex of my quest for that nice, good life I was ever to get. 'Feels like being in heaven,' I murmured to myself. Turning my head, I found Alan beside me. He smiled. The sun on his glasses had made them go dark, so I couldn't see his eyes. I squinted, trying to read them and he must have felt my need, somehow, for a more immediate connection.

He took my hand and squeezed it. 'Yes, he said, 'it does.'

Carla and a few of the others began to play a hilarious game of boules with the children's set. It got quite combative in a rumbustious, good humoured way. Presently the light was so poor that it became impossible to tell the colours of the balls. Carla became almost helpless with a fit of giggles and sank onto the cool grass to give way to them. Her laughter was so infectious that the rest of us joined in without really knowing what she was laughing about. Soon we were just rolling around, holding our sides, tears pouring from our eyes. Next door, at *Hazelwood,* windows were slammed shut all over the house. It just made us worse. Then, as the

151

cool blue twilight finally chased the sun away, Pete swooped down on Carla, scooped her off the grass and dropped her into the pool. She screamed of course, and began to fling ineffectual handfuls of water back at him, while her dress, made transparent, clung to every contour of her body. Finally Pete just stepped into the pool, fully clothed as he was, and sank down into the water. It was only thigh-deep, but as he lowered his bulk the surface rose up and began to lap, gently, over the sides.

Gary and Marcus opened more beer and threw themselves, spent, onto chairs. I made a gesture towards Carla with a towel but she waved me away. Anya went indoors to get herself a soft drink.

Katrina said, 'By the way, I'm going to have a baby.'

There was a moment of stunned silence, before I, speaking, as I believed, for us all, said, 'Oh Katrina, that's wonderful news. I didn't even know you had a boyfriend.'

Then everyone started to laugh again.

Everyone except me. I looked from one to the other, bewildered. Carla, still in the pool, was too far away to help me but she threw me a sympathetic if indulgent smile. Marcus, taking pity on me, threw a significant look across at Gary, suddenly intent on the strings of his guitar. I found the gist of what he was trying to tell me profoundly shocking but I knew it to be true. The dynamics of the effortlessly balanced tripartite relationship in Gary's house suddenly made perfect, though scandalous, sense. To spare me, I like to think, the others began to chat amongst themselves, but I had never felt so alien, so completely out of step with the rest of them before and it was a sensation both embarrassing and rather frightening. I felt marooned, almost abandoned, very nearly betrayed. For the first time I felt like I wanted to be somewhere else. I thought I might cry.

Anya re-emerged from the house. 'What were you all laughing at?' she asked.

'Molly said something funny,' Katrina said and gave me what I interpreted, in my newly vulnerable state, as a rather withering, patronising smile.

Later Alan found me in the kitchen washing glasses. 'Are you alright?' he said, quietly.

'Doesn't Anya *mind?*' I blurted out. I couldn't get over it. It was so unconventional, so disturbing, so wrong. The revelation had swept me away in a tsunami of disapproval which came straight from my mother's straitlaced conservatism.

'Well,' he said, mildly, picking up a tea towel, 'we'd have to be clear about what Anya *knows,* wouldn't we, before we knew if she minded.'

'You think she might not even *know?'* I was appalled.

'She knows about the baby, of course, in the same way that Colin (Pam's oldest) knows about them; they turn up from time to time. But further than that she doesn't enquire.'

'But....' I paused to wipe my forehead with a sudsy hand. 'You mean that she doesn't know that..' I lowered my voice to a hoarse whisper, '...that Gary and Katrina....?'

Alan placed another glass down on the counter. 'She knows that she loves Gary and Katrina. She can't imagine life without either one of them. Just as importantly she knows that they love her; absolutely and unconditionally. I think that's all any of us needs to know, isn't it?' If I had been less caught up in the blow of the evening's disclosure I might have heard the note of sadness in his voice.

When I went back outside the mood of the evening had changed. All the house lights were off to discourage insects. Only the feeble glimmer of a few candles illuminated the night, which was black and moonless, still very warm. Gary and Anya were snuggled onto one lounger. This disturbed me as I still felt that he had betrayed her and yet no one could

153

be a more loving, indulgent, attentive husband than Gary. I felt, too, for reasons I could only dimly explain, that he had in some way betrayed *me* – his oldest friend here in the Close; that our long association – that *I* - was tainted by his nefarious goings-on.

Pete and Carla were still in the pool and they had been joined by Marcus. I had a wild, sickening idea that they were *all,* in some sordid but non-specific way – my experience, even my imagination, falling far short of such things – *at it.* They were whispering and giggling and the water was slightly turbulent, suggesting furtive fumblings.

Then, aloud, Carla panted, 'Oh please, please hurry.'

'I can't quite get it in,' Pete cried, to raucous laughter from the other two.

'Try harder,' Carla urged, gasping.

'Shall I help?' Marcus wheezed.

'I've never needed any help before,' Pete guffawed, 'have I Pammie, love?'

Pam tutted and turned to me. 'They've knocked the plug out,' she said, quietly.

There was a slight noise behind us, coming from the house, and the click of a light switch. I half turned, expecting to see one of the children, woken up by the noise, but it was Stan, still dressed in his suit and clutching his brief case. He was standing stiffly just inside the patio doors, a stark and proper contrast to the rest of us as we lay about, crumpled and awry, more than slightly inebriated, blinking in the sudden glare. I felt, all at once, faintly compromised. At that moment Katrina rose from her seat. I expected her to offer Stan a drink or some food, one of those fulsome *including* gestures which I had noticed them use to make Stan feel special. But what she did took my breath away: in one swift, seamless motion, she pulled her shift dress over her head. Underneath, instead of the wispy bikini I had expected, she was wearing nothing; absolutely nothing at all. She laid her dress down on her seat without any sign of haste and walked slowly across to the pool, twisting her luxuriant hair up into a knot as she went. There was no sign of the pregnancy other than a delicate map of bluish veins visible just under the skin of her breasts, their aureoles large and dark and puckered. They, and her rounded, voluptuous bottom were as brown as the rest of her. Her groin – clearly on view as she lifted her leg over the side of the pool – was hairless. But it was not so much her body – unarguably beautiful and powerfully erotic – which provoked her audience, but her manner; her poised, languid movements, the roguish glint in her eye as she swept us all with her glance. She *intended* to stun, to enrapture us.

Carla stood up to make room for Katrina as she sank down into the water alongside Pete and Marcus.

'I have been promising myself this,' Katrina said, 'all day.'

On the patio, Stan stood rigid, his face, darkened anyway by his habitual shadow of stubble, was absolutely engorged with blood, almost purple with some inner, raging potency. His lips were dry and feverish and his eyes, steely points of light, burned with an acquisitive, famished flame. Beads of moisture broke out across his brow. At last, with an effort that was almost physical, he dragged his eyes from the pool and met mine. 'Going home,' he croaked, and was gone.

That night Stan made love to me with a frenzy that was almost violent, leaving me aching and sore. But as he pounded and writhed above me I felt a curious detachment; I knew with a deep and hollow certainty that it was not me that he was fucking, at all.

Later, as I lay sleepless beside him, I considered the revelations of the evening and it occurred to me - following Stan's earlier passion - that Gary and Katrina might consider their physical liaison in the light of a kindness to Anya, sparing her – child that she was – the carnal reality of adult intercourse. I could imagine Gary loving Anya; cuddling, stroking, kissing and petting. I could imagine him pleasuring her. But I could not imagine him doing to her what Stan had just done to me. Katrina, on the other hand......

It was very soon after this that Anya came to me for help with baking a cake. While we waited for it to cook I brought the subject round to Katrina's baby.

Anya hugged herself with glee about it. 'It's *so* exciting,' she thrilled, 'isn't it?'

'Oh yes,' I gushed, 'only I can't help feeling a bit sorry that,' I hesitated, on risky, uncertain ground.

'What?' She held the wooden spoon poised in front of her mouth.

'Well,' I said, 'babies need Daddies as well as Mummies.'

'Oh!' she laughed, 'you mustn't worry about that. Gary says that *he'll* be the Daddy, so that will be alright, won't it?'

That's when she gave me the look; utterly frank and unencumbered by the shadow of suspicion. Either she did not know that Gary was the father of her sister's child, or she had no notion of the irregularity of such a situation. Either way everything in her world was well and if she didn't mind, I thought to myself, why should I?

Present Day: Doing the Laundry

Julia and Gerald's place is rather far out for an unannounced visit so I ring them in the evening when I can be sure to catch them in. I express, dutifully – my mother's stringent codes on these things being well embedded – my thanks for the invitation and for 'a lovely evening.'

'Charmed! Nothing to it!' barks Gerald, who has answered the 'phone, and quickly puts Julia on the line. I repeat my thanks.

'Oh well, yes,' Julia snorts, 'although something of an unexpected denouement.'

'Perhaps things got *a little* out of hand, right at the end,' I say.

'*Some* individuals forgot themselves, certainly,' Julia trumpets indignantly, 'and I have told them so.'

'Have you?' I tread carefully. I can think of quite a few at the party who stepped out of line. 'And what did they have to say for themselves?'

Julia sniffs. 'Not much, I'm sorry to say. Other than to suggest that one might mind one's own business. Which is hurtful, frankly. I only had her interest at heart.'

'Of course you did,' I soothe, my mind working furiously. Who did she speak to? Pam? Sheila? Or am I way off target? Perhaps it was one of the yokel women.

'The trouble with that boy is, he can't say no,' she says with a sigh of fond forbearance, 'and, as Gerald says, with that kind of provocation, who can blame him?' Then I know exactly where she is. She's always been dotty about Pete, with an indulgence almost motherly in its nature, because of what he managed to do for them financially but also just because of his large, genial character, his great appetite, his open, giving nature, so uncannily like her own. An image of poor pudgy Pam comes vividly to

157

my mind's eye. *She*, I think, might blame him. I wait, hoping Julia will say more but she embarks on a long story about a hen coop before, with much throat-clearing, getting round to the favour she wants to ask.

I have left the two most difficult visits to the last and even as I set out I question what on earth I am doing embroiling myself in other people's affairs. Last time things were different; the marriages newer and fresher and worth saving, the children younger and more vulnerable to disruption. I was still deeply imbued with my mother's vinegary version of morality. Even then, increasingly aware of the flaws within my own marriage, deeply conscious of dissatisfactions and incompatibilities, the idea of separating had never occurred to me in my wildest imagining. In my family, you just *didn't*, and since, by then, I considered the neighbours as extended family, I went in like an avenging angel wielding a sword of righteousness. But I know now that what I was really fighting for was myself, my own comfortable Combe Close world. It was *my* applecart I didn't want Pete and Sheila to upset.

The marriages are twenty-odd years older, now. And the children are all grown, well able, you would expect, to take into their stride any surprising aberration the old folks might embark upon. I am different; older of course, wiser perhaps, and very much aware of my own frailties which would stand up to no scrutiny at all. And the world I wanted to protect all those years ago has disintegrated – I must, at last, acknowledge it. The visits I have made so far have shown me not only the geographical separation but also the unnavigable landscape of different life-styles which lies between us all. Carla and Marcus in their chocolate-box idyll of village shows and homely hoe-downs, their door always on the latch, while Anya languishes in their remote rococo mansion, imprisoned behind electric gates. Julia and Gerald – I can only imagine it – perched on some wild and barren hillside, weathered and hoary, rescuing lambs from snow-drifts and perpetually smelling of sour milk and slurry, Alan and Sheila in their immaculate show-home, Pam and Pete, as I will find them today, in their rambling Victorian semi. The Combe Close set is gone; dead, and beyond reviving, leaving me the sole survivor.

And yet I do set out, for conflicting reasons which I am not able to resolve. On the one hand I am still, even after all these years, absolutely ham-strung by an in-bred instinct to do what my mother would call 'the right thing', to be unimpeachable in the mess which, I fear – or feel – is more or less inevitable, now. I will lift no finger which will release my secret peccadillo although since Saturday it has been raging and roaring within its cage. In fact, I will make this last attempt to condemn it to life imprisonment. But it is a bitter inner battle. The temptation to do nothing – to let things take their unavoidable course – is almost overwhelming.

More insidious is the inducement to give things a helping hand – what ninety nine women out of a hundred would do, I suspect, in similar circumstances. Why can't I be like them? Why can't I just take what I want?

Pam and Pete moved from Combe Close to an enormous but dilapidated semi which is in fact not too far from where I live now. It has three storeys and a huge but over-grown garden. I think the initial idea was that they would renovate it and, as the boys began to leave home, convert it gradually into flats which they would rent out; it was a project. Needless to say, the scheme never got off the ground and the house is still full of creaking floorboards and doors which don't close properly and ancient radiators which alternately seep and scald. It isn't in a 'good' area and I am sorry to say that the older two boys became embroiled with some unsavoury characters and squandered their early potential. Colin, the oldest, lives on Pam's top floor now with his girlfriend and their child. He calls himself a musician but I do not think he has done a day's paid work in his life. His brother, Stuart, did a spell in rehab but did manage to pull things together to a certain extent and is now holding down a manual job but also still living at home. Andrew, the third boy, however, is doing brilliantly, articled to an accountant in Sheffield. Quentin, who turned out to be so difficult, is a quiet, rather secretive young man. He is a night

159

porter in a large but seedy hotel; the slightly disreputable nocturnal, goings-on there suit his guardedness. He has accommodation at the hotel but arrives home regularly for food and to collect clean laundry. So even all these years later, Pam is still cooking and cleaning and permanently besieged by mounds of ironing.

That's exactly how I find her, in the cavernous, draughty kitchen of the house. Fresh baking is cooling on wire trays on the vast scrubbed kitchen table and a baby of about eighteen months is playing on the tiled floor with a collection of battered cars.

'I knew you'd come,' Pam says when I appear in the doorway, and I cannot read her expression: relief? Pleasure? Resignation? She is vastly overweight, poor thing, her chin has disappeared into the doughy cob of her face and it looks to me as though her eyes will be the next to go; they peep out at me from what are now only folds of flesh on her face. The result is that she is unreadable; her face a flattish, semi-catatonic mask. But she has the same swift, warm affection and instinct to nurture as ever and I am instantly embedded in a wheezing, bosomy hug before she busies herself with the kettle. The child gives me a cursory look and then goes back to his game.

'Are his Mum and Dad out?' I ask, thinking, optimistically, about job interviews and social housing applications.

'Oh, no,' she makes a stiff, neckless motion with her head to indicate that they are upstairs, 'but he likes being down here with me. They seem to find it hard to settle him, somehow.'

'Good as gold, now,' I observe, slipping off my coat.

'He always is, for me. If only all the men in my life were as good, eh?'

She has got right to the crux of the matter and although I have come to discuss exactly this issue, her precipitate reference to it throws me off balance; I still, I realise, am not certain which road I will take. Rather cravenly, I reach for her one cause for pride. 'Andrew's doing well,' I say, buying time, making a statement; giving her a solid, reliable handhold in a world of flux.

'Oh yes,' she says, placing our tea mugs on the table and shifting laundry so that we can sit down, 'working very hard. He and Pete were talking about a partnership, at Christmas, once he's qualified.'

Pete's name brings him squarely back into the frame of our discussion. Pam bends her lips into a wan, faltering smile and says again, 'I knew you'd come, Molly, after Saturday.'

I give a helpless little shrug. 'I felt for you. But I don't know what to say, or do.' These, perhaps, are the most honest words I will speak to her today.

'No, but you can listen and you, at least, really *understand*. Most of the time it isn't too bad, is it? I mean I'm busy with the boys and the house and everything, and I've always been able to just – I don't know – block it out. But then when it's right in front of you…. when you come across the evidence…it sort of hits you all over again, doesn't it?'

'Evidence?'

'If you needed any more than they gave you on Saturday! But, oh, *you* know. Restaurant bills. Hotel receipts. When *his* conference coincides with *her* soft-furnishing course…'

Clearly things between Pete and Sheila have progressed much further than I had anticipated. I had thought that Saturday's shenanigans were just the start – the re-ignition – of their old flirtation. 'So this,' I venture, 'this isn't a *new* thing?'

She sighs. 'Let's say that this is a new chapter in a very long book. And what's more, it might interest Sheila to know that she is by no means the only female character!'

I eat one of the buns from the wire tray while I assimilate this information, folding the paper case up neatly. Suddenly I recall Pam's

161

oddly reserved attitude towards Carla and me when we first met – years ago, in Combe Close. Now, at last, I understand it; she had been trying to decide if either of us might become 'the other woman.' While I absorb this new understanding the child has taken one bite of his cake and abandoned the rest on the floor. Pam has eaten three and is reaching for another. It is no wonder she is the size that she is. She is loving herself, I think to myself, and who can blame her? Nobody else is doing it. But then I wonder, callously, what Pete's excuse might be.

'Years ago,' Pam says, 'you persuaded me that this was just a mistake, a moment's madness: "a brief deviation from the norm," were your exact words, I think.' She gives a harsh, bitter laugh and shakes her head, 'I don't think you were right, Molly, were you?' But then she sighs and relents. 'I'm not blaming you – you know that, don't you? You, after all, know how it feels.'

I don't much like her inclusive language. It probes a deep sore. 'I'm not sure I know what you mean,' I say, evading her eye.

'Oh please! I don't know why I should be the only one whose dirty laundry gets an airing. Aren't you sick of being mollycoddled?'

Her unintended pun lets me laugh off her remark, but it disquiets me. Nobody has *ever* trespassed on that forbidden ground. I wonder if she resents me for my involvement all those years ago. With hindsight, I clearly didn't manage to mend anything. Would it really have been easier on them all, I ask myself, if it had all fallen apart back then? Would we be looking back on it now and agreeing that it had all been for the best? I reach for another cake even though I don't really want one.

'It *hurts*,' she says at last, and all at once her moonish face sort of deflates, and two fat tears ooze from her tiny, lashless eyes. I reach across and squeeze her hand. The baby plays on, oblivious.

'The question is,' I say, quietly, 'what are you going to *do*?'

'*Do?*' She looks at me through eyes which are red even though she has been crying for only a moment. 'Do? What *can* I do?'

'Well,' I lean back slightly, giving myself a kind of mental run-up to what I am about to say, girding myself. Even then, as I open my mouth, the words 'I was wrong, Pam, it would have been better to give him his marching orders. I think that's what you should do now,' are doing battle in my throat with the alternative, 'remind him of his obligations, ask him to go to marriage guidance counselling with you.' Before I can say anything at all Pam repeats: 'What *can* I do? Look at me, Molly. Look around you. What do you see?' She indicates the kitchen, the laundry, the child and, beyond those things, the house and the lingering, malingering children. I see them all as keys, ready to lock away my dreams; the ties, the dependents, which must be protected. 'Do you think,' she goes on, 'that I haven't reasoned with him? Again and again? It doesn't do any good! These things are beyond reason. I've learnt *that* much. Haven't you?'

When I don't reply, she throws up her hands. 'Well,' she cries, 'I give up.'

It is, at one and the same time, exactly what I *do* and what I do *not*, want to hear. For a moment my selfishness gets the upper hand. The sense of responsibility shifting from my shoulders is almost physical. From that new, unencumbered point of view I can almost see my way; a clear, blameless path along which I can travel untainted. In my head I have a sudden vivid picture of myself changing horses, like a circus performer in a spangled costume and a tall feathered headdress, leaping lightly from one broad, cantering back to another. (This is so much more appealing than the other images of treachery I could use.) 'So ...You're going to...' I try, speculatively, '...throw him out?' I say it very quietly, almost in a whisper, not knowing how much the child might understand, not wanting to hear myself make the suggestion, the rattle of silver coins in my pocket, 'No one would blame you.'

But Pam just gives me a bewildered look. 'Why would I do that?' she asks. 'That isn't what I want at all. I mean,' she indicates again the

163

kitchen, the child, the house and all its contents, 'everything I want is right here.' I realise then that my journey here today has been quite unnecessary. The shining path of possibility I had glimpsed only a moment before has faded as quickly as it appeared. I have come to preach to the converted but I am conscious of a residual flame of anger on her behalf. What about her? Doesn't *she* matter? 'You could still have all that,' I say in a voice which I don't recognise as mine, 'or nearly all of it, anyway.'

But she seems to have no instinct for self-preservation; it seems not to have occurred to her that Pete might leave *her*. My expression must betray my frustration at her myopic grasp of the situation.

'I want *him*, Molly,' she says distinctly.

'I can see that's what you want, Pam.' I reach across the table again to take her hand in mine. 'But I'm worried, I mean, I'm wondering what Pete…..' And genuinely it is her I'm thinking of, now. She has, unarguably, been treated dreadfully.

'Oh!' she says, taking – almost snatching – her hand from mine, jumping up, grabbing the kettle and taking it to the sink, 'Oh I see. But you mustn't worry about *that*, Molly. Pete will never leave *me.'*

I wonder that she can be so sure, but there is something about her on this ground which makes me believe her; a glimpse of flinty certitude in her tiny congested eye.

'Oh yes,' she goes on, picking the child up and settling him in her arms, (and I feel like she has put up a shield between us), 'the business, for one thing, is all tied up in my name as well as his; our tax affairs are inextricably linked. And, after all, none of the others love him like I do.' She gives me a gimlet look - a speaking, frank look. She isn't talking about devotion, or, at least, not just about that. She is talking about physical love of which their four children and, indirectly, this one in her arms, are the manifestation. I have never thought about dumpy, plain Pam as a sexual entity but the actuality of it is in the kitchen with us, now. It has sprung, like a genie, from the lamp of Pam's confining.

Then she hugs the child to her and addresses her final word to him. I can see that the child symbolises for her the cement which has bound and will continue to bind her and Pete together; their children, their home, the security of their livelihood, and now also their gargantuan, tectonic plate-shifting sex-life, and it is by no means imposed upon her; it is only and absolutely her choice. 'He has too much to lose, doesn't he, my poppet?' For all Sheila's allure I am suddenly sure that she cannot offer Pete anything better than he already has, just more of it. She is adding to a plate already heaped high with all the good things he enjoys and because he is greedy he cannot say no.

Which, I recall as I drive away, is just what Julia said.

I stop at a café on the way home. I want to be able to think without any distractions. The café is deserted – it is almost five, already dark – practically closing time. Because the proprietor looks annoyed at me for coming in so late in the day I order, alongside the tea, an omelette, thinking to myself that it will save me cooking when I get in, but by the irritated way he sets about beating the eggs I gather that I have compounded, rather than mitigated my offense. But my sense of failure would be hard to augment. I have wasted my afternoon, I think. The day had already been saved, and not by me; I can't cast myself in that role a second time; there is no pride in it, no martyrish whiff to perfume my days of singleness that *I*, at least, did the right thing.

I hope that by now you will realise what that means to me – I have scruples; I must be innocent as far as my actions and words go. For my thoughts, and for the visceral urges of my poor hapless heart I can take no responsibility. For a tantalising moment, *they* had glimpsed another outcome, but it is not to be. Perhaps you will call me a hypocrite. At the very least you will accuse me of gross dishonesty. Well, I will not contradict you. It is the compromise I have had to live with. But it has not been easy.

165

Combe Close: Three is Company

After the revelations at the pool party it took me a while to adjust to the situation across the road at Gary and Anya's – or, as I supposed I must think of it now, Gary and Anya and Katrina's, since, after this time, any alternative domicile of Katrina's, real or pretended, ceased to play any role. She was there all the time, bare-facedly coming and going for all the world to see.

'Did *you* know?' I asked Stan one day soon afterwards. It was a Saturday but Stan was working, as he did all hours these days, on schematics for the by-pass.

'Know what?'

'About Gary and Katrina.'

He didn't look up from his plans but cleared his throat with a sort of strangled cough and fidgeted in his seat. 'Of course,' he said.

I let a moment or two pass, hoping he would say more, but he remained stubbornly glued to his work. Eventually, I spoke again. 'And what do you think about it?'

He reached up and scratched his head with a distracted, irritated frenzy. 'She's just that kind of woman,' he said at last.

'Which of them? What kind of woman?'

'Katrina. *That* kind. Oh for God's sake, Molly, what would *you* know about it?'

The whole situation preyed on my mind. It wasn't just the unorthodox nature of the arrangement that I struggled with, but the route by which they had arrived at it. Had Gary, I wondered, been unable to make up his mind between the two girls and simply determined that he would have them both? Or had he married Anya and discovered afterwards Katrina's proclivity for passion – that she was, as Stan put it, *that* kind of woman?

More disturbing, perhaps, than the irregular ménage at number 3, was the vision of myself that had been thrown into sharp relief at its discovery. It occurred to me – but I could hardly credit it – that it was *my* knowing, at last, the truth of their unconventional relations which had brought them, as it were, out of the closet. Could it really be that it was *me* they had been hiding it from so that, now I was finally apprised, concealment had become unnecessary? I worried over the possibility, like a dog with a bone. What kind of person did they think I was, then? Did I really come over as such a prude? Or just as hopelessly naive? Stan's jibe – what would *I* know about it – rankled. I compared myself systematically with the other women of the Close. Sheila had been to University, had spent time travelling and had twice been married; Pam was the oldest of a large and relatively impoverished family and had become acquainted with the harsher realities of life at an early age; Julia – pretentions to minor nobility notwithstanding - had been a farmer's daughter, with all the arduous hours and brutal realities that implies; Carla's all-girl education had made her alarmingly at home with the basics of the body's functionality; clearly Katrina had learnt early on to handle the possibilities – and also perhaps the problems – of her more-than-average quota of sensuality. That left Anya - for whom, as I have explained, normal criteria did not quite apply – and me. Put like that they did all seem – Anya aside – to be worldlier than me. My pursed, suspicious upbringing, a narrow field of travel, my youthful lack of friends, added to an inherent desire for life to be sunny and smooth-edged had made me constitutionally unable, perhaps, to see the seamier side of things.

Coming to this conclusion, I became anxious that my friends should not mistake my ignorance for disapproval. I *did* disapprove, of course – I found the whole thing fundamentally distasteful and shocking – but I didn't want to distance myself from the others so I became positively zealous in my attention to Katrina and Anya and the burgeoning baby. I knitted baby clothes and donated baby paraphernalia, I cooked nourishing meals. I offered – tactfully (clearly such a thing was going to be beyond Anya and I wasn't sure how overt Gary's involvement would be) to be Katrina's birth-partner. I condoned, I supported, I affirmed their unusual affiliation with every word and gesture.

Once I had embarked upon my scheme it was no trouble to me, truth be told. I found considerable solace in directing my care and attention towards my neighbours during those months, and afterwards. Things between Stan and myself were difficult – I am conscious, even though they are now far behind me, of girding myself up to describe them to you - and any outlet I could get which took me out of his orbit was to be welcomed. He was on a constant short-fuse, like a volcano threatening to erupt. He couldn't sit still, couldn't sleep and found fault with everything, especially me. I was expected to put up with his fulminating attitude during the day and at night submit to attentions I can only describe as positively priapic; he was subject to some terrible and driving imperative which no amount of sex seemed able to assuage. The night after the pool party was only the beginning. Things weighed on him like a leaden pall, squeezing the enjoyment and brightness out of every aspect of his life. His great coup over Bernard, the vote of confidence from Mr Abel now seemed like only a poisoned chalice. Nothing pleased or satisfied him. Lucy began to shrink from his heavy-handed contribution to bath- and bed-time and his brusque, critical contributions to her whimsical, experimental conversation. He had taken to prowling round the Close at night.

It was my attentiveness across the road which caused me to be on the spot when Katrina went into labour one Saturday the following March. Gary was working on one of the houses which he and Katrina had bought for development. Anya was away, at Crufts with Julia and Gerald. By this time ground had been broken for the by-pass and traffic throughout the borough was catastrophically disrupted by road closures and tortuous diversions; Stan and his department letting the huge-scale project of the by-pass go absolutely to their heads. It would have taken Gary an hour at least to cross town and half as long again to get Katrina to the hospital so I left a protesting Lucy with an equally reluctant Stan, alerted Carla and Pam and drove Katrina to maternity myself. Gary arrived about forty five minutes later, his hair full of plaster-dust and his face full of genuinely spousal concern.

Suffice it to say that Katrina had a terrible time of it. I remained at the hospital throughout, sometimes in the labour room, administering cool flannels and rubbing her back, sometimes in the waiting room drinking the evil brew dispensed by the machine, or feeding a fortune into the pay-phone to keep the neighbours updated. All that day she laboured through stage one, alternatively moaning and shrieking, sometimes livid, at other times limply inert. It wasn't until late into the evening that she was declared fully dilated and there followed a period of truly colossal effort although by that time I had discreetly withdrawn from the scene of travail to the corridor outside. Finally she was rushed down to theatre for an emergency caesarean; the baby – Austin – was just too big for her tiny, doll-like frame. It was later – well into the small hours – when Gary joined me in the waiting area. He was dazed with fatigue – the high of pride and relief and achievement would come later – but for now he was simply drained.

'Nothing Mrs Brewster (our old biology teacher) taught us prepared me for *that*,' he said, pulling off the little mob-cap he had had to wear in theatre.

'Ah. No. Chicks hatching from eggs doesn't quite compare, does it!'

'Katrina was just brilliant,' he said, 'so brave. What a woman!'

'But you always knew that,' I observed, wryly.

'Oh yes,' he agreed. We exchanged a significant glance.

'I can't help wondering, sometimes…' I began.

'Why I didn't marry *her*?'

'Don't get me wrong,' I interjected, hastily, 'Anya's *lovely*..'

169

'Yes she is – and truly I do love her…'

'Of course you do.'

'But Katrina,' he shook his head slowly, 'surely you understand that no man will ever really *have* Katrina.' He held his hands out in front of him. I hadn't noticed before how fine they were, his hands, long-fingered, immaculately manicured. 'I might have held her for a while,' he mused, 'but sooner or later she would have slipped away.'

I was beginning to understand. 'Whereas,' I put in, 'between Anya and Katrina..'

'Oh yes, that's unbreakable.'

We didn't speak of it any more, or, indeed, ever again. It was left to my own nascent conception of these things to gather that Gary, in taking Anya, had secured Katrina as far as anyone ever could. It would have been a despicable bargain if there had been any sense in which Anya was disadvantaged by it; had she been no more than a lure, sacrificed to net the prize. But anyone who ever witnessed their little family – which Austin augmented and completed to perfection – could ever have levelled that accusation. Anya was always in the centre; cared for and considered, guided, protected, petted and indulged. It was all about her, and if Gary from time to time took a sabbatical from the pure linen and wholesome duck-down of Anya's virgin bower to tangle in the black silk of Katrina's boudoir, which man will blame him?

But I'm sure you'll appreciate how difficult it made things for me, when the time came, to deal with the situation between Sheila and Pete. If I was complicit in turning a blind eye in one direction, why couldn't I be equally unseeing in another? The difference, of course, was the question of casualties.

Present Day: Coffins

Alan and Sheila, as I have mentioned, moved from Combe Close to a large and in my opinion rather soulless out-of-town development. An ironic consequence of Stan's by-pass, it occupies a relatively isolated hillside site geographically far from the commercial hub and yet only twenty-five minutes or so drive on the broad and uninterrupted sweep of the new road. Described as a 'village' with a square green, a modern community hall and a general store, the houses are built of identical pale stone and are uniform in design. They loop round in bewildering concentric circles and I struggle to find the right one. Finally I spot Sheila's car and also – something I had not anticipated – Alan's, on the double driveway of their home.

When she answers the door to my ring her face betrays the fact that I am intensely unwelcome and there is a swift moment when I almost think that she won't even ask me in. She barely opens the door, but stands with it like a shield between us. 'Molly!' she exclaims, and I can hear the unvoiced but unmistakable adjunct 'Just when I thought this day couldn't get any worse!' But she manages to suppress it in favour of a heavily loaded 'Just passing?'

'No,' I proffer a bunch of early daffodils, my disguised olive branch, 'I took a chance of your being in and came on purpose.'

'Who is it?' I hear Alan ask, wearily, from somewhere inside.

'It's me!' I call past Sheila, before she can reply, before she can hiss at me that it isn't a good time and to go away, and crane my neck to look beyond her into the gloom of their hallway. He appears behind her and gives me such a look that it will take me hours to decode it. That I have caught them in the throes of something unpleasant goes without saying; he looks like a man in – well, I can only describe it as turmoil. Always pale, the skin of his face is whiter than ever, his lips almost blanched, but it is his eyes which arrest me the most. They are red-rimmed and bloodshot, behind his glasses. Whether from tears or from lack of sleep or even from anger with difficulty controlled, I am unable to say. He gives me a look which is perplexing beyond anything, a stream of communication that I can't decipher at all; as jumbled as tongues; semaphore glimpsed through fog. But there is some imperative behind it; I am almost sure that he is trying to tell me something. When he slips my coat from my shoulders his hands linger in the task, briefly squeezing my arms, as though they too would reinforce whatever message his eyes would speak. For my part I give a smile which I hope will impart reassurance and understanding but it misses the mark; he heaves a heavy sigh, frowns, blinks those roseate eyes and gives the slightest possible shake of his head. I follow Sheila into the kitchen and am surprised that he doesn't come in behind me, but instead mounts the stairs with a weary, defeated tread.

Sheila slaps the daffodils down on her immaculate draining board and reaches for the kettle. 'I suppose you've come about Saturday,' she says, 'but before you even start I need to tell you that I've already had an *extremely* hard time about it.'

'A hard time?'

'Yes. From *everyone*, just about.' She is fiddling with cups, arranging biscuits on a plate, avoiding looking at me in the face.

'Everyone?'

'Julia, for one.'

'Julia?'

She spins round to face me at last. 'Molly! Are you going to repeat *everything* I say by turning it into a question?'

A question? I want to ask, but resist. 'For God's sake why don't you just come out with your *sermon?*' she spits. 'I'm sure you have one prepared. Is it a new one? Or the one I got twenty years ago?' Her tone is quite venomous, loaded with accusation which erupts in her next salvo. 'Didn't you do enough damage back then?' Damage? I am confused. I thought I had saved them. 'Have you any idea?' she goes on, 'what it is like to live every day seeing someone, *loving* someone, that you can't have? To see him coming and going, playing with his children, kissing his *wife*, for Christ's sake; so close, Molly,' she holds her finger and thumb up, a millimetre apart, 'but a million miles away?' Of course I have. I *have*, I want to cry out. 'You have *no* idea,' Sheila rasps, 'but you come here to pontificate about what's *right* and set yourself up in judgement above us all.......'

'I haven't! I haven't' I burst out.

'You have. It's what you do. You interfere, you meddle, Molly. Do you know that's what we call you, Meddlesome Molly.....'

Perhaps this is what Alan had been trying to warn me about. My mouth flaps uselessly for a while. Meddlesome? Mollycoddled? What unpleasant images of myself I am being bombarded with. I can feel the prickle of tears. Can it – can any of it - be true?

I manage to croak out 'I've.... I've only come,' before I recall, miserably, that I don't know why I have come.

'Well?' Sheila challenges me, across the polished granite of her crumb-free kitchen surface. The kettle has boiled now but she makes no move to pour water onto the tea bags in the cups.

'To listen,' I finish, lamely.

That deflates her angst. She slumps against the fridge. 'Well,' she says, 'you're the only one who's offered *that.*'

A very tentative step across the highly polished floor tiles is enough to break her. She crumples like a sack, sliding down the fridge until she is kneeling on the floor, her abject misery pooling around her on its glossy surface. Her shoulders and head droop until her forehead touches her knees, as though her skeleton has simply melted away. She is not so much crushed as completely eviscerated by agony.

'I love him,' she sobs, the words racking her like an expulsion of bile. 'Oh Molly! Oh! Oh! I love him, I love him, I love him....'

I am so acquainted with her hopelessness that I forgive – although I do not forget - her earlier jibe. Knowing what I know from Pam, that Pete will never be free, my sympathy and its much more painful sister – empathy – is overwhelming. I crouch next to her and wrap my arms around her as she rocks and moans, and her words, scarcely articulate, resonate through our two bodies as if our diaphragm and vocal cords are shared. 'How can it be wrong?' she moans. 'How can it? Why must my heart be broken when I love him so much and I've waited so long?'

'I don't know,' is all I can say. And it's true. I don't.

Later, when I have poured the tea, she pours out to me the latest history of attempts to fight against the avid attraction; the accidental meetings, the deliberate meetings, the guilt, the lies, the ecstasy. Her practice is my theory. Hers is the story which I have not allowed to be written, the shadow-narrative of my desert-days and insignificant trig-points. When she has finished we sit in silence. I will not, now, for anything, offer advice, even if I had any. We are as miserable as each other, I, who did the 'right' thing and she, who did the 'wrong', equally punished. There is no comfort for me in my abstention, none at all, and no satisfaction for Sheila in her participation, nor any prospect of it, I fear. Presently Sheila falls into a troubled doze against the appliquéd cushions of her sofa. Since Sunday morning she and Alan have been in almost constant discussion, I gather, night and day. No wonder they both look so awful.

While Sheila sleeps I creep upstairs and knock gently on the door of Alan's study. He opens it cautiously and his eyes are still transmitting the urgent messages which I can't read. I step into the room and he closes the door softly behind me. The room is warm, lined with books and shadows now that the short January day is drawing to its close. Only a reading lamp casts a splash of light over an old easy chair in the corner by the window, but I can't see any reading material, any spread sheets or lists of figures – such, I imagine, is the stuff of Alan's business – and his computer monitor is black. He has just been sitting up here, I realise, quietly, alone, thinking. Very unusually he is not wearing his glasses and the effect is at once to unveil – I almost want to say unmask – and to unshield him; there is a new candidness and correspondingly an endearing vulnerability about him which makes me feel very privileged and also a little afraid.

Secrets are like coffins: there is a world of difference between a closed one and an open one. A closed coffin is awkward to skirt around at first, perhaps, but disguised with an embroidered cloth and a vase of flowers it becomes as innocuous as an old sideboard. It ceases to attract notice and is soon familiar and unremarked. But an open coffin calls attention to itself. It is impossible to ignore, irresistibly, horribly drawing every eye in the room. Its grisly contents provoke extreme emotional reactions which are unpleasant and traumatic. It is only a matter of time before something has to be *done*. It must be dealt with; it cannot under any circumstances be closed up again and re-covered with its cloth. That's how it is with a secret which has got out into the open and that, I realise, is what Alan is doing up here, alone in his study. He is mounting vigil, he is mourning the dead, he is staring the bloated corpse in its ghastly face before the time comes to take action. What form that action will take I cannot tell although I still have the powerful and perplexing impression that he would tell me if only I could read the sub-text of his expression. Will he proceed to the calm resignation of burial? Or will he attempt to effect a resuscitation?

I could help him, of course. I *should* help him, I know. Only I have the elixir which can revive the corpse. I ought to say it, out loud, here in the gloom. I would be a revelation, a life-line, a miracle.

'You're quite safe,' I should say. 'Pete won't leave Pam. Pete will *never* leave Pam. So you don't need to worry. She'll stay. Of course, she'll stay with you.' But something chokes the words in my throat, Sheila's earlier taunt; do they *really* call me Meddlesome Molly?

While I am considering these things Alan has taken two steps across the room and put his arms around me. In fact I think it is more accurate to say that he places himself in my arms; that is what I feel – that I am being called upon for comfort and for strength. He rests his head on mine, his arms are heavy on my shoulders, he leans into me in such a way that I am giving physical as well as emotional support. He is bone-weary, poor man; his world has collapsed around him and it is to me that he has turned. I give myself up to it, melting into the contact of skin on skin, the nearness, the delight of human warmth. Within that closeness there isn't room for words. There is no space even for the smallest whisper.

It is downstairs, five minutes later, while he helps me with my coat, that I find my voice, and I only speak the words to remind him that outside of this vortex the ordinary world spins on more manageably.

'I am going, next week,' I say, 'to Julia and Gerald's place. They've asked me to look after things for them for a few weeks.'

'Their big cruise?' It comes out almost as whisper, his voice is so weary.

'That's right.'

When I get home there is a message on my machine from Lucy, full of laughter and excitement and the kind of disjointed rambling which happens when you had expected to speak to someone who isn't there. 'Oh, Mum, you're out – you're always out, you old gad-about – anyway, I wanted to talk to you. Freddie (you remember Freddie? From the hotel at Christmas?) well he and I have been – you know – anyway, it seems that there's this cottage... somewhere..... in the country – can't think where, now. Cotswolds? Anyway, we've got the chance to use it – it's too complicated to explain just now – but anyway, if you'd like to – oh! This is impossible. Why aren't you *there*? Call me, will you? Call me soon! Soooooooooon.'

I pour myself an enormous gin and tonic – even though it isn't Friday – and light the fire and throw a ready-meal into the oven before calling her number. She is so full of all her news; a particularly successful time at work, a new gym she's joined, the thrills of Zumba ('you absolutely MUST try it') and her burgeoning relationship with Freddie - about whom she gets all giggly – that mercifully no in-put is required from me as she chatters on. Her youth and exuberance are a real tonic after the week I have endured and when she gets to the crux of the call – an opportunity to use a friend-of-a-friend's cottage for a long weekend – I accept at once without really assimilating the details. I want to get away – from this pokey, friendless house and from the complicated lives of the Combe Close set and, as much as possible, from myself, the sadness of my unfulfilled dreams, my adorable, dangerous tiger which must pine away behind its bars.

Combe Close: Cracks in the Pavement

Looking back I see the night of the pool party more and more clearly as the zenith of those Combe Close days – only three years, but they had been for me, till then, a kind of arcadia. The circle of friendship and trust between us had been – had seemed – complete, my place at its hub satisfying my yearning to belong. I had found it, I thought; nice *and* good.

Afterwards, although I was often happy, and indeed was conscious in myself of enlargement on every level – social, intellectual, emotional – which was all to the good, I was yet aware that in that Combe Close world I was making compromises I hadn't had to make before. I was, probably, seeing my neighbours in a less rose-tinted light. They were not quite the perfect people I had thought, and wanted, them to be. The household across the road was just the beginning.

Things were on the up for Carla and Marcus. His business got a huge order from abroad and profits soared. This, combined with the promise of a sizeable inheritance from Carla's parents when they passed away – which they did, around then – led to a noticeable increase in spending including a number of exotic holidays. They were very generous with their money. Carla treated me on a number of occasions to manicures and facials, and often gave me bits and bobs of clothing she said she had grown tired of but which she said would suit me to a tee. At the same time they were dismissive of it in a way which I am sure was meant to draw attention away from it but which in fact had the opposite effect. Carla developed a tendency towards ostentation – it all went, in my opinion, a bit to her head. She wanted more and more *things* – clothes, jewellery, a red sports car (she had always envied Katrina's), a time-share property in the Balearics. She joined a Country Club and took golf lessons – spending goodness knows how much on clubs and clothing. Although she frequently offered to take me along as her guest, on the few occasions I accepted I felt uncomfortable, out-classed, as she lounged by the pool with her new cronies.

Sheila felt the same. She attempted, on more than one occasion, to engage me in critical comment on Carla's new life-style, a practice which prompted me to defend, rather than to attack Carla, much to Sheila's chagrin. She was jealous, I concluded, identifying a sour, resentful layer beneath the brittle veneer of her habitual cheerfulness.

The money didn't change Marcus at all, and he did his best, within the elastic limits of his generosity, to curb Carla's extravagance – he denied her, anyway, for the time being, the sports car although that too, eventually, he allowed her to have. He resorted more and more often to his garden and his shed after work, as Carla filled the house with expensive prints and electric gadgets and her own, hedonistic aura of bright laughter and chaotic, playful fun.

Pete had been heavily involved with a local amateur dramatic group before he ever moved into the Close. He took comedy parts - bumbling police officers, clumsy Vicars and the occasional ham-fisted thug. The problem with Pete was that he had such a potent, forceful personality of his own that it was virtually impossible to subsume it into anything smaller-scale. However hard he tried every role just turned into a facsimile of Pete. But he was enthusiastic, a power-house of hard work when it came to set-building and light-rigging and a positive evangelist in the matter of publicity and ticket sales. He did am-dram on the same scale that he did everything – large. Sometime during the period of Katrina's pregnancy the erstwhile leader of the group moved away and Pete found himself at the helm. In this role he persuaded Sheila to lend her skills to the wardrobe department, and it became a regular occurrence to see them drive off together on Thursday evenings, and then, as a production approached, at weekends too, for technical and dress rehearsals. And of course we all went dutifully to watch the performances – some of them cringingly awful, others surprisingly good. I think two seasons went by in this manner as the group put on a pantomime at Christmas, a musical or review in spring and an Alan Ayckbourn or similar in the autumn.

By the time this pattern was well established it became apparent to me that Pam was experiencing some kind of decline. All our children except for Austin and Quentin were at school and we shared the school runs between us. There were a few occasions when I would call for her boys to find them not dressed, or their packed lunches not ready. When it was her turn to do the pick-up she was frequently late. She was constantly on one or another doorstep to beg cooking ingredients that she had forgotten to get at the shops. Her figure – never, as I have indicated, what you would call slender – began to increase quite noticeably while her complexion became pasty and her hair even more lank and lifeless. At the time I took Pam's degeneration to be caused by anxiety over Pete's business and the on-going problems with the youngest child. Quentin, since birth, had been of a querulous, difficult bent and, although getting on for two by then, was continually subject to various non-specific ailments. He didn't sleep well, was a fussy eater and was altogether lacking in the general generic of rumbustious behaviour and overall pell-mell which characterised the other boys and, indeed, Pete himself. I did everything I could to help bar the one thing I *should* have done: sit down to listen.

To be honest with you though I had problems enough of my own, around about then. Freda had had a stroke and Stan and I were backwards and forwards to the hospital and then the nursing home, juggling Lucy and her busy diary of school and Rainbows and ballet and swimming lessons between us. Then Freda died – quite peacefully – and we had all the business of the Will and the sale of her house to handle. I must say Carla was a tower of strength; having recently lost her own parents she really made an effort to engage with Stan on the subject of Freda's death. I often found them together, mulling over the complexities of Probate.

The by-pass was still very much with us, apparently occupying all of Stan's waking attention, but Freda's death seemed to exacerbate his state of agitation. He often tossed and turned at night and roamed the house and the Close with a tortured restlessness I just couldn't mitigate. He started to find social situations almost intolerable, even though he was mixing now – so he told me – with some very high-powered chaps through work. I had to virtually force him to the Combe Close socials. He would make any excuse not to go but I feared that if not pressed he would turn into some kind of weird, socially incapacitated recluse or, worse, begin to insist that I too, stayed behind. So I usually made him go, but often he exhibited behaviour that was bordering on rude; standing aloof, barking out responses to questions, and giving every impression of being engaged in some terrible personal conflict.

My neighbours were magnificent, especially the women. Anya invariably picked him for her team in any game. Pam would ply him with second helpings of pudding. Katrina always made much of him, sashaying over on her high heels, clad in some figure-hugging number, to take his arm and draw him to the buffet or to enlist his help in choosing the music. Stan was putty in her hands, and if I had thought he stood even a glimmer of a chance with her, I might have been a tiny bit jealous, but I had resigned myself to his fascination and on the whole rather enjoyed than otherwise the halting, bluff attempts at chivalry that she provoked. The harsh fact was that when we all got together it gave me a break; I could slip away for half an hour's respite with my friends knowing Stan would be sufficiently distracted not to miss me.

It was one afternoon at Julia and Gerald's when it was forcefully brought to my notice that things between Pete and Sheila were not at all as they should be, and that I linked this state of affairs with Pam's altered demeanour. It was summer and the doors to the garden stood open but a sudden shower had driven us all indoors. This was awkward – but also highly amusing – as we crammed ourselves in around the supernumerary furnishings juggling plates of hors d'oeuvres, rugs and cushions rescued from the rain. Pete, tightly wedged between an ornate bureau and a Chinese lacquered cabinet clasped the punch-bowl to his chest. It was one of those enormous and frankly hideous silver-gilt artefacts, richly embossed and a pig to clean, which comes with a dozen little punch cups which attach to the rim. The table was full of food and every other surface was cluttered with Julia's collection of fussy, innumerable nick-nacks; there was nowhere Pete could put the punch-bowl down. We were all struck with the hilarious irony of this situation: Pete, always the thirstiest amongst us, couldn't take a drop of the punch, and we took great delight in filing past to fill up our glasses, which we raised to him in a number of cynical toasts, thoroughly enjoying the joke. He growled and fumed in mock indignation, and even attempted lifting the bowl to his lips to drink.

'Thirsty, old man?' Gerald wheezed eventually, 'can I get you a drink?'

'Oh well, just a small sherry, if you have one,' Pete boomed, 'but I'll have to have it intravenously.'

We all roared with laughter, except Stan, who stood in one corner behind an elaborately carved chair, scowling at a spot on the richly figured carpet and Sheila, who stepping forward, filled one of the punch glasses and put it to Pete's lips, feeding him the drink, drop by careful drop. It was nothing, really, just part of the joke, but there was, in her gesture – I wonder if I can describe it to you adequately - something so shockingly, so unwarrantedly familiar, far over-leaping the boundaries that even our warm and comfortable relations allowed, that all our laughter dried in our throats. The close confidentiality of her posture - her bosom pressed carelessly against his arm as he clasped the bowl; the unhesitating assurance of her hands as they proffered the glass to his mouth, the frank, direct way their eyes connected.

Their attitude shouted intimacy; long-standing, habitual, inappropriate intimacy.

Pam, entering just then with a tray of hot *vol-au-vents*, - Quentin, the querulous child, clinging to her skirts and emitting the kind of incessant whining which is calculated to get on your nerves - stopped in her tracks. The child's shrill complaints filled the silence of the room. I think if I hadn't stepped forward to take the tray off her she would have dropped it. Alan stood in the opening of the patio doors, his back to the room, resolutely surveying the rain. Sheila and Pete continued oblivious, their eyes fixed on each other, closely contained in an exclusive, sequestered bubble; her hands, his mouth, the wet, suggestive noises of his sipping and swallowing and his little mews of appreciation appalling in the sudden hiatus. Presently a trickle of punch escaped from the glass and ran down Pete's chin. Sheila caught it with her finger, offered it for Pete to lick off and then, slowly, suggestively, put the finger into her own mouth. A gust of excruciating embarrassment overwhelmed us — it was palpable, as tangible as a bad smell, impossible to ignore, imperative to over-look. Suddenly Pam turned to the dragging, whinging child at her hem and dealt him a swift slap which sent him flying into a long-case clock. Pete and Sheila leapt apart. Punch slopped down his shirt-front. The weights and pendulum inside the clock set up an alarming jangle and the child, of course, began to yell. We were all galvanised into frantic action, our busy hands - fussing with cloths, soothing the child, checking that no damage had been done to the clock's innards - masking our busy minds: what had just happened?

The afternoon progressed ostensibly as though nothing had happened. Pam took Quentin home, declaring him 'poorly'. The shower passed over and Pete went out to light the barbeque. Julia let the latest litter of puppies out of the whelping room, to the delight of the children. Katrina teased Stan about the diversions through the town centre and pouted prettily while he tried to explain their rationale until I thought he would either stammer himself into an apoplexy or ejaculate into his trousers. Then Carla took him off to a quiet corner to look through a *Which? Sports Car* magazine she had brought with her. (She was still hankering for a sports car but she wouldn't have got much sense out of Stan on the subject, he knew next to nothing about cars.) The rest of the men played cricket out on the Close with the children whilst the women washed up. It was a normal Combe Close get-together except the incident with the punch bowl had set the whole thing into a minor key. Sheila was in over-drive, gushingly full of over-enthusiastic, exaggerated sweetness that began to put my teeth on edge. Alan spent almost the entire afternoon in a minute examination of Julia's artefacts.

Stan and I walked home as the sun was going down. The disputed Mock Orange on the front lawn was in glorious flower, showering petals like confetti over the turf. Lucy ran to it and began to cover herself in them. 'I'm a bride!' she announced. The shrub was seven or eight feet tall by then and a real pleasure to observe from my bench, a source of welcome shade and wafts of sweet perfume. As we stopped for a moment to admire it, Stan began to scuff at something on the pavement with the toe of his shoe; a tiny crack in the tarmac.

'It's the roots of that thing,' he fulminated, nodding at the shrub, 'it'll have to come out.'

'Oh Stan! No!' I protested. 'It's only just coming into its own.'

'If it's doing this to the pavement, what do you suppose it will be doing to the foundations of our house? I'll ring the council on Monday.'

He strode off with the air of a man entirely vindicated and went into the house, leaving me alone on the pavement to consider the fissures opening up beneath my feet.

You might ask me why I considered it my responsibility to tackle the situation between Sheila and Pete and the only answer I can honestly give you is that I did it because it was clear to me that nobody else would. It was the kind of lead I was by no means in the habit of taking, even in the Close, where I felt so secure. I did it, nominally, out of loyalty to Pam and Alan and also, I told myself, out of kindness for Sheila and Pete. They would be grateful, I thought, when they realised the hurt they were inadvertently storing up. But mainly I think it was an in-built reflex, fall-out from those dry, judgmental days of my childhood; there was hardly any thought and certainly no kindness in my interference, only a default setting of finger-pointing. It wouldn't do, I crowed. It wasn't good and must be stopped before things went too far. That they had already progressed beyond that point I didn't doubt, calling to mind, now, with a sick chill, various ribald stories of the men's dressing room during the Christmas production of Robin Hood. Pete had played Little John, grotesque in a leather jerkin and a pair of women's tights, and there had been several jocular references to Sheila's obsession with his hose. How we had all laughed, then, thinking it only innocent banter. I cursed them both for their blind and reckless selfishness, flinging themselves without a moment's thought to the consequences, into a sordid and underhand affair. I imagined them thrilled with the subterfuge, caught up and careless in the moment.

I went round to Sheila's the very next day, Sunday, mustering every ounce of outrage and indignation I could. Alan had taken the girls to their horse-riding lesson (I had carefully timed my visit to coincide with their absence) and I found Sheila on her hands and knees shampooing the lounge carpet, a position I rather took advantage of as, dispensing with preliminaries, I launched in with 'That business yesterday with you and Pete. It was a bit near the knuckle, wasn't it?'

She had the decency to blush through a half-hearted protest, 'Poor man. He couldn't have a drink!' as though that was all there had been to it.

'I've never known Pete let himself go short – he'd have managed. But even if he couldn't, don't you think it was up to Pam to help out, if anybody had to?'

She looked up at me, startled, I suppose, by my unsmiling demeanour. 'Molly?'

My face remained obdurate. She tried to stare me down for a moment or two. Presently, she went back to the carpet, scrubbing at a particularly stubborn spot – one that was invisible to me – before giving a forced laugh. 'You're making too much of it, Molly.'

'I don't think so,' I pressed on, 'in my experience of these things…' (a

185

ridiculous notion – I had no experience of them), '…. there's no smoke without fire.' I moved to stand directly over her. My mother's voice, issuing from my mouth, made me blanch, but fortunately Sheila, still industriously scrubbing, didn't see my face. 'How could you *do* such a thing?' I almost spat out. 'Poor Pam. Not to mention Alan and your girls……' I let the rest of my sentence speak for itself, allowing Sheila a period to fully assimilate my meaning; not just the consequences of the affair itself, but the consequences of it's being out, as it were, in the open. If this was to be mild, milksop Molly's reaction, what might the stronger personalities around the Close make of it?

Stepping across to her lounge window, I pushed home my point. 'It's so *nice* here, so *good.*' I let her take it in. Not just the Close, which looked especially lovely after the previous day's rain, the hanging baskets and flower tubs refreshed and vibrant, the houses all neat and pretty, but her own house, perfectly clean and as carefully dressed as a feature in *Woman and Home* and her own situation in the midst of it: amongst friends, such nice, good friends; next to Alan, her nice, good husband, with her girls - safe and secure. Surely an enviable situation, and not one to put at risk for a passing, whimsical fling.

Sheila remained crouched behind me but her restless rubbing of the carpet had stilled. My work was as good as done; half a dozen sentences had accomplished it. I had conjured up for her, I hoped, so sufficiently vivid a picture of what there was to lose that further dwelling on the seedy details would be superfluous. She made a small sound somewhere between a sniff and a sob, and I knew, with a mixture of relief and disturbing triumph, that I had broken her. From that victorious position I threw her a life-line. 'To think that a moment's silliness might spoil it,' I mused, almost to myself. We both understood my reference to 'a moment's silliness'; I *knew* (and she knew that I knew) what she had been up to, but I had given it a euphemism we could both live with. Slowly, like a woman whose every bone has been ground to powder, she hauled herself to her feet and came to stand with me where her pristinely polished windows displayed the Close in all its precious order. What I said next was unnecessary and perhaps cruel. 'I'm very worried about Pam. Aren't you?' I spoke in a conversational tone which suggested a whole new topic but which was, of course, umbilically linked with what had gone before. 'The poor thing looks absolutely worn to a frazzle. I must go over, later.'

I had intended that the threat would hang over her: what, she would agonise, would I say to Pam? Would I expose her? What, now it really came to it, had she intended to be the outcome of the dalliance? Would she – *could* she – see it through? But in fact what happened next provided a reality-check more potent than any I or even my shrivel-hearted mother could have come up with. As we stood together in the window Pete's car pulled into his driveway directly opposite and Pete levered himself out of the driver's door. Besides me, Sheila gave an involuntary lurch and a stifled gasp as though shot-through by a sudden current of electricity. Tears, perhaps pent up for the last moments, sprang from her eyes with such velocity that they sprinked the glass in front of us. The next moment the front door of Pete's house was yanked open and the four boys exploded from the threshold as though propelled by some hidden cannon, hurling themselves into his capacious arms. It was always this way whenever he came home and I, certainly – and I speculated Sheila, also, on many a vigil at this very window – had witnessed it on innumerable occasions. The boys simply adored their father and to remove him from the elevated pedestal on which they maintained him – as any continuance of their affair would certainly do – would be unspeakably cruel and perhaps permanently damaging.

Confronting Pete was beyond me and I didn't even attempt it. It is impossible to maintain a position of superiority when no one will take you seriously and I knew that Pete would simply laugh me out of court, decimating any dignity I could muster with hot, fleshy hugs and a series of patronising pats on the head. The prospect of being sent away like a

187

silly school girl was intolerable and in any case, for some men, being told that they can't do something is like a red rag to a bull. Cleverer tactics were called for, so the following day I went to see Pam with an entirely different strategy.

I found her at almost lunchtime still in her dressing gown eating the cold remains of a left-over pizza and watching some mindless day-time soap opera. Quentin, the awkward child, was mercifully asleep under a grubby blanket on a threadbare settee. When I broached the subject of my call she immediately began to cry with huge, stifled sobs. Clearly the pain of recent events was exceedingly raw and hovering very close to the surface. This, I realised (much too late) was at the root of all her distraction over recent months. I knelt down beside her chair and took her hot, pudgy hand in mine. Our whole conversation was conducted *sotto voce* so as not to wake the toddler.

'Pete's been behaving so oddly,' she wheezed, mopping her streaming nose with a sodden tissue, 'and now I know why!'

'You don't know why at all!' I cried in a theatrical whisper, 'not if you think it's anything to do with Sheila. I can think of a hundred reasons why men behave oddly!' It was a wild and ridiculous assertion: I knew nothing of men and their psychology, but Pam was so desperate for a benign explanation for Pete's peculiar conduct that she was willing to overlook it.

'Really?'

'Of course. Look. You told me yourself, when Pete first set up the business, that it was going to cause stresses and difficulties, that you'd miss the security of a salary. Naturally Pete's aware of that. It's bound to put extra pressure on him.'

'I suppose so,' she sniffed, 'but he hasn't *said* anything...'

'Do they ever?' I gave her what I hoped was a worldly, rueful grin.

'I suppose not.'

'And is it any wonder? When you look at the hours he works? He's out virtually every evening, isn't he? It isn't unusual for his car to be missing as late as ten at night! I don't suppose you *ever* have time for conversation, do you?'

'People like him to visit them at home, and often the evenings are the only times they're free.'

'Well there you are then. Poor man. I expect he's exhausted, missing time with the boys, time with you. No wonder he's behaving oddly.'

'He still makes time for the drama group,' she muttered, bitterly.

'Don't even get me started on that! Seems to me he runs the thing single handed these days...'

'They're never enough people to help out backstage. Everyone wants to *act* and then they're forever falling in and out with petty little spats...'

I sat back on my heels and held my hands out, palms up in an 'I rest my case' gesture. Pam surveyed the picture I had drawn for her, of a man worn to a frazzle trying to succeed in a new business, working fourteen hours a day, desperately missing the domestic comforts he had previously enjoyed, put-upon by a troupe of temperamental and self-seeking thespians. I wondered if she would recognise him, this poor harassed creature, in the figure of her burly, gregarious, irrepressibly buoyant husband (I scarcely did).

I decided to add another layer to the image I had projected. 'Are you sure he's entirely *well?*' I enquired. 'How long is it since he had a check-up?'

Pam blanched quite visibly. Her hand shot to her mouth. 'Ages,' she mouthed, 'do you think there's something *wrong?*'

I hoped I had sown enough seeds of mitigation. I took her hand again. It was damp, now, as well as hot. 'We mustn't jump to *any* conclusions, Pam,' I said with laboured significance. 'All I'm trying to do is to show you that there is any number of explanations for Pete's unusual behaviour recently, and these are only ones that *I* can come up with. Heaven knows that *you'll* be aware of lots more...'

'Well there is something we haven't quite seen eye to eye on...' her eyes made a mute appeal, 'although it seems *terrible* to admit it...' I gave her hand a squeeze. She cast a swift look across the room to the sleeping child. 'Quentin's been *such* a handful, Molly. Really, if he'd been the first I'm sure he would have been an only child.'

'I know,' I soothed. 'So there's *another* strain we can add to the list. Broken nights...'

'Yes. And I really have come to the conclusion that enough is enough. I mean, *four* children is enough, don't you think?'

'*Two* would have done me, Pam,'

'And I've been trying to get Pete to go – you know...'

'For the snip?'

'Yes. But he absolutely refuses.'

'He wants *more* children?'

Pam shook her head. 'It's the operation itself. He seems to think that it would make him less of a man. Oh Molly. We have had some arguments about it. And when I saw him with Sheila on Saturday, I thought 'So *that's* why...' She started to cry again and I handed her a clean tissue from my pocket, imagining, as I am sure Pam was doing, the blighting effects a vasectomy would have on impromptu clandestine couplings.

'Their behaviour on Saturday was appalling,' I said. 'There's no getting round it. It made us all feel very uncomfortable and I know it upset you a great deal. I think it upset Alan too. But I've been to see Sheila and...'

'You've been to see her?'

'Of course I have. Somebody had to.'

'Oh Molly,' Pam said, dissolving again, 'you're so good. I wouldn't have dared...'

'Well I *did* dare. You're my friends! What else could I do? Anyway, the fact is, Pam, that Sheila *assures* me that it was just a moment of thoughtless stupidity. She's devastated to think that it might have spoiled the lovely friendship we all have here, really she is.' Pam, though still snivelling a little, was hanging on my every word. 'And I must tell you, Pam, that after what we've just discussed, I do believe her. Poor Pete is dealing with so much at the moment – you *both* are – that he forgot himself. It was an aberration, a brief deviation from the norm.'

'Do you really believe that?' her small, bloodshot eyes craved reassurance. I had got to the crux of the matter and I needed to nail it. In a leap of psychological insight I hit on what I instinctively felt would be the right note. Pete wasn't the kind of man who would respond to haranguing. He could schmooze his way around the coldest cold-shoulder. But an appeal to his manly credentials would undo him every time; he was a sucker for a helpless damsel and an unconditional declaration of belief in his noble heart would send him out to face dragons. 'It doesn't really matter what I believe, Pam,' I said. 'Who am I? I'm nobody. I'm irrelevant. Pete needs to know that *you* believe it, that you believe *in him*. I think that with all the pressure he's under he's losing a sense of his own capacity as a man. He's worried about providing for you, through the business. He's anxious about supporting you with the boys, especially Quentin. He's desperate to keep it all together for you – that would explain his reluctance to have a vasectomy and his dogged perseverance with the drama group. He's always been the life and soul of our parties and what we saw on Saturday was just him trying to do the same as he always does. He just misjudged it. We both know he'd *never deliberately* do anything to let you down, to hurt you or distress you in any way. Tell him you believe in him, Pam. Tell him you trust him. I think perhaps *that's* what he needs to hear.'

Yes, I thought, tell him that, and he'll never have the heart to stray again.

Present Day: Cotswolds Weekend

The days leading up to my weekend away with Lucy are spent swinging in dizzying arcs of mood, from periods of dull, indolent torpor to prolonged states of near hysterical frenzy. Some days I can hardly bear to get out of bed. I pad around the house in my dressing gown and subsist on stale cream crackers and things out of the fridge past their use-by date. One night I get morosely drunk and wake up in the small hours on the bathroom floor with the sour smell of vomit in my nose. On other days I am strict and spry; cleaning and washing, sorting clothes for the charity shop, swimming with stiff, quick, inefficient strokes up and down the pool as though pursued by the Kraken.

The past few months have been fraught with disappointment, like those water meadows which, seen from a distance, seem verdant and appealing, but close to, turn out to be sucking, stinking bogs. The thrill of my lunchtime adventure, the anticipation of Julia's party, that oh so brief moment under the strobe were only deceptive coverings for the poisonous decomposition beneath; the dissolution of the Combe Close set, my friends' beleaguered marriages, the inevitable tragedy of Carla's debilitation, not to mention the arid wasteland of my own utterly futile and terminally doomed love. Sheila's misery has convinced me, if I needed it, that whilst the hair-shirt of my self-discipline has been agony, the guilt and heartache pursuant on any affair would have made it self-defeating.

Whatever will come of it now is out of my hands. I absolutely give it up, but in the same way that an addict gives up her narcotic – with many a backward glance. The Close has sustained me for the past twenty five years; even after we all moved away, I strove to keep its connections alive. My friends became my reason for living. Without them, who am I? Apart from Lucy – upon whom I will not be a burden – I am without association, support or purpose. The silent inhabitants of the houses either side of mine, the disembodied voices of my students, the nameless naked bodies in the changing rooms at the pool are nothing to me. I have made no effort with them, I haven't needed them, because I have had Combe Close.

I go cold-turkey. I don't call, or text or email yet I speculate ad nauseam on the possible sequence of events. Sheila, perhaps, will pack her bags and leave; Alan will come home to an empty house and a note. Pete will fail to show up at the rendezvous; Sheila will be left high and dry at the airport or the hotel or wherever she might have designated as their trysting point. She will go back home and let herself in, and set to polishing her draining board as though nothing has happened while Alan hovers in diffident bewilderment, imprisoned in the status quo, for what, under these circumstances, can he decently do, other than just carry on? That is one scenario I imagine.

Here is another. Carla's health will decline. She will prove unreliable when left alone even for the briefest periods and Marcus will book her into some exclusive asylum where he will visit her, daily, bringing gifts and bright snippets of news from the village. She will receive him with increasing confusion as moments of lucidity grow more sporadic until he is no more to her than the nurse on night duty or the occasional curate fulfilling his pastoral quota. But Marcus will carry on with his visits, sitting by her chair, and then by her bed and at last by her grave, squandering his tenderness on dust and ashes, a criminal waste of his huge and generous capacity to make a woman happy.

I imagine a period during which Pete's return to the marriage-fold will be the Sumo equivalent of a second – or third, or fourth – honeymoon; the rapture of their elephantine love-making causing the house to quake to its crumbling foundations. Pam will cook and clean herself into a home-making frenzy while Pete reclines in his favourite chair, a beer in one hand and the TV remote in the other, his wife and boys within booming distance, the luckiest man in the world. But inevitably in time his luck will bring some further irresistible offer within reach; a cherry for the icing on his cake, rendering poor Pam once more cuckquean.

I cannot speculate on the future for Gary and the girls; their arrangement – odd as it is – seems perfectly satisfactory to them. I am only sure that they will go on without me. And although it is me that Julia and Gerald have asked to look after their small-holding while they go away, I am sure that it is only because their local friends are all far too busy with their own rustic concerns and because I am – let's face it – so wholly available. I will do it for them – of course I will – but expect nothing beyond it.

In all the flux, amid the mutability of their situations, I see no glimmer of a respectable opening for me. This, of course, from any upright point of view, is exactly as it should be, and what I have always, at considerable personal cost, striven to achieve; it has been the battle-ground of my moral struggle, the basis and the beneficiary of my heart-break; couples staying together through thick and thin, in sickness and in health. But it is a Pyrrhic victory, for me and for them, I see that now. And if I cannot see them happy, the recipients of my sacrifice, what, after all, has been the point of it?

Truth be told I am heartily sick of flogging the dead horse of Combe Close, particularly now that I discover that nobody appreciates the effort it has cost. Meddlesome? Mollycoddled? Let them all go to hell!

It feels imperative to find something else, something new, and certainly something more solid, to anchor myself on to. This is the conclusion I come to as I pack my bag and tidy the house the night before my departure. I will move house, I think, emigrate, perhaps – my Far Eastern students are always telling me that I could make a success of teaching full time out there. I will talk it all through with Lucy over the weekend.

This resolve occupies my feverish mind the night before I travel and it is with a thorough-going determination to start afresh that I put myself on the train on Friday morning, to be met, after several changes and much loitering on draughty platforms, at a tiny deserted station in a remote country village by a curiously coy Lucy. Although she is as affectionate and effusive as ever in her greeting, and as habitually full of chat and laughter, I am immediately aware of something held back – a barely suppressed excitement, some mischief afoot. Her eyes – very bright – continually slide off mine. I know that I mustn't ask – nothing would infuriate her more than that. Lucy must be allowed to pull the rabbit out of the hat in her own time and way. At the same time I am avid to do or say something which will put a conclusive stamp on my new beginnings.

It isn't long before I am given the opportunity. Lucy is driving a car that turns out to belong to Freddie; sleek, silver and frighteningly speedy, with a roof that concertinas at the touch of a button and disappears into a compartment at the rear. She demonstrates the roof, along with sundry other gadgets before we set off through the narrow streets and then out into the Wolds, Lucy negotiating the route directed by an on-board satellite navigation system.

'We drove up last night,' she says, and I notice that she almost swallows the pronoun. 'Wait till you see the cottage, Mum. It's actually for sale. Mac's thinking about buying it off this friend of his. He wanted to clock it from home and from the office. So Freddie and I drove straight from town and Mac came from home. Obviously it needs to be within reasonable commute of both, for weekend visits.....'

'Obviously,' I say, a little dryly. The rabbit, I think, is precipitately out of its hat. Or perhaps it would be more accurate to say that the cat is out of the bag. My weekend with Lucy has turned into a weekend with Lucy and Freddie and Mac. Little minx, I think, I bet she has been hatching this plan since Christmas. I am inclined to be awkward – I have, after all, been lured here under false pretences – but then I notice again her air of hugged-in excitement, the same manner of secret harbouring she had had as a child just before Christmas or my birthday, and I decide, with a resignation which is almost gung-ho, that I will simply go with the flow. Clearly this weekend is to be about Lucy, not about me. What the hell, I

195

think to myself, while Lucy witters on about the cottage's accommodations – two bathrooms, a range oven, beautiful views – I had wanted something new and perhaps here it was.

'Freddie's *here*? And his father too? What a lovely surprise!' I cry effusively.

'You don't mind?'

'Why should I mind, darling?'

She breathes then, and flashes me one of her loveliest smiles. 'I *do* want you to like him, Mum. *I* do, so much.'

I identify it then, of course; she is in love. It is love which is lighting her up, and although I am happy for her I feel a small contraction in my heart, a shrivel of self-pity. She is my last, my very final hand-hold, but here is confirmation, if any had been needed, that that, too, I must let loose.

The cottage nestles between a gentle hill and a dark green coniferous plantation about half a mile from a tiny village. The silver car's bigger and altogether more grown-up brother is parked on an area of shingle besides a wooden, creeper-strewn garage. Dusk has already fallen as we pull up but the sound of our tyres on the gravel brings a flood of light to the path as Freddie and his father spill out of the door to greet me and to take my bags. Mac is taller and more handsome than I recall, attractive as only a man wearing cashmere can be. Very much mine host, he gives my hand a meaty shake before leading me inside. Freddie is as charming as I remember, and I am glad to see that he puts his arm around Lucy at the earliest opportunity. The two men look very alike – which is more than I can say for Lucy and I, she has her father's dark good looks – so you can see, in Mac, the man that Freddie will become, and it is by no means unpromising. They are both broadly set, with the kind of solid frame which could turn to fat if not kept under close control, much more at home, I would say, on a rugby pitch than a golf course. We crush into the miniscule hallway for a moment, exchanging greetings, before Lucy leads me into a low-ceilinged sitting room where a bright fire burns in the grate and a tray is ready with the makings of gin and tonics. Freddie takes my bag away and Mac disappears through the door at the other side of the hall which I presume to be the kitchen; certainly it is the source of a quite delicious smell of cooking.

While they are out of the room I think it judicious to make enquiries as to the sleeping arrangements; the cottage, as far as I have seen it, doesn't seem to promise more than two bedrooms, but I make my request for information in as off-hand a manner as I can manage, eyeing the sofas with an apparently phlegmatic eye. Even in the muted firelight, I see the blush which creeps up Lucy's neck. 'Well,' she falters, 'Freddie and I will share. But only if you're entirely comfortable with it, Mum,' she says. 'I know it might seem a bit weird but you must remember that, since Christmas, Freddie and I have been seeing a great deal of each other.'

'Oh!' I laugh, waving a careless hand which serves, at once, to blithely bless my daughter's extra-marital sexual union and to slap down the voice which tries to raise the objection that she has only known the man six weeks, 'I assumed that you would. I meant, really, what will the arrangements be for me?'

'Oh!' she smiles, 'well don't worry. We don't expect you to bunk in with Mac *yet!* There's a very nice single en-suite up in the attic. Mac did offer to let you have the master, but I thought, since he's paying for the whole shebang, that was a bit much.'

'I wouldn't dream of it,' I reply.

The old Molly would have been horrified by Lucy's throw-away suggestion, even in jest. The new Molly, I find, is surprisingly unperturbed by it. Mac is very personable, after all, and I *do* need something new in my life......

I am in a kind of free-fall, without the hand-holds which my place in the Combe Close set has previously provided, and it is curiously liberating.

197

Nobody expects anything from me. Freddie and Mac don't even know me; I am a blank canvas, and determine to allow them to paint me in whatever colours they choose. I will do, I will say nothing because it is expected of me. Before I am half way down my second gin and tonic I am conscious what a relief it is not to have to be the one who holds everything together, of what a gargantuan effort it has been, these past few years, to push the Combe Close connection along against its will.

Most of all it is wonderful not to have to watch my body language, words and gestures for fear of giving my secret away.

We progress from the sitting room to the kitchen across the hallway where Mac serves up a delicious bœuf bourguignon and manages to bump his head repeatedly on a low beam, an occurrence which gets funnier with every repetition until I almost begin to wonder if he is doing it on purpose. Freddie splashes Merlot into our glasses. Lucy shifts her chair fractionally closer to his. They throw around ideas for the following day – a run into Bath, a walk, a trip to Sudeley Castle. The only fixed point is a table booked for dinner at the village Inn. Freddie and Mac are like Lucy and I – close, comfortable in one another's company, and as the meal progresses I can tell that Lucy has spent a great deal of time with them both; she has been absorbed into their familial relation, knows the people they talk about, shares their common ground. Mac treats her very affectionately, like a father, and in some curious way this attracts me to him; I feel that, through Lucy, I, too, might find a connection here.

The room is warm – a log-burner glows in one corner and there's an Aga (of course) – and lit by candles. After dinner I push my chair back a little and take it all in – the chintz, the dark patina of the dresser, the flickering shadows on the ceiling and the three of them, bright-eyed, laughing at some remark. I watch Freddie's hand as it languidly strokes Lucy's arm, note Mac's hands – nicely manicured, a heavy ring on his right pinkie. Now I have opened the door, just a crack, to the possibilities Mac presents, I find my eye drawn more and more through it. He is articulate, but not a waster of words, a quiet foil for the livelier banter of the young people. He drinks quite his share of the wine but I detect no sign of inebriation in him; he is steady and solid and not the kind of man, I think, who will lose his equanimity very easily.

After a while we all help to clear the table and then move through to the sitting room. Lucy and Freddie have a fiendishly difficult jig-saw in the early stages of completion on a table towards the back of the room. Mac and I sink down into comfortable chairs by the fire. I am powerfully reminded, all of a sudden, of the library at the cliff house where we had had our autumn holiday, and Lucy's interrogation.

'I wouldn't marry a man because he was available,' I had said.

Well, perhaps I had been wrong.

Mac is very pleasant company. He wants to know all about my work, how it is funded and organised, to whom I am accountable. In return he explains about his role as the MD of an advertising agency. We debate – politely – the moral questions implicit in presenting some patently predatory products – like payday loans and sugary snacks – as harmless.

'What would *you* like to do, tomorrow, Molly?' he asks me as we say our goodnights – the question, earlier, had not been resolved. I am momentarily flummoxed; I don't think anybody has ever asked me that, before.

'Well, if nobody else minds,' I stammer, looking from one to the other of them, 'Bath, you know, has a Jane Austen museum....'

'Perfect!' Mac ejaculates (drowning out Lucy's muffled groan), 'Bath it will be, then.'

My impression of the rest of the weekend is not of falling but of floating. The company is so easy that, in the morning, we drift in common accord from the breakfast table into the garden, where Freddie and Mac survey the property in pursuance of their opportunity to buy it, speculating about a possible extension, the state of the guttering, the age of the roof, while

199

Lucy and I link arms and stroll around the garden. It is cold but bright, late snowdrops and early crocuses carpet the lawn. Despite the sunshine, Lucy seems to me to be the source of all the light as she pours out to me, in breathless detail, the sequence of texts and emails, the first date, the bouquets of flowers, the late-night telephone calls, the dinners, the surprise weekend in Paris where she was fed with champagne and strawberries in the honeymoon suite of a boutique hotel on the Rue de Rivoli.

'And the *sex*....' she squeaks, but I hold up my hand.

'I can imagine,' I say, although, in point of fact, I can't. Good sex is a blank page in my lexicon.

Later, as promised, we stroll around Bath and visit the Jane Austen museum and the Roman Bath and the pump room, now a restaurant. Lucy and Freddie flip from being super-cool and sophisticated savants amongst the exhibits to acting the giddy goat in the gift shop. Mac smiles on indulgently and puts his hand in his pocket at every turn, buying our tickets, paying for tea, feeding the parking meter. It occurs to me with a stab that we must look like a family; Mum, Dad, two kids; it is a forcefully engaging idea; the thought of not being, for once, *alone*.

'We must pay for dinner,' I hiss to Lucy after Mac has presented me with a new Austen biography which had taken my eye in the book shop.

Lucy cocks a cynical eyebrow. 'Good luck with *that*,' she says.

Sometimes Lucy and I walk together, ogling outfits in shop windows (as is our wont), while the men bring up the rear. Sometimes I find myself next to Freddie, charmed by his eagerness to point out things of interest. Occasionally Mac is my chaperone, keeping me to his left, taking my elbow to steer me to our table, putting out a gently restraining hand as we attempt to cross a busy road. I am gob-smacked (also, perhaps, a little suspicious – has Lucy made him read 'Jane Austen for Dummies?') to discover that he is conversant with the entire Austen canon.

'You don't look like an Austen aficionado,' I remark.

'Looks can be deceiving,' he replies.

Lucy had been right, I think to myself, at Christmas, when she said I hadn't given Mac much of a chance. What other opportunities have I let slip by, I wonder, in these last lonely years, in pursuit of a hopeless dream?

Lucy wants to make an entrance for the dinner so she brings her clothes and make-up to my room and we get ready together, leaving the men to shift for themselves but with strict instructions to be ready in the hall at the appointed time with our coats.

'Oh,' she says, over her shoulder, as we mount the narrow stairs, 'and, naturally, we'd like a cocktail while we dress.'

'They won't really bring us one, will they?' I ask, a little awed. Freddie and Mac's sheer amiability is beginning to seriously impress me; the way they had loitered, without a glimmer of complaint, while Lucy and I tried on shoes; Mac's willingness to retrace three miles of dual carriageway so that Lucy could buy some Jerusalem artichokes from a road-side stall.

'Of course they will,' she laughs.

I have brought the silver dress with me – as much to show Lucy as to wear – but she insists that it will be perfect for the restaurant and thankfully it is none the worse for being scrumpled in my weekend bag.

'Are you sure it won't be too much? Aren't we just going to the village pub?'

'Ah, Mother,' Lucy sighs, towelling her hair, 'how little you know of Mac and Freddie. I predict a minimum of one Michelin star. Mac's probably had to bribe the Maître d' to get us a table.'

'Oh dear,' I smile. 'I think they're a bit out of my league. You mustn't let your poor old mother hold you back.'

201

She gives me a swift, fierce hug, then. 'You'd never do that.'

There's a knock at the door and two gin and tonics are handed in.

'Isn't this fun,' Lucy says, clinking our glasses in a toast. 'Like a double date!'

'Don't be ridiculous,' I retort, slipping the dress over my head.

I know what she is up to.

I search myself for a tremor of betrayal. After all this dress was bought for *him*. But I find my conscience is clear; I have wasted enough time on him. Whatever opportunity there might have been has been squandered, but *this, here*, is within my grasp. The gin – or something – ignites a tiny flicker, a frisson, in my belly.

Lucy does my make up for me, and blow dries my hair ('Loving the new style, Mum,' she says) and fills me in on the gossip from the office, her flat-mate's latest crisis, endless trouble with her little run-around. Almost every sentence is punctuated with 'Freddie thinks', or 'Freddie says', showing me his omni-presence in her thoughts. Happily she makes no enquiry into how the weeks have passed in my life since we were last together; I do not under any circumstances want to open up that can of worms; this alternative is far too pleasant.

At the appointed hour Lucy makes her grand entrance, descending the stairs with theatrical aplomb, and Freddie is sufficiently loquacious in his admiration to satisfy both of us. I scurry down after her with as little fuss as possible, am folded into my coat and hurried out to the car which Mac has waiting at the gate with its engine running. The restaurant, as predicted, is a very classy affair with obsequious waiters and heavy damask table linen and eye-popping prices. Mac is made much of and ushered to a sequestered table where the chef-patron (of TV fame) comes out personally to make recommendations and take our order. Lucy catches me in the act of trying to collect my jaw from my lap and we dissolve into a fit of inappropriate giggles while a po-faced sommelier comes with complimentary Kir Royales and suggestions from the cellar.

I repair to the lavatory to compose myself. Lucy follows close behind.

'Who *are* these people?' I ask her, 'I mean, am I missing something? Are they famous?'

Lucy smiles, delightedly. 'They associate with famous people all the time – you should see their client list, Mum. And of course,' she pauses to apply more lipstick, 'they're wealthy, which always helps. But the main thing is,' she turns and runs her fingers through my hair, settling it back into its style, 'they're just very, very *nice*. I mean genuinely kind, good, decent men.'

'And they've taken you up,' I murmur, almost to myself.

'They've taken *us* up,' she qualifies.

Food arrives – although I do not recall having ordered – wave upon delicious wave of delicacies, and I manage – with difficulty – to present an approximation of someone who eats out in places like this every week. Mac is an assiduous host, topping up our glasses, enquiring after our comfort and enjoyment. He occupies my whole vision; my eye is drawn, like a magnet, to his genial, open countenance, dark, alluring, brown eyes, a small cleft in his chin, good teeth. He smiles with his whole face.

The tremor in my belly is expanding, shooting quivers of excitement outwards, upwards, down. It has a life of its own. I take a quick peep beneath my napkin, almost expecting to see a dull, reddish glow through the material of my dress.

'Dropped something?' Mac enquires.

'Oh, no,' I blush.

Freddie and Lucy leave the table to dance on the stamp-sized square of parquet. Without the distraction of their company I have to drag my eyes

203

off Mac and take refuge in a survey of the room. The restaurant is pure 1930s and peopled by E.F. Benson characters; heavy-jowlled Brigadiers and buck-toothed Bishops, wafer-thin women with brittle smiles and out-sized, multi-chinned matrons encrusted with ancient gems.

'It's nice to see the home crowd in,' Mac remarks. 'Usually you can't move in here for Americans.' His voice has a particularly attractive timbre which I try, but fail, to identify; deep and dark without being at all gruff. Velvet? Chocolate?

'So if you do buy the cottage, these people will be your neighbours,' I smile. 'How do you think you'll fit in?'

He shakes his head. 'Not well. I'm new money,' he says. 'I expect they'll black-ball me.'

'Surely there'll be *some* in-comers,' I say, craning my head. 'What about that chap over there, in the loud shirt?'

'The one with the monocle?'

'No, next table, the one with the Simian companion.'

He frowns. 'You do have an odd idea of the kind of person I might like as a friend, Molly. I seem to recall you tried to palm me off with some wholly inappropriate types at Christmas.'

I laugh. 'The bridge widows?'

'And the brass-rubbing lesbians!'

'Oh no,' I demur. 'Not *them*, at least.'

We sip our wine. 'I probably ought to apologise,' I say. 'I wasn't very friendly at Christmas. If I'd have known what was in the air,' I indicate the two love-birds, 'I would have been a bit more forthcoming.'

Mac shrugs. 'I just assumed you were spoken for. But, interestingly, Lucy says not.'

'Oh. I....' I am very tempted to tell him the truth. 'But even so, for Lucy's sake, I should have...'

Mac leans towards me. 'I wasn't interested in Lucy and, as you can see, Freddie can shift for himself.' He gives me a very direct look. I can hardly meet it. A small valve in my solar plexus gives way and there's a warm, syrupy flood in my pelvic organs. 'Perhaps you *were* spoken for, but Lucy didn't know,' he speculates.

'Perhaps,' I murmur.

'But now it's over?'

I nod, glassily. 'I think it is.'

He takes my hand in his, and raises it to his lips.

'Good,' he says. Just that.

And I am absolutely smitten.

After dinner we move to the lounge and drink cognac, and the vapour of the strong spirit lifts me until I think that I am afloat, only half corporeal, carried on some diaphanous cloud of dizzying desire. This, I decide, is how Cinderella felt when the fairy's wand had done its work. I am transformed, charged, a corpse brought back from the dead.

Back at the cottage, though, he and I are left with the dull embers of the fire, and the shrill squeals of laughter from the other two as they romp in their room above our heads brings me sharply back to earth. From being thin, and heady with theory, the air in the room feels oppressive with the awkward incongruities of rusty mechanics. The iridescent bubble bursts with the midnight chime. Because I am nervous, I witter inconsequentially about inanities which I can tell half amuse and half annoy him. I am waiting, in sick dread and also in breathless hope, for him to make a move, telling myself in the same sentence that it is impossible and also imperative. I am only Molly, after all, prim and provincial and this kind of thing doesn't happen to women like me.

Why would he?

When will he?

If he does, I think, I'll slap him.

If he doesn't, though, I'll scream.

Since that moment at the table my whole body has been coursing with electric currents of desire and anxiety, skin a-fire, my short-circuiting brain sending sparking waves of charged pheromones hurtling to long-dormant receptors in areas of my body I have forgotten that I possess. I have all the breathless, trembly symptoms of a sixteen year old virgin, an incapacitating sense of gauche, angular greenness underscored by a rabid, wanton impatience for the voltage of his touch. Where, I wonder, is the seasoned, sensible 49 year old I am supposed to have grown into? Suffice it to say that she is lamentably absent; I am over-come, undone, and, all at once, I have gabbled my goodnights and made a dash for the stairs, leaving Mac behind me – bemused? Amused? I have no idea. I only know that I have to get away before I explode.

Later, more calmly, in my room, stripped of my dress and make-up, showered and restored to some semblance of normality, I stand for an extended period of time in front of the long mirror with all the lights unflatteringly a-blaze for a much-needed reality-check. I am nearly fifty years old and although the swimming and a healthy diet and my recent weight-loss are all pluses, the negatives far outweigh them. My hair is grey. There are permanent creases around my mouth and my brow is furrowed. The skin of my neck has a mottled appearance. I have good breasts but they are decidedly sagging. My stomach is pouched and stretch-marked. Recent depilatory efforts have been somewhat piecemeal, it would seem, resulting in pubic mane it will take a lion-tamer to subdue. There is an area of skin on my inner thighs which is puckered and laced with purple thread-veins. I have an ugly bunion on my left foot. What, I ask myself, would a man like Mac – an attractive man, an interesting and intelligent man, a prosperous man – want with a woman like me?

I sigh and get into bed. I have allowed myself to be toyed with, I think, crossly. Schmoozed. I have mistaken his natural gallantry for a more particular attention.

But all night long, I am listening for his tread on the stair.

The next day I deal with the rabbinical pubis but I don't apply any make-up. Over breakfast I absorb myself in the Sunday papers and then take Lucy off for a long walk while Mac and Freddie prepare lunch. After lunch Lucy and Freddie begin to pack their things – they have theatre tickets for tonight and need to leave by three. Mac is to drop me at the station for my train and I spend a long time wandering round the garden trying to get a signal for my mobile so that I can see if there's an earlier train that Lucy can drive me to catch. In this way I avoid Mac for most of the day until we have waved the children off and are left alone by the gate. Then my composure, sternly summonsed up and given a pep talk to equal Henry V's on the eve of Agincourt, deserts me in droves, leaving me only with a hollow, bowel-clenching panic.

The path by the gate is made narrow by unpruned rose bushes and I cannot move without brushing against his body, a prospect only the thought of which threatens to render me instantly down to hormonal soup. So I stand like an idiot, unable to speak, unable to meet his eye but staring stupidly at the path, at his feet – large, and shod in expensive leather brogues – until the fixity of my gaze is helplessly obscured by tears. One of them drops, a glassy pearl, and lands with a splat on the toe of his shoe.

Then he hands me his handkerchief. 'It's always hard to see them off, isn't it?' he says, kindly (he could, with some justification, I think, upbraid me for my rudeness, for my recalcitrance the night before. Hadn't he bought a little gratitude, he might say. How much did it cost, these days,

207

to get a pouched, raddled, middle-aged widow into bed?) His kindness makes it harder for me to maintain any sort of grip on myself.

'I'm..... I'm....' I stammer out.

'I know,' he says, and takes my face between his hands, 'I am, too.'

I hardly know the woman who goes back into the house with Mac and as the afternoon and evening wear on she becomes less and less known to me; metamorphosed, the wide gaps in her small experience filled up, her lacks abundantly supplied. As food and wine follow tea, and the fire is rekindled in the grate, and as evening closes in, the train un-caught, the beauties – and the unarguable imperatives – of human desire are revealed to her at last. He discovers her, inch by inch – blind to the raddles, the pouches, the sags and furrows, and under his approving eye and appreciative hand she is reconfigured, cell by cell, with newly-forged, conductive connections pulsing life to organs which have been desiccating for want of use; synapses snap and sizzle and shower sparks across the hearth-rug. At last, as languid as a bee in honey, the black-and-white uniformity of her narrow understanding is re-projected across the low, fire-dappled ceiling in rainbow hues of shimmering, tolerant grey.

Later, when I come back to myself, I will wonder at it all, and half believe it was a fantasy summoned up by the drowsy thrum of the wheels of the slow, Sunday train; that I heard only the roar of the express as it buffeted past and the cry of distant whistles in far-away tunnels, and that the ache in my body is the combination of draughty platforms and the crippling curl of train seats designed to suit the ergonomics of the average dwarf. I pinch myself, and palm myself off with explanations such as these, because it seems impossible that such a thing could really have happened to me.

Combe Close: Mock Orange

I remember that luckily, when the Council engineer called round the following week, Stan was out and Julia was in. I don't know if it was even legitimate for the Council to be called to a shrub in a private garden, do you? I suppose Stan had just called in a favour, or thrown his weight around at the Town Hall. Anyway, the engineer surveyed the surface drains in the Close and declared them to be free of impediment. He examined the slight crack in the pavement and expressed doubt that it was caused by the Mock Orange's roots. But he had been asked, by the householder, as a favour, to remove the bush and was well up for it until Julia sailed out with her deeds to prove to him that *she* was as much the owner of it as anyone, and to send him away with a flea in his ear. We stood together on the lawn as his van pulled away.

'Did you know about this, Molly?' Julia demanded imperiously.

'Stan mentioned something. I honestly didn't think he'd do anything about it, though. He's worried the roots might be undermining our foundations,' I replied, miserably.

'Stuff and nonsense,' Julia fumed, 'it would never even have been planted if there had been the least risk. Architects do *know* about these things, you know.'

'*I* don't want it taken away!'

'No, I know, poppet. Stan's had a bee in his bonnet about this plant from the beginning, hasn't he?'

'It's what he does, I'm afraid, makes mountains out of the silliest molehills...'

'Well,' Julia sniffed, 'we'll have to have it out, once and for all. Gerald and I will call round, if you don't mind, before supper.'

When Stan got home he was in a towering temper. No doubt his friend the engineer had been in touch to complain about the fool's errand Stan had sent him on. My stomach had been churning all afternoon in anticipation of the scene which I knew was inevitable. I had called Carla to fill her in on the details and to ask if she would have Lucy over for tea with Sophie. 'There's no telling what he'll do,' I concluded, grimly.

'My goodness, what an *ogre* you make him sound,' Carla laughed. 'Send Lucy over by all means, before Stan chops her up into pieces and bakes her in a pie!'

'Julia and Gerald are coming over,' I gabbled as Stan strode into the house, 'to talk things over. They're *sure* there's no problem with the foundations, and so was the engineer.'

Stan flung his briefcase into its cubbyhole under the stairs and yanked at his tie. 'That isn't the *POINT*' he snarled. 'Do you *still* not get it?'

I opened my mouth and then closed it again. That was a rhetorical question, I realised.

He stepped towards me, across the carpet, until his face was right in front of mine. 'The *point* is, you stupid woman, that it isn't *their fucking tree*. It's *OURS* and if we want it cut down *they* can't stand in our way!'

'But Stan,' I stammered, considering the phrases 'I don't think you're right,' and 'I think you're wrong' and rejecting both as equally incendiary. 'Julia and Gerald don't seem to think so,' I muttered, lamely. 'Anyway, when we all get together over the deeds, I'm sure we'll all agree.'

Stan blanched, a little. 'They have their deeds?'

'Oh yes. Julia had them, today. Haven't we got ours?'

'No.' From being white, Stan's face had gone dark. 'The Building Society has them.'

'Those plans you've got – aren't they deeds?'

'No. They're builders' blue-prints.'

'Isn't that the same?'

He gave me, then, one of his most withering, reptilian looks, and left the room.

Julia and Gerald arrived about half an hour later. Stan was upstairs, changing, and even though I called him a number of times, failed to make an appearance for so long that I had to offer my guests some refreshment. This, I knew by now, was a favourite ploy of his. He liked to keep people waiting. He liked to give the impression of being too busy on *much more important matters* to be able to spare them any time. Ideally I should have kept them waiting in the hall, feeling like awkward trespassers on his valuable time. Inviting them into the lounge, which I had done, would smack, to Stan, of craven capitulation. Even as I drew the cork from the bottle (we did not, in those days, keep spirits in the house) I knew with a terrible, sinking certainty that my hospitality would be heavily frowned upon as a gutless pandering to the enemy. We all sipped our wine. Gerald clamped his un-lit pipe between his teeth. Julia blew her nose into a man's handkerchief. I wallowed in a wretched morass of embarrassment and awkwardness and sadness which had, at its centre, a hot flame which I identified, with a shock, as hatred for Stan, that he should put me, and these poor, lovely, harmless people, through such a trial.

Eventually, I heard his footsteps on the stairs. We all stood up. Gerald cleared his throat and put his pipe away. Julia clutched a sheaf of documents to her capacious bosom.

'Will you have a glass of wine, Stan?' I enquired in a faltering voice.

'That would hardly be appropriate,' he said, archly, proceeding to the dining table and taking a proprietorial seat. 'As I understand it, this isn't a social call.' His comment was calculated to put the rest of us in the wrong. Gerald and I put our glasses down, exchanging shame-faced looks of commiseration. But Julia, a better man than either of us, held on to hers and bore it before her, like a ceremonial chalice, as she followed Stan through the archway.

'What else could it be, my dear man, than a social call?' she boomed theatrically, pulling out an adjacent chair and easing herself down on to it. 'Good Lord, this is just a little misunderstanding. We'll have it cleared up in a jiffy. Come on, you two, and sit down.'

Gerald and I scuttled through and took our seats. Julia spread out her papers, a half dozen or so double spaced sheets in legalese and an outline plan of their property, cross hatched and colour-coded. 'Now,' she said, 'I think this will make things clearer.'

'I'm *quite* clear, in my mind,' Stan said, darkly, but he pulled the pages towards him.

'What *my* understanding is,' Julia said, 'and I think I'm right in saying, Gerald is in agreement...'

'Oh yes, *quite* right,' Gerald put in, restoring his pipe to his mouth.

'... and what's more, what seems to be confirmed by the relevant clause in the deed, is that it's an unequivocal fact that the shrub does, or at least is supposed to, demarcate the *shared* border between your plot and ours in a scheme which, by right of covenant, disallows any fence, hedge, gate or boundary marker to be erected in, across or around the front landscaping. See, here it is.' She pointed to the relevant paragraph.

Stan perused the pages with fussy attention to detail while we all waited in breathless anticipation. Finally he sat back and pushed them away. 'I can categorically state that I have no intention of erecting a fence,' he declared, as though that was the main point at issue.

'Of course not,' I agreed, feeling that I ought to say something.

'No, alright,' Julia nodded, 'perhaps that's something of a red herring...'

'And we resent the inference,' Stan pushed on, capitalising on her admission.

'Alright, yes, quite. Withdrawn.'

'Quite withdrawn,' Gerald seconded.

Julia regrouped and made another sally. 'But the *positioning* of the plant – that point I stand by absolutely, and I think it's at the crux of the issue. It's in the middle, and, as such, we must both agree before any remedial action is taken.'

'I dispute that it's in the middle.' Stan leaned back in his chair and folded his arms. Something in his demeanour told me that he had us right where he wanted us, on this point. In an effort to evade anyone's eye, I drew one of the pages towards me and made my eyes scan the verbiage.

'Do you?'

'Yes,' he nodded. 'I believe that it's wholly and entirely on my property.' He stretched his lips around an unpleasantly unctuous smile, 'And that being the case, I believe that I have absolute say over what happens to it.'

'It's *supposed* to be in the middle,' Julia asserted, but with a tremor of uncertainty in her voice.

Stan actually laughed. 'That's as may be. But it isn't.'

'Well,' Julia sniffed, and made recourse once more to her handkerchief. 'If that's the way you want to play it, Stan, it's easily determined. Gerald – fetch your tape measure.'

Gerald rummaged in his jacket pocket and brought out a large retracting tape measure. 'As a matter of fact I brought it along with me, just in case.' He placed it significantly on the teak veneer of my dining table. He and Julia exchanged a look. Clearly they had anticipated this development. We all looked at the tape. It was large, of what I would call commercial or even professional quality, and appeared to be brand new. It had, as it sat there before us, all the latent significance of a pregnancy test or a telegram; the potential to change everything for ever.

213

Julia sighed and threw me an apologetic look. Then she stood and zipped up her body-warmer with a firm, decided gesture. 'Excellent,' she said, briskly. 'And while we're out there, I think we should also check the siting of the rear fence. I've always felt that there's some inaccuracy in its positioning.' She fixed Stan with a gimlet eye. 'Shall we?'

I looked across at Stan. His face was an unreadable mask but his upper lip was beaded with perspiration. His eyes flickered wildly from one indeterminate point to another; he looked like a cornered animal. Julia's neck and chins were mottled with red blotches and they quivered with barely suppressed emotion. Next to me, Gerald gnashed his pipe stem.

'I can't help thinking,' I said, into the pregnant silence which denoted the stand-off, 'that, in some ways, we're missing the point.'

'Oh yes?' All three of them looked at me, all, I realised, desperate for some way out of the uncomfortably tight spot we had manufactured for ourselves.

'Well,' I said, pointing to a paragraph on one of Julia's documents, 'I'm no expert of course but this phrasing seems contradictory; how can the bush *denote the boundary* on a piece of land which, by right of the covenant thingy you mentioned, Julia, *isn't allowed to have a boundary put in, across or around it?* And this cross-hatching here, across the whole area of the lawn, if you look at the key underneath, it says 'in common ownership, nos 4 and 6'.'

Gerald fiddled to get his spectacles out of their case. 'By jingo! She's right,' he said at last. 'That seems to clinch it.'

I thought Julia was going to cry with relief. Stan shifted in his seat. I raised my eyes to meet his. Hanging in the balance between us was the trade off between the front lawn and the back. He would accuse me, no doubt, of selling out to the enemy, and I anticipated ramifications to come, but five minutes in the back garden with Gerald's inarguable tape measure would land us, I thought, in even deeper waters. I pleaded with him, silently, to take the compromise I was offering.

'I'll have that wine, now,' was all he said.

When I came back with a glass and the bottle, the tape measure and the documents had all been cleared away.

'In the light of developments,' Julia was saying, 'I think it only right that we should both have our foundations surveyed, just in case. And naturally, we'll share the expense.'

'Oh yes, I think so. Wise precaution.' Gerald nodded emphatically.

'I'm sure *you'll* know the man to do it, Stan?'

'Oh yes, of course he will,' Gerald assented, 'nothing surer. Man in his position? Bound to know the right chap. Leave it to him! He'll sort it. Safe pair of hands and all that.'

The remainder of that incident is marked out in my memory by two separate but equally significant developments. After Julia and Gerald had made their departure, I went into the kitchen. Since Stan never cooked and rarely contributed to anything in that room, I did feel that it represented 'home ground' for me, and I instinctively took up a defensive position there, preparing a hasty supper. If I had hoped that he would not beard me there, however, I was disappointed. He followed me in.

'I had to do it, Stan, you know that. There were bigger issues at stake,' I said, pre-emptively, shredding lettuce with shaking hands.

'The back garden?' He gave a bark of derisive laughter. 'I told you at the time, I *showed* you, for God's sake, that the fence had been put in the wrong place.'

I had my back to him, but I could feel him, the hectic warmth of his body close behind me, his hot breath on my neck. I found myself pressing against the work-top so hard it was beginning to hurt. 'I know that's what you wanted me to believe. Perhaps you believed it yourself but...'

'Believe?' He roared so loudly that my instinctive reaction was to duck, so that I banged my head on the wall-cupboard in front of me. 'It's a case of geometry, pure and simple!' he went on.

I began to cry, partly from the pain in my head but mainly from fear. I was frightened of him, I realised, and the truth of it curdled the wine in my empty stomach, soured everything, in fact. 'But Stan,' I sobbed, as I felt it all ebbing away from me, 'this is our home. These are our neighbours.......'

I turned to him, then, hoping, I suppose, to convince myself that I was wrong about him, that my feelings were just an irrational over-reaction to the trauma of the afternoon and the evening which had just passed, and to appeal, as well, to whatever remnant of humanity I hoped I might see in his face. I saw none, absolutely none. His eyes were as dead and cold as marbles and I can only describe his expression as murderous. The anger saturating the air around us was intolerable. I wanted to do something – anything – to incarnate it, even if it was to materialise as violence.

'If you were so *sure*,' I goaded, 'why didn't you just go outside with the tape measure?'

You read about people being 'swollen with pride' and 'engorged with lust' don't you, but take it just as a figure of speech. But I watched Stan, during the next few moments, literally suffuse with anger. He reared up in front of me so that I was pressed back against the counter-top, his livid face right against mine, his chest swelling and swelling, pushing against me so that I could hardly breathe. A vein in his neck pulsed like a purple worm under his skin, his forehead bulged and in the white of his eye I saw a tiny capillary erupt and flood his eyeball with blood. His hands, gripping the work-surface on either side of me, were shaking uncontrollably. I really thought that he would explode, that some over-loaded internal mechanism would detonate him into a fit, a heart attack, a stroke. It seemed impossible that his frame could sustain whatever cataclysmic phenomenon was taking place.

I am ashamed to say that at moment, whatever it was, and whatever its outcome, I would have welcomed it.

But the event was never to come to its natural conclusion. The loud click of the front door and heavy footsteps along the hall and Carla's cheery 'Hellooooo' caused an instant deflation in Stan. He took a step away, releasing me from the prison of his arms. His high colour faded, the throbbing artery in his neck subsided, the circumference of his chest resumed normal proportions. It was quite uncanny, the speed of his rehabilitation, and I almost doubted that the foregoing episode had actually occurred, until I saw his hands, in his pockets, now, but still trembling, slightly. As Carla entered the kitchen, and helped herself to the last glass of wine from the bottle, some light of humanity rekindled itself in Stan's stony eye. It was remarkable the restorative effect that she had on him, like a balm, she simply soothed his angst away. Within two minutes he was leaning affably against the breakfast bar while she regaled him with some story or other. The only revenge he took on me was to push away the plate of supper I put in front of him some fifteen or twenty minutes later.

'Oh, not for me, thanks,' he said, coldly. 'I've already eaten.'

I had time, over the next few days, to make some sense of that evening. Stan was away and Lucy was also absent for a few days on Brownie camp. I avoided my bench on the lawn; for the time being it was in some way tainted for me, that place I had so loved, now the ostensible source of such myriad unpleasantness. And, in any case, I wanted to be on my own, to think.

The first thing I had to come to terms with was the new depths my feelings for Stan had fallen to; hatred and fear, and although, in the calmness of the days which followed, I was able, to some degree, to excuse or at least explain them in a general way it was inescapable that, for those moments, I had tasted them, as bitter as gall. They sounded bleak, sour notes in the concert of my marriage, so much more difficult to get past than those which had gone before. I was used to a mildish sense of irritation at being set tasks that were impossible from the start; last minute calls for a certain suit to be dry-cleaned, or a sudden imperative hankering for some obscure foodstuff which would send me out to scour the borough for retailers who stayed open late at night. I had often caught myself, recently, feeling hopeless, or even, in some indefinite way, doomed. And yes, at times I had felt intimidated; his increasing irascibility over quite mild infractions could be daunting. We had had a terrible scene, for example, over a silk tie which I had inadvertently washed along with the rest of the laundry because it had been wrapped – I would almost say *hidden* – in the folds of a shirt. Apart from these occasions I was conscious of a general tone of ennui at a burden which must be borne; the need to *manage* Stan. But fear, fear of physical harm, that was a new and deeply unsettling development. And my sensation of hatred, though brief, like an icicle plunged into the gut, had shocked me; I had not known myself capable of it. I told myself sternly that I would have to be more careful, guard against the occasions which gave rise to such feelings, be more diligent, a better wife.

The second aspect of that unpleasant evening was far more difficult to fathom and lay, in any case, out of my control. It was this: the uncanny effect which Carla had wrought on Stan that night; her arrival had signalled a complete and astonishing change in his demeanour. It was almost as though she had waved some magic wand and transformed him from a vicious, club-wielding beast to the closest approximation to a Prince that Stan could manage. I thought back over the innumerable occasions when I had been glad to hand him over to her cheerful, no-nonsense hands, been relieved to hear her bright laughter chase away his darkness, to hear her 'Oh Stan, thank goodness you're here. Could you be a darling and help me with this?' and to think to myself, 'that's *him* settled. *Now* I can enjoy myself.'

But in freeing myself for that short time of the trouble of him, what greater trouble, I wondered now, had I been storing up?

And now I began to make the connection between those times that Stan had spent with Carla and the worst excesses of his carnality. I had misconstrued entirely, I realised, the source of Stan's inflamed appetites; not Katrina, but Carla. Even that night by the pool, I remembered, beyond Katrina's naked body, Stan would have seen Carla, wet to the skin in her skimpy frock and engaged in word-play – or worse – laden with lurid innuendo.

My response to this newly discovered situation was complicated and took me some time to iron out. Whereas I had felt assured that Katrina was out of Stan's reach I couldn't say the same of Carla; not because she was a less attractive woman, but just because Carla's impetuous, blasé spirit might stop her from taking Stan – and his infatuation – seriously; a mistake anyone would make at their peril. Sex, to Carla, was perfectly natural and lots of fun (and this, of course, was in itself a potently alluring characteristic), not something that she could ever imagine getting out of hand. I felt that it was possible that she might unwittingly allow Stan to embroil her in relationship which she wouldn't recognise – until it was too late, or, perhaps, at all - as improper. I began to wonder if Stan had been telling Carla things – private things, perhaps untrue things – about me, to engage her sympathy. I believed him absolutely capable of spinning a classic 'my wife doesn't understand me' line if it was in his interest to do so. And while I couldn't think of much that he could tell Carla that I hadn't hinted at to her myself, I began to query, now, her motivation for those nuggets of advice she had, from time to time, handed out, not to mention the beauty treatments and cast-off clothing. Had they, I considered, been for *my* benefit, or for *his*?

I didn't like the fact that I suddenly distrusted my dearest friend, and resented the wedge that Stan, however unconsciously, had potentially driven between us. And I was jealous; not of Stan, but of Carla. This discovery unsettled me considerably. It was not my husband of whom I was covetously possessive, but my friend. She was *my* friend, not his. I did not like the idea that she might begin to prefer him to me.

At the same time, I envied Carla her easy control over Stan. It made me feel cringingly inadequate. Those hours I had spent bemoaning his behaviour, had she, in her own mind, been thinking, 'you hopeless dolt, Molly. Give *me* half an hour in a darkened room with him and I'd have him eating out of my hand.'

The afternoon that Stan was due back I sat once more on my bench in the sunshine and surveyed the Close, but my vision of it, in every direction, was fissured. Sheila, next door, and Pam, opposite to her, had avoided me since my intervention in their concerns. I struggled, still, to be comfortable with the strange ménage across the Close from me at Gary's house. Stan's dispute with Julia and Gerald had bruised that relationship and now I felt on unsure ground with Carla.

I sat there, the whole afternoon, but none of the neighbours came near.

Combe Close: At Arm's Length

You'll be glad to know that following the debacle of the controversial shrub and its aftermath, the next period in the Close passed more calmly for us all and especially for me; I allowed the intensity of my initial dependence on the neighbours to wane and was much less pro-active in seeking their company and in organising get-togethers. Perhaps the slightly more arms-length interaction we achieved was more normal; we became less of a commune and more of a community. I missed them all, I missed the sense of being at the hub of something sociable and affirming, but I recognised how close I had come to having it all blow up in my face.

Pete continued to work as hard as ever but he rented an office above a hair-dressing salon on the parade of shops opposite to the children's school so that he was more successful in keeping what began to be called, around then, a work-life balance. Even so, Pete had, very reluctantly (he said), to give up the amateur dramatic group for the time being. So far, Pam gained her point, but, as far as I know, Pete never did go for the snip.

Pam put her problematic toddler into the nursery which was attached to the school and started going three days a week to help Pete with his paperwork and to deal with callers when he was out. With Quentin off her hands at least for part of the time, and more time both to herself and with Pete, Pam regained her former sanguine nature and lost some of the weight she had put on during the time of her great unhappiness. They were both as friendly as ever towards me but mainly too busy running the boys to football or cubs or music lessons to have much time to chat.

Sheila also resigned from the drama group in order to begin coaching the Junior Harriers, into which she had enrolled both her girls who were by then aged 12 and 15. They were away a lot, at meets all over the country, leaving Alan in sole possession of the stencilled and cross-stitched homestead. Sheila was always to be guarded in her manner with me. I suspected her of harbouring a deeply held resentment against me, a fact I found astounding, and, frankly, rather hurtful, but she masked her feelings with her habitual brittle, empty smile. She, too, was always toweringly busy (but never too busy to batik me a wall-hanging, if I needed one).

Gary and Katrina's property development business went from strength to strength and Anya took on more or less full time care for Austin while Katrina went out supervising plumbers and plasterers and showing prospective purchasers round their refurbished properties. Anya was home alone with the child a great deal and I am sure she missed her sister and her husband but she never complained. I continued to spend time with her, but I increasingly found she was not a person whose company was supportable for long periods and in any case I frequently got the impression that my arrival had interrupted some game that she and Austin had been playing and were eager to get back to; there were often semi-constructed forts or railway layouts strewn across the parquet, or all the tinned goods would be out of the cupboards and stacked onto make-shift shelves for a game of shops. I could quite imagine Anya entering into this make-believe quite as enthusiastically as Austin. I thought of them as Hansel and Gretel, those two; innocents left to fend for themselves, and wondered how on earth she would cope when it was time for him to begin school.

Julia and Gerald lost one of their precious Bearded Collies and mourned her as though she had been a child. They buried her in the garden and planted a flowering cherry over her grave, and I often found Julia there, jowls quivering with emotion, and Gerald too, snuffling into his handkerchief, while the two remaining dogs quartered the garden listlessly looking for their lost companion. But come spring Dolly – or Polly, I could never tell one from the other – was in pup again and this time the best bitch of the litter would be kept. The intricacies of Julia and Gerald's financial affairs had been sufficiently untangled by Pete and a considerable sum clawed back from the Inland Revenue and they began to enjoy a species of semi-retirement, taking trips to the country and so on, and between these and dog shows and a few hours work, they were often absent.

The Mock Orange remained in situ on the shared lawn and no surveyor was ever engaged to inspect its possible deleterious effects on our respective foundations.

Marcus was absent also, for long periods of time, setting up a manufacturing unit in the Far East, and, during the school holidays, Carla took Sophie out to visit him, leaving Lucy and I bereft. Apart from that Carla and I continued in apparently steadfast friendship when she was not at her Country Club, but I never confided in her about Stan again and when she asked about him I changed the subject abruptly. A raw, treacherous chasm had opened up at our feet, a no-go area. I am sure Carla was as aware of it as I was. We viewed each other across it warily. I caught her looking at me sometimes with an expression I was unable to positively decode; hurt, suspicion, guilt, confusion. I don't know. She didn't broach the topic, which seemed to me to be more indicative of a secret, not less. Wouldn't you think someone with nothing to hide would have tackled the thing head-on?

Stan travelled rather less but still worked long hours. The by-pass was ploughing its way through the green fields which surrounded the town, and sending out tentacles which would eventually connect up with a north-south motorway and the main east-west trunk road and provide a link to the airport. Stan had been issued with a computer which intimidated and infuriated him by turns. He was constantly turning it off, then quickly on again, to make sure it hadn't lost his precious spread-sheets and memoranda. He was paranoid about breaking it, or losing data on it. Lucy and I weren't allowed to touch it. On Freda's death we had moved Lucy into the second bedroom and he took over the box room as

223

his office. Many an evening he would be closeted up there, arranging never-ending site meetings and then writing up the minutes of them while I sat downstairs alone.

For all his belief that he was so wily and clever, he made a poor job of hiding his penchant for Carla, dropping her name into our conversation with insistent regularity, positively quizzing me, at times; had I seen her? What had she said? Was this her recipe? Would she be dropping round? On the rare occasions when we were all in company he would watch her from under his beetling brows as she served drinks or laughed at someone's joke. Sooner or later he would pounce, and she would engage in conversation, just as she always had. His face would take on a flushed, eager expression, and he would lean in close to her and speak into her ear as though the room were crowded and noisy, even when it wasn't. I even saw him take her arm and steer her out to the patio or through to another room, on the pretext of needing some private concourse. At these times I noticed her take a fleeting look over her shoulder, a gesture I chose to interpret as an attempt to reassure herself that nobody was watching. Once or twice I made myself catch her eye; I don't know why. Stan's marked partiality for her wasn't very flattering to me but my feelings for him were at such a low ebb by that time that it scarcely mattered. I suppose I just wanted her to know that I had seen. The look she returned to me was inscrutable; I couldn't read it. She didn't blush, neither did she smile, but she held my eye until he had steered her from sight in a way which suggested powerful sub-text. The neighbours seemed wilfully blind to it all and privately I upbraided them for their determined attitude of laissez-faire.

But, since that evening when Julia and Gerald had come round, there had been a kind of truce between Stan and I. His ravening sexual appetite – or, perhaps I should say his demands that I quench it – had diminished. Of course I wondered, pondered endlessly, with very conflicted feelings, if he had found an alternative outlet, but apart from the examples I have given you, could find no evidence of it.

As a huge concession he allowed me, that September, to enrol in an Access course at the local College which would refresh my A levels and qualify me, theoretically, for University. I was reading; devouring books from the library and from Alan's collection, everything from Smollett to Follett, writing essays and presentations for our seminars and thoroughly enjoying my college days. I was one of the few mature students but the teenagers good-naturedly included me in their social circle and took me with them when they went to the cafeteria for lunch. They ate chips and I ate salad and listened in shock and awe as they described their brutal feuds with their parents, their interminable dilemmas over fashion, their constant fallings in and out with various friends, their Saturday night Cider binges and especially their promiscuous encounters. Often I itched to give them motherly advice but instinctively knew that to do so would signal the end of my inclusion in their group, something I wanted, on balance, to avoid. I was lonely without my Close friends. The society of these youngsters provided a sort of placebo.

Stan never asked me about my studies or showed any interest in my results.

That year, the children wanted to attend the bonfire at the Scout hut so we had to forego our usual gathering with sparklers and slices of Parkin in the Close. Our Christmas get-together was cancelled when one of Pam's boys went down with Chicken Pox (all the children caught it anyway and so did Gary, who was actually quite poorly with it). We had New Year at Gary and Anya's house, Gary still crusty with calamine lotion, but our numbers were swelled by their friends from elsewhere and although the entertaining was on a lavish scale, it was somehow impersonal and unsatisfactory to me. When midnight came I don't think I was the only one to keep a careful eye on Pete and Sheila, but they exchanged hugs with no more or less cordiality than the rest of us. I watched Carla and Stan too. In such a crowd it had been more difficult to monitor Stan's alcohol consumption and he was flushed and wild-eyed by then. He made

225

a bee-line for Carla but then it was time for *Auld Lang Syne* so I lost sight of them both as Marcus swept me into the circle.

It was a mild winter so there was none of the usual snow-man building or trips into the hills with toboggans. Easter was early and wet, so the Easter egg hunt was something of a wash-out. Stan and Lucy and I went away for Whitsun – that, I think, was the holiday when Stan grew his beard – and then I had my head down revising for exams so that it was summer again and the Mock Orange heavy with waxy white flowers, and I sat underneath it and lamented that in the year which had passed we had enjoyed none of those informal, hilarious games evenings, those impromptu Saturday night cook-outs, no languid afternoons by Pete and Pam's pool, no day-trips to the coast for roller-coaster rides and ice cream. The constant interaction, the comings and goings, the droppings in and poppings out which I had so enjoyed had virtually ceased. It saddened me to think what riches had been squandered. Perhaps, I thought, despondently, nice *and* good just weren't compatible.

Combe Close: The Fun House Party

As far as I can recall – isn't it odd, how the years meld into each other? – things in the Close continued in this low-key vein for a further two years. We had our moments, but they were in some way muted; there wasn't the openness – perhaps I ought to say the trust - there had been, our numbers were often augmented by interlopers from other circles which made the sense of intimacy less. Maybe this was a good thing. In any case, I know that I was more reticent; less willing to assume that everyone would have the same standards as me.

The children grew, of course, and took to playing out in the Close at weekends and after school if it was fine. They, at any rate, seemed unaware, or unaffected, by any currents of tension which might have existed between their various parents. The little posse was soon deserted, anyway, by Sheila's girls, as they became proper teenagers, more interested in shopping and boy-bands than in hanging out on the Close. Pam's two older boys were happy to take responsibility for the younger ones and led them on expeditions along The Crescent and forays onto the golf course to look for stray balls or other plunder. There was a little stream which ran along the periphery of the course and the lads liked to fish in it in the summer and pull semi-decomposed, malodorous objects from it in the winter. Lucy and Sophie tended to watch from the sidelines although once or twice they did come home soaking wet and filthy dirty, but in general I had no anxiety about Lucy when she was out and about with the boys and I believe that Pam and Anya were happy to know that Austin and Quentin would have the girls' sensible eyes upon them.

We had continued to share the school run but things were due to change in the year which I am now calling back to mind. That coming September Pam's second son Stuart was to join his brother at the High School, Sophie was (to Lucy's dismay) to start at an expensive prep school some way out of town and it seemed to me, that as they began to go their separate ways we, in the Close, were threatened with losing one of the strongest cords which had tied us together. Hadn't I, after all, played an instrumental role in the birth of three of the Close's children? I had always felt that my being on hand during those crucial periods had somehow given me a special status, and although I had never been asked to officiate as God-mother I did consider myself, informally, to fulfil that role for Andrew, Sophie and Austin. The Close children were the closest thing to brothers and sisters that Lucy would ever have; I didn't want her to lose that vital connection which early years establish between children.

So for her birthday that year, her ninth, I decided that we would throw a party. We had endured three years of purdah, I told myself, surely, by now, whatever so-called ungovernable flames of desire had scorched us would have cooled, and, at a children's party, what danger could there be?

Amazingly, in those first three years of frenzied socialising in the Close, Stan and I had never hosted a party. I had had the women over for lunch often enough, and we'd had the neighbours, one couple at a time, to dinner. These modest sorties into the world of entertaining had seemed sensible for us; I was no cook and Stan no host, so we kept things very informal. Even so Stan always dreaded these occasions and made stubbornly little effort; keeping his slippers on, staying resolutely in his favourite arm-chair and allowing me to greet our guests, take their coats and serve their drinks while all the time trying to keep my eye on things in the kitchen. He even insisted on keeping the television on until we moved to the table, I suspect to fill up any awkward silences that might arise while I was out of the room.

'But we absolutely must return people's hospitality,' I would cry, as he threw his hands up in the air and rolled his eyes at the news that I had issued an invitation to this or that couple.

'I'm sure they don't expect it,' he would grumble.

'No, but it's good manners,' I would state, primly.

On this occasion, however, he made surprisingly little complaint when I outlined my plan to him. A day-time party, in the garden, predominantly for the children, with children's party food and just wine or beer for the grown-ups.

'Why include the grown-ups at *all*, if it's for the children,' he objected, but without much energy.

'Carla and I were only saying the other day, it's been so long,' I answered, untruthfully, and left my assertion to do its inevitable work. This was a strategy which I had taken to using whenever I needed Stan to agree to something. It was cynical, perhaps, but it worked. He liked the clothes I bought at Carla's recommendation. New recipes *from her*, even quite exotic ones, were usually acceptable, even though he was in general a plain, meat-and-two-veg kind of man.

Stan's labour on the by-pass had redoubled in recent weeks. By now parts of it were open; the motorway link and the connection to the airport were already carrying traffic. The main portion of it was very close to completion and Stan's department was, at that time, in the throes of organising a grand opening. There was to be a ribbon cut by the Minister for Transport and a convoy of local dignitaries, private hauliers and the press to make the inaugural run before it was opened to the public. Timing the actual completion of the project with the pre-designated date of this event was causing some chagrin. It was a part of the project which had nothing to do with Stan, really, but naturally he loved a crisis especially if it was somebody else's and so there was much gnashing of teeth and hyperbole about shoddy procedures and laughable ineptitude. The problem was not that the by-pass wouldn't be ready on time, but that it would be ready days – even a week or so – ahead of time, but *that*, of course, was strictly 'need to know.'

'We don't want the public finding out,' Stan warned, 'or they'll insist on access.'

'Heaven forbid,' I said.

'I'll need to be available at a moment's notice,' he informed me, pompously, when I reminded him of the party. 'Don't rely on me to even be there.'

'Don't worry,' I said. 'I won't.'

I wanted this to be a really special occasion, mainly for Lucy, of course, but special also in the annals of the Close; something new and different to signify a new era on a different tack to the one which had decimated our company three years before. Lucy's favourite TV programme at the time was Fun House, a fiesta of chaotic games and slithery obstacle courses, and I decided to try to emulate it. I cannot say, now, whether subliminally I was trying to get across the message that wild and even messy fun could be perfectly legitimate if we approached it right. Even then I think I wanted to impose some sugary, sanitised facsimile of real-life onto the inhabitants of the Close

The prospect of Stan's absence didn't throw much of a shadow. That's the kind of detail which, afterwards, makes you feel very guilty.

Lucy wrote out the invitations, careful to specify that adults and children alike should 'wear old clothes and bring a change' and delivered them round the Close. I began to plan the activities, which would involve quantities of goo and water and assorted other paraphernalia. It was ambitious of me but so long as the weather was fine, and the guests entered into the occasion, I thought I'd be able to see my way through. I bought a long length of visqueen from a builders' merchant and arranged to borrow hockey sticks and other bits and pieces of equipment from the primary school of which I was, by then, a parent-governor. I started saving up cardboard boxes and other items of trash, and I raided the local charity shops. Lucy and I spent a few evenings making an enormous banner from a redundant roll of wallpaper with the words 'Welcome to the Fun House' emblazoned across it in every colour of felt tip we could muster.

The day of the party dawned bright, dry and warm. Predictably, Stan had to go off for a site meeting. He dashed off even before Lucy had opened her presents. Poor little thing; I will never forget the look on her face. What a hurtful impression it must have left her with.

We got to work on making mounds of sandwiches, sausages on sticks, fairy cakes and all the usual children's party fare. Julia, bless her, came round to help me and I set Gerald to mixing up pints and pints of green jelly that I had made the day before with a bottle of washing up liquid and several tins of peas in a large galvanised bucket. Alan had agreed to come and do some of the manly, outside preparations. He arrived early to string some fairy lights up across the apple trees at the top of the garden and to rig up a music system for me. Pam brought over the birthday cake she had been keeping for me and stayed to help out as well. It was almost like old times. I remember quite distinctly thinking to myself, 'I'll always be able to count on my friends.'

Lucy was in her element, skipping between the house and the garden, playing with her new toys and helping me to set out the trays of water and flour, the ping pong balls and the other gear we would need for the various games. We hung our banner out of Lucy's bedroom window and fixed it with string to the window-catch. Then I went into Stan's study and climbed onto his desk to dangle a length of string out of that window. Lucy fixed it to the banner and I hoisted it up so that it covered the front of the house. It looked splendid. I left her filling half a dozen old Fairy liquid bottles with water while I hurried away to get changed.

There was a super-charged, hectic ambience to the party, right from the start. I know I felt it; a sense of taking a momentous step of faith into the future of the Close. I was holding out an olive branch. My banner might as well have read 'Let's make a new start.' People arrived with a will to enjoy themselves, to throw themselves into the fray. It was as though they saw the afternoon as glowing with portent, as I did. In spite of the enormity of the task ahead of me I felt suffused with a sense of buoyancy and confidence. Nothing will go wrong, I thought.

231

How wrong could I be?

News of the afternoon's activities had leaked out and the children arrived almost sick with excitement; little Austin was pale with it, solemnly holding out a beautifully wrapped parcel to Lucy as though proffering a ceremonial artefact. Pam's two older boys rushed straight through to the garden to survey the stuff for the games. Pete went to join Pam in the kitchen where she and Julia had, to my relief, offered to supervise the catering. He was soon levering tops off cold beers and filching sandwiches from the plates. His big, booming shout of laughter at Pam's playful smack made the glasses in my cupboard rattle and sent little thrills of excitement racing round my solar plexus. Sheila and her girls arrived next, the girls (and, indeed, Sheila) dolled up to the nines in attire wholly unsuitable for the kind of afternoon they were in for. They gave Lucy a make-up set (also, in my opinion, wholly unsuitable, although Lucy loved it). They went through to the garden where Alan was busy hauling the hose pipe to the top of the garden.

Just before three o'clock, Carla, Marcus and Sophie roared up in a new, red sports car – she had got her way at last - which they parked on our drive so as to save time. They leapt out of it, full of apology for being late, but of course every eye was on the splendid new vehicle and I felt a stab of annoyance that they should have drawn all the attention to themselves on what should have been Lucy's special day.

There was no sign at all of Stan.

The games began. One rank of children armed with water-filled washing-up liquid bottles had to rinse off an opposing rank, dressed in bin liners and swimming goggles and covered in shaving foam. The children entered into the activity with whoops of enthusiasm, taking turns to squirt and be squirted. It was clear from the off that the matter of fastest and slowest was going to be academic; nobody seemed to care except the wetter the better and Gerald soon put his stop-watch away. In the warm sunshine the enjoyment of the children quickly spread to the grown-ups. The tone for the afternoon was set. To my delight, and the untrammelled joy of the children, Gary and Pete insisted on having a go at the game. Pete threw aside the bottle and grabbed the hose pipe instead. Carla and Katrina kicked off their shoes and threw themselves into the spray. Anya shrieked and tried to hide behind Julia, who had emerged from the house barefoot and dressed in a capacious safari outfit topped by an ancient pac-a-mac. Alan and Marcus brandished dustbin lids as shields. Before long almost everyone was happily soaked. The children were in their element. The squeals and shouts issuing from our garden must have resounded throughout the Crescent.

We stopped only briefly for drinks before moving on to the next game. Pete, already dripping and stripped to the waist, was in amongst them all, organising the teams. Only Gerald, on account of his heart condition, remained peripheral. Sheila and her girls hurried home to change.

Soon everyone was pasted with flour, twirling round hockey sticks until they were dizzy and then off up the garden in as straight a line as they could manage – not very – where a ridiculous pile of out-sized, oddly assorted jumble awaited them. Watching little Quentin struggle into the 38DD sized bra made us all roar with laughter but not as much as the sight of Pete cramming himself into a pair of fishnet tights.

'This is the best,' Gary guffawed. He had brought his camera and was taking dozens of pictures. 'We've missed all this, haven't we Anya?' Katrina said, adjusting a frilly apron across her bosom. Anya perched a child's sun bonnet on her head. 'Oh yes. Very much.'

Pam brought out jugs of squash for the children, and punch for the grown-ups. 'Lovely party,' she whispered, squeezing my arm. 'Just what we all needed. I think everything's going to be alright, don't you?'

We both looked across at Pete, covered in flour and still wearing the tights over his shorts, mock-wrestling his boys on the grass, and over at Sheila and her girls, who had started on the junk-sculpture activity with Lucy and Sophie on the patio.

'I think so,' I smiled.

Presently Alan and Marcus unrolled the visqueen and laid it down the slope of the lawn almost the full length of the garden. Alan wet it down with water from the hose and Marcus larded the whole thing with the bright green mess of jelly and peas. As I had planned, the detergent in the mix foamed up in the water to make a lurid green lather to equal any toxic-looking goo that the ITV studios manufactured.

Lucy was beside herself with joy. 'It's just like the real thing, Mummy,' she said. She and the other children set about the task of scrambling up the slope to deposit an egg, unbroken, in the box at the top. It was virtually impossible, of course. The adults, hauling the children up the slippery slope, only found themselves pulled onto the treacherous vinyl, slipping and sliding with a delightful lack of dignity to the bottom. We all squirmed and floundered in a mess of flailing limbs, adults and children together, like new-hatched invertebrates emerging from the primal ooze, laughing and gasping and clutching at one another. Oh the mess of green goo and slimy egg! The garden rang with laughter, we were helpless with it, wet and weeping. It was cathartic, I suppose. I was filled to the brim with affection for them all, back in my place at the heart of the Close.

And that's how Stan found us.

He stood for a while on the patio like Banquo's ghost, his mouth opening and closing, looking starched and stuffy and out of place, and I blinked at him a couple of times, willing him to throw off whatever stiff and unyielding carapace it was which kept him imprisoned in its humourless restraint.

'Go and get changed,' I urged, at last. 'Come and join in!'

There was a beat, and then he barked, 'Somebody's parked on the drive!'

Carla struggled to her feet and wiped the worst of the gloop from her face, 'Oh Stan, sweetheart, that's me, I'm afraid.' She looked down at herself, ruefully. Her t shirt was transparent, thick with gunge, her shorts and thighs slick and dripping. She gave that musical, mischievous laugh of hers. 'I don't really want to move it while I'm covered in this stuff. If I give you the keys... would you mind?'

Stan looked at her with a fixed, almost hypnotised stare; his eyes livid with a dark, avaricious fire. The knuckles of his hand were white. His tongue passed quickly across dry lips. One leg, inside its sharply creased trouser sheath, was trembling, slightly.

'Park on ours m'dear,' carolled Julia, blinking through a generous larding of gunk. 'Plenty of room there.'

'By all means,' Gerald seconded.

Stan gave a hard swallow. 'It doesn't matter,' he muttered. 'It'll do later.'

He turned and went into the house but an uncomfortable pall lingered behind him. We all, even the children I think, began to feel, suddenly, very silly and in some way compromised.

'Let's eat,' I cried, a shrill, emotional edge to my voice. 'Have showers if you like, and get changed.'

'I'll just hose 'em all down,' Pete blustered.

I bustled about with paper plates and napkins. The neighbours were all breezy co-operation but it was strained and awkward. The shady garden, ideally cool for our earlier exertions, felt, all at once, gloomy and chill. Alan, sensing it too, illuminated the lights he had put up earlier. They made, I am afraid, a feeble amelioration. The Fun House theme tune which had played all afternoon, energising the children, had become brassy and strident and Marcus changed it for something more laid-back.

Stan did not soon join us and eventually I slipped inside to face him.

I found him in his office. En route I was confronted with the unforeseen fall-out from the party activities; a trail of greenish slime across the carpet towards the cloakroom, gobs of grey, floury mastic adhering to door

235

handles and in evidence on pieces of furniture. The floor in the cloakroom was awash where the children had been refilling their detergent bottles. Stan would have seen it all, I reflected, miserably, as I trailed up the stairs.

As angry as these things would undoubtedly have made him, though, worse was to meet him in the office. A breeze from the open window must have dislodged a vase from the window ledge. His desk, monitor and keyboard were littered with tiny shards of glass. As I entered he picked up the keyboard and cradled it as though it had been the corpse of a tiny child. His face, his lips, even the rims of his eyes were white, emptied of all human pigmentation. Only the eyes themselves radiated with the cold fire of his temper. 'What have you *done?*' he asked in a voice scarcely audible.

'It's just an accident,' I replied, shakily. 'No harm done, I'm sure.'

'No *harm?*' he repeated, his brows furrowed in incredulity. 'How can you possibly know?'

Unbeknownst to Stan I had used computers at college and Alan had let me use his for my essays, on occasion. I pointed to the grey box which stood, unharmed, under the desk. 'All the information's in there,' I said. 'Look. There's no glass at all on the floor.'

'And what the hell,' he shouted, on surer ground, waving his arm in the direction of the garden, 'what the *hell* is going on out there?'

'Please don't raise your voice, Stan,' I pleaded. 'People will hear.'

He glared at me and would have repeated his question so I stammered, 'It's Lucy's birthday party, just party games, but they're all finished now. I've started to serve the food. Then we'll have the cake and everyone will go home.'

'It looks like an orgy,' he roared. 'It looks *disgusting*. And have you seen the state of the house?'

'Yes,' I mumbled. 'It's a mess. But it'll all come clean again.'

He turned to his desk and began methodically sweeping the glass from its surface onto the carpet. I could tell, from the hunched set of his shoulders and the livid colour of his neck, that he was highly charged; whatever happened next was likely to be explosive, and I waited, hardly breathing, for the detonation to issue from the alembic of his warped neurosis. But once he had cleared the desk his voice was surprisingly and unnervingly calm.

'Come over here, Molly,' he said, and it wasn't until I was half way across the carpet that I began to feel the slithers of broken glass under my bare feet. I winced and hesitated, but he was without mercy. 'Come *on*,' he urged, and reaching out, took my arm and yanked me the rest of the way to the desk. Cruel shards of glass impaled themselves in the soft flesh of my sole. I began to cry out but he clamped his hand across my mouth and pressed me backward until I was half way bent over the desk. Then I recognised the look of furious imperative which characterised his periods of unassuagable sexual desire; swollen, dry lips, engorged eye, hypertensive, shallow breathing.

Only a soft knock at the door and Carla's gentle 'Helloooooo! Can I come in?' arrested what I am certain would have been a serious sexual assault taking place right there and then. Stan released me and threw himself across to the other side of the room as Carla entered, leaving me spread-eagled and semi-compromised on the desk. She was quite magnificent, I must say. She must have assimilated the situation in that one fleeting glance but she glided smoothly over it as though it were nothing.

'Oh *there* you are, you naughty noodles,' she cooed. 'Lucy wants to blow her candles out!' She reached out and took Stan's hand. 'Come on,' she crooned. 'You're missing all the fun.' With that she led him from the room. He followed her like an obedient puppy.

When I got downstairs again the visqueen and messy residue of the games had been tidied up and the children were busy building rockets from the accumulation of cardboard boxes and plastic bottles I had been amassing in the garage. Most people were changed and calmly enjoying the last of the food. I lit the candles of Lucy's cake and managed to carry it out, my voice quavering the first notes of 'Happy Birthday to you' until the neighbours lustily took it up. As I had predicted, soon afterwards the guests began to make their excuses and gather their belongings. The late afternoon sun was still bright out on the Close but now the house blocked it entirely from the garden and the few lights in the trees did nothing to dispel the dank pool of gloom.

Stan spent that last half hour or so standing rigidly apart; no amount of the usual cajoling could lighten his mood. He expressed no interest in the gifts Lucy tried to show him and refused both food and drink even though both were repeatedly pressed upon him. The neighbours seemed both anxious and reluctant to quit the scene; Julia and Pam took an inordinate amount of time clearing away the food and wrapping the remains in cling film; Marcus and the other men took pains to hose down the patio and haul the visqueen into the shed. The others, even while clutching their napkin-wrapped cake and carrier bags of sodden clothing and making sounds of imminent departure, yet lingered to encourage last additions to the space rockets and to say again what a wonderful afternoon it had been. I could see them exchanging sidelong looks with one another. Nobody, I realised at last, wanted to leave me alone with Stan.

Then Carla took me to one side. 'I'm taking Stan for a drive,' she said. Her eyes were empty of their habitual sparkle. Her mouth, usually wide and full of smiles, was grim and pursed; bleak with resignation. The look she gave me made a last attempt to cross the no-man's-land which had existed between us for the past two years and I could see what the trespass cost her. Clearly, it was, for her, as for me, a place of ghosts and whispers and shadows.

I wish, now, that I had stopped her. That I had laughed away her offer and told her that it would be fine – it had been before – and that I could handle Stan. But I watched them race off in the little red car, its top down, Carla's golden hair tousled by the breeze, a bright, carefree smile plastered across her mouth and Stan beside her; coiled, primed, and staring straight ahead. They rounded the corner and disappeared from view. Then Alan stepped up and slipped his warm hand into the crook of my arm.

'You're frozen,' he said. 'And your feet are bleeding.'

The police came much later – to Marcus' house first, of course, and then to mine. The car had been found on a prohibited stretch of the new by-pass. Security cameras had picked it up travelling at high speed. Then it had swerved, flipped over and come to rest on its side in the soft soil of the newly seeded verge. The driver had sustained serious head injuries and was unconscious. The passenger had been thrown from the vehicle and found some yards away. He was dead.

Present Day: In the Wilds

Following my tryst in the Cotswold cottage, I bombard myself with accusations; I had been 'loose', 'easy', 'a tramp'. At other times I am positively effervescent with some inner geyser of intoxicating euphoria. I am a woman released, relieved, freed. 'So *that's* what I've been missing!' I say to myself, in guilty, delighted, wicked, astounded awe. Between these two extremes of indictment and exhilaration the workings of my physiology are on over-drive, energised, hyper-active. My guts coil and roil like a basket of snakes, my heart is tap-dancing, my mouth is perpetually dry. I have no appetite. Sleep is a stranger.

I am perilously poised on a high cliff; apprehensive, ecstatic, tangled helplessly in cords of heady, romantic love without a grain of solid foundation to secure them to. I am pole-axed by the body's mutiny against the sensible and protective restraints of the mind.

During those few, fevered hours there hadn't seemed the time, there hadn't seemed the need – there hadn't really seemed even to be the vocabulary – for spoken exchange. Communication had been sensory - skin cells and nerve endings responding in instinctive concert to deeper, unanswerable, primal impulses – and in some profound, mystical way, spiritual. A numinous melding had taken place – a coalescence of the personal, emotional essence. I had given way to the promptings of my body, and of his, and, more than that, I had answered, with the cries of my soul, the cries of his.

What we had trafficked that night had been mutually self-sufficient. There had been no talk of the future, no indication of the from-now-on which would follow. I had broken the restraining bonds, the onerous taboo. As ridiculous as it seemed, for a widow of forty-nine and a mother, I felt as though I had come through some long-overdue rite of womanhood.

But I hardly know the man. Surrounding the cataclysm of our fusion is a void of history, blank pages of biography flap restlessly in my ears even while I thrill and quiver in the recollection of the biology. It troubles me, but not too much. There is time, I think, to redress the balance, and in the meantime a brightly shining beacon of instinct leads me onwards.

When I arrive home, and open the door, that mysterious sigh, the whisking away of whispers, is absent. I recognise it at last as the sound of my own loneliness. A constant ghostly presence, it had lurked in the gloomy corners, hovering just out of view, scuttling into the shadows as I moved from room to room. It had attended me at my single place-setting at the table, impregnated the dinners-for-one with the taste of its sourness. It had cowered under my single sun-chair on the bare square of yard by the bins and trailed behind me in the wash of my solitary swims. It had crept into bed with me at night. It had been my companion, I thought, pretty much my whole life.

Now it is gone. I have made a connection and I am, as I have never been before, complete. In some way that I cannot begin to fathom, my itinerant yang has at last been brought to counter-balance my over-dominant yin; the impulsive, instinctive, spontaneous facet of my personality has come into its own after a lifetime of dominion by strait-laced, over-analytical timidity. I am in awe of this new-found part of myself. It is indeed like discovering a long-lost twin, an essential component without which life had only been half-seen, half-understood, half-experienced, half-lived.

The strength of my new self-assurance banishes for good the bitter echo of my mother's parched, carping voice croaking 'You slut!' and 'Get out of my sight.'

I have only a very few days before my trip to the country and throughout these I am filled with expectation. Moment by moment I expect – something. A 'phone call at the very least, an email, a bouquet, perhaps Mac himself on my doorstep, smiling and holding out his arms. But there is nothing. I pound on the send/receive button by the hour. Eventually it yields an email from Lucy: 'Mac has asked for your email address,' it says. 'Is it OK to let him have it?'

'Oh yes,' I reply, fingers fumbling and stumbling over the keys. 'It is.'

Julia and Gerald's small-holding is reached via a steeply inclining, narrow trail up a kind of fire-break, cut into a dark, sinister coniferous plantation. The heath above is exposed, a broad flank of peaty upland, tufted with heathers and fissured by black bogs, evocatively Wuthering. But their property is situated in a crater-like depression, like a colossal bowl, pressed deeply into the surrounding moor. It is in a micro-climate of its own, contained by the rim of the bowl, which also provides the horizon in every direction, giving the place an oddly unreal, remote, perhaps almost dream-like aura of intense isolation. From no point within the perimeter of their holding can any road, building or sign of habitation be seen – not so much even as a smear of smoke rising from an unseen chimney. Their own rugged, pot-holed track leads down the seam of the depression and, from the time I watch them leave, it is empty of other traffic.

I feel suddenly overwhelmed by solitude, intimidated by the overarching silent sky. It is as though I have been abandoned on the moon. The low moan of the wind above the crater's edge and a single, wheeling, keening bird are the only sounds. In the house, the static of poor radio reception sounds like lost voices light years away.

The muddled collection of farm buildings are all huddled at the bottom of the bowl, as though they have given up trying to cling to the sides and have slipped down there resigned to rest wherever gravity has drawn them. The low-roofed house is whitewashed, with a central porch and entrance giving access to a beamed sitting room. Off this there's a dining room and, through a narrow doorway, a dark, panelled hall with stairs off to the right. Through the hall is the kitchen, a large, practical room with quarry tiles and an oil-fired range cooker, and a sort of study, chaotic with papers and magazines like *Dog Breeders' Weekly* and *Poultry World*. It is all very solid and prosaic, and I pat the rough masonry of the walls with the flat of my hand, and tell myself that I am safe.

A glazed passageway leads from the back door to the outhouses, a motley of single-storey sheds and lean-tos whose original purpose I cannot even guess at but which now house the kennel accommodations for Julia's own Bearded Collie breeding programme and for her paying doggy guests. I venture through them clutching a torch and the poker, unnerved to find occasional pieces of Julia's unwieldy household effects standing incongruously juxtaposed with gardening implements and a long row of coat pegs draped with assorted haberdashery. In the half-light, the impression is terrifyingly like a row of garrotted children.

The passageways go on in a maze-like bewilderment of unexpected openings and awkward corners, little flights of steps connecting their various levels; dark, windowless corridors lined with superfluous pictures and mirrors suddenly opening out into light, bright spaces scrupulously tiled for the preparation of canine comestibles. A cavernous parlour divided by half-height concrete partitions – perhaps a former milking shed? – has been converted to provide large enclosures for the dogs. A heavy, sliding door gives access at last to the outdoors, a wide, secure yard. From here, a fenced track leads off to the exercise paddock. This slopes up and widely outwards in the shape of a fan, almost to the rim of the crater, and incorporates most of the few trees on the plot, a noble stand of Scotch pines, and a boulder-strewn area of ancient quarry from which I suspect that the very stones of the house were long ago mined.

Opposite the house, across a cobbled courtyard, is a corrugated metal barn. Its rusty sheets lift and groan and flap in the wind which chases itself like a restless dog in pursuit of its own tail, round and round the bowl in endless, howling circles. Inside the barn it is eerily still except for the straw on the floor which shifts and rustles and whispers with disembodied voices. Behind the barn are the chicken run and the sheepfold, the oil tank for the central heating and a rusty old generator which, I have been assured, will spark into instant life at the turn of a key.

In addition to the three dogs I have been left in charge of a dozen or so ragged hens, six sheep and the telephone, via which enquiries for kennelling and offers of stud from the owners of boy-beardeds are supposed to arrive. I am deeply distrustful of the telephone, however. The dialling tone sounds like the sizzle of distantly frying bacon. The 'good broadband connection' I have been absolutely promised seems a dim probability. For work purposes this isn't an insurmountable obstacle; for now it is half term and my students are working on their assignments. But, given my personal situation and my daily – indeed hourly – expectation of an email from Mac, it is a blow. The farm feels more and more desolate to me with every hour that passes.

The first night I have hardly the heart to climb to the little chamber at the top of the house which is to be my room. The heavy slate roof seems suddenly to be flimsy protection against the gusting maelstrom of wind. I lie awake for what seems like hours, but in the morning the wind has subsided and the sky is clear. I get up, shower, and dress. I have work to do.

Julia hasn't left me with any kennel tenants, I'm happy to say, other than their own three trusty Collies. I can't tell them apart and take to calling them by the collective pronoun 'girls', a nomenclature they respond to willingly enough. These dogs aren't relegated to the outhouses but lounge around the house, helping themselves to the warmest spot by the fire or the softest cushion on the sofa and regarding me with expressions of offended surprise when I suggest to them that this isn't allowed. They have their own mats, after all, but are by no means disposed to sit on them when more comfortable accommodations are to be had.

From my first hour alone in the house I wage a one-woman war on dog-hair. I know Julia is no slave to housework and I'd expected that there would be some remedial action to be taken to make the place habitable but the full extent of the task has been so far beyond my wildest imaginings that, by day three, I am beginning to wonder if *any* of the kennel dogs ever make it as far as those pristine enclosures but in fact spend their entire holiday here in the house. The floors in the farmhouse are flagged with stone, which is easily swept and mopped, but the occasional rugs are matted with moultings which Julia's vacuum is barely man enough to tackle. Likewise the upholstered furniture is thick with dog hair both where they have been allowed to lie and where they repeatedly brush past. I find balls of fur, like tumbleweed, lurking in corners and under the heavy armoires and sideboards and lying in greyish lines along the tops of the skirtings. I find dog hair felting the curtains and lacing the lamps. All the sink and bath plugs in the house are semi-choked by long, soap-slimy tendrils of dog hair. It forms a composite of the dusty, doggy dander which coats all Julia's ornaments and photographs. I find it in my bedding. I find it in the bath. I find it inside the drum of the washing machine. I even find it in the fridge. This is not to mention the muddy footprints, the bloom of greasy lanolin at exactly dog-height which greys all the walls and furniture, the doggy-nose-smear on the glazed doors or the pungent smell of dog which permeates absolutely everything.

I would not like to suggest that Julia and Gerald don't try to keep on top of things; the sorry state of their mop and broom and the vacuum's exhaustion would indicate that they have been in frequent use. But with *three* such hairy dogs as these, plus interlopers, and with all the work to do around the farm, I am guessing it isn't their first priority and in any case the dogs are so much family, to them, that perhaps they don't care. But I do, rather. I see it as *my* problem, not theirs, and I certainly don't blame the dogs who, after all, are such lolloping, good-humoured, easy-going creatures.

As fast as I am cleaning the dogs are making more mess, bounding around, making feints and lunges towards me as though I am on my hands and knees only to play. Clearly, no amount of cleaning is going to

245

solve the problem while the dogs, the source, are allowed to remain indoors, throwing themselves from one spot to another, romping on the rugs, scratching and licking and shaking. So I start putting them in the exercise yard for quite long periods of the day while I am working. In the afternoons I take them for long walks up the track and through the woods and round the entire perimeter of the farmstead. Then I groom them all thoroughly and I move their mats and bowls to the glazed corridor which leads from the kitchen. They are fed and corralled firmly in that locale until the evenings. Only then do I allow them into the house, by which time they are so exhausted that they can be relied upon to remain more or less in one position.

The process of cleaning and getting things straight is therapeutic, and the routine of the days – cleaning out the hens, feeding the sheep, walking and grooming the dogs – soon blurs into a mechanical, mindless monotony. Alongside the physical excavation of hair and debris, the sweeping and dusting and polishing and mopping, I go over, in my mind, and in the light of my new incarnation, the course of events which has brought me to this pass; my narrow, frowning childhood and adolescence, the initial whirlwind and then bitter doldrums of my marriage to Stan, my hopes for the Close and the manner in which they had all, inevitably, one way or another, failed to live up to my ridiculously green, simplistic aspirations. How shallow had I been! How dull my understanding of human nature! And what one-dimensional people I had supposed them all to be! Anyone would think that I had mistaken Combe Close for Camberwick Green. I think, now, what extra-ordinary patience they all had with me, as I trimmed them to fit my tame expectations and squeezed them into the regular, predictable boxes of my own, restricted vision. Pam had been right – they had mollycoddled me.

In the afternoons, I range across the landscape wrapped up against the bitter interminable wind which seems to be as trapped in this pocket as I am. The delirious dogs romp and run in happy pursuit. The days progress and with them the sky, a high dome above me, a passing projection of weather; sometimes charcoal and boiling with imminent rain, other-times pale and thin, sucking the heat from the ground and leaving it adamantine with ice. Afterwards, as darkness falls, I drink tea and stare into the flames of the fire as a biblical rain pours down or the ice-glazed windows creak and murmur.

My mobile has no signal. The telephone works only intermittently. Broadband is non-existent. There is no sign of a postal delivery. I think of it as a kind of retreat. Against the background of the rain-blurred, amorphous landscape and the diaphanous sky the things of the mind are taking on a starker, clearer-edged focus.

My communion with Mac has made sense for me of the irresistible power of human desire, its urgent imperative. Of course I had known – with a mealy-mouthed, shrinking distaste - the theory of it, but now I comprehend at last the power of the feelings which had drawn Sheila to Pete. I had been naive to think them just a whimsical, thoughtless flirtation. If she had felt, in her body, what I had felt in mine, I had been wrong – very wrong - to interpose my dry morality between them. Add to that, she had had (as I had not, with Mac) prolonged and – thanks to my relentless provision of social events – numerous opportunities to establish a real basis of relationship. I remember, now, they were always in animated discussion, laughing together. Breaking things off must have been like gnawing off a limb. It is no wonder to me that she has grown another appendage and is even now reaching out again, seeking that essential union. I think of her, sobbing helplessly in my arms that day hardly more than a week ago: 'Oh Molly! Oh! Oh! I love him, I love him, I love him....' I hadn't *really* known what love was, then. Perhaps I don't even now. But I understand much better the sexual constituent of it, and I am coming to understand the fine balance of love in its most perfect, most beautiful form; the mind, the body and the heart in equal, reciprocating, harmonious accord. Who, I think, as I look out across the wide, wild moor, has a right to stand in its way?

247

It is such a fine, such a delicate equilibrium, though. Let one component overpower the others, let the poise of the scales over-balance and the result is a twisted facsimile of love; abuse, obsession, rape, emotional blackmail, dragging dependency, overweening control; the kind of warped impulse which drove Stan, that afternoon, to undo his seat belt and lunge across at Carla. He had wanted her for a long time, wanted her very badly. I knew only too well the insatiable nature of his appetite and his capacity for self-deception. He would take her invitation for a ride in the car as a come-on, the opportunity of the deserted stretch of road would have seemed too good to miss. That ravening craving of his *must* be assuaged, the gnawing, the clawing of his inner beast was too strong and he was helpless in its fangs.

I have misjudged Carla, I realise. Probably she had known, all along, the destructive nature of Stan's obsession. While the no-man's-land between us had been characterised, on my side, by suspicion and mistrust, for her it had been about patient endurance and generosity – and all for my sake. At last, I decipher the meaning of Carla's departing expression; fear of what might come, mingled with a sacrificially loving determination to face it. 'Don't you,' she had said to me once, in relation to her fling with Marcus' brother, 'do anything for the people you love?'

As night falls I battle my way against the biting wind, or through the deluge, or across the frozen wastes of the yard, to the area behind the barn. I have had a world of adverse meteorology in this isolated globe of mine – this lonely hollow of earth and the overarching vault of sky. The hens are already in their house, shuffling and fluttering a little as they settle for the night. One evening I glimpse a fox, furtive in the long grass at the end of the field, predatory, stalking, and it comes to me that Stan must have been the same, prowling round the Close at night, peering in at Carla through the bright uncurtained windows of their lounge. I batten down the hatches for the hens and coax the sheep into their little shelter with a rattle of the food bucket. A couple of hay bales and a metal gate across the entrance will keep out the weather. I send the dogs out to scour the field and see off the fox.

One morning, the sky is swollen and so low it almost seems stretched across the bowl like a skin across a kettle-drum. The air is eerily still, as though waiting, and there is the unmistakable tang of snow. In a panic I start up the car, and hare up the rutted track, my fingers fumbling with the clasp of the gate which keeps the small-holding enclosed and the world at bay. The little town is grey and almost deserted and I have to fight weird feelings of being in a dream – of being insubstantial, a ghost – as I hurry from the car park to the shops. I buy milk and bread and the least wizened-looking fruit and salad stuffs from the scantily-stocked green grocery shelf of the sorry little supermarket. Addressing the cashier I almost expect her not to reply, to look through me. My voice sounds peculiar, exchanging laboured pleasantries; I haven't used it, I realise, in over a week. On impulse I ask her if there's a cyber café in town. She looks at me as though I have asked for a massage parlour or a lap-dancing joint.

"Ere?' she queries, moving her gum from one side of her mouth to the other. Then an idea dawns – I watch it as it slowly illuminates her dark intellect to a dull glow. 'There's 'puters in't library,' she says.

'And where *is* the library?' I ask, slowly.

'Up street. T'other side o' t' car park,' she intones.

The library, like the rest of the town, is deserted. The gargantuan librarian indicates a row of computers in a draughty corridor without looking up from her Mills and Boon and I log into my email account. I dash off a quick email to my students and one to Lucy explaining why I haven't been on line while the bing-bong of messages landing in my in-box sends my blood pressure sky-rocketing. Outside, though the high, grimy windows, the first flurries of snow begin to fall.

249

There are three of them, separated by spam and students' assignments and trivial notifications from on-line shops, the first sent on the afternoon of the day of my departure, the second a day or so later and the third only this morning.

'Is there a printer?' I yell, heedless of library protocol.

The librarian waves the other arm in the direction of a gloomy alcove and barks '20p per sheet.'

I hit 'print' without opening the emails, listening for the whir of the printer. But the last – the most recent one - I do open; it contains only four punctuation marks. I press 'reply'.

I am marooned on a remote small-holding I type *while its owners are on a cruise. Communication with the outside world is very sporadic. Blizzard conditions imminent.* I hesitate, type *please send rescue without delay* and then delete it again before finishing *I will reply properly when I am able. Molly.* I add *X* recklessly and press 'send' before I can change my mind.

The streets are already slick with snow as I run to the car, and the winding, little-used lane up the hill has become quite treacherous. The wipers go ten to the dozen, compacting the large, fat flakes into a thick shelf along the bottom of the windscreen. I almost miss the turn up through the woods, come skidding to a stop and end up slewed across the lane. The wheels spin, trying to get a grip, then I'm bounding up between the trees. It's still reasonably clear of snow, here, but preternaturally dark. Out on the cusp, the boom of the howling wind hits me as I get out to open the gate. The snow is already as deep as the lowest bar; I can feel it round my ankles. Above me, the sky glowers purple with its unshed weight. Beyond me, the moor rolls into the blizzard, thickly frosted, smooth and deceptively benign. In front of me the track down to the farmhouse is only barely discernible in the enveloping smog of thick, woollen white. Even from here, up the amphitheatre of the crater, I can hear the dogs barking. I edge through the gate, shut it securely and begin the jolting descent. Down in the hollow, through the swirling maelstrom of eddying flakes, the house looks cold and small and unspeakably bleak. But when I arrive at last at the front of the house, there's a car in the yard and a figure sheltering in the lee of the barn. He steps forward as I climb out of the car. We look at each other as the snow billows around us and my past and present collide.

'She's gone. And I'm here,' he says, his voice unnaturally charged and strangely projected across the space between us, as though we are actors speaking words in a play.

My line escapes me, although I have rehearsed it a thousand times. Eventually he gives me a prompt. 'Shall we go into the house?' he asks.

'Oh, yes,' I falter. 'Come in, Alan.'

Combe Close: Tiger in a Cage

The pool party hadn't been quite the beginning of it but it was a significant moment. In describing all these things to you it seems clear to me that even on the occasion of that very first party, the night of Stan's disgrace, Alan had revealed himself as something of a hero, escorting me home and whispering, on the doorstep 'You'll be alright?' It seems to me quite likely that in a subliminal way I was conscious of him right from that moment; a benign, watchful presence. It forged, I think, the first, tentative connection. At the pool party he had reached out to me, seemed to share with me my brief moment of blessing and had taken the time and trouble to help me understand the curious arrangements of Gary's ménage. Because that evening proved to be so momentous in other ways, I think Alan's actions, that night, welded him into my consciousness of its noteworthy significance.

After Stan's death the neighbours couldn't have been more supportive. All of them, even Marcus, who had, from then on, his own terrible cross to bear, rallied to support Lucy and I in our loss, but it was Alan, especially on the day of the funeral, who remains in my mind like a guardsman on alert, a safe sentinel, always at my elbow to pass a clean handkerchief, to add or dispense with a jacket, to let me know that this or that person needed my attention. Pam and Julia stayed behind at my house to handle the refreshments for the funeral tea, the rest of them filled in the rows at the crematorium, swelling the woefully small numbers. Lucy and I sat at the front with a distant cousin, Stan's only other relative, an angular, socially awkward woman with a dreadful squint and appalling halitosis. Mr Abel and a bare handful others from the Traffic Management Office attended along with Bernard, brought back from retirement for the occasion. Their wreath, if you can believe it – I scarcely could – had been made to resemble a traffic light. Mr Abel offered his condolences with a limp, fish-like handshake. Three or four people variously affiliated to the by-pass project arrived at the last minute, their shoes filthy from the morning's site visit. A man in a shabby Macintosh and a scruffy tie who I did not recognise turned out to be a reporter from the local paper. He circulated after the service making obsequious notes of people's names and pumping them for information about the circumstances of the accident, particularly the identity, and Stan's relationship with, the lady driver of the vehicle. Alan bent and said something in a low voice and I didn't see the man again.

I had been firmly discouraged from visiting Stan in the chapel of rest. Reluctantly the funeral director admitted to me that in the process of being thrown from the vehicle Stan's head had become detached from his body. Throughout the service I wondered, with a vague, inconsequential interest, whether they had tried to reattach it in some way or just chucked it into the box with the rest of him and screwed down the lid, a procedure, which, I thought, on the whole, would rather irritate Stan.

After the service – very brief and impersonal – everyone repaired to the house, their faces a study of fixed, grim determination, as though this were an ordeal like a court appearance or a root canal filling, which just had to be borne. Julia and Pam – bless them – had prepared enough food to feed three times as many mourners. Sophie, at Lucy's special request, came across to join us, and the two little girls sat in solemn but mutually supportive silence side by side and held each other's hands. Poor Sophie, she was in as much shock as Lucy; Carla was still in hospital, unconscious, her prognosis as yet in some doubt.

After what seemed like an interminable time, people began to take their leave. Pam took Lucy and Sophie home with her while Julia finished the washing up. I went upstairs for a rest. When I came downstairs only Alan remained, in vigil.

I know that, to the reporter, the neighbours were tight-lipped and defensive about the details of the accident. His article, in the following week's paper, was brief and barren of any salacious import. Carla was described as 'a close friend of the family' and their joy-ride along the barely completed by-pass had become 'a routine tour of inspection.' What the neighbours, privately or collectively, thought about it all I never knew. I liked to assume that they were genuinely shocked, surprised and unable to account for the peculiar circumstances of the accident. On the other hand it's possible that they berated themselves for allowing Carla to take Stan off in the car that day, knowing - as I did not, then - the usurping power of sexual impulse, the way it could silence reason and break the chains of social restraint.

The neighbours never referred to the accident to me – or, I presume to Marcus – as anything other than a terrible tragedy. Only Marcus and I attended the inquest and neither of us ever mentioned the paramedic's euphemistic reference to the state of Stan's clothing; 'in some significant disarray.' The Coroner's verdict of death by misadventure exonerated Carla of any crime. I am sorry to say that for a time I was unable to share the same view. I couldn't get out of my head the idea that on their ill-advised jaunt along the deserted tarmac they had indulged in furtive glances and sordid fumblings, that Stan, in his pent-up urgency, had guided Carla's hand to his crotch. I speculated that she, with that roguish nature of hers, exhilarated by the speed of her new car and the thrill of the empty, unrestricted highway, and given her notoriously carefree attitude to sex, had complied with his urge to the detriment of her concentration on the road. At my lowest ebb I found those old suspicions reawakened – that she and Stan had been involved for years, that the neighbours had all been in some way complicit and that none of them had had the balls – as *I* had, for Pam and Alan - to step in. At those times I conveniently forgot Carla's last, bleak expression as we parted company on the drive and I construed the neighbours' tireless visits and offers of assistance as gestures of guilty restitution.

I'm glad to say that this unhappy response lasted no longer than Carla's stay in hospital – which was, however, of a not inconsiderable duration. When she came back to the Close, a wan, pale reflection of the old Carla but still, then, recognisably the same person, I was happy to hand over the mantle of chief sufferer to her, and to join the others in supporting her as and when I could. She was underweight, and often very tired. Severe headaches assailed her at the site of her injury. She was sometimes a little absent-minded but then she always had been a bit unpredictable and prone to sudden impulses, so we didn't think anything of it. To all intents and purposes she was adorably the same jocular, whimsical, charismatic Carla. She purported to remember nothing at all about the accident or indeed anything about the entire day which had preceded it and insisted that her first recollection was of a 'George Clooney look a-like, oh my God Molly, you should have seen him, gazing down at me. I thought I'd woken up in an episode of ER. I could have cried when I realised they'd shaved my head. Can you imagine what a fright I looked?'

In the end I chose to think of the escapade in its most charitable light, as an intended act of kindness on her part; that she had had the idea that if she took him off for a while it would give me time to clear away the mess of the party which had clearly irritated Stan so much, and I left it at that.

My shock at Stan's death had been immense but as the severity of it lessened I found that my grief, beneath the shock, was not profound, and in some ways I became almost glad of it. Pete and Alan, in a co-operation which would have been unthinkable six months earlier, took upon themselves the sorting of Stan's financial and legal affairs (I had completely forgotten that at the time we had taken out the life insurance policy we had also made Wills naming Pete and Alan executors). It gave me pleasure to see them with their heads together, consulting documents and arranging meetings at the bank. Pete expedited the payment of the life insurance money and advised me about investing it; 'to provide an income, my lovely. If you're careful you'll never have to work a day in your life.'

Sheila seemed inclined to bury the hatchet, after Stan's death. She invited me to go to Aquarobics classes with her, two afternoons a week, which I found I thoroughly enjoyed. I suppose it was this which led to my love of

255

swimming, so I owe her that. In a huge gesture of good-will Sheila included Pam in these occasions also, healing up, to all appearances, the rift in their relationship. Sheila was also kind enough, from time to time, to ask Lucy and I round for tea with the family. The older girl had already left home to attend University but Lucy enjoyed hanging out with the younger one doing 'big girl' stuff - flicking through magazines, playing music and experimenting with the clothes in the wardrobe - and so I generally accepted these invitations. Sheila and I would never be close friends but I took her acts of reconciliation at face value. Often, having eaten, she would have to dash away to a training session or to measure up for someone's curtains or to deliver stock to one of her agents (she had, by this time, risen a considerable way up the party-plan pyramid). At first I took her departure as a signal that Lucy and I should leave, but then Alan said to me, as I went to call Lucy downstairs, 'do you *have* to go, just yet?' and so I began to stay on, for a while.

With the reinstatement of cordial relations in the Close, and Carla out of danger and back home amongst us, and after a respectable period of mourning for Stan, we recommenced our social activities. We kept them low-key and very informal.

'Come and have pot-luck on Saturday, I've a glut of strawberries needs eating,' Julia might coo over the fence, 'pass the word along. Everybody's welcome.'

'There's a big match next week. Pete's invited the blokes over,' Pam would wheeze between gyrations in the pool. 'I don't see why the girls should miss out, do you?'

'Molly, do you know what 'Raclette' is?' Anya asked me once. 'No, neither do I. Only Gary's bought a machine. Will you come and try it with us? I'm asking everyone. Hopefully *somebody* will know what we're supposed to do.'

We gradually eased ourselves back into our routine of regular get-togethers, marking off the calendar together; Shrove Tuesday, Easter, something at Whitsun to herald the start of the summer, a walk and a picnic over August Bank Holiday, Halloween, Guy Fawkes, Christmas and New Year, interspersed with special birthdays and spur-of-the-moment gatherings. One way or another it worked out that we found ourselves sharing a glass of wine or something to eat every four or five weeks and although I enjoyed the cosier afternoons or mornings I spent in between with just one or two of the others, I found myself looking forward to the comprehensive assemblies with real eagerness. They were becoming, even then, the peaks which enlivened the general low-land of my widowhood.

In time I was to add to them the annual Combe Close holiday. Lucy and I tried holidaying on our own, with varying success; beach-type holidays bored us both, we found British camping nothing short of penal whilst European camping challenged our Entomophobia to its breaking point. Cultural tours turned Lucy into a frowning, foot-sore misanthropist. In the end we signed her up for an annual school-organised holiday and settled for a week with our neighbours in a country house. They all enlisted in the scheme enthusiastically enough as long as I did all the organisation. Whether they felt sorry for me, or were still dealing with guilt, or genuinely looked forward to it, as I did, I don't know.

Two, perhaps three years rolled by. They were peaceful and uneventful years and I wasn't unhappy; just vaguely dissatisfied, with a feeling that I had missed out on something. I was mournful, but not for Stan. Regardless of the warmth of my welcome when I arrived, I didn't like setting out to events on my own, or that achingly forlorn moment when I would have to separate from my friends and take the lone path home. I tackled this formless, hollow sensation by trying to fill it up with busyness and in fact I assuaged it somewhat in the exercise of my new autonomy. I commenced a programme of refurbishment in the house, tearing up the hateful carpet which Stan and Freda had foisted on me and replacing the cheap, old fashioned – and, incidentally, excruciatingly uncomfortable –

257

lounge suite. I got used to making decisions on my own, or with Lucy, but did not hesitate to call in one of the neighbours if I felt I needed help. Katrina put me on to a decorating contractor and I had the anaglypta covered in warm, earthy shades. Marcus helped me come up with a design for the back garden, with some manageable borders and areas of practical hard landscaping. Alan finally built the long-promised barbeque with the bricks Stan had dug out of the garden ten years before and Julia helped me establish hardy, shade-loving plants in the beds. I found I thoroughly enjoyed spending time outdoors. I continued with my Governorship of the primary school even when Lucy left it to begin her career at the local secondary. From being a rather mediocre performer she began to shine in mathematics. I am notoriously awful with numbers and when she needed help with her homework it was Alan that we tended to turn to.

In fact, because of his proximity, or perhaps because, of all the neighbours, he was the least encumbered with supernumerary family responsibilities (the second girl had just embarked on a gap-year expedition to South America), or just because he showed himself to be so very happy to fulfil the role, Alan became my first port of call in any kind of need. He could always fix things or offer advice. And it was Alan who encouraged me, around that time, to apply to the local University to do my degree. My Access course results, combined with my old 'A' levels, were more than adequate academically, but he gave me, with his quiet support, the confidence that I needed to take the step. Once I had started, he was avid to know what texts I was studying, listened rapt while I read out my papers and could usually come up with an obscure piece of literary criticism to reinforce, or to challenge a line of argument.

I began to find, almost imperceptibly, that Alan, never the largest personality in our group, had, in my mind, stepped out of the shadows. From the comfort of knowing I could call on him if I needed to, the instinctive sense in any dilemma that 'Alan would know', he became a sort of champion, a real boon. I was nothing short of blown away by his competence, his quiet wisdom, his endless patience; his diametric difference to Stan was as refreshing as a sea breeze. I was grateful to him, of course – he had, after all, been wonderful in a hundred small but significant ways. I revelled in the kindred interest that we had in literature. I liked his dry, sometimes acerbic wit. The genuine kindness in his eye comforted me. But there came a point when these natural and, I think, wholly legitimate reactive responses to his kindness underwent a significant change. I found that I was becoming *proactive*; looking out for his car on the drive so that I could tell him about the mark for my latest essay; engineering a seat for myself next to him at the dinner table or on a sofa; seeking him out at parties to regale him with some academic anecdote I thought would amuse him; coming out with literary witticisms, which only he and I would understand. I wanted to provoke his slow, slightly uneven, quirky smile and when I succeeded I was conscious of a deep, thrilling satisfaction which would buoy me up for days. I was flirting.

The unwelcome truth crashed in on me one night at Gary's. We had had a huge dinner in celebration of something. As usual wine had been poured with a liberal hand. It was a dinner *party* as opposed to the less formal catch-as-catch-can type of evening, and we had all dressed up. I was wearing a low-cut, sleeveless dress (even that, I realised, in retrospect, had been chosen to please Alan. Carla had helped me choose it for a Mayoral reception I had attended with Stan a few years before and her effusive approval 'Look at you! Sexy lady!', although laughed off at the time, had always stuck with me). Our places at the table had been pre-determined (cards in Anya's round, immature hand) and I had found myself opposite Alan towards the bottom of the room. I had been talking with animation about a particularly avant-garde production of *Marat Sade* that I had been to see with my fellow students the previous week, when I looked around to find that everyone else had left the table apart from the two of us. My description faltered to á halt.

'Where's everyone gone?' I stammered.

259

Alan smiled. He had a way, I noticed, inconsequentially, of lifting one side of his face in an expression of ironical amusement. 'They've gone into the other room. About ten minutes ago. Didn't you notice?'

'I've had too much wine,' I blushed. 'I must have bored them all silly.'

'Not at all,' he demurred.

I don't know what came over me, then – a sort of rush; heady, devil-may-care. I reached for the wine bottle and emptied the rest of its contents into our two glasses. Alan looked taken aback but then leaned back in his chair and placed his hands behind his head, waiting to see what would happen next. He was surprised, I think, but not discomfited.

'Do you think we ought to join the others?' I asked, in a low, silken voice I hardly recognised; I had turned, in an instant, into a Siren.

'Oh yes, probably,' he replied, but made no move other than to lift his glass and sip his wine.

'I don't think I want to,' I said, my voice, by now hardly more than a whisper.

'Tell me more about the play,' Alan said.

I leaned well forward onto the table, knowing full well that this would give Alan an ample view of my cleavage. I rested my chin on one hand and with the other hand reached across the table to toy with a shred of ribbon which trailed from the table decoration. It is difficult to conceive of a more coquettish ploy. With hindsight it was laughably unsubtle but I was in the grip of a sudden wicked rebelliousness. Alan's eyes widened for an instant and then he whipped off his spectacles and commenced an assiduous programme of polishing.

That's how Sheila found us, a few moments later. She stood on the threshold of the room as I spoke a sentence which ended with the words 'inciting the audience to sexual acts.'

'I came in to blow out the candles,' she said, having taken in the situation at once. 'Perhaps you'll do it, when you're finished.'

The recollection of it, the following day, was painful, and I spared myself no castigation for my appalling behaviour. I was shocked at how easily I had drifted into an insidious position, astonished and rather disgusted with myself, to tell the truth, that I had not only developed but also acted upon a decided preference for a man who was patently and unarguably off limits. I recalled how I had hauled Sheila over the coals for precisely the same offence (the words 'blind and reckless selfishness' came stingingly back to mind). In addition to being thoroughly ashamed of myself I was also seriously hung-over but I forced myself out into the garden even though it was raining, and spent the day turning over the compost heap and raking up leaves as a punishment. Later, after a hot bath and what Lucy and I had begun to call 'sofa supper' in my pyjamas (how my mother – not to mention Stan - would have disapproved of such slovenliness) I had an early night, but not before I had given myself a severe talking-to and determined that I must absolutely ensure that I never did anything so wicked and irresponsible ever again.

I declined the next invitation to tea round at Alan and Sheila's house and refrained from asking Alan's opinion on my next assignment. When Lucy got stuck with her Algebra I sent her round to Alan by herself. At the next gatherings I allowed myself no private conversation with Alan and did my utmost to make sure that we were not seated together at meals. When he dropped round with books, or just to see if everything was OK (a habit he had got into), I pretended to be 'just on my way out', or 'rather in the middle of something.' All these gambits he took, as he took everything, calmly in his stride.

I swam for miles, up and down the pool, studied hard and redoubled my involvement with the PTA. I haunted the houses of the other neighbours and shut my lips whenever Alan's name came up.

Of course it was absolutely hopeless. The less I saw of him the more he was in my mind. I developed a kind of emotional radar for him, instinctively registering the sound of his car on the drive, noting a square of light on their lawn which indicated that he was busy in his office. At weekends my ears were alert for the sound of his mower, or for the whirr of his drill in the garage. As resolutely as I kept myself out of his way, a sixth sense monitored his movements. I could always pin-point his position in a crowded space even as I planned my own circuit of the room to avoid him, and I recorded, almost subconsciously, who he spoke to and for how long, which sweater he was wearing, whether he had had – or needed – a haircut. I came to know the scent of him – a particular brand of soap; I inhaled it, greedily, one evening at their house, like an addict snorting cocaine. My ear was attuned to his voice; even while ostensibly listening to somebody else I honed in on the timbre of it, catching snatched phrases of his conversation and gathering them in like precious nuggets of contraband. I watched and listened with an oblique, involuntary assiduousness, and learned his preferences for food and drink and music. He liked camembert but not brie, preferred Shiraz over Merlot, thought John McLaughlin a better jazz guitarist than George Benson. I found he liked to be the boot in Monopoly and Professor Plum in Cluedo. His favourite Monty Python sketch was *The Cheese Shop* as opposed to *The Dead Parrot*. He had a little depression, an old piercing perhaps, in one earlobe, and a double crown, which explained the endearing cowlick which grew over his forehead when his hair got long.

I never allowed myself to touch him – even the perfectly legitimate bodily contact involved in passing food round a table or squashing into a taxi. I almost thought that if I permitted my hand to brush his arm or our fingers to touch, even for an instant, some seditious spark would leap out, a blue, contagious volt, the dark current of my desire made manifest. It coursed around me potently enough whenever he was near, and at night, between sleep and wake, my imagination pursued fantastical lines which left me hot and breathless, and wanting, with a sharp, intimate ache.

Christmas, Easter, Whit. Another year rolled over the Close. And then another. Lucy, aged 14, had and lost her first boyfriend and was earmarked to take her maths and physics GCSEs a year early. Gary finally left the Estate Agency and devoted all of his time to the property development business. House prices were due to rocket, he said, and it was time to cash in. Julia's bitch won 'Best of Breed' at Crufts and she was inundated with requests for puppies. I completed my second year at University and was approached by my Professor with the offer of a research post leading to a PhD to commence immediately after my finals the following year. I was desperate to tell Alan my news privately but I kept myself in strict check until I could announce it publically, at a time when his undoubted hug and kiss of congratulation could not compromise my sangfroid.

Pam and Pete's oldest boy left school with good 'A' levels and began his dilatory attempts to get into the music business by practicing day and night. His nearest sibling left school without any qualifications at all and promptly got involved with a shady gang of bums and ne'er-do-wells who took to hanging out at Pete's house in the guise as 'roadies' for the older boy. The tortured clamour of agonised guitar strings from their house, and the frequent nocturnal comings and goings of motorbikes and pizza delivery vans was a constant annoyance. Pete and Pam were full of apology. Pam took on that harassed, doughy look again. I watched carefully but could see no signs that the affair between Sheila and Pete had been reignited.

I wrestled, daily, with my nemesis, yearning for Alan and rebuking myself for yearning. I suppose I experienced something of what it is to be a reformed addict; wanting something, with a fierce and unquenchable desire and yet denying oneself with an iron, sometimes even destructive determination. It is no wonder to me now that all those rehabilitated alcoholics and drug-addicts wear such wan, haunted expressions. It is a terrible battle that they wage, each and every day.

Alan and Sheila celebrated their twentieth wedding anniversary with a party at the local tennis club in the year to which my memoires have now brought us. That evening is marked out in my memory for three distinct but equally dreadful reasons. We all attended, of course, in our finery. Alan stayed by Sheila's side as they received their guests and an assortment of china figurines and porcelain ornaments which I imagined would be judiciously disposed of, at a profit, by Sheila when the dust had settled. We in the Close had taken the 'china' theme more figuratively and booked them a banquet at a fashionable and expensive Chinese restaurant in town.

'I think it's a great idea,' Carla had chimed, when I had suggested it.

'And at least she won't be able to sell it on,' Pam had muttered, stumping up their share of the cost.

Organising their gift, and picking a romantic and effusive card had been another tool in my arsenal of self-discipline which was supposed to arm me against swingeing assaults of conscience. Likewise I dressed myself for that evening with great care and went out of my way to dance and have a good time. I thought my face would crack with the effort of maintaining a carefree smile and my supply of hyperbole almost ran dry as we agreed again and again what a lovely couple Alan and Sheila were, how happy they made each other, how well suited they were, what an ideal family they had....... But watching Alan, as I couldn't help doing, from the corner of my eye, plotting the course of his progress around the room in order to stay one step ahead, eyeing the way his hand rested in the small of Sheila's back or took her elbow, admiring the smooth line of his jaw, the impeccable cut of his suit, the flash of a (new) gold watch from beneath the crisp cuff of his shirt, his easy smile and the hospitable way his gaze, from time to time, scanned the crowd to check that everyone was enjoying themselves, I found myself plunged into an abyss of hopeless misery. Later, as they made speeches ('he really is the most lovely, kind and wonderful man', 'she's a fantastic woman, boundlessly energetic, very creative. I'm a very lucky man'), toasted each other in champagne and danced to 'their' tune (Eric Clapton, *You look wonderful tonight*) I wanted to howl with abject despair. In spite of all my efforts I felt my eyes fill with tears. I was in love with Alan and there was no point in denying it. I had fought against it in vain; my tactics of avoidance, my frenzied programme of study, my punitive attempts to exorcise my feelings out of existence had been a complete failure. I stared it in the face, there in that hot, noisy, smoky room. However I might attempt to discipline myself, whatever the strength of my willpower, no matter what strategies I employed or with what vehemence I might chastise myself again and again, the truth remained; I could on no account control my heart. My tiger was born.

Carla, at my side, took my hand, thankfully misconstruing the cause of my sadness. 'How long would you and Stan have been married?' she asked.

'Erm, sixteen years,' I mumbled, working it out on my fingers.

'We're the same!' she exclaimed, as though our cases were exactly similar and I was not condemned (and at her careless hand, I thought, bitterly) to a lifetime of arid widowhood. 'And by the way,' she went on, with one of those conversational leaps she was prone to these days, juxtaposing disparate subject matters into the same sentence, 'did I tell you that we're moving?'

'*Moving?*' It was the second cataclysmic shock of the evening. I thought my heart would break. 'Where to?'

Marcus shot me an apologetic look and, taking Carla's hand, gave it an admonishing shake. 'We were going to tell you privately, Molly. We knew you'd be upset.'

The tears which, until now I had managed to keep balanced on my lower lashes, spilled unchecked down my cheeks. The prospect of the break-up of the Close was too much, after all I had done, all I had sacrificed, all I *would have to* sacrifice, in the light of my earlier revelation, to keep it together. The idea of Marcus and Carla, even this altered Carla, living elsewhere, somewhere I would not be able to see them, and strangers coming in their stead was like a violation. I rummaged fruitlessly in my bag for a handkerchief. Someone behind me passed me theirs and I turned to say thank you to find Alan hovering at my shoulder. The shock was enough to stop my tears.

'Thank you.' I mouthed, and turning back to the table repeated my question: 'Where to?'

Carla named the village, forty minutes drive or more from Combe Close. 'You know I can't drive anymore and Marcus just can't manage the school run for Sophie,' she said, briskly, totally caught up in the practicalities of her own situation, as though we had not been friends for all those years, as though I had not been the one to find her in labour, as though she had not been privy to the most intimate details of my life. 'It's too much for him. So this way we'll be much nearer the school and Sophie can get the bus.'

'I see,' I sniffed. 'I can see that will be much easier for you, Marcus. But won't you.... won't you *miss* us?'

'Oh!' Carla laughed. 'We'll make *lots* of new friends.' Her coldness astounded me.

'I'm sorry, Molly,' Marcus said again. 'We didn't want you to find out this way.'

I scanned the table; Gary, the twins, Julia and Gerald, Pete, Pam. None of them had evinced the least surprise at Carla's news. 'They've kept it from me,' I thought, angrily, and felt, all at once, betrayed.

Just then the music changed tempo – a slow number.

'Come and dance with me, Molly,' said Alan, and against all my self-imposed rules and restrictions, I took his hand and followed him onto the floor.

As if that evening could have got any worse, when I got home, in the small hours, I found all the lights of my house ablaze and the two girls, Lucy and Sophie, cowering under a blanket on the sofa. They had insisted that they were too old to need a babysitter and could look after each other. Marcus and I had agreed to give it a try, and they had been left, on their best behaviour and as a special privilege, with stringent instructions as to what was and was not allowed, and the contact number of the tennis club in case of need. There was a strong smell of disinfectant and air freshener but it could not mask the underlying reek of sour beer, cigarette smoke and vomit. They stammered out their sorry tale. The boys from across the road had come over; they had brought the beer and smoked the cigarettes. They had persuaded the girls to smoke as well – that's what had made them so sick. The boys had tried to get the girls to go upstairs with them ('into the bedrooms,' Sophie gasped, round-eyed with horror,) and when they had refused the boys had raided the drinks cupboard, poked around in the drawers and threatened to make off with some few jewellery items. It wasn't until Lucy had picked up the telephone to call the tennis club that they boys had laughingly made their exit.

'We've known Colin and Stuart all our lives,' Lucy sobbed. 'How could they have been so horrible?'

What could I say? Just then I was in absolute accord with her sense of betrayal.

I stared past her into the Close. Other cars were arriving. Soon Marcus would be here to collect Sophie. The whole sorry business would have to be dealt with tomorrow, the two lads made to apologise, another fissure in the disintegrating fabric of our neighbourhood to be shored up. But what was the point? Marcus and Carla's departure would be the thin end of the wedge, I predicted. What would it matter if we all fell out?

Later that night, with Lucy asleep, I kept vigil at the window, looking out at the peaceful, slumbering houses. A light was still on at Alan and Sheila's. I imagined them reliving the success of the evening, viewing their presents, taking a last glass of champagne upstairs, making love... It made me queasy with longing and caustic, crippling envy but I forced myself to watch, a sad, sick voyeur.

At three, four o'clock – I don't know – long after it was feasible to think of going to bed myself, their lights were all extinguished and I heaved a heavy sigh. I had painstakingly retraced the whole history of my relationship with Alan and come to the conclusion that his kindness, his interest in my studies, his gestures of good neighbourliness, his involvement in probate and every incidental evidence of friendship all sounded a pure and unassailable note. He was, as Sheila had testified, simply 'a lovely, kind and wonderful man'. I couldn't, much as I might like to, identify any instance whatsoever of his demonstrating any particular, any inappropriate preference for me. I couldn't in all honesty think why he should; I could certainly lay no claim to the kind of energy or creativity which he admired in Sheila. Even that night, as I had clung to him on the dance floor, and rested my bewildered head on his shoulder, aching for comfort, his hands had remained chastely in the small of my back, his arms had exerted no iota of pressure or warmth, he hadn't murmured words of consolation into my ear. That being the case, I decided, with a sorrowful but an iron resignation, no harm could befall except to me. As long as only I would suffer, only I would be hurt, then I could carry on, nursing my private infatuation and disguising the marks of its claws.

You might accuse me, at best, of woeful self-delusion, or, at worst, of specious dishonesty. At times I have accused myself of both. Be that as it may, it's the decision I came to and, as dawn broke, I put my tiger into its cage.

Combe Close: Falling Apart

It all fell apart in a relatively short time. Marcus and Carla's house sold quickly and they moved out to the idyllic rural village. Gerald and Julia followed perhaps a year later; they needed much more space for their breeding programme, now that Poppy (Polly?) was in such demand for pups. Gary's business went viral, escalating house prices brought them money in hand over fist and they moved to their gated community not long after Julia and Gerald had departed for the hills. Their houses were bought by perfectly nice folks and those of us who remained did our best to extend the hand of friendship, but by this time houses right left and centre on the Crescent were being demolished and little enclaves like ours were springing up all over. The old guard Crescent Set had moved away in disgust, leaving what was left of the ivied gables and ancient stucco to the swathes of in-coming hoi polloi. Only the barrister and his shrewish wife at *Hazelwood* stayed on, daily affronted by the relentless cacophony of rock which gusted from Pete and Pam's house.

I finished my degree and did the first year of my PhD as Lucy finished her GCSEs and began 'A' levels. I thoroughly enjoyed my research, (into Jane Austen's use of ill-health in characterisation and as a narrative device), and the teaching responsibilities which came with it; small, earnest groups of students who guzzled coffee in my 9am tutorials and tried to palm me off with plagiarised FR Levis in their neatly word-processed essays.

Pete and Pam brazened it out with their mob of unruly boys for another year or two before moving to the dilapidated semi on the wrong side of town. The neighbours' oft repeated promises to 'keep in touch' and 'always be dropping in' turned out to be without substance. I did my best to get everyone together as often as possible and doggedly continued to organise the annual Combe Close holiday, then even more important to me than ever.

Meanwhile I continued to pet and groom my guilty pleasure, raking him with sidelong glances and oblique peeks when nobody was looking, sliding my gaze away when our eyes met. My thoughts and intentions were encrypted beyond translation, disguised as throw-away words and casual gestures. I would happen to fall into a seat he had vacated to feel his warmth permeate my chilled, restless bones, and carelessly stroke the nap of a sweater he had left over the arm of a chair while I seemed to be lost in a book. Meanwhile I served him camembert instead of brie, and Shiraz instead of Merlot and became conversant with the canon of John McLaughlin although I never could see the funny side of *The Cheese Shop*. My poor incarcerated creature received never a meaningful look or a suggestive word; I fed it no hope at all. I left myself bruised beyond healing, the woeful gaoler of a pitiful, starved obsession, which raged and clamoured and importuned and pleaded, but which I never, for a second, let out.

Then, one evening, everything changed; the stakes were raised and all bets were off. It was summer, the end of a long, languid, golden day. Lucy was away on holiday with a group of girls from school; I was getting used, anyway, to losing her – in the autumn she would leave for the London School of Economics. I had spent the day in the garden. It was well established, now, and the orchard area at the top of the slope got a dappled glimmer of sun since the new owners of *Eventide* had done away with the towering leylandii hedge. I sat in it by preference even over my bench in the front garden – that had lost its pleasure for me, since the neighbours had moved away. I had showered and poured myself a gin and tonic, and had been looking forward to the last hour of sunshine in a deck chair, when a step on the patio made me look up. The sun was in my eyes and I had to shield them to identify my visitor. I knew him from the shape of his tall, willowy frame and the silhouette of his head and the faint, icy glint of the glass of his spectacles. It was Alan.

I placed a marker in my book and put it on the table before half rising to my feet, 'Is Sheila with you? Will you have drinks?' I said, establishing a shield of respectability.

He hovered in the shade and didn't answer me.

'Alan?' I said, getting up properly and going down the steps to meet him. 'Is everything alright?'

You know how it is when you step out of bright light into shadow; it takes your eyes a moment to adjust. I stood in front of Alan for perhaps a full minute, peering through the gloom, trying to read his features. Still he said nothing, but his body was coiled in a sort of awkward agony, his Adam's apple working restlessly, whether to bring words to his lips or to suppress them, I couldn't tell. Every so often he opened his mouth but then he closed it again. He removed his glasses with an exasperated motion and wiped them on the hem of his shirt.

'Alan,' I said at last. 'You're frightening me now. Has something happened? Is it Lucy?'

'Lucy?' he gave me a quizzical, myopic look. Without his glasses he seemed vulnerable and defenceless. He settled them back in place. 'Oh no. Nothing to do with Lucy.'

'Well what, then?'

He took a step backwards – I thought he was going to leave – but then he seemed to shake himself and summon his resolve. He stepped towards me and put his hands on my shoulders; they were cold, in spite of the heat of the day, I could feel their chill through my summer dress. 'You're frozen,' I said quickly, in a feeble final attempt to deflect him from his purpose, because I could see it, then, in his face, which was taut, without a hint of that flicker in his cheek which presaged his smile. He pressed his lips together, and I thought I had succeeded in getting him to restrain the words which were stockpiled on his tongue.

But no.

'Molly,' he said, with a look of intense, almost religious fervour in his

271

clear, kind eyes, 'please Molly, tell me, just this once, so that I know...' His voice was reedy with repressed emotion. At the end of his sentence it almost broke, like a school boy's. He took a sharp in-take, a sob, of breath.

'Know what?' I croaked, although this was craven prevarication on my part – of course I knew very well what he meant.

His eyes rolled skywards and he took another breath. The tip of his tongue moistened his parched lips. 'So that I *know*,' he said, half pleadingly, half emphatically, 'so that I know if it's only me.'

The glory, the unutterable relief of his implication – I had thought, for so long, that it was only *me* – was as heady as wine and I drank it in. He saw it, I suppose, in my face, the answer to his question, but he waited, still, for some reply. Time stretched out into the forbidden territory between us; this was the hallowed ground I had denied myself. It opened up between us, a crater of longing, a sultry pool of delicious, soothing waters, balm to my injured heart. What the hell, I thought to myself, what do I care what anyone will think, what *they* think? They've all turned their backs on us, haven't they? Don't *I* – don't *we* – have the right to be happy? But hard on the heels of this hedonistic response came the antiphonic counter-part. How could I give way, after all I had said and done? Hadn't I put my stake in the lonely high ground all those years before – yes, and chained myself in perpetuity to it? It would be false and hypocritical, now, to slink down from the eyrie. I had set myself up as a beacon and if it burned me in its flames, who had I to blame but myself?

I looked into Alan's eyes and saw there the mirror of my own tormented soul; the torture of trying to do the right thing.

'Molly!' he cried, giving my shoulders a little shake as he saw me slipping away from him, the iron of resolve in the alembic of my eye.

'I don't know....' I burst out at last, in a voice racked with agony, and taking a step backwards so that his hands fell uselessly to his sides. 'I don't know what you *mean*.' The tears in my eyes gave the lie to my words. His, too, were awash. His shoulders, his whole body drooped, crushed by my rejection. He stared at the ground.

'Alright, then,' he nodded at last. 'Yes. Alright.' Then he turned and walked away.

I put the house on the market the next week. I needed to be nearer the University, I said, and with Lucy away from home I didn't need anything nearly so big.

'We've been thinking just the same,' Sheila said, brightly, 'although not about size; the girls are sure to want to come home sooner or later. There's a big new development off Stan's by-pass. Alan says we should have a look at it and I want to get a good plot, this time.'

'I'm sure it's the right move for all of us,' I said, bleakly.

*

Recently I have doubted that it happened at all – that tortured interview in the gloom of my patio. I must have dreamt it, in the end-of-day languor that hard gardening and a stiff gin and tonic will bring. Heaven knows I have a stockpile of similar fantasies, dozens of scenarios, but their unvarying end is that wonderful justifying moment of finding that he feels the same. Wasn't that just one more? Certainly, year has followed year and he has made no renewed approach. I have told myself that I am glad to be able to rely on his strength as well as my own to shore us up. But at times I have up-braided myself for betrayal; I had that one isolated moment, as inviolable as a confessional, to be honest – to meet his courageous honesty with mine – and I let him down. At other times I have up-braided *him*; how could he have let his armour slip, even for those few moments, and placed us both in such danger? As time has gone on, in spite of my tendency to pick apart his every sentence and decode the intention in his every passing glance I have convinced myself that if he had ever felt anything he is long over it now. Only the occasional nugget ('you are not plain,'; 'you look *so* lovely,') has glimmered in the dark, impenetrable mine of his partiality.

Present Day: Tiger Set Free

Here it is; the culmination of my years of secret hoping, but it doesn't feel like the stuff of dreams – not the stuff of *my* dreams, anyway, those wide-awake day-dreams which I have, sometimes, guiltily pursued. This is more like one of those crazy juxtapositions – the wrong person in the wrong place – that dreams sometimes present us with, and a line from Hamlet springs clamouring into my head; 'the time is out of joint.'

Alan, in the kitchen, as I put the shopping away and make coffee, is more awkwardly corporeal than I had expected, hovering diffidently in the doorway, polishing his glasses which have steamed up in the sudden warmth. Despite the heat, from the Aga and the central heating, he looks as white and frozen as the view from the window. Goodness knows how long he was waiting, out there, in the cold. It is clear that he has come here on impulse, in a blind hurry, desperate, in his distress, for company, for comfort. He is wearing only a thin coat. The bottoms of his jeans are soaked, his shoes wholly unsuitable for the prevailing conditions. I assume that he is in a kind of shock; his world, after all, has just been wrenched from under his feet. But his coherence, out in the yard, gives the lie to this, the cause and effect between his two clauses: 'She's gone. And I'm here.' I find myself wittering about my morning's excursion, the dogs, the cleaning, anything to give me time to find a foothold. I pour out strong coffee and add a splash of Gerald's best brandy to our cups.

'After all,' I smile, indicating the driving snow outdoors, 'we won't be going anywhere for a while, will we?'

We sit on opposite sides of the kitchen table. Alan puts his hands round his mug and stares into the depths of it, a seer seeking truths in the grounds. The girls whimper and fret out in the passageway.

'When did Sheila leave?' I ask, quietly, at last.

'I got home on Thursday and she'd gone,' he says. 'But it wasn't a surprise. I knew she was going. It was just a question of when.'

I don't know when Thursday was, or what today is, except that it can't be Sunday or the library would not have been open. 'And have you heard from her, since?'

'Just a text.' He gropes in his pocket for his 'phone, and shows me the screen. '*Am ok. Don't worry. Sorry,*' he quotes. 'There's no signal here,' he observes, switching his 'phone off and returning it to his pocket.

'No,' I say, with a dry laugh. 'There isn't much of anything, here.'

'God-forsaken place. Thought I'd never find it. I wonder why they picked it.'

'It's probably nicer in the summer,' I conjecture, 'and there's nobody to complain about the dogs.' The brandy is doing its work and I am beginning to see my way, to see the narrow window of opportunity which is being given to us. 'I'm glad you've come, though. I think I was going a bit mad here on my own.'

'I'm not surprised. Nobody to hear you scream.'

'Perhaps that's the beauty of it,' I suggest, obliquely. 'You'll stay, for a while?'

We look at each other properly, then, in the unflattering, bluish fluorescent light of the kitchen. His kind, kind, sad eyes gaze back at me, needing something that only I can give him, here, in this distant, dismal place.

There's a catch in his voice when he replies. He has to cough to get his answer past it. 'May I?' he manages at last, a hoarse whisper.

'Of course,' I nod.

Then the lights go out.

We blink at each other in the sudden gloom. The abrupt absence of all those humming, ticking, rumbling background noises which go on in a house but which never get noticed heightens my sense of being cast adrift in a dream.

'Alright,' I say, pushing my chair back. 'Siege tactics.'

I collect the log-baskets and coal-scuttle from the sitting room and start getting back into my sodden coat and boots.

'What can I do to help?' Alan asks.

'Come with me,' I say.

I lead him through the glazed corridor where I select a dry, waterproof coat for him from the row of pegs and a pair of wellingtons from a stash underneath an old settle. Then, we venture out into the storm. The girls, reluctantly, follow us out. Round the buildings we're relatively sheltered but once out of their lee the wind assaults us with a battery of fat, wet flakes and we have to lean against it to make any progress. We open up the hens' coop, collect the eggs and fill up their feed and water trays. The birds put their heads out into the blizzard and then quickly back in again.

'I don't think hens like snow,' I shout.

'I can't say I blame them,' Alan mouths, but his words are snatched away.

The sheep are snug enough in their shelter. I make sure they're well off for food and water and cut the twine on a hay-bale to replenish their bedding. Alan helps me add another layer of bales to the ones across the entrance, to keep out more of the weather.

We walk round to the back of the barn where the logs are stacked. We have to brush away quite a bit of snow before we can get to them. The wind, here, is particularly strong and cold, with a penetrating rawness that chafes the skin. It bays and howls like a demented dog at our backs.

'Let's a get a few good loads and put them behind the house,' I suggest. 'It's more sheltered there, I think.'

'Does the Aga take solid fuel?'

'No. Oil. But, without electricity, its pump won't work. We'll have the generator, hopefully, but we must keep that for emergencies.'

'How resourceful you are, Molly!' Alan exclaims, giving me a quizzical look.

The physical work warms us and gives us something to focus on apart from the elephant between us. We barrow several loads of wood round to the back door and dump them in a heap. Our tracks are obscured by fresh snow almost as soon as we have made them and it's hard work forging new ones with every trip, and resisting the relentless bluster of the gale. The dogs bark at shadows and keep getting under our feet, clearly on edge, and indeed there is an unsettling air of Armageddon about the place. It is premature evening, the sky grimly grey and without a glimmer of relief, a lid of doom over our barren, boiling cauldron of blizzard. The storm has draped a manic, ashy-grey curtain across the landscape, closing us in. Beyond the reach of our vision, weather-ghouls shriek and moan like tortured souls.

Alan and I stand together in front of the geriatric generator. I pull the key, on its matted length of hoary twine, from a niche between two sheets of the barn's corrugated skin, insert it and turn it. Nothing happens. Alan dips the tank for fuel and adjusts the choke. We try it again. This time the generator gives a bronchial splutter, much, indeed, like Gerald's, and chunters into life. We could be without power for hours, or days and I don't know how long the fuel in the tank will last out. Even at this early stage it is clear, though, that there will be no prospect of leaving the farm for supplies of any kind until the snowstorm subsides. Neither Alan nor I have four wheel drive vehicles and the job of clearing the track by hand would be impossible. The enormity of our predicament strikes me forcefully but I reach out with a determined hand and switch off the generator.

'We'll just have to sit it out,' I say.

Alan puts his arm around me, then, and pulls me in to his side. 'We'll be alright,' he says, with the first glimmer of his old, capable, reliable self I have seen since he arrived. 'Don't worry.'

Inside, I dry off the dogs and allow them, for once, into the sitting room with us. I find Alan the first of the series of ridiculous outfits he will wear over the next few days. Everything of Gerald's is too big round the waist and too short in the leg. I do slightly better with Julia's wardrobe – she tends to wear practical, mannish clothes so although these also are too big and baggy and Alan feels intensely uncomfortable wearing them, they are a closer approximation to a reasonable fit. He comes down that first afternoon, after a tepid shower, in a pair of lilac sweat-pants and an ancient though capacious Arran sweater. He stands on the hearthrug and gives a hopeless, rather endearing shrug. 'Not quite the look I was hoping for,' he smiles, ruefully.

'It'll be pitch dark, soon,' I tell him, stifling laughter, and then add, wildly; 'I'll just imagine you in your tux.'

He matches my gambit unhesitatingly. 'And I'll imagine you in that beautiful pearl-grey dress,' he rejoins, quickly. It is our first approach – the first of several we will make – to the crossing-place into untried territory, the land beyond our relation as we have so far lived it out.

While he builds the fire, I deal with things in the kitchen. I need a torch to see my way around the room. Any light which might remain outside is shrouded by a thick pall of falling snow. I have lost all sense of time – the digital clocks, of course, have all stopped. The assorted long-case and French mantel clocks have all been chiming crazily out of sync since I arrived and can't be relied upon. My wristwatch is upstairs, somewhere. I haven't worn that, it occurs to me, for days. It could be mid-afternoon or midnight, for all I know. It all adds to my sense of being in a kind of parallel reality, remote and disconnected from the world, out of sight, out of mind, out of time and, most oddly of all, out of myself. The arrival of Alan, rather than diminishing this sense, has added to it. My earlier alarm has given way to a calm, almost detached interest in whatever is going to happen. Whatever prudish, cripplingly proper moral tenets have hamstrung me in the past they have no place here and I cast them away with a careless flick of a languid hand.

There's enough heat in the Aga to boil the kettle and I cut huge wedges of Julia's cake to eat with the tea. (I am famished, I realise, having missed both breakfast and lunch.) I put two potatoes to bake in the residual heat of the oven, thinking that we can always finish them off in the fire if necessary.

I sit on the hearthrug, overwhelmed by a philosophical inertia. Alan is in the armchair behind me. We drink our tea and stare mesmerised at the leaping flames in the grate. The girls, on their best behaviour, or perhaps, like, us, under some enchantment, curl onto their mats. Apart from the snap of the logs and the roar of the chimney, the house is quiescent, its thick, sturdy walls keeping the tempest safely at bay.

'Have you always known?' I ask Alan, in a drowsy voice which doesn't sound like mine. It is a forked-road of a question and I wonder with an odd aloofness which direction he will choose.

'About Sheila and Pete?'

I nod, thinking, 'If you like.'

He sighs. 'There were signs. I chose not to read them. Sheila is a woman of...' he considered his next words carefully, '....serial *enthusiasms*. One week this thing, next week something else. Tupperware, crochet, cosmetics, amateur dramatics....I let them all wash by me. And by the time I realised that Pete was more than just a passing phase, it was too late.'

'Too late? For you?'

'Much too late. For her.'

A log in the grate collapses with a shower of sparks. One of the girls is chasing rabbits in her sleep, twitching and giving throaty little yelps.

'Was that why you moved away from the Close?'

'We moved because *they* did, and......and because *you* did.'

'You know why I moved.'

'Do I?'

'I thought you did.'

We are back again at the metaphorical border-crossing, a new frontier. He shifts fractionally in his seat behind me. His knee touches my shoulder. His warmth is like potent wine, seeping through me.

'I didn't see any of the signs,' I murmur, presently.

'The signs?'

'About Stan – they way he felt about Carla. Well, that's not quite true. I saw them, but I misread them.'

'Easily done. Stan was an inscrutable sort of bloke.'

'But *you* all knew. Like you all knew about Gary and Katrina.'

'I suppose we did.'

'Even that he was stalking her?'

'No, we didn't know about that until it was too late.'

'You all protected me, especially Carla, beforehand *and* afterwards. She knew that I didn't understand about sex – I thought it was all just silly, just self-indulgent and weak.'

He answers me with a long, thoughtful silence. We are at the boundary again, considering the terms of crossing. Eventually he says 'But now...'

'I understand it *all*, now. These last few weeks, my eyes have been opened. I've grown up, ridiculous as that sounds.' I screw my head round to look at him, to see what he makes of what I have said, but his face is in shadow and I cannot read his expression. It isn't until I have turned back to face the fire that I hear his low reply. 'I see.'

Later, while the potatoes scorch in the embers of the fire, we squint through the crusted windows to see our cars in the yard, almost entirely encapsulated by snow, and a drift against the end of the barn which must be two feet deep. The wind must have shifted a little or perhaps our moving inside the house has in some way altered its dynamic. The front door begins to whistle, a dissonant, mournful note.

'Heathcliff! Let me in! Let me in!' Alan quotes as we stop up the key hole and the gap at the bottom with bits of cloth. The house is like a drum, pounded without, resonating within, and Alan and I are in some way part of it; skins tight-stretched and vibrating with every nuance; almost – but not quite, yet – in tune. There has been, between us, so much unsaid, a whole lexicon of sideways glimpses and oblique body-language. Our communication has been Jamesian ('It doesn't matter what he means. What matters is what the other person THINKS he means.'), an idiom of inference, its meaning shrouded. Now that the necessity for code has past, now that we can talk straight and plain, we find our tongues are struggling to adjust. Alan opens a bottle of Gerald's good claret while I fumble in the kitchen to cut cheese (camembert, of course, I never buy any other kind) and wash salad. We eat our meal cross-legged on the hearthrug. Alan clinks his glass against mine, but we make no toast.

'Did Sheila ever speak to you about her first husband?'

I think for a moment. 'No. I don't believe she ever mentioned him.'

Alan fixes me with a significant look. I can see the flames of the fire reflected in his glasses. 'She needed a lot of putting back together, afterwards,' he says, and then adds, heavily, 'he was another one, like Pete.'

I consider all the ways I could describe Pete, and which one of them Alan might be particularly referring to. 'Greedy?'

He laughs. 'Ha! Yes, well, that's one way of putting it.' He lifts his glass in salute and then drains it, setting it on to the hearth with a gesture of finality. 'Ah yes, there it is. History repeats,' he sighs, almost to himself.

Then I understand. The sub-text is decoded and plain before me. What he means is: Pete will hurt her, and I will have to go back. 'I see,' I say, clearly, and I, too, finish my wine.

And there, in a muffled room, deep inside the battened house, in a hidden crater in a wide sweep of snow-bound earth, I set my tiger free.

All that night, and throughout the following day, and through the next night, we scarcely sleep. We talk and laugh, and feast on cake and hot buttered toast, and experiment with bizarre cocktails and beautiful, lingering kisses. We scour Julia's bookshelves and read each other our favourite passages. Alan recites sonnets, perched on the edge of the sofa, ridiculous in Gerald's tartan pyjamas and a pair of walking socks. He massages my feet; the soles are still faintly puckered with a dozen small white scars. We talk about that Fun House party, and I confide, folded safely into the crook of his arm, the worst excesses of Stan's behaviour. Alan rocks me gently and strokes my hair while I cry cathartic tears into his shoulder.

In the morning the snow has stopped and the sky is an exhausted voile of white, empty air. Alan puts his jeans on and we walk the girls round the whole farm, ploughing through the heavy snow, shaking the boughs of the Scotch pines to cover each other in snow and pine needles. Like the dogs, we romp and roll in the snow, shrieking like idiots. We restock the log pile by the back door, and fire up the generator for long enough to warm the farthest extremities of the house and a tankful of hot water. I boil kettles and fill every thermos I can find. The hens venture out into the vast, crusted landscape and peck suspiciously at their corn. The lambs frolic around the fold and bleat at the strangeness of it all. In the late afternoon the air turns arctic blue, the temperature plummets and I fear for the water pipes. We take to running the taps periodically, to keep the water moving, even the ones in the outhouses. We venture there, in the dead of night, our wavering torch picking out the odd angles of a wellington chest, the flourishing curlicues of an ornate armoire. The water falling into the low sink sounds like a cascade in Eden; primordial water on prehistoric rock, and Alan and I, shivering beside it are like Adam and Eve, sole inhabitants of a newly created world.

At night we snuggle into the folds of the myriad quilts and blankets I have dragged off the beds and camp by the fire. Alan spoons me, or I him, and we drowse between sleep and wake, or perhaps it is only me who dozes; whenever I open my eyes his are regarding me with a soft, steady, absorbing gaze. Once, in the night, he turns to me and says 'It wasn't only me, was it Molly? All those years? It wasn't only me?' The echo of his question – how long? Nine? Ten years ago? - sounds a sorrowful note.

And I pull him closer and whisper clearly – as I couldn't do then - 'Oh no, darling. It wasn't only you,' untying the tight knot of my betrayal.

Our love-making is slow and very deliberate; every touch, each kiss must count. No stroke is insignificant, no caress without value because they are all we have, all we will have. The smallest movement – the slightest brush of finger-on-skin – is infused with a quality of valediction. With every fresh opening we foreshadow closing; the joy of our joining is subtly coloured with the sadness of our imminent separation. Each orgasm is a thorough-going culmination, fulfilment of our years of wanting. We realise every unspoken promise of the years gone by, and make good on all our secret expectations. No fantasy is left un-enacted; I have him burst through the door and ravish me on the carpet. He has me slip without a word into his bed and make love to him stealthily and in complete silence. We wallow in Julia's bath by candlelight and drink crème de menthe. We re-play our lunch, and this time he bundles me upstairs and into one of the bedrooms. Every moment is a massive finale, an achingly overdue tying up of a thousand loose ends. Our mouths stop up the lament of bitter hindsight, our hands smooth over the wasteland of crippling regret.

Mid morning of the second day, the lights in the house flicker back into life and we look at each other across the morass of our tumbled sheets. Later, a neighbouring farmer comes in his tractor with fresh bread and milk, and offers to give Alan a tow up the track.

He looks at me helplessly. 'I ought to check.... get clean clothes...' he stammers.

'Don't,' I say, shaking my head. Our little time-warp has straightened itself out again and we're back in the continuum. We have taken the dregs of the cup we were too afraid to taste, the life together that we might have had if our cowardice, our crippling loyalty and a terminal inhibition about what people would think hadn't stood in the way. We both know that when Alan gets home Sheila will be waiting, her heart in a thousand pieces, and he will patiently put it back together for her. That's the noble, honourable man that he is and that, in the end, is why I have loved him. He always does the right thing.

At the top of the track the little convoy pauses while the farmer opens the gate. They pass through and then I see Alan as he comes to close it, the sun on his pale hair, the glint of light on his spectacles and the indistinct contours of his hand, raised in farewell.

Present Day: By broad, bright daylight

It takes the snow about three days to thaw; the celery-pale green of the grass gradually re-emerges, the wind drops to a whisper, the sky is innocent and empty. Within a few days more, a rash of crocuses sprouts from the area around the quarry; their silky trumpets glow in the sun as though lit from within. It is still cold at night but during the day it is warm enough to leave the house doors open so that fresh air can sweeten the interiors and blow away the ghosts. Some afternoons I take a chair out to the yard, tilting my face up to the sun. The atmosphere within the crater is unlike anything I have known, in some way lighter, thinner, almost without gravity. I feel as weightless as gossamer, a wisp of being winnowed by the air; and the silence has a soft, vibrating quality to it which hums through my bones. I spend a lot of time outdoors, just roaming, and at night I feel at home with the silence and solitude, the crackle of the fire, the contented sighs of the dogs, the occasional rasp of my turning page.

Julia's house is back to rights; the bedding restored to the beds, the clothes I had borrowed for Alan laundered and returned to their drawers. The telephone is in order and, with it, a broadband connection. I work, steadily, through the back-log of students' assignments, and we begin work on the texts for the final term. I am happy to hear their voices again, across the ether. I take reservations from dog owners for kennelling and note the names and numbers of people wanting puppies. Twice a week the postman's van comes jolting down the track with mail and once a girl from a neighbouring croft comes to buy surplus eggs, to take to the farmers' market.

Alan does not return; I hadn't expected him to. There are no tears, no angst, no railing at the sky or haranguing the hills. I feel deeply peaceful; what the psychologists call closure. My tiger is free and his cage is gone.

After a week or so I unfold your emails from my bag. It isn't that I had forgotten about them, or about you, Mac, only that I wanted some time, an interval, breathing space. I am sorry if you were left hanging while I sorted myself out. I think you will understand, now.

The first one says:

Dear Molly

It wasn't until after the train had left that I realised that I didn't have any way of getting in touch with you. I suppose it shows our age. A younger man would have had your mobile number off you before you'd taken off your coat on Friday. I hesitated to ask Lucy for it in case you didn't want her to know. I spent a long time trawling through your University's website and I can say that I am now minutely conversant with the prospectus of the Distance-Learning department's English faculty; particularly the 19th century literature course which I assume is yours. I considered signing up! Needless to say they don't give out the personal contact details of their tutors so faced with that dead-end I had to ask Lucy. I hope you don't mind. I fear your secret – our secret – won't remain secret for long; your daughter has a way of wheedling things out of a person, doesn't she? I am holding out so far but she threatens to cook curry for us this weekend, which she knows is my favourite, and I think I may weaken.....

In fact, Molly, - and here, at last, is the point – I *have* weakened. You have weakened me. I'm weak for you – and, (oh God) now I'm beginning to quote song lyrics, which only goes to show you how bad I've got it – I want you to know, because I think I might not have really made it clear, that although what happened on Sunday afternoon (and evening, and, if I recall, also – not bad, for an old bloke - on Monday morning) was amazing (truly) that isn't just – isn't only – what I want. I'm not that kind of man. I thought you were a beautiful, interesting and exciting woman when I met you at Christmas and I think so even more now. I am more of a Colonel Brandon than a Willoughby.

I don't know how – or, indeed, if – you wish to proceed from here. I will leave that up to you. I just want you to know that I want us to proceed somewhere, somehow, please.

Mac

I smile when I read it, of course – the idea of you combing through the University's website in the hopes of finding my email address! Even the possibility of finding you enrolled as one of my students! I like the Jane Austen reference – as I am sure you hoped I would - although I'd say I was more of an Elinor than a Marianne.... I wonder at your assertion that I have weakened you – me? I feel humbled and, at the same time, massively empowered.

I *do* want to proceed. I'm quite certain of that. I should have done it years ago – moved on and let Combe Close do the same. I have been flogging a dead horse, all these years, keeping something on life-support which I should have allowed to peacefully slip away. There's tenacity in it, I suppose, but no dignity.

The second email is a little shorter and more poignant.

Dear Molly

I haven't had a reply to my last and am wondering if you got it – these things do get lost, sometimes, and you wonder, in idle moments, where they go to. In some ways I'm hoping that it *did* get lost – it was a bit rambling and incoherent, and didn't present me in a very flattering light, perhaps. The alternative – that you did get it but chose not to reply – is too difficult to contemplate.

Is that what's happened?

Perhaps you're uncertain, a bit disorientated by the way things happened. I know I am. I'm blown away by you but I'm also a bit nervous; a new relationship is a big step for people like us. Are you worried that we inadvertently hit fast-forward and missed out on all the important preamble - got started where we should have ended up? In an ideal world I'd like to have taken you out to dinner a few more times. I mean in real-life. I've taken you out to dinner in my mind a hundred times since I met you at Christmas. (You always look lovely, by the way. Why do you always choose asparagus?)

If you feel that we don't know each other very well, why don't you tell me all about yourself? Lucy's sick to death of me pumping her for information. 'Why don't you just ask her yourself?' she says. (Yes, I am afraid her world-renowned Biryani did the trick. I spilled the beans....) So I am doing.

Molly, darling Molly. If you want to start again, at the beginning, that's fine with me. Let's start and then let's move forward, ever so slowly if you like, but let's do it.

I can't stop thinking about you.

Please reply. Even if it's to say that you don't want to hear from me again. Put an old dog out of its misery.

Mac.

289

I think there is a virtual depository somewhere where all the lost emails go. It is manned by a pimply YTS employee who enjoys putting things in the wrong pigeon holes and who probably reads the personal stuff on the sly. I know for a fact there are dozens of my students' assignments there, which they swore were sent but which certainly never arrived.

Yes, I think we got things a bit back to front but there are some excellent novels which use that technique very successfully.

I *am* partial to asparagus, as a matter of fact.

My response to your invitation to tell you all about myself has turned into quite a tome, hasn't it? Writing it, in the mornings once the hens are out and the dogs in the yard, and during the evenings when everyone is tucked in safe and warm, has been therapeutic as well as instructive – I see things, now, so much more clearly than I did then – and I have felt, as the words spooled out of me and onto the screen, and then, by some magical time-travelling trick through the ether to land with a 'bing-bong' into your in-box – that they have been weaving us together, you and I, that I have in some way threaded you into the pattern of my history. I have found your replies comforting, illuminating, reassuring.

My six weeks here is almost done; Julia and Gerald are due back tomorrow. Now the daffodils have been and gone and the slopes of the hollow are carpeted with wild primroses. Soon the woods will be full of bluebells; I can see their dark, glossy spikes emerging through the tilth and litter of last year's leaves. I wondered, you know, when I got here, why Julia hadn't built a garden, but now I see why – she doesn't need one, this entire farm is her garden.

Next week I will go back to the dour little terraced house – it has never, interestingly, really felt like 'home' – pack up my books and make arrangements to find a tenant. The following week I will travel to your cottage in the Cotswolds and stay, as you suggest, just as long as I like. Thank you for your carte blanche: 'anything you want to do to the place is good with me, Molly; nice *and* good.' Your choice of words is not lost on me.

And we will see.

There's nothing at all for me here, now. Even Carla is gone, disappeared into some grey-walled world of her own confusion. I'd like to visit her and let her know that I'm sorry – that I understand, at last, what Stan put her through, how much I owe her – but I fear she is beyond my reach. I can only hope that he doesn't haunt her, that her sleep is untroubled.

The final email is short, and sad:

? :-(

But since I did reply to that one, I assume your sadness was short-lived.

98,553

AC

19th March 2014

Coming soon

by the same author

The Hoarder's Widow

Suddenly-widowed Maisie sets out to clear her late husband's collection; wonky furniture and balding rugs, bolts of material for upholstery projects he never got round to, gloomy pictures and outmoded electronics, other people's junk brought home from car boot sales and rescued from the tip. The hoard is endless, stacked into every room in the house, teetering in piles along the landing and forming a scree up the stairs; yellowing newspapers, and obsolete maps, back copies of Reader's Digest going back twenty years, rusted bikes, a rotten greenhouse, moth-eaten clothes… It is all part of Clifford's waste-not way of thinking in which everything, no matter how broken or obscure, can be re-cycled or re-purposed into something useful or, if kept long enough, will one day be valuable. He had believed in his vision as ardently as any mystic in his holy revelation but now, without the clear projection of his vision to light them up for her as what they *would be*, they appear to Maisie more grimly than ever as what they *are*: junk.

As Maisie disassembles his stash she is forced to confront the issues which drove her husband to squirrel away other people's trash; after all, she knows virtually nothing about his life before they met. Finally, in the last bastion of his accumulation, she discovers the key to his hoarding and understands – much too late – the man she married.

Then, with empty rooms in a house which is too big for her, she must ask herself: what next?

31979550R00176

Made in the USA
Charleston, SC
04 August 2014